SUNRISE

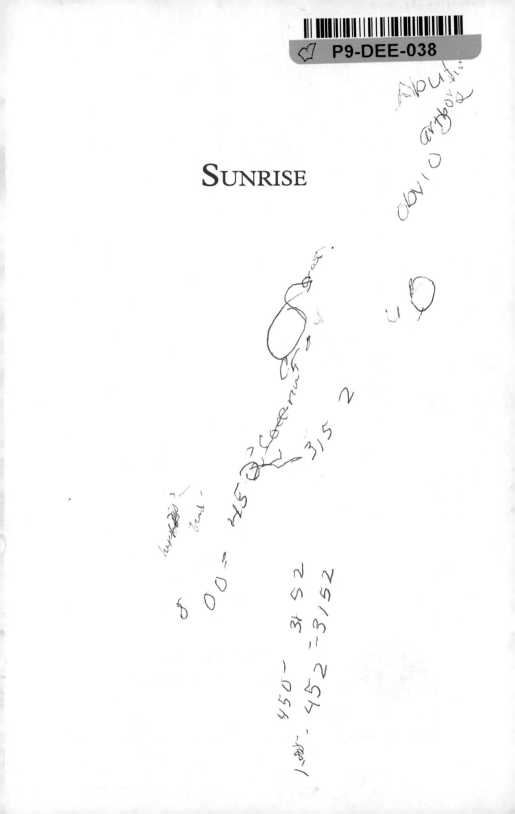

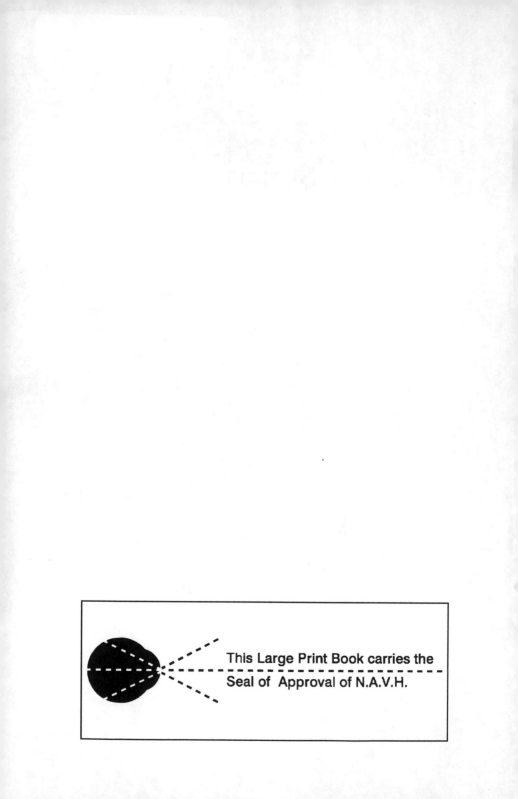

This Large Print Book carries the
Seal of Approval of N.A.V.H.

SUNRISE

KAREN KINGSBURY

THORNDIKE PRESS
An imprint of Thomson Gale, a part of The Thomson Corporation

THOMSON

GALE

Detroit • New York • San Francisco • New Haven, Conn. • Waterville, Maine • London

LIBRARY OF CONGRESS CATALOGING-IN-PUBLICATION DATA

Kingsbury, Karen.
  Sunrise / by Karen Kingsbury.
    p. cm. — (Baxter family drama-Sunrise series ; #1)
  ISBN-13: 978-0-7862-9748-1 (lg. print : alk. paper)
  ISBN-10: 0-7862-9748-4 (lg. print : alk. paper)
  ISBN-13: 978-1-59415-208-5 (lg. print : pbk. : alk. paper)
  ISBN-10: 1-59415-208-X (lg. print : pbk. : alk. paper)
  1. Family — Fiction. 2. Celebrities — Fiction. 3. Weddings — Fiction. 4. Large type books. I. Title.
PS3561.I4873S86 2008
813'.54—dc22   2007039156

Published in 2008 by arrangement with Tyndale House Publishers, Inc.

Published in association with the literary agency of Alive Communications, Inc., 7680 Goddard Street, Suite 200, Colorado Springs, CO 80920.

Printed in the United States of America on permanent paper
10 9 8 7 6 5 4 3 2 1

Donald, my prince charming

I look at all we've been through, and I'm amazed. Amazed at the faithfulness of our God and amazed at the way we grow closer, more in love with every passing season. You continue to be my strength, my rock, the leader of our home. We marvel together over the blessings and weep together over the losses. I am, my love, forever yours. Now and always. God has given us the most beautiful sunrise. Now I pray that He might grant us the privilege of walking hand in hand through the journey of parenting and into the sunset beyond. Thanks for dancing with me. I love you forever.

Kelsey, my precious daughter

You are very nearly eighteen, a young woman all grown up. Gone are the pigtails and braces, the middle school moments and high school heartaches. College life beckons, just as we always dreamed it would, and I'm breathless from the ride, from the speed of it. But I've learned this, my beloved daughter: When I look at you, I see more than the beautiful, godly, grown-up girl you've become, more than the one-in-a-million we always knew you to be. I see the three-year-old blonde, blue-eyed pixie who couldn't say her *w*'s, jumping up onto my lap on a freezing cold day at the park and telling me, "Mommy, with you I'm warm." I see, too, the kindergartner all girly with pink ribbons and puffy bangs and the eight-year-old with tears on her cheeks asking Jesus to forgive her for lying and making a promise to love Him forever and always. Your childhood years have brought me millions of moments of joy and laughter, Kelsey. I can only imagine how many more we'll share in the years ahead. Keep dancing for Jesus, and if you ever get lost, check back with the little girl inside, the one who has always known right from wrong. I believe in you, honey. I love you so much!

Tyler, my beautiful song
Somewhere along the way we switched

places. Once upon a yesterday you could run to me and jump into my arms. Now you are a six-foot-two teenager, and when we watch a family movie, I can rest my head on your shoulder. Just thinking about that makes me smile through teary eyes, because I love this; I absolutely do. I love the confident young man of God you're becoming, Ty. And I love that somewhere inside that grown-up-looking body is the heartbeat of a wide-eyed, happy kid, a boy who still bursts into song as he walks through the house. One of so many things I love best about you is that you're so kind and loving, that you care about the Lord and others. And of course I love how you are with Kelsey. Could a brother and sister be better friends? When I thank God for all He's given me, that special laughter and like-mindedness you share with Kelsey is high on my list. The sound of you two dancing and singing to "Friendship" will stay with me forever. Keep using your gifts to glorify Jesus, Ty. I love you, precious oldest son. Always.

Sean, my wonder boy
At the end of a day of writing or when life has sometimes thrown me something I

wasn't expecting, I can always count on your hug to lift my cares. Years from now when I look back at our short season of raising children, the picture of you will always be one of your arms outstretched, a smile stretched across your face as you come to me for one of our hugs. God knew you belonged in our family, and I will be grateful forever. It's that way on the soccer field, too — you leading the way in kindness and team unity. "Strange," one parent said at our team party last week. "This team has been more closely bonded than any my son has been on." I wanted to wave my hands and say that I knew why. It's because of that special something you bring to the group. I saw that during the state cup tournament when you gathered the guys — a bunch of twelve-year-olds — in the middle of the field to pray before the game. Afterwards when your team lost 8-1, you found me and gave me that big, wholehearted smile. "Mom! Did you see that? Everyone on the team wanted to pray with me!" Keep that, Sean, and you'll always find your way. I love you so, dear child.

Josh, my tender tough guy

I've watched you shoot up this past year, and I smile at the glimpse of tomorrow you're giving me. I love your easy smile, the way you are by nature a leader and a peacemaker and the picture of quiet confidence all at the same time. For a boy who's good at everything he does, you are remarkably easy to get along with, kind, and compassionate. Hold on to that, Josh. When I peek ahead at the things God may have for your future both in sports and in academics, I'm convinced you'll need humility and a dependence on Christ above all things. I'm so grateful God brought you to us and that He knew which little boys from that Haitian orphanage belonged here with us. I love you and I cherish the way our relationship is growing closer as the seasons pass. The hugs and smiles, the connection between us is one that will take us into the next chapter of your life and the next after that. I'm so proud of you, Josh. I love you always!

EJ, my chosen one

What amazing changes in you these past months! Dad asks me which of our sons I think might've aced their math test and the answer — more often lately — is you! You who struggled with learning when you arrived in our home now excel at it! Isn't God so great? But beyond your academic successes, I'm grateful for your kind and servant heart, EJ. You offer to help on a daily basis, and often you're the one handling a task before Dad or I know that it needs doing. You have a quiet way of showing that heart for God you've been given, and I'm so glad. Your sense of humor is also at the center of our unforgettable moments. Don't ever lose that ability to make people laugh, because we all need to spend a little more time laughing. I thank God for you, EJ, for leading us to you at the very beginning of our adoption journey. You are my child through and through, no question. I love you forever.

Austin, my miracle child

Last year when you celebrated that ninth birthday, I rested assured that I still had another year, another set of seasons before I needed to say good-bye to single digits. But here we are on the brink of your tenth birthday, and I feel dizzy at the thought. Dizzy and grateful in a way that cannot be defined by mere words. I remember how it felt when Daddy and I held you in that small, curtained-off area at Children's Hospital, how it felt to have just a few minutes to say good-bye — maybe forever this side of heaven. I remember placing you into the arms of the heart surgeon and seeing that he, too, had tears on his face. Five hours later God gave you to us a second time, and I've been mindful of that fact ever since. We were given a miracle that day, and with each month and year that pass, I smile to see the zest for life that makes up that special heart of yours. You try hard at all you do, and I can see the gift of learning you've been given. Somewhere down the road I'll know more about the reasons God saved you that long-ago day. But for now I cherish every moment, knowing that none of them would've happened if not for the grace of our Savior. They had to sew your IV into your wrist in the days after your infant heart surgery, and even now the scar remains — a scar on the inside of your wrist in the shape of a cross. Never forget what it stands for, Austin. I love you always.

And to God Almighty, the Author of life,
who has — for now — blessed me with these.

ACKNOWLEDGMENTS

This book couldn't have come together without the help of many people. First, a special thanks to my friends at Tyndale, who have believed in the Baxter family books and worked with me to get this book to my readers sooner than any of us dreamed possible. Thank you!

Also thanks to my amazing agent, Rick Christian, president of Alive Communications. I am amazed more as every day passes at your sincere integrity, your brilliant talent, and your commitment to the Lord and to getting my Life-Changing Fiction out to readers all over the world. You are a strong man of God, Rick. You care for my career as if you were personally responsible for the souls God touches through these books. Thank you for looking out for my personal time — the hours I have with my husband and kids most of all. I couldn't do this without you.

As always, this book wouldn't be possible without the help of my husband and kids, who will eat just about anything when I'm on deadline and who understand and love me anyway. I thank God that I'm still able to spend more time with you than with my pretend people, as Austin calls them. Thanks for understanding the sometimes crazy life I lead and for always being my greatest support.

Thanks to my mother and assistant, Anne Kingsbury, for her great sensitivity and love for my readers. You are a reflection of my own heart, Mom, or maybe I'm a reflection of yours. Either way we are a great team, and I appreciate you more than you know. I'm grateful also for my dad, Ted Kingsbury, who is and always has been my greatest encourager. I remember when I was a little girl, Dad, and you would say, "One day, honey, everyone will read your books and know what a wonderful writer you are." Thank you for believing in me long before anyone else ever did. Thanks also to my sisters Tricia and Susan and Lynne, who help out with my business when the workload is too large to see around. I appreciate you!

And to Olga Kalachik, whose hard work helping me prepare for events allows me to operate a significant part of my business from home. The personal touch you bring to my ministry is precious to me, priceless to me. . . . Thank you with all my heart.

And thanks to my friends and family, who continue to surround me with love and prayer and support. I could list you by name, but you know who you are. Thank you for believing in me and for seeing who I really am. A true friend stands by through the changing seasons of life and cheers you on not for your successes but for staying true to what matters most. You are the ones who know me that way, and I'm grateful for every one of you.

Of course, the greatest thanks go to God Almighty, the most wonderful Author of all — the Author of life. The gift is Yours. I pray I might have the incredible opportunity and responsibility to use it for You all the days of my life.

FOREVER IN FICTION

A special thanks to Sandra L. Agueda, who won the Forever in Fiction auction at the Canyonside Christian School auction in Jerome, Idaho. Sandra chose to honor her husband, Joe Edgar Agueda, forty-three, by naming him Forever in Fiction.

Joe Agueda has been married to his high school sweetheart, Sandra, for twenty years. They have three children — Sarah, eleven; Greg, nine; and Lori, six. Joe is the oldest of three siblings. In his spare time, Joe loves fishing or playing games with his kids and attending football games.

Joe also enjoys vacationing in Santa Cruz, California, and going to professional Portuguese bullfights in Stevinson, California, each summer. He likes all Portuguese festivals and attends them throughout the year in Wendell and Jerome, Idaho. He cherishes his time with his family and drives his kids to school every day. Joe finds great

17

pleasure in working on his dairy farm, rolling up his sleeves alongside the other employees. He speaks three languages — Portuguese, English, and Spanish.

Joe's friends know him for being loyal, honest, bighearted, and a devoted Christian family man. He's a big guy with big hands and a big love for the people in his life. He has a great sense of humor. Joe came to the United States in 1974 at age eleven from São Jorge, Azores Islands, Portugal, where he was born. He moved to Jerome, Idaho, with his wife in 1989 to realize his dream of starting a dairy farm. He considers the births of his children among the most significant events in his life.

You'll notice that Joe Agueda's character in *Sunrise* is a retired police officer who volunteers to work the sidelines of the Clear Creek High School football games. His character is influential in helping the football players realize the dangers of underage drinking and drunk driving. I chose to name this character after Joe because my fictitious retired police officer seemed much like Joe in his love for football and kids and family and faith. I have a feeling if Joe were asked to run security at his town's local football games in Idaho, he would do it, and along the way he would offer whatever advice he could to the young players.

Sandra Agueda, I pray that your husband, Joe, is honored by your gift and by his placement in *Sunrise* and that you will always see a bit of Joe when you read his name in the pages of this novel, where he will be Forever in Fiction.

Also thanks to Forever in Fiction winners Anthony and Diane Monterisi, who won the item at the Eastern Christian auction in Wyckoff, New Jersey. Anthony and Diane chose to honor their niece Jaclyn Michelle Jacobs, fourteen. Jaclyn is a pretty redhead with freckles, braces, and glasses. She is easygoing and loves reading books and babysitting. She is one of the top honor students in her class and can spend lots of time on the computer instant-messaging her friends.

Jaclyn loves her family — her parents, who have been married for twenty years, and her brother and sister, whom she counts among her best friends. In *Sunrise,* I named a young, talented actress after Jaclyn, mostly because Jaclyn is a girl who is also known for her transparency and genuine kindness. Whether she is babysitting or playing games with her brother and sister, she is the sort of girl others want to be around. For that reason, the young actress character seems to truly depict the teenage girl that Jaclyn is. Anthony and Diane, I pray that Jaclyn is honored by your gift, and as you imagine the young actress mentioned for Dayne Matthews' next film, you'll always see a bit of Jaclyn.

For those of you who are not familiar with Forever in Fiction, it is my way of involving you, the readers, in my stories while raising money for charities. To date this item has raised more than $100,000 at charity auctions across the country. If you are interested in having a Forever in Fiction package donated to your auction, contact my assistant, Tricia Kingsbury, at Kingsbury desk@aol.com. Please write *Forever in Fiction* in the subject line. Please note that I am able to donate only a limited number of these each year. For that reason I have set a fairly high minimum bid on this package. That way the maximum funds are raised for charities.

CHAPTER ONE

A wintry wind blew across Bloomington the day after Thanksgiving, and it reminded Katy Hart that the seasons had changed. Not just in the air around town but in her life as well. After all they'd been through, after every good-bye they'd ever told each other, this time Dayne Matthews wasn't going back home.

He *was* home.

The walk around Lake Monroe was Dayne's idea — returning to the place where their hearts first connected, the place where they could always find their own world no matter what paparazzi or media circus waited for them at the other end of the wooded path.

They held hands, their pace slow and easy. The shock of the past week's events wasn't wearing off, but it was sinking in. For the first time in his life, Dayne had a family waiting for him around the corner, people he could visit after Sunday church services or invite over for a barbecue. Sisters and a brother and a father who would welcome him and listen to him and laugh with him. People who saw him not as Dayne Matthews, Hollywood star, but as Dayne, the missing member of the Baxter family.

Katy breathed deep and looked up through barren branches to the bright blue sky beyond. "We're dreaming, right?"

Dayne chuckled. His arm brushed against hers as they walked. "I keep asking myself the same thing." He tightened his hold on her hand. "I thought we'd be on a plane back to LA this morning."

Katy smiled. "I hate to say it."

"I know." He laughed again. "You told me so."

A burst of wind swept along the path, and Katy moved closer to Dayne. He was warm and strong, and the hint of his cologne mixed with the smell of distant burning leaves. The feel of him against her filled her senses. Even in the darkest days, when Dayne's accident looked as if it would kill him or leave him permanently injured, Katy had always believed that somehow, someway, they would wind up here.

When Dayne woke up from his coma, when God's miraculous powers became brilliantly obvious in Dayne's recovery, his doctor and therapist had never thought for a minute that today he would be well enough to walk around Lake Monroe.

But here they were.

Dayne released Katy's hand and put his arm around her shoulders. "We need to shop."

"For the house?"

"Yes." He stopped and faced her. "Every room. You can pick out what you want, and we can have a designer do the rest." He grinned and framed her face with his hands. "As long as it's ready before the wedding."

Katy felt suddenly light-headed. This was the part of being engaged to Dayne that she rarely thought about. The lifestyle change. She would go from her apartment above the garage at the Flanigan house to a beautiful estate on a bluff overlooking Lake Monroe. Whatever furniture, whatever bedding and linens and dishes and entertainment systems she wanted would be hers. The thought was overwhelming, more than she could comprehend. Not that she would change because of it. Her tastes would remain simple; she was sure of that. But still her new budget was something she'd have to get used to.

"The house could stay empty for all I

care." She eased her arms around his waist. "I only need you."

"Mmmm." He came closer, his breath warm on her face. He worked his fingers into her hair, cradling her head with both hands. Smoldering desire filled his tone. Slowly, with a restraint that didn't show in his face, he kissed her. Then he pulled back enough to see her eyes. "You and a big bed with down comforters and satin sheets —" he kissed her again, longer this time — "and a dozen pillows."

"Dayne . . ."

He chuckled low in his throat and swayed with her, dancing to the sound of an occasional passing flock of geese and the whisper of the breeze around them. He pressed his face lightly against hers. "Maybe we should change the wedding date."

She felt dizzy with the nearness of him. "Okay."

His lips met hers. "Let's get married this afternoon."

Katy's body reacted to his, and she almost dropped the teasing and told him yes. But she kissed him instead. Long and slow, a kiss that told him he wasn't the only one looking forward to the honeymoon, dreaming about every day that followed. She could feel him trembling. How easy it would be to get into trouble between now and then. She ran her hands up the small of his back. "We have to be careful."

Dayne kissed her again. When he pulled back, his breathing had changed. "Very . . . very careful." His eyes were smoky, filled with passion and a longing that was more about love than lust. He moved a strand of her hair and looked deep into her eyes. When he spoke again, there was control in his tone once more. "And we *will* be careful." He smiled. "The wedding's going to be beautiful, Katy."

She put her hands on his shoulders. A cool wind blew through the space between them. "I was sort of looking forward to your other idea."

"The courthouse this afternoon?"

"Exactly."

He laughed. "I love you." He kissed her again, but this time he was the one who stepped back. "For now, though, this —" he gave her a pointed look and exhaled hard — "will have to happen in small doses."

Katy laughed and fell into place beside him. For a while it was all they could do to keep walking. She ached to kiss him again, to stay lost in his embrace for an hour. But Dayne was right. They'd made a promise to God and to each other to wait until they were married — a promise that was bound to be more difficult for Dayne, whose past had robbed him of the innocence Katy still cherished. In her private moments with God, she had vowed not to tempt Dayne. For that reason, their tender, intimate moments needed to be brief.

"So . . ." Dayne raised his brows. His expression told her that he was still cooling off. "About the wedding . . ."

She smiled and turned her gaze toward the water. "The real one?"

"Right." He slipped his arm around her shoulders. Their strides were casual and in perfect unison.

"You really think we can keep the media away if we have it at the country club?"

"I'd like to try."

She'd been thinking about the logistics. They wanted a beautiful, traditional ceremony without the chaos of circling helicopters and paparazzi jumping out of the bushes. Especially now, when the chase of media had nearly cost Dayne his life.

Even so, Katy had no idea how they were going to keep the wedding a secret. She looked at him. "I can't get past the impossibility of it."

"I've got someone working on it." His voice was deep, soothing. "I guess the rule of thumb is fifty people. Invite fifty or fewer, and the press usually doesn't find out. Invite more . . ." He shrugged. "It's just about unheard of."

"Fifty?" Katy winced. "CKT alone has more than twice that." She wanted to invite her ailing parents from Chicago, the Flanigans, the Baxters, and everyone involved with her Christian Kids Theater group. Then there were a few dozen Hollywood friends and business associates Dayne hoped to invite.

"I know. We need to plan on a hundred and fifty." Dayne narrowed his eyes and glanced at the path ahead of them. "That's why we need to talk." He stopped and drew a long breath. "I have an idea."

Katy looked into his eyes, and her heart soared. Dayne wasn't willing to settle in any way, not when it came to her. "Tell me."

"Okay." His eyes danced. "Here's what I was thinking. . . ."

John Baxter didn't usually jump into Christmas shopping the day after Thanksgiving. But Elaine had suggested the idea. Now it was Friday morning, and he was waiting for her to pick him up so they could drive to Circle Centre mall in the heart of Indianapolis. Elaine told him the trip could take most of the day. They had fifteen grandkids between them to shop for.

John wandered into the living room and looked out the front window. She would be here any minute. Elaine Denning was never late. He leaned against the sill and thought about last night.

Elaine's visit with him and his kids over pumpkin pie marked the first time he'd included her around any of them. The outcome had been dramatically better than he'd ever hoped. The entire family had accepted Elaine with kindness and grace, making conversation with her and helping smooth over any awkward moments — like the time Maddie walked up, took Elaine's hand, and said, "Are you Papa's girlfriend?"

Rather than looks of shock or disapproval, everyone chuckled, and Ashley walked up to her niece. "Yes, Maddie." She smiled at Elaine. "She's Papa's friend and she's a girl. So that makes her a girlfriend." She cast an unthreatened smile at John and Elaine.

"See." Maddie looked at Cole, satisfied. "I thought so."

As his granddaughter walked off, John had looked at Ashley, awed. The animosity she had always expressed about Elaine seemed to have been totally replaced by warmth and acceptance. Her hospitality toward Elaine had been one more way the Baxters' Thanksgiving was marked by God's presence.

After Maddie's innocent remark, the topic of Elaine and him hadn't come up again. Everyone was busy connecting with Dayne and Katy and the Flanigans, who had also joined them for dessert. Elaine's presence felt natural, and John believed they'd found a new level of friendship because of it.

Late last night, when she was ready to leave, he had walked her to her car. Their conversation replayed in his mind.

"I felt welcome tonight, John." Elaine seemed careful to keep some distance between them.

John pulled his jacket tighter around himself and looked at the half-moon hanging over the Baxter house. "I guess they're ready for me to have friends."

Her expression changed but only slightly. She smiled. "I'm ready for that too."

"Good." He reached out and gave her hand a single squeeze. They'd avoided each other for two months, because John was determined to give Elaine the space she seemed to want. If she was looking for more than friendship, he was the wrong man. He wasn't ready to love again, and he had a strong sense he might never be.

The memory dissolved as Elaine's car pulled into the drive. A slight thrill passed through him. He was looking forward to the day more than he'd expected. Elaine made him laugh with her subtle sense of humor. Spending a day with her would get him out of the house, away from the memories of a lifetime of Thanksgivings past.

John took a last look at the house before he stepped outside. This was the day each year when Elizabeth would haul out the Christmas decorations and turn the Baxter house into a wonderland of red and green and twinkling lights.

Since her death, the banister had gone without garland, the mantel without pine branches and bows, and three decades of decorations had stayed in boxes. Last year this had been one of the hardest days of all. He'd spent most of it sitting in his recliner — the one next to her rocker — looking through photo albums of smiles and laughter and loving moments lost forever to yesterday.

He would not spend the day that way this year, though. He turned and closed the door. As he did, he left behind the trace of cologne he hadn't worn in years. Today he would find another kind of smiling and laughter, shopping and joking and enjoying time with a woman he couldn't wait to spend the day with — Elaine Denning.

His friend.

Someone was knocking at the door, but Bailey Flanigan could barely open her eyes.

"Bailey . . . get up. Come on!" The voice was Connor's.

"Please . . ." She groaned and turned over. "Let me sleep."

She had stayed up late Thanksgiving night, going over audition songs with Connor and texting Tim Reed. It was three in the morning when she'd turned off the lights and finally fallen asleep.

The door opened and Connor leaned in. "Bryan Smythe's here. I'm serious, Bailey. You have to see this."

Bryan Smythe? Bailey sat up. It took only a few seconds before her body responded. She jumped out of bed and ran into her bathroom. "What in the world?" She looked over her shoulder at her brother. "Why?"

Connor grinned. "You need to see for yourself."

"Ugh. I can't go down looking like this." She ran her fingers through her hair and splashed cold water on her face. The mirror told her she still looked half asleep. There were pillow creases across her right cheek.

31

"It doesn't matter." Connor's tone was almost frantic. "He's waiting. Come on."

After Connor left, Bailey darted into her closet, water still dripping from her face. She pulled off the T-shirt and flannel leggings she'd been sleeping in and slipped into a sweatshirt and the first pair of jeans she could find. Ever since she and Tanner Williams broke up, her social life had been one extreme or the other. Meanwhile, Tanner had been seeing a senior girl with a reputation for sleeping with her boyfriends. Bailey and Tanner rarely looked at each other when they passed in the halls, and many weeks Bailey could come home from school five days straight without so much as a single call or text from any guy.

On those days, Cody Coleman, the senior football player who lived with them, would pat her on the shoulder and smile at her as if she were a child. "Don't worry, Bailey. They'll be lined up one day."

Her attraction to Cody had cooled a lot since he moved in with them. He dated a different girl every few weeks, and he treated Bailey like she was thirteen instead of sixteen. Sometimes she couldn't wait for next year, when he'd leave for college and they could be finished with him.

Bailey pulled her hair back in a ponytail

and hurried out her bedroom door. The text messages from Tim the day before ran through her head. *Do you ever think about the future, Bailey? . . . How things might wind up?* She had kept her answers short. Tim Reed was rarely in such a pensive mood, and she wanted to know what he was thinking. A few texts later he wrote, *Let's go to the park tomorrow. You and I need to catch up.*

What was this with Bryan? She rounded the corner and headed down the hallway. Sure, he'd acted interested a few months ago. But he'd been out of the picture for a while. Rumors around CKT had him seeing someone at his high school. So why was he here this morning?

She made it to the entryway, and there, standing just inside the front door, was Bryan. He held an enormous bouquet of roses — red and yellow and white. A small note card was tucked in near the middle.

Bailey gasped softly and looked from the flowers to Bryan. "What . . . what's going on?"

He shrugged. "I finally had a morning to myself." He took a step toward her and held out the bouquet. As he handed it to her, he grinned. "I might not call every day, Bailey, but I'm thinking about you." Bryan hesitated; then he moved back toward the door. "I wanted you to know."

She wasn't sure what to do next. "For no reason?" She lifted the flowers close and smelled them. "You brought me roses for no reason?"

His eyes answered her question before he did. In them she could see confidence and determination directed entirely at her. "You're reason enough." He gave her one last smile and raised his hand. "Bye. See you around."

Then, before she could hug him or thank him or get any more information than that, he turned and jogged down her walkway.

Bailey went to the door, stepped outside, and raised her voice so he could hear her. "Thanks. They're beautiful."

He waved and flashed a grin that said he enjoyed this — being mysterious and unexpected and beyond romantic. He was in his car and back down their driveway before she could catch her breath.

What was he up to? And why this morning? She pulled the card from the bouquet and opened it.

White because I will always treasure your innocence, yellow because we were friends before anything else . . . and red for all that I hope lies ahead.

Always,
Bryan

Chills passed down Bailey's neck and spine. "Okay, Bryan," she whispered as she smelled the flowers again. "Could you be any more amazing?"

She was heading back inside, still trying to make sense of it, when from the far left side of the house she heard her mother scream.

"Mom?" Bailey set the flowers down and raced toward the sound. She heard her father and the boys running behind her.

They arrived at the guest room door at the same time, and Bailey covered her mouth. Her mother was kneeling on the floor, her eyes wide and scared. "Call 911. Hurry. He's barely breathing."

Connor jumped into action, racing past their mom and grabbing the phone.

Her dad rushed into the room and knelt near her mother. "Does he have a pulse?"

"Barely."

Her dad looked like he was going to cry. He moved in closer. "How could he?"

"Pray, Jim." Tears spilled onto her mother's face. She looked at the rest of them. "Pray!"

"Is he . . . ?" Bailey couldn't finish her sentence. She stayed frozen near the doorway.

Cody Coleman was sprawled on his back, his face and arms gray. The entire room was filled with a pungent smell. That's when Bailey spotted it. Only then did she have a clue what had happened. Lying next to Cody was a bottle of liquor — hard liquor.

The bottle lay on its side, and from what Bailey could see it was no longer full.

It was completely empty.

CHAPTER TWO

Jenny Flanigan stood at the window in the fourth-floor waiting room at Bloomington Hospital and stared at the rainy sidewalk below. Jim was in with Cody, watching his vital signs, praying for the kid to wake up. Bailey was on her way back from the cafeteria with coffee and hot chocolate, and Jenny was trying to understand what had happened. Why it had happened. And how they could've possibly missed the fact that Cody was still drinking even though he'd left his mother's home in search of a safe place, a place where he wouldn't even be tempted to drink.

The doctor had told them the score earlier today. If Cody had been brought to the hospital an hour later, he would've died. The alcohol in his body was enough to kill him. When a person passes out, the doctor had explained, alcohol stops metabolizing in the body, stops dissipating from the person's system. Even so, alcohol in the stomach continues to be released into the bloodstream. By pumping Cody's stomach, they'd stopped this process in time to save his life. But it might not have been soon enough.

Jenny gripped the windowsill. The scene was like some sort of macabre joke. Cody was in a coma. Every day that Dayne Matthews fought for life in his coma in LA, Jenny had prayed for him and imagined what it would be like to hold vigil near the bed of a loved one, not knowing when or if he'd ever wake up.

And now here they were.

There was a noise behind her, and she turned around.

Bailey walked in and set the drinks down on the closest table. "Any change?" Worry shaded her eyes, her expression.

"Nothing. Dad's still with him."

Bailey sat in the nearest chair and folded her hands. She stared at her feet and let out a shaky breath. "Why would Cody do it, Mom? I don't get it."

This was the hard part. She and Jim believed in being invested in the lives of kids — not just their children but others whom God brought along. That was the reason they'd adopted three boys from Haiti, and certainly it was why they'd welcomed Cody into their house. The situation with Cody reminded her that there was a price to pay for helping people. Bailey's fear and anger, her deep worry, was one of the costs.

But there were lessons, too.

Jenny sat next to her daughter. She put her hand on Bailey's knee. "We told you about Cody."

"I know, but he's been with us long enough." She leaned back and looked at the ceiling. "You told him he couldn't drink one time, not once." A single tear slid down her cheek. She cast angry eyes at Jenny. "So he brings it into our house and drinks a whole bottle? I mean, who does that?"

The question hung in the air for a moment. Then, her hand still on Bailey's knee, Jenny told her daughter the truth. "Alcoholics." She slipped her arm around Bailey's shoulders. "When a person drinks like that, there's no other answer."

Bailey straightened her back, and for a few seconds her eyes glazed over and she stared at the opposite wall. Her teeth started chattering. Not loudly but enough that Jenny could see her daughter's fear growing. "So . . ." She swallowed. "So Cody's an alcoholic?"

"Yes." There was no downplaying the fact.

39

Not anymore. "We always thought he was, but after this we know."

Bailey leaned her head against Jenny's shoulder. "My health teacher said that once a person's an alcoholic, they're an alcoholic forever."

"That's true." Jenny rubbed her daughter's arm, doing her best to ward off her chill. "Cody needs a lot of help."

"That's why you didn't want me liking him?"

"It's a big commitment, honey, falling in love with someone who has a drinking problem, someone who's an alcoholic." Jenny tried to be careful with her opinions. "People can get help and they can change, but with an alcoholic it takes time to know how serious they are."

"About not drinking?"

"Exactly." Jenny released her gentle hold on Bailey and took her coffee from the table. "Want yours?"

"Thanks."

She handed Bailey her hot chocolate.

A few minutes passed while they sipped their drinks in silence. Jenny cherished quiet, comfortable moments like these with Bailey. Even here, in the midst of praying for Cody and struggling with his alcohol overdose.

Bailey lowered her cup to her knees. "Is he trying to kill himself?"

"No. I don't think so." Jenny felt the sadness of the situation deeper than she'd felt it all morning. "Remember when we went around the table during Thanksgiving dinner? Everyone talked about what they were thankful for."

"Hmmm." Again Bailey's eyes grew dim. Her voice filled with fondness at the memory. "Cody was thankful for our family and his future. And most of all for second chances."

"He wasn't suicidal. Cody Coleman's an open book. In the years we've known him, he's always worn his emotions for Dad and me to see. When he's down, he tells us. And when he's desperate, he cries." She sighed. "Thanksgiving? He was happier than I've seen him in a long time."

Bailey released a long breath. "Stupid parties."

"Yes."

After Thanksgiving dinner, the Flanigans had gone to the Baxters' for dessert. Cody was invited, but he declined. "I don't care about meeting some movie star." He'd chuckled, his voice full of teasing. "Especially when Katy Hart's making such a mistake." He puffed out his chest. "

41

she should be marrying."

Is that right?" Jim had given him a 𝗂endly punch on the shoulder. "I'll tell 𝒥ayne you said so."

For a moment, alarm showed on Cody's face. "Uh, yeah . . . don't do that." He allowed a nervous laugh. "I'm just kidding."

So instead of going to the Baxters', Cody had gone out with his friends to celebrate Clear Creek High's third-place finish in regionals the week before. "We'll probably make a bonfire and talk about how much turkey we ate."

As he left the house that night, Bailey had muttered under her breath, "He'll probably find some girl to make out with, he means."

"Bailey . . ." Jenny was constantly warning her daughter about being judgmental. "Give him the benefit of the doubt."

"I am." She had frowned as they climbed into their van and headed off to the Baxters'. "I definitely doubt him. No question."

Now Jenny wondered if they might've avoided all this if they had doubted Cody a little more. Parties were almost never a good idea for Cody. Not as long as they'd known him.

Jenny took another sip of her coffee. "Has anyone texted you about what happened?"

"Heather." Bailey took her cell phone

from the back pocket of her jeans and flipped it open. "She said Cody was making out with Grace most of the night." Bailey rolled her eyes. "Which I predicted, by the way."

"And drinking?"

"Heather didn't know." Bailey leaned on the arm of the chair. "But it's always the same at those parties. People show up and start drinking; then they hook up with someone, and half the people finish out the night throwing up in the bathroom or in the bushes. The next day everyone's talking about who did what with who and how much this person drank over that person and whether anyone was smoking weed or hookah." She shook her head. "Stupid parties."

"They're still smoking hookah?"

"Oh yeah. Everyone's into it."

Jenny wasn't really surprised. Every generation had their form of rebellion, and Bailey's was no different. Hookah — flavored tobacco smoked from a water-filled pipe — was often passed around at parties.

"You know what I hate?" Bailey took the lid off her hot chocolate and smelled it.

A lot, Jenny wanted to say. Bailey w opinionated on the decisions her cla made, which was a good thing. Jenr worry for a minute that Bailey wanted to go to one of the parties her friends attended, let alone drink or smoke. But sometimes Bailey's attitude bordered on a critical spirit. She studied her daughter, the tension in her posture and the way her brow was knit. "What do you hate?"

"I hate when everyone blames drinking." She tossed one hand in the air and let it fall back to her lap. "Like getting drunk is some sort of license to do whatever you want."

"Kids your age drink so they'll have a reason for what they do."

"Exactly. It makes me so mad." Bailey's voice grew thick, and there was no hiding the way she was suddenly fighting tears. "These are my friends, Mom. Three years ago the worst thing anyone did was cheat on a test. Now everyone's changed. I have maybe a handful of friends who haven't slept with their boyfriends or gotten drunk at a party." She hung her head and pinched the bridge of her nose. After a long time she looked up again. "At least I have CKT."

Jenny thought about her husband and how earlier this football season he'd been tempted to move the family across the country for an NFL coaching position. He had coached for years and retired to give the kids stability. But he was getting the itch again. One of the reasons he'd agreed to stay another year was because of the Christian Kids Theater group. A drama club like theirs was available in only a handful of states. If they moved, Bailey and Connor would lose their friends and a place where they could explore theater in an environment that made faith and family priorities.

She had prayed several times since then that they might stay in Bloomington, Indiana, another five years — so Connor could finish high school with the benefit of CKT in his life. Jim wanted that too. But coaching at Clear Creek High was no longer the challenge it had been at first.

Jenny had agreed that if Jim felt God leading them away from Bloomington, she would leave without looking back. For now, though, she could only agree with Bailey. Her daughter's involvement in CKT was often the rainbow across an otherwise stormy sky. The kids weren't perfect. Gossip and criticism sometimes reared their heads among the group. But a Christian theater program simply didn't attract kids who partied or lived on the wild side.

"You think Katy will keep doing CKT? Even after she's married?" Bailey finished her hot chocolate and tossed her empty cup in the trash.

"It depends." Jenny met Bailey's eyes. "Marriage changes things. I guess we'll have to see."

She was about to ask Bailey how Cody had been acting around her the week before Thanksgiving when Jim returned.

He looked five years older than he had that morning. The fine lines around his eyes were deeper, his face haggard and drawn. He shook his head. "Nothing's changed."

Being a coach's wife always had its highs and lows. But being married to a high school coach meant emotional drama Jenny had never experienced before. During Jim's first year coaching football at Clear Creek High, a third-string running back had locked his bedroom door and shot himself with his father's gun. The kid was a loner, a guy most of the players didn't know well. Even so, his death stunned the school and left the team reeling. Counselors were brought in to talk to the players, but most of the burden of helping kids through the trial fell on Jim and the other coaches.

For a month afterwards, Jenny would catch Jim staring into space. "What're you thinking?" she'd ask.

His answer was always the same. "How come I didn't see it? Why wasn't there a sign?" Once he had confided in her that

46

maybe if he'd let the boy start a game or two, he might still be alive.

Now Jim leaned against the doorframe. "You can go in." He pulled his cell phone from his pocket and flipped it open. "A few of the players texted me. They're coming down to the hospital to talk."

"Who?" Bailey looked like she was holding her breath, her eyes glued to Jim.

"Tanner Williams, Jack Spencer, Todd Carson. The captains."

"Other than Cody." Jenny stood and went to her husband. She put her arm around his waist and leaned her head on his shoulder. "I'm sorry. This is so hard."

Bailey got up slowly and looked at the floor. When she lifted her eyes, Jenny saw the mixed emotions there. Ever since she broke up with Tanner, she'd had hours of regretting her decision. He had been a good boy while he was dating Bailey, but recently Jenny had heard rumors that Tanner had joined the ranks of partying players. Because of that, Bailey was angry with him.

"Don't tell Tanner I'm here, okay?" She leaned up and kissed Jim on the cheek. "I don't want to see him."

"You think he's been drinking?" Resignation filled Jim's tone.

"I do." Bailey bit her lip. "Maybe that's

47

why he wants to talk."

Jenny had to agree, but she said nothing.

"Whatever's going on, we need to get rid of it." Jim raked his fingers through his hair and hugged both of them. "Go see Cody. He needs people praying around him."

Bailey nodded and then moved into the hall.

Jenny let a long sigh fall across her lips. "Have the doctors said anything?"

"They're not sure. He needs to come out of the coma."

"Weren't we just saying that about Dayne?" Jenny kissed her husband. "When will the guys be here?"

"Any minute."

"We'll stay away until they're gone." Jenny gave him a sad smile. The guys wouldn't open up if she and Bailey were in the waiting room. And the drama between Bailey and Tanner would definitely bring a halt to any meaningful talk.

Jenny went to Cody's room. As she stepped inside, she felt her heart breaking. Bailey was standing at the far side of Cody's bed, gripping the bed rails. Her head was bowed, and she was quietly sobbing, her shoulders shaking. She looked up and found Jenny. "I don't understand —" her voice was choked by tears — "why he won't wake up."

They'd already been over this three times since the ambulance had come for Cody. Jenny moved closer to the bed. Her daughter didn't need another lesson on alcohol poisoning. Just the support of knowing that she wasn't alone, that Jenny would walk her through every step of this trial. The way she and Jim had always walked their kids through the hard times.

Bailey stared at Cody. "Why'd you do it?" Her whispered words were angry and drenched in pain. "Why?" She looked across the bed. "What would make him do it? drink a whole bottle like that? And right in our own house." She pushed back from the bed, crossed her arms, and shook her head. "He knew this could happen."

"He did." Jenny kept her voice down. She understood Bailey. Clearly fear was at the root of her daughter's feelings. The angry outrage was only her way of dealing with it. "He thought he needed another drink, but that wasn't what he needed at all."

Bailey sniffed, and the anger lifted for a few seconds. "He needed us."

"When Cody wakes up —" Jenny took his hand and ran her thumb along the top of it — "he'll need Jesus more than us."

And there it was. The lesson Jenny and Jim talked about so often with their kids. Nothing truly good could come from life without the help of God. Not a single good deed or accomplishment, not the ability to succeed or to even draw a breath. Certainly not the strength to get help at an alcohol treatment center. None of it was possible without Jesus.

Jenny felt tears in her own eyes as she stared at Cody's still form.

Now they could only pray that Cody would have a chance to learn that truth for himself.

CHAPTER THREE

Jim was praying for Cody when his players entered the waiting room. Without their pads and uniforms and bravado, they looked young and small, like three forlorn kids with their heads hung.

"Hey, Coach." Tanner Williams took the lead. He was the starting quarterback, the guy Bailey had liked since fourth grade. Tanner was always one of the first to find Jim at practice or in the weight room so they could catch up on Tanner's life or the latest news on the Indianapolis Colts. But since he and Bailey had stopped seeing each other, Tanner hadn't come around. When he did, he seemed too busy to talk to Jim.

"Guys." Jim nodded to three empty seats across from him. "Why don't you sit down."

Jack Spencer was a senior, the team's punt returner and backup quarterback. He looked pale and nervous. "Is he . . . is he gonna make it?"

"It's too soon to know." Jim pursed his lips. In some ways he wanted to gather the guys into a hug the way he would with his own kids. But they weren't here for a hug. Tanner had said in the text message that they had something to tell him.

Tanner cleared his throat. He linked his hands behind his neck and stared at the floor. When he looked up, the pain in his eyes was raw and consuming. "We were at the party — the one Cody went to. We . . ." He gave an angry shake of his head. Jim could see that his emotions were too strong to get the words out.

Todd Carson sat in the middle of the three. He took a shaky breath. "We wanted to tell you before you heard it from someone else." He was six feet six, the team's best lineman. But here he looked like a little boy who'd lost his way. "We were at the party and we drank." He looked at Jack and then Tanner. "All of us."

The other two nodded, shame clouding their faces.

Jim felt his heart sink to his knees. His worst suspicions were true. His three captains drinking at a party on Thanksgiving night. A memory came back, something he'd gone through when he was in high school. When the timing was right, he would share the story with the guys. Because drinking had been a part of high school football since the sport began. If only he could get this group of players to understand what was at stake before it cost one of them everything.

He studied his players, and a dozen questions came to mind. Why hadn't they been home with their parents? How many football players had actually been there? But he settled on the one that mattered most. "Why?" He met their eyes one at a time. "Why'd you do it?"

Tanner started to say something, but his chin was quivering too hard. He coughed and determination came over his features. "Everyone was there, Coach. Only a few guys didn't go."

"We didn't drink until later." Jack shrugged. "Doesn't make it right, but we weren't the first."

"We weren't gonna do it." Todd filled his cheeks and exhaled slowly. "The girls kept pushing us, telling us to go ahead and drink. Just one or two beers." He pursed his lips. "It was stupid."

Jim surveyed the threesome. They were pathetic, and what they were saying made him furious. But at least they were honest. He leaned over, planting his elbows on his knees. "So there you are, my captains, at a party where people are drinking." His tone screamed his disappointment, but he kept his anger in check. "You know what I would've expected from you?"

The boys stayed silent, but they didn't look down, didn't look away.

"I would've hoped my captains would tell the other guys how wrong they were." Jim pointed at Tanner. "If you had left, just about every guy on the team would've done the same thing. That's the sort of pull you have, Tanner." He looked at the others. "You too, Jack . . . Todd." He worked to lower his voice. "You were named captains for a reason. Because the other guys look up to you."

"It was stupid." Tanner folded his hands and stared at a spot on the floor again. "Nothing but stupid."

"It was." Jim sat up straight and crossed his arms. *God . . . give me wisdom. I don't want to crush them, but I want them to understand . . . please.* He exhaled and another thought hit him. "How many of you drove home after you drank?"

"Lots of us." Todd seemed the most ready to spill the entire story. His cheeks were red, and he looked mortified. His expression told Jim that he wanted to come completely clean before this moment passed. Todd gestured at Tanner and Jack. "I drove these guys home."

A sick feeling twisted Jim's gut. His players hadn't only been drinking; they'd driven drunk. He remembered something he'd seen online a week ago, and he wondered if he could show them. He'd brought his laptop with him because he was fielding dozens of e-mails from Clear Creek students wanting to know about Cody's condition. Now he pulled it from its case in the corner of the waiting room. He sat back down and motioned for the guys to gather around him. "There's something I want you to see."

Jim had come across the video when he was surfing the day's news stories. A trial was taking place for a drunk driver who, a year earlier, had entered a highway going the wrong way. Driving seventy miles per hour, the drunk driver hit a limo bringing home several members of a wedding party.

The horrific crash was captured on the limo's dashboard security camera, and the video was being used as evidence in the trial against the driver. The Internet news services had the short video available for anyone to see, and Jim had taken a look. The images were not graphic so much as they were dramatic in their speed and finality.

Now, with his three captains gathered around him, Jim ran a Google search and found the link. Then he looked at the guys. "This video shows you what can happen when you drink and drive." He explained about the wrong-way driver and the limo carrying the members of the wedding party.

He hit Play and the video came to life. First there was the image as it had looked through the limo's windshield that late night. Then, from out of nowhere, headlights appeared bearing down on the limo with a speed that left little time for reaction. The limo driver started to turn his wheel, but it was over before he could get out of the way.

Next, the screen went black, but there were four more seconds of screeching tires and breaking glass and twisting metal. Mixed in with those sounds were human cries and moans and then nothing but silence.

Jim quit the Web site and closed his laptop. "Just like that —" he looked at his football players — "the seven-year-old flower girl in the back of the limo was killed. One minute she was giggling with her family, pretty in her flower girl dress and fancy shoes." He paused. "The next she was dead." He made eye contact with each of them. "All because some guy made a decision to drink and drive."

Tanner and Todd were both pale. Jack's face was red and splotchy, and he looked sick to his stomach.

Jim stood and returned his laptop to its bag. Then he faced them. "How many football players drove drunk last night?"

Todd swallowed hard. He crossed his arms in front of his big gut. "Fifteen. Maybe more."

"And by the grace of God, none of you killed someone on the way home." Jim was shaking, imagining the flower girl and how easily one of his players might've killed someone on the road, maybe a family coming home from Thanksgiving dinner. He shuddered before turning his attention to Tanner. "How did Cody get home?"

"Some girl." Tanner looked shaken. The memory of the images from the short video clip hung in the room. He licked his lower lip and swallowed hard. "She goes to another high school, but she was hitting on Cody. She had the hard stuff." Tanner seemed too embarrassed to go on.

"So what happened?" Jim was upset with all his players, but he had more interest in Cody's actions. The players knew Cody lived with their coach. "Tanner? Finish the story."

Tanner gripped the arms of the chair and breathed in hard through his nose. "He and the girl went off for a while. Into one of the bedrooms." He looked humiliated at having to tell the story, but he kept on. "After an hour or so, she led him back into the living room. She . . . she had a full bottle of some kind of liquor, and she held it up." He massaged his brow and caught his breath. "She said it was a gift for Cody."

Jim's nausea grew stronger. Why would Cody do this? For a girl? He'd come so far in the last few months that it was hard to believe there wasn't more to the story. Jim cleared his throat. "At that point Cody could still walk?"

"Barely."

"He was pretty drunk." Todd winced and stared at his trembling hands. "More than the rest of us."

"And the girl left with him?"

"Yeah, but I don't think she took him straight home." Tanner couldn't make eye contact with Jim. "She said something about taking a drive."

Jim's anger resurfaced. He gritted his teeth. He wanted to ask why none of the players had tried to stop their friend, but there was no point. They hadn't stopped each other, either. The rest of Cody's story was easy to piece together. The girl had stayed with him until late that night, then brought him home. He must've still been sober enough to give her directions.

The bottle they'd found empty beside him must've been the girl's gift.

And now — because he wasn't strong enough to resist the pull of the bottle — Cody was fighting for his life. Jim stared at the guys one at a time and scrambled for an idea. A plan that would make a difference to his players. He could be coaching in the NFL, but he was working with high school kids instead. Maybe seeing Cody would be enough to change things for his three captains, but what about the other players?

Suddenly he remembered something. Officer Joe could help him make the point. The retired policeman loved the kids and was a weekly presence on the Clear Creek High sidelines. Joe Agueda was forty-three, a hardworking family guy whose first language was Portuguese. A handful of years ago, he'd retired from police work in Los Angeles so he and his family could open a dairy farm on the outskirts of town.

The guy was crazy about football, and long before Jim and his family came to

Bloomington, Joe Agueda had taken on the job of maintaining security at the football games. Every Friday night throughout the season, Joe and his wife, Sandra, could be found on the sidelines with their three grade school kids — Sarah, Greg, and Lori. Joe and his family hadn't missed a game in years.

"Don't worry about your security," Joe would say whenever Jim or the other coaches walked by. "I've got everything under control."

In the last few years while Jim had been Ryan Taylor's assistant coach, the only security issue that had ever come up was a fistfight between a couple of Clear Creek students and a few boys from the crosstown rival. Joe had taken care of the fracas and spent half an hour lecturing the kids on the dangers of fighting. That's how much Joe loved his job. He volunteered his time, and the players saw him as something of a mascot.

Now, with his three captains struggling to make eye contact, Jim remembered the offer Joe had made him at the end of the season. "It's that time of year." Joe gave him a wary look.

"Play-offs?" Jim chuckled. The more comfortable Joe had become around Jim, the more he offered his suggestion on a play or a defensive set.

"Not the play-offs." Usually Joe's smile never left his face as he joked with players and line judges alike. But in that conversation he had been deeply serious. "The holidays are when the guys drink. I've seen it with other football teams. They finish the season, and it's one party after another." He made a light jab with his pointer finger at Jim's chest. "When I worked as an officer, I saw enough to scare the guys away from partying. Let me know if you ever need me."

So maybe Joe was the answer.

Jim clenched his fists. "As soon as Cody —" A surge of emotion grabbed him by the throat. He squeezed his eyes shut and waited until he had control. When he did, he focused on Tanner. "As soon as Cody comes out of this thing, we're having a meeting." He looked down the line at Jack and then at Todd. "I'll want you three to say a few words to the guys."

There was a round of "Yes, Coach" and "Definitely."

Todd was the first one to stand. "Can we see Cody?"

"I'll check." Jim knew that Bailey didn't want to run into the guys, but by now she and Jenny would be ready to take a break, maybe head down to the cafeteria for lunch. Jim rose and faced the captains. He wasn't sure whether to yell at them or pray with them or wrap them up in a hug. He settled with putting his hand on the shoulders of Tanner and Jack. "You guys know where I stand, my faith, my convictions." He heard the sincerity in his tone. "I won't stand for drinking on my team. Not another day."

The guys nodded.

Tanner gulped and squinted at him. "We're sorry. Really, Coach. That's why we came here."

"I know." Jim felt his shoulders relax a little, and he lowered his hands to his sides. "I respect you for that. Still, we've got a lot of work to do. All three of you have families that attend churches in town. Right now . . . Cody could use your prayers." He excused himself and went down the hall.

Jenny and Bailey were standing next to Cody's bed. They both looked up when Jim entered the room. He met Jenny's eyes. "The guys want to come in."

"Okay." She didn't ask any questions.

Jim told her with his eyes that he was grateful she didn't need details now. He didn't want to talk about his players in front of Bailey.

As she and Jenny filed out of the room,

Bailey stopped. "Daddy . . . what if he doesn't wake up?"

"He will, baby." Jim hugged her for a long time.

Jenny came up beside him and put her arm around Bailey's shoulders.

When Bailey took a step back, she had fresh tears in her eyes. "Thanks for giving me a warning. I really don't want to see the guys."

Jim watched them leave, then returned to the waiting room and led Tanner, Todd, and Jack to Cody's room. Though they had arrived contrite and wanting to confess their wrongdoings, Jim wasn't sure they fully understood the seriousness of their actions. But now, as they gathered stiffly around Cody's hospital bed, Jim saw the gravity of the matter hit each of them at the same time. Jim suspected they would feel the seriousness of their troubles at an even deeper level when he asked Officer Joe to talk to them and the rest of the players. Joe had explained that he had videos from his days on the police force. Yes, there would be difficult days ahead for the entire Clear Creek football team.

But for now, Jim could tell the reality was taking its toll on these three. Not because of anything they said to each other or to

Cody as they hovered near his bed. But because each of Jim's toughest football captains was doing something Jim had never seen them do before.

They were crying.

CHAPTER FOUR

Dayne Matthews' breath hung in the freezing air, but he moved carefully on the sloped, grassy lawn, staying in the pocket as he searched for his receiver. "Shawn . . . get open!"

Shawn Flanigan ran as hard as he could past the three-man defense. "Here! Throw it here!"

Dayne took two long steps, winced at the pain that remained in his left leg, and fired the ball downfield. It soared through the air, and twenty yards away Shawn jumped as high as he could, snagged it, and brought it to his chest. "First down!"

Ricky, the Flanigans' youngest, raised both hands in the air and hooted his approval. He high-fived Dayne. "We did it! I knew we could do it!"

Dayne was out of breath and mindful of the ache in his leg. Though he'd come far in rehab, the doctor had told him to take it easy, and he would. He had. There was a chance his leg might never be as strong as it had once been, but none of that mattered. Not the pain in his leg, the way he still tired easily, or the scar that ran from his knee to his thigh.

He was alive and he was here, well enough to play the game the way he'd played it as a boy in boarding school. If God had given him this much, what more could he want?

Dayne walked down the yard to the new line of scrimmage. "Another one just like it, okay?"

Ricky's cheeks were red from the effort. "One more score and we win!"

The teams weren't that evenly matched. Dayne, Shawn, and Ricky against Katy, BJ, and Justin. More than once, Justin had given Katy a look that said they might as well have Bailey on their team for as great a job as Katy was doing. "No offense," Justin had said before the last play, "but you play football like a girl."

Katy tipped back her head and laughed. "I'm not sure I'm even *that* good."

She was bundled up in a nylon down jacket, red scarf, gloves, and snow boots. She was so bogged down that she didn't so much run as lumber from one part of the yard to another. But her eyes shone, and her blonde hair hung halfway down her back. Dayne couldn't keep his eyes off her.

Dayne nodded across the line to Justin, the most athletic of the Flanigan boys. "We're in the red zone now!"

Justin tossed his hands in the air and gave Dayne a look of comical defeat. The four youngest Flanigan boys — all athletes — knew better than to expect much sporting talent from Katy Hart. The game had been going for half an hour, and already Dayne's team was up by three touchdowns. If they reached four, they'd agreed they would call it a day.

In all, the game had been a great diversion.

Jim, Jenny, and Bailey were still holding vigil for Cody Coleman at the hospital, where they might stay all day. Connor was at the Reeds' working on his voice recital performance, and Jim had asked Dayne and Katy to watch their four younger boys.

Dayne was spending the week at the Baxter house until he and Katy had time to buy furnishings for the house on the lake. When Dayne had learned about the emergency with Cody, he joined Katy at the Flanigan house. Katy was heartsick about the teen, and the four youngest boys had been sitting around the living room, somber and teary eyed.

The football game had been Dayne's idea.

Shawn stayed at receiver as they lined up for the next play. Dayne didn't want to make it too easy, so rather than go out for another pass, they agreed the ball would go to Ricky, the youngest. He was the only Flanigan child who had actually played football that fall. The other three boys were playing advanced club soccer — a sport that went almost year-round.

"You're mine." Dayne pointed at Katy. They were lined up opposite each other, and as soon as Shawn hiked the ball, Dayne passed it off to Ricky. Then, moving in dramatic slow motion, Dayne ran at Katy and pulled her backward onto the ground. Katy let out a yelp as Dayne fell next to her.

On the other side of the yard, Ricky took off with Shawn blocking for him and Justin and BJ on their heels. Shawn threw himself in front of Justin, giving Ricky just enough edge to speed across the imaginary line formed by two trees on either side of the yard.

"Touchdown!" Dayne was on his feet. He moved toward Shawn and Ricky, and the trio exchanged another round of high fives.

Ricky held the ball high and danced around in the end zone.

"Not fair." Justin laughed and put his arm around BJ's shoulder. "We were set up."

It was well after lunch, and the temperature was below freezing. The forecast called for clouds and possibly snow by tomorrow. Katy cupped her hands around her mouth. "Let's get inside before we freeze."

Back in the house, the boys were still chattering about the game as they headed up to their rooms to change out of their wet, muddy clothes.

Dayne had brought an extra pair of jeans and a sweatshirt. He changed in the downstairs bathroom and took his dirty clothes to his car.

When he met Katy in the kitchen, she took a deep breath and leaned on the raised kitchen counter. "We never stood a chance."

"No." Dayne pulled a couple of glasses from the cupboard and went to the sink. He filled both with water and handed one to Katy. Then he looked through the great room, out the window toward the yard where they'd just been playing. His eyes met hers again. "That's all I want, Katy. You and me and a bunch of kids. Playing football and rolling in the mud and being the kind of family I always dreamed about."

"Hmmm." She took a drink of her water. "Where does Hollywood fit into the picture?"

"I don't know." He downed his water and set the glass on the counter. "I already told you what I think about my next movie."

"You're serious?" Katy angled her head. She was standing across from him, a few feet separating them.

"I want you to read for the part. If the director likes what he sees, you should consider it."

Katy released her next breath slowly. "I don't know, Dayne. I love what I've got here. CKT, the theater kids, and their families."

He smiled. "God will make it clear. Whichever way it's supposed to go."

They heard the sound of pounding feet on the stairs, and Dayne felt a wave of sorrow. He spoke softly so the boys wouldn't hear him. "I hope Cody comes out of it soon. I'd love to give those guys some good news."

Katy finished her water. "For now let's give them dinner."

The boys came into the kitchen talking all at once. By unanimous decision, they decided on sloppy joes.

"I'll get the mix!" BJ ran for the pantry,

disappeared inside, and came out balancing four cans in his arms. "This should be enough!"

Katy laughed. "For most of the neighborhood."

"Where're the pans?" Dayne had washed his hands and rolled up his sleeves.

Katy pointed to a cupboard and directed Dayne to find the pan and a pack of buns in the refrigerator while she went to the garage for a frozen package of ground beef. "It'll thaw as we cook it." She peeled off the plastic wrap, dropped the icy block of meat into a frying pan, and turned the burner on. Bright flames licked the sides.

Dayne studied the situation. "Maybe turn it down a little. Since it's still frozen."

"Nah." Katy found a lid and covered the pan. "I've seen Jenny do this a dozen times. The high heat thaws it." Her eyes danced, and she gave him a look that said she knew what she was doing. "I know about cooking."

From the other room, Justin called to them. He was the second oldest of the three boys the Flanigans had adopted from Haiti. In addition to being the most athletic, Justin was the tallest boy with the largest build of the four youngest Flanigans. Dayne had noticed that around his brothers Justin could slip into a teasing mode that bordered on cockiness. But for the most part he was a gentle kid who took it easy on his siblings.

Today, though, he'd been beaten at football. Now he was chalking up a cue stick and standing near the pool table. "Who thinks they can take me?"

Ricky ran up to Dayne and grabbed his sleeve. "You can do it, Dayne! You can beat him."

Dayne had heard the stories. Some days even Jim couldn't beat Justin at pool. He shrugged in Katy's direction. "Someone has to do it."

They moved into the great room, and not until the game was tied with two balls left apiece did Dayne smell something burning. At the same time, Katy gasped and raced back into the kitchen.

Dayne saw a ribbon of smoke drifting from the direction of the stove. "Is it on fire?"

"Not yet. Hurry, Dayne," Katy yelled. She sounded frantic. There was the sound of her rushing around the kitchen, then the crash of something dropping.

Dayne left his cue stick balanced against the table and jogged toward her as fast as he could, the boys close behind. As they rounded the corner, Dayne saw the problem. With the flame still on high, the bottom of the frozen block of ground beef had burned to a crisp, sticking firmly to the pan.

Katy was picking up the pieces of a large glass mixing bowl as Dayne reached the stove. "I was trying to dump it in this."

"Just a minute." Dayne rushed toward the open cupboard, grabbed another big bowl, and tried to grab the pan handle. But it was too hot. Meanwhile, the smoke was getting thicker. "The flame's still on." He flipped the burner to the off position and set the bowl on the counter next to the stove. "Where're the pot holders?"

"Right." Katy jumped up, darted around the corner of the island, and opened the first drawer. "Watch the glass!" From the stack of hot pads, she grabbed an oven mitt and tossed it to Dayne. "Here."

He barely caught it, slipped it over his hand, and finally removed the frying pan from the stove. The lid was still in place, though it wasn't enough to keep smoke from curling out around the edges. Using his gloved hand, he lifted the lid and set it down.

Ricky and BJ began coughing and waving their hands, trying to clear the kitchen air.

"Stay back!" Katy ushered them into the great room. As she did, Dayne heard her slide open both patio doors.

But the fresh air didn't come fast enough. Before Dayne could thank her, the smoke alarm went off.

The siren pulsed through the house, and the boys covered their ears. Shawn made eye contact with Dayne and said above the noise, "This happened last time Katy cooked."

Katy put her hands on her hips and gave the boy a wry look. "Thanks, Shawn." She turned her attention to Dayne. Her smile said she wasn't capable of a defense. Especially over the roar of the alarm.

Dayne took the lid from the pan and tried to sweep fresh air toward the monitor. "Are you hooked up with the fire department?"

"I think so." Katy was doing her best to fan air into the house. "What should we do?"

"Last time, Mommy called the firemen." Ricky folded his arms in front of him. "She said you have to do it fast or they come with their sirens and everything."

Katy dodged the broken glass and hurried to the phone at the other end of the kitchen. She opened a drawer and sifted through a stack of papers. "Ugh . . . the false alarm stuff's supposed to be in here."

"Is it in a folder or just loose?" Dayne

moved to her side, helping look through the documents in the drawer.

"Maybe I should call Jenny. Except her cell phone's probably off since she's —"

She never had the chance to finish her sentence. Sirens sounded in the distance and grew closer every second.

"They're coming!" Suddenly Dayne took stock of the situation, and he felt himself starting to laugh. The picture was hysterical. The boys covering their ears in the next room, Katy frantically looking through the drawer, and shattered glass all over the floor — while the burned block of frozen meat sat in the middle of the counter looking less like dinner all the time.

Through the front window, Dayne watched a fire engine pull into the Flanigans' driveway.

Katy threw her hands in the air and blew a sharp breath at her bangs. "Great. Jenny'll never let me watch the kids again."

"I'll handle it." Dayne gave her a quick hug. As he walked by the smoke alarm, he fanned fresh air at it once more. This time it was just enough; the relentless siren fell silent.

"Does that mean there's no fire?" BJ blinked, his brown eyes so wide that Dayne could see the whites all the way around them.

"There's no fire." Dayne looked at each boy as he passed by. "Stay here." He ran down the short hall toward the entryway and opened the door just as three firefighters came up the tiered sidewalk.

The man at the front of the trio was Landon Blake, Dayne's brother-in-law, his sister Ashley's husband. "The call came through, and I figured it was a false alarm." Landon's face was taken up with his smile. "We've had a few others here."

Dayne leaned against the doorframe. "Let me guess . . ." He made a face that suggested he already knew the answer. "All when Katy was cooking?"

"Afraid so." Landon stopped on the porch and peered into the house. "What's she making this time?"

"Frozen beef." Dayne massaged his brow with his thumb and forefinger. "Charbroiled frozen beef."

"Mmmm." Landon gave him a light punch on the shoulder. "Sorry I can't make it, friend." He looked at his watch. "We have to get back. You know, in case someone else sets off a smoke alarm."

Katy must've heard Landon's voice, because she came down the hallway toward the open front door, her hands on her hips. "Did Dayne mention that I was distracted?"

Dayne gave a mock serious nod. "It's all my fault." He waved off the firefighters. "She was too distracted to remember she had ground beef thawing over a high flame." He pressed his fist to his chest. "All my fault."

Katy opened her mouth as if she might try to defend herself further. But then her shoulders sagged, and she gave the firefighters a sheepish smile. "Sorry, guys. At least the smoke alarm works."

Landon laughed hard. "It was a slow day at the firehouse anyway. We needed to get out." He patted Katy on the shoulder. "Don't worry about it."

"Here's a tip." One of the firefighters nodded at Katy. "Don't use a high flame unless you're standing right by the stove."

Dayne wasn't about to say he'd told her so. He only saluted the firefighter. "We'll try to remember that."

Landon made a few more minutes of small talk. "You and Katy coming to the big leftover dinner tomorrow at the Baxters'?"

"Definitely." It occurred to Dayne then that Landon might not know about Cody Coleman. He allowed a few seconds for the silliness to fade. Then he explained about the boy and his drinking and how Jim and Jenny and Bailey were at the hospital.

Landon's face lost some of its color as the story sank in. "I'm sorry. Please . . . tell them Ashley and I'll be praying."

"Us too." The quieter firefighter raised his hand. "If he pulls out of it, pray it's the last time he does something like this."

After the conversation ended and Dayne and Katy bid the firefighters good-bye, Dayne hesitated just inside the door. "You'd never see that in LA, not for a minute. Firefighters come to the door, laughing about a false alarm and sticking around to shoot the breeze?" Dayne reached out and pulled Katy to him. "I love this place. I love everything about it."

"Dayne? What about dinner?" Shawn peered into the hallway. "Me and the brothers are hungry."

Katy laughed. "Dayne's going to think up something this time."

As it turned out, the beef was salvageable. Dayne sliced off the burned bottom and finished the job, slow cooking it the way he'd suggested in the first place. Every time his eyes met Katy's, they laughed again.

"It's not funny." Ricky was still concerned about the fire truck coming to the house. As the youngest Flanigan, he acted brave for his brothers. But his concern showed now that the danger had passed. "The whole house coulda burned down."

"I know." Katy put her hand over her mouth. "It's my nervous laugh. Used to drive my parents crazy."

Dayne slipped his arm around her waist. "I know the feeling." He leaned in close to her ear. "Everything about you drives me crazy." He kissed the tip of her nose and winked at her. "But in a different sort of way."

Katy managed to pull off a salad without dropping anything or slicing her fingers. BJ prayed for the meal, and the sloppy joes tasted only mildly like smoke.

All through dinner Dayne kept reminding himself that he wasn't on the set of a movie. This was real life for the Flanigans — a houseful of kids with merriment and boys teasing each other while they ate. Yes, they would have to deal with their concerns about Cody Coleman at some time, but for now the dinner was full of life and love and everything Dayne had always thought a family should be about.

"Hey, let's play the Three!" Shawn raised his fork.

"The Three?" Dayne gave Katy a look. "Help me out."

"It's a dinner game the Flanigans made up. Someone picks a category, and we go around the table. Everyone has to say three answers." Katy shrugged. "Simple."

"I called it. I get the topic." Shawn grinned at the others. "Three favorite moments of all time." He went first, naming the time he'd scored the winning goal in a championship soccer game, the day he arrived in the United States from Haiti, and the afternoon a year ago when their dad took them to get Mandy, their yellow Lab puppy.

Ricky went next. "Christmas mornings and birthday mornings and every time we go swimming!"

"No, no." Justin leaned his forearms on the table. "That's tons of moments. Shawn was talking about three moments."

"Those are three!" Ricky halfway stood at his place. He held up one finger. "Christmas mornings." The second finger. "Birthday mornings." And a third finger. "And every time we go swimming." He looked at his three fingers. "See, three moments."

"I think we can call it three." Katy dabbed her mouth with her napkin and smiled at Ricky. "Very good, buddy. I like the same three."

And so it went. Finally it was Katy's turn. She looked at her plate for a moment as a soft laugh came from her throat. "I have about three million." She glanced at Dayne. "In the last few years, anyway."

"But you need three exact ones." Justin was still defining the rules, keeping them on task.

"Hmmm." Katy tilted her head. "Okay, looking across the theater during opening night and seeing Dayne there, knowing that he had come to see me when he should've been in LA. And the second, when Dayne pulled that dusty old Christmas tree off me after I fell on the stage, and then he took out a ring and asked me to marry him." She looked deep into Dayne's eyes. "And the third was when we came home a few days before Thanksgiving and found half of Bloomington had fixed up our house. Even Dayne's brother, Luke."

"Your turn." Ricky pointed at Dayne. "Three best moments."

Dayne held Katy's gaze a little longer. He loved her so much, and she was right. It was impossible to limit the number of amazing moments to three. Each of hers was still very much alive in his heart as well. But the boys were waiting, so he needed to give an answer. He gave Justin a silly look and jabbed his thumb in Katy's direction. "She stole mine."

"You have to think of different ones then." Justin nodded at his brothers. "Right, guys?"

"Yeah." Ricky giggled. "Stealing doesn't count."

"Okay." Dayne sighed and looked at the ceiling for a moment. "The first time I saw Katy — the time when I walked into the theater and heard a bunch of kids singing a song from *Charlie Brown,* and then when the show ended, Katy climbed onstage and thanked the kids and families." He looked at her. "I haven't been the same since."

"What's the second?" BJ bounced in his seat. The boys clearly had no time for mushy stuff.

"Second, when Katy and I walked to the top of the Indiana University stadium. We were all by ourselves, and at the far end of the football field the band was practicing."

"There was a breeze, and it was the first time —" Katy stopped short, as if she suddenly realized it wasn't her turn. She put her finger to her lips. "Oops."

"Yeah, come on! Dayne isn't finished." Justin gave Katy a pretend look of warning.

Dayne chuckled, but he shot Katy a look that said he knew what she was about to say. It was one of the first times they'd ever kissed, a moment when their feelings for each other had never been more clear —

even with all the obstacles that stood in their way.

Dayne cleared his throat. "And the third —" he felt his smile fade — "was when I was working myself as hard as I could in rehab, and something inside me snapped."

"Like your arm?" Ricky's eyes grew wide.

"No . . ." Dayne kept himself from laughing. "Something inside my heart. I stopped working out for a minute and talked to Katy, and I knew — from that moment on — that nothing would come between us ever again. No matter how things worked out or where they worked out, the two of us would be together."

Ricky made a face. "That's yucky girl stuff."

"Yep." Justin gave Dayne a knowing smile. "But Dayne's old. That's okay for him and Katy."

"I'm old, yes." Dayne put his arm around Katy's shoulders and grinned at Justin. "But this old guy just beat you in a football game."

They all laughed, and Ricky pointed at Justin. "Oooh! You got served!"

"Yeah, okay." Justin held up his hands in Dayne's direction. "Tomorrow we get a rematch."

The upbeat atmosphere continued while

they cleared the table and washed dishes and counters. The boys were upstairs brushing their teeth when Katy took a call from Jim Flanigan. There wasn't much news. Jim and Jenny and Bailey were staying a little longer at the hospital. There had been a few changes in Cody's vital signs, but nothing drastic enough to be a real encouragement. Jim asked them to keep praying.

When the boys came down in their pajamas, Dayne and Katy cuddled with them on the leather sofa in the great room, and they watched the Indiana Pacers take on the Cleveland Cavaliers. The boys were immediately glued to the action, cheering whenever LeBron James did a monster dunk.

"I thought you'd be Indiana fans." Dayne loved their enthusiasm.

"We are." Justin didn't take his eyes from the screen. "But we're LeBron fans first."

The game came down to the final minute, when LeBron led the Cavaliers in a surge that gave them the win. The boys celebrated by reenacting LeBron's dunks and talking all at once about how they were going to play like that one day.

When the energy died down, Katy made the announcement. "Okay, guys . . . time for bed!"

"Can you read to us?" Ricky took Dayne's hand as they walked up the stairs.

The feel of Ricky's little-boy fingers stirred the strongest feelings in Dayne. Feelings of fatherhood and family and all that he wanted to share with Katy in the years ahead. He looked back at her, bringing up the rear next to BJ. "Do we have time?"

"Sure." Katy put her arm around BJ's shoulders. "Your mom reads to you, right?"

"Almost every night." Justin went ahead of the group.

The boys' rooms were at the end of the hall — Justin and Ricky's on the left and Shawn and BJ's on the right. They settled on reading in Shawn and BJ's room, since everyone agreed it was their turn.

Shawn picked up a book titled *The Encyclopedia of Animal Facts.* "We could read this, but the brothers always say no."

"Is that right?" Dayne loved how they called themselves "the brothers." Katy had explained that it was something they'd started the week the boys came home from Haiti. The name had stuck, and now they considered themselves the brothers.

Dayne sat next to Shawn and looked at the book. "What are your favorite animals?"

Shawn's eyes lit up. "All of them. But the Bengal tiger and the cheetah and the el-

85

ephant are my favorites. Did you know that a cheetah can run seventy miles an hour, and one time they clocked a cheetah running eighty yards in 2.25 seconds?"

Dayne raised his brow. "I didn't know that."

"Yeah, only they can't run their top speeds for more than a hundred yards or they overheat."

Justin put his hands on his hips. He had a Dr. Seuss book tucked under his arm. "Dayne doesn't care about the cheetah."

"Actually, I do." His heart went out to Shawn. He was the oldest of the three adopted boys but easily the smallest. His love for animals was clearly a God-given gift, something the Flanigans obviously encouraged. Even if Shawn took a little razzing from his brothers. Dayne patted the cover of the animal book. "How about you and I take some time tomorrow, and you show me the best stuff?"

"Cool!" Shawn set the book on his nightstand. "I'll tell you about the lion and his den and all about the life span of the sea turtle."

Katy sat on the other bed facing Dayne and Shawn. She thumbed through the pages of the Dr. Seuss book and smiled. "I like this one."

"Me too." BJ scooted in and sat next to her.

Justin sat on the other side of Katy, and Ricky joined Dayne and Shawn.

Ricky swung his legs and sat at the edge of the mattress. "Show us the pictures, please."

For a few seconds, Dayne felt as if ten years had passed by and these were their kids, this warm house their home. Would it be like this? The normalcy of a bedtime routine? Or would he be gone half the time filming movies? Once he fulfilled his current contract, the choice would be his. But if he didn't make the decision sometime soon, his agent would sign him up for another six films, and there would be no getting out of it.

Katy turned to the first page and began to read. " 'The Star-Belly Sneetches had bellies with stars. The Plain-Belly Sneetches had none upon thars. . . .' "

The story went on about the Star-Belly Sneetches feeling superior because of the stars on their bellies and how Sylvester Mc-Monkey McBean, a clever charlatan, came through town and — for a price — offered the Plain-Belly Sneetches stars on their bellies.

Ricky laughed at the part where McBean

offered to remove the stars from the Star-Belly Sneetches so they could still be different.

When the story ended, the Sneetches were broke, having run in and out of the star machines, but they were also wiser, and they made a decision. It no longer mattered whether a Sneetch had a star or not — they were all the same on the inside, and they all deserved to be viewed with respect.

"Know what it's really about?" BJ brought his legs up under him and looked at Katy. "It's about how people shouldn't judge you on how you look."

"Not the color of your skin or your eyes or your hair or if you have freckles." Ricky touched his freckled face. " 'Cause God made us all and we're His kids — no matter how different we look."

Dayne took in the scene, and he felt himself choke up. Here were four boys — three black, one white — all with different birth parents and backgrounds, each one with his own unique look. And yet clearly they'd heard this Dr. Seuss story many times before. Because the moral had been spelled out for them by their parents, and the boys believed it to their very core.

Katy closed the book and glanced at the little faces around the room. "You're right.

God made us all different, but He loves us the same."

"God has the biggest box of crayons ever." Justin laughed. "That's what Mom says. He wouldn't be a very creative God if He made everyone look alike."

"Yeah." BJ yawned, and the dawning of a realization came across his features. He stopped and looked from Katy to Dayne. "Have we heard from Mom and Dad?"

Dayne had known this moment was coming. He and Katy could only keep the boys distracted for so long. He glanced at Katy, and she took his cue. "Your dad called after dinner. Cody's still very sick. I said we'd pray that he gets better."

Next to him, Dayne could feel Ricky start to shake. He looked, and sure enough, the boy had covered his face and he was crying.

"Why'd he have to go and drink that alcohol?" Anger colored Justin's expression. "He promised he wouldn't do that."

"Could he die?" BJ blinked back tears.

This wasn't the time for nice-sounding answers. These boys were only years away from facing the same kinds of decisions. Dayne bit his lip. "Yes, he could die." He looked at the sad and scared faces around him. "When people drink too much alcohol, they sometimes die because of it." He

89

reached out and took hold of Ricky's hand. "That's why we're going to pray for him right now."

Justin was the natural leader among the brothers, no question. It showed in everything he did, and this was no exception. "Can I pray first?" Katy told him yes, and he folded his hands and bowed his head, drawing a shaky breath. "Dear God, Dad says You brought Cody into our lives for a reason. But now he's sick in the hospital, and I don't think we had enough time to help him." Justin's voice broke, but he continued anyway. "Please don't let him die. He needs to learn about You so he can see that he doesn't need to drink that junk. In Jesus' name, amen."

Justin's prayer started a chain reaction, and the boys took turns asking God to heal Cody. Ricky prayed that the Lord would "give our friend Cody just one more chance."

When they were finished, everyone had tears on their cheeks, and Dayne was sure he'd been part of something very special. The room felt filled with the presence of God in a way Dayne had never experienced before. Because until now he'd never been around children whose faith was so sweet and strong.

Dayne and Katy tucked the boys into bed and shifted the conversation to the front yard football game. By the time they turned off the lights, the boys were still sad, but they weren't crying.

After the doors to both bedrooms were shut, Dayne and Katy headed for the stairs. When they reached the first step, Dayne stopped and leaned against the wall. "That was amazing."

"*You* were." Katy eased her arms around his waist and rested her head on his chest. "I think I love you more right now than ever before. You're so good with those boys, Dayne. I was watching you and thinking of everything we have ahead of us, and . . . I don't know. I could barely breathe."

Dayne kissed the top of her head. "I felt the same way. Watching you read to them." He pulled back a little and found her eyes. "And that talent you have in the kitchen . . . wow, Katy."

She gave him a light punch on the arm. "Thanks." She took his hand and led the way down the stairs. "We'll be married fifty years before I ever live that one down."

Dayne laughed. "Maybe not even then."

As they reached the bottom of the stairs, Dayne could hardly wait until Katy was reading Dr. Seuss to their own children, kids who would understand God and trust Him the way the Flanigan kids did.

Now it was a matter of holding tight to real life in a real place like Bloomington and enjoying every moment along the way.

CHAPTER FIVE

Katy's heart was full as she reached the bottom of the stairs and headed for the sofa where they'd watched the basketball game earlier. Dayne could tease about her cooking, but she could sense what he was feeling, how the bedtime ritual upstairs had touched him the same way it had touched her.

When he was seated on the couch beside her, she pulled up her legs and faced him. "You're going to be a wonderful dad someday, Dayne Matthews."

"I've played one in the movies." He grinned and reached for her hand.

"Never mind the movies. I mean right here in Bloomington in our lake house, with me and whatever kids God blesses us with down the road."

His look went deep, to the private areas of her heart where only he was allowed. "Thanks. That means a lot."

"It's true. The boys could've been upset all day. You knew just what it would take to make the day fun and still have Cody on their hearts when it was time for bed."

"I loved it." Dayne's smile faded. "It's what I would've had if I'd grown up here." The seriousness of his tone, his expression, didn't last long. The corners of his lips curved again. "But at least I have it now." He leaned close and gave her a tender kiss, just brief enough to be careful. "And one day we'll share this same kind of life with our kids."

"But first we have to get married." Katy loved this — the way she and Dayne could tease each other. "I haven't heard much about the plans."

"Ah, my secret weapon." Dayne turned and brought one leg onto the couch. "Everything came together this morning. I was going to tell you, but, well . . . a football game broke out instead."

"And a basketball game."

"That too."

She laughed. "Okay, so tell me."

"Her name's Wilma Waters, and she's the best wedding coordinator in Hollywood."

A wedding coordinator? Katy gulped and tried not to show a negative reaction. Of course they'd have a wedding coordinator.

That's what people with money did, right? And now that she was marrying Dayne, she fit into that category. But she hadn't thought about a wedding coordinator. She tried to think of something to say. All she could come up with was "Wow."

"I know. I can't believe she was available."

"Lucky for us." Katy did her best to sound sincere, but she was struggling. She'd figured Dayne was talking to someone who could help them pull off a secret wedding. But a coordinator? It sounded so . . . so impersonal. The people she knew didn't hire wedding coordinators. They gathered their friends and family and planned a wedding themselves. "Meaning . . . she handles everything?"

"Everything!" Dayne didn't pick up on her hesitancy. "She takes care of the guest list and the location, the flowers and the theme colors, the decorations and whatever else you need for the perfect wedding." He held out his hands. "But the best part is, she's an expert at keeping the whole thing a secret from the media."

Katy reminded herself to exhale. Here was the first piece of good news, news she could relate to. "We'll need that."

"We will." Dayne rested his arm along the back of the couch. "Wilma agreed the breaking point is usually fifty people. If your list is fifty or fewer guests, she can almost guarantee the press won't find out. But when it's more than that, it takes a full-blown plan to pull it off."

"But she thinks we can do it?"

"She does."

Katy heard the patter of little feet on the stairs and the muffled sound of tears. Before either of them could ask who was out of bed, Ricky rounded the corner. His blond hair was messy from the pillow, and he was rubbing his eyes. Ricky was a sleepwalker and he slept light, though he'd been doing better lately. But every now and then he found a way back downstairs after lights-out.

Katy whispered in Dayne's direction, "He has a hard time getting to sleep."

Dayne nodded. "Hey, buddy. What's wrong?"

Ricky squinted. He came close and looped his arm around Dayne's neck. "They won't let me win."

"They won't . . . ?" Dayne directed a questioning look at Katy.

"Sleepwalking," she mouthed.

Understanding filled his eyes. He put his arm around Ricky's waist. "They won't let you win?"

"No." Ricky did a dramatic shake of his head. His eyes were open and filled with fear and frustration. But he had that look he always had when he sleepwalked. "Every time I try they won't let me."

Dayne hesitated. "Okay . . . now they said they'll let you. The next time you try you'll win for sure."

Katy's heart melted. Dayne was compassionate with the child, and she realized that other than her CKT kids, she hadn't seen him interact with children before. They'd talked about kids, but this was the first time she'd seen Dayne act like a daddy. She kept watching.

The fear in Ricky's eyes faded, and he yawned. His arm was still around Dayne's neck, and now he added his other arm for a full hug. "That's all I wanted." He pulled back and shrugged. "But they wouldn't let me win."

"They will now." Dayne's voice was confident, his tone reassuring.

"I don't have to win every time." He blinked, and his face looked more alert, as if maybe he was waking up a little.

"I know." Dayne stood and took Ricky's hand. "Let's go back to bed."

Katy smiled. She pulled one knee close to her chest and watched Dayne lead Ricky across the room and around the corner up the stairs.

After a few minutes, she heard Dayne quietly coming back down. When he came into view, he stopped and pressed his hand to his heart. "I love that kid. We get to his room, and he asked if Cody was home yet."

"Really?"

"Yeah." Dayne took his place facing her on the sofa again. "I told him that Cody was still in the hospital, and we'd have to keep praying for him." He smiled. "So the little guy yawns and says Cody's going to be fine. Jesus already told him."

"He's a sweetheart." Katy looked at a portrait of the Flanigan family that hung on the wall near the patio door. "It's always interesting to me how Ricky was the one who had emergency heart surgery when he was three weeks old, and now he's the one with the most tender heart."

"I forgot about that."

"His scar goes from the middle of his back and curves around his shoulder blade to his side. He's perfectly fine now. A real miracle boy."

Dayne put his arm on the back of the sofa and leaned his head against his fist. "How many kids, Katy? Two? Three?" He grinned. "Six like the Flanigans?"

Katy laughed. "Probably not six." They'd talked about this before, but their answers changed every time. "Jenny told me they planned on two, but God planned on six." She raised one shoulder. "That could happen, I guess."

"I guess." Dayne looked like he felt dizzy at the thought. "We could have ten, and the way God's been with us, He'd see us through somehow."

"He would." Katy reached out and took his hand. She loved that here away from Hollywood and the pace of his filming schedule, their conversations sounded like they belonged to people with perfectly normal lives. Not the insane paparazzi chase and movie contracts and filming schedules that had dominated their talks when he lived in Los Angeles.

Katy ran her thumb over Dayne's fingers. "As long as you get your little girl."

Dayne gave a slow shake of his head. "I can't imagine how it would feel, watching you have a baby and holding my daughter for the first time. It's something I barely let myself dream about. Especially after . . ."

He didn't have to finish the sentence. Katy knew he was thinking about the baby he lost, the one that had been aborted. "That moment will be special in a lot of ways."

"Yes." After a few seconds he grinned. "I can only say heaven help the boy who tries to date any girl of mine."

Katy wanted to slide closer and kiss him, tell him she felt the same way and that — girl or boy — she could hardly wait for that day. Instead she leaned back against the arm of the sofa. "I guess we better talk about the wedding."

"Before we plan the nursery, you mean?" A crooked smile flashed on his face.

"Yes. Before that. Now this wedding coordinator . . . do we get input?" Katy kept her tone light. "Or do we tell her what we want and she does the rest?"

Dayne released her hand and sat straighter. There was no denying his excitement as he talked about having Wilma on their side. "She'll do as much or as little as we want." His eyes lit up, the way they always did when they talked about the wedding. "She's flying into Indianapolis on Monday, meeting us at the Hyatt."

The meeting at the Hyatt had all the makings of a media circus. She wrinkled her nose. "What about the press?"

"Wilma's coming with ideas." Dayne slid a little closer. His voice told her there was nothing to worry about and no need to talk about the wedding further until they had their meeting with Wilma. "The main thing is privacy. After my accident . . . I want to keep it a secret from the tabloids. If they find out . . ." He looked away for a few seconds. "If they find out, it'll be like having the person who tried to kill you crash the biggest day of your life." His tone was still gentle, but the muscles in his jaw flexed. "I won't have it."

Katy understood. Until Thanksgiving, they'd been so consumed with getting Dayne well enough to walk, well enough to fly to Bloomington, that there had been no talk about the wedding or flowers or cakes or churches. None of the usual things an engaged couple talked about. And now — clearly — Dayne trusted Wilma Waters. They could share their ideas with her, and she would have the momentous task of helping them plan a secret ceremony. It didn't matter where that would take place — at Bloomington Community Church or on the lawn of their lake house — so much as that they pulled off that one crucial detail.

Keeping it from the press.

Dayne was rubbing his leg, the one he'd nearly lost in the accident.

"Does it hurt?"

"A little." He smiled, but his face was shadowed by a look that was common since he woke from his coma. "The game was probably a little much."

Feelings welled up inside Katy. Pride for how far he'd come since the accident and sorrow over how close she'd been to losing him. In some ways, she still couldn't believe that they were here, having the most normal of days. Katy put her hand on his knee. She wanted to know if she was right about the look in his eyes. "You're thinking about the accident."

Dayne's emotions were raw and easy to read. Indebtedness for all the hours she'd spent by his side, praying for him, believing he'd pull through. And a love so strong and honest it almost hurt. He covered her hand with his. "Am I that obvious?"

"There's a look you get." Katy tilted her head, hoping he could feel the way her heart went out to him. "I always figure you're thinking about the accident when I see that look."

Dayne averted his gaze. "Sometimes I see it happening again. I'm driving along, and Randi Wells is in front of me, and I see the paparazzi come up on either side of her." He blinked and turned back to Katy. "They're pressing in on her, trying to snap a picture at forty miles an hour, and she's jerking her car left and right, all nervous.

The rest of it happened too fast to remember, except for the truck . . . the way it came straight at me. I can see that the same as I did when it happened."

Katy didn't say anything for a while. She held his knee a little tighter and swallowed back a wave of sadness and terror. The accident so easily could've killed him. "Sometimes I can't believe you're really here. That you're well enough to even sit beside me."

"The part that still needs work is my heart." He made a frustrated face. "I keep thinking I'm over it, not angry at the paparazzi anymore. They were just doing their job, you know?"

"But they were doing it illegally." Katy felt her own anger ignite. "What happened that day was completely their fault."

"I said that exact thing to Bob the other day when he called. And Bob told me I had to be careful." Dayne was still having weekly conversations with Bob Asher, his missionary friend in Mexico, and he was glad for the challenge of getting to know God and understanding His Word better.

Katy wasn't sure where Dayne was going with this. "About what?"

"Getting a hard heart. Staying mad at them and holding it against them anytime I'm around a photographer. Bob said all that'll do is hurt me."

Again Katy thanked God for the wisdom of Bob Asher. The guy seemed to always come through at the right time with the words Dayne needed to take the next step in his faith. Katy hadn't thought much about it, but Bob was right. Dealing with his feelings toward the paparazzi was something Dayne would have to do — especially once he returned to Los Angeles.

Maybe sooner, if the banquet manager at the Hyatt hadn't kept quiet about their Monday meeting.

Dayne lowered his leg to the floor and ran his fingers along Katy's face. "I've just had the best day ever." He cupped the back of her head with his hand and studied her. "I don't want to talk about the paparazzi."

Katy was always amazed at how quickly her feelings could intensify when Dayne was close to her this way. Suddenly she couldn't think from the nearness of him. "Dayne . . ." She was going to tell him that maybe they should step outside, sit on the front porch glider, and look at the stars — anything to keep from getting too close to him.

But before she could say anything, Dayne brought his other hand up alongside her face. "I love you." He breathed the words against her face. They weren't filled with the familiar desire but with a desperation, especially in light of all they'd been given, all they'd almost lost.

He brushed his lips against hers, and for the sweetest minute they let themselves be lost in the moment, in the rush of everything they felt for each other.

When she came up for air, she sat back. "So . . . you think Jenny'll smell the smoke in the kitchen?"

A chuckle filled his throat. "In other words, we better take a break?"

Katy drew a quick breath and released it slowly. "I know *I* better."

The house was quiet except for the occasional sound of the ice maker and the subtle hum of the heater. Tonight was supposed to get down into the twenties, and Jenny and Jim kept the house cozy.

"Maybe we should light the fireplace in the living room." Dayne grinned. "Then the smell wouldn't be so obvious."

"Thanks." She gave him a playful push. "Seriously, it's not that bad, is it?"

Before he could answer, the phone rang. For the past hour she'd almost forgotten about Cody Coleman and the battle he was waging against alcohol poisoning. Now she looked at Dayne, and fear painted broad strokes across her heart. "Probably Jenny."

She hopped up and ran to the kitchen, picking up the receiver on the third ring. "Hello?"

"Katy?" The relief in Jenny's voice filled the phone line in as much time as it took her to say Katy's name. She uttered a quick cry. "Cody's awake. His doctor said he's going to be okay."

"Oh, Jenny . . . thank You, God." She closed her eyes for a few seconds and silently prayed. Every year kids died from drinking too much. But by God's grace alone, Cody Coleman wouldn't be one of them. Not this time.

"He's groggy and nauseous and embarrassed." Jenny sounded drained from the vigil. "He can't believe he nearly died and all he put us through."

Katy turned and caught Dayne's eye. She nodded and gave him a thumbs-up. Then she gripped the phone a little tighter. "He needs help. . . . Does he realize that?"

"He's still pretty sick, but yes. He's more broken than I've ever seen him. He's been awake for about an hour, and the tears keep streaming down his face."

"Maybe this'll turn things around for him."

"I think so." The relief was back in Jenny's voice. "We almost lost him. Another hour and the stomach pumping might've been too late."

Katy shuddered.

They talked another few minutes, and Jenny said that though Cody couldn't come home until Sunday, the rest of them would be back in the next half hour. "Everything okay with the kids?"

"We had a blast. Played football and made dinner together. Read *The Sneetches.*" Details about the fire department could wait until later. "Dayne loved it."

They finished the call, and Katy returned to the sofa. "Cody's been awake for an hour. The doctor said he'll be okay."

Dayne stood and faced her. "He woke up an hour ago?"

"Mmm-hmm." Katy slipped her arms around his waist and searched his face. "Why?"

"That's when Ricky told me he wasn't worried about Cody. Jesus had already told him that Cody would be okay." Dayne shook his head. "I figured he was still half asleep."

"Makes you wonder." She held his gaze for another couple of seconds, then led him toward the living room. "About that fire . . ."

They lit the fireplace and sat on the rug and talked until the Flanigans came home.

But even then, Katy was taken Ricky's words, how he'd been so confident that Cody would be okay. All because Jesus told him so. Ricky had a pure, untainted faith — the faith of a child. Exactly the sort of faith God called all His people to have.

Katy was still pondering this after Dayne had gone to the Baxter house for the night. Without question, Ricky believed in God's power to make a difficult situation work out. If she and Dayne were to navigate the paparazzi between now and the wedding, without the bitterness Dayne had talked about, one thing was certain.

The two of them would have to do the same.

CHAPTER SIX

They called it Laughter and Leftovers, part of the Baxter tradition. Ashley was stirring milk into a pot of mashed potatoes, working alongside her sisters, Kari, Brooke, and Erin.

Ashley pressed her spoon against the lumps in the potatoes. The familiarity of the night was comforting. Especially on a day when she was missing her mom more than usual. Laughter and Leftovers was her mother's idea, after all. Every Thanksgiving weekend, the entire Baxter family would gather at their parents' house on Saturday night for another round of turkey and the stuffing, salads, and vegetables that went with it. Usually one or more of them had a story to tell about hanging up the Christmas lights or shopping in the mad dash the day before, and always the family found a reason to laugh.

Ashley moved her spoon slowly. As long

as she had breath, she would see that they kept the tradition. It was one more way they could keep their mother's memory alive.

"You're quiet." Kari took the spot beside her. She was adding water to the green peas, which Ashley had already placed in a saucepan.

"Missing Mom." Ashley kept her words quiet, so only Kari would hear. Her dad's friend Elaine Denning was here. She was sitting in the family room with Reagan, Katy, Ashley's dad, and the other men, all of whom had been placed on dish duty for later tonight. Landon was holding Devin, rocking him to sleep before dinnertime.

"I know what you mean. Thanksgiving was such a rush, so exciting with Dayne home and all the work on the lake house."

"But today it's hitting me." Ashley stared at the potatoes. "How she'll never be with us at a time like this again."

"This morning Jessie saw Mom's picture — you know, the framed one I keep on the kitchen counter." Kari found a spoon in the drawer beside the stove. She stirred the peas and then stopped and looked at Ashley. "I asked her if she remembered Grandma. She looked at the photo for a long time, and then she said, 'I think so.' "

Ashley smiled, but her eyes filled with

tears. "Jessie was only two when Mom died. All the kids are bound to forget eventually." She blinked, and a single tear fell onto her cheek. She wiped it with the back of her hand. "Even Cole, and Mom practically raised him until Landon came back into my life."

"I think we're all feeling it today. When I got here, Brooke was in the guest room looking at that painting, the one you did of Mom and Dad walking the path behind the house."

"I love that old painting." The potatoes were starting to bubble. Ashley turned down the heat. "I painted it for one of their anniversaries."

"Because they were always out back walking together."

"Whenever us kids had issues, they either sat in their chairs in the living room or out on the porch or they went on a walk." The memory warmed Ashley's heart. "I can still remember looking out the back window and seeing them out there, hand in hand."

On the other side of the kitchen, Brooke and Erin were slicing fresh cucumbers for the salad when one of the slices shot across the room and hit the floor just as Ryan came in.

Ryan's heel landed squarely on the cucumber slice, and his foot flew out from underneath him. He grabbed the refrigerator handle to keep from falling.

For a moment, Brooke and Erin tried not to laugh, but then the image of big, strapping Ryan hanging on to the refrigerator handle as if his life depended on it was too much to take. Before he found his footing again, Ashley's two sisters burst into laughter.

"That reminds me." Kari elbowed Ashley. "This is called Laughter and Leftovers for a reason." She whispered the next part. "If it weren't for the cucumber, I'd be ready for a long walk and a good cry."

"I'm sorry." Ashley watched Erin pick up the mashed cucumber from the floor. She felt a ripple of laughter stir inside her. "Hey, Ryan, could you do that again?"

Ryan was cleaning off the heel of his tennis shoe with a napkin. "That's what I'm here for — to keep you girls entertained." He bowed toward Erin and Brooke, who were now doubled over laughing. "Glad to be of service." He found his cup of coffee and reenacted his near fall before leaving the kitchen.

Brooke was trying to catch her breath. "I've never . . . seen a cucumber shoot . . . so far."

"Like . . . as soon as you sliced it, the thing was desperate to get away." Erin dabbed at her eyes. She drew a long breath. "My goodness, we're silly."

Yes, Ashley thought. And if the night was going to be celebrated the way their mother would've wanted them to celebrate it, then Erin and Brooke couldn't be the only ones laughing.

While they finished fixing dinner, Ashley forced herself not to think about her mother or the fact that Elaine Denning was in the other room sitting in the seat where her mother was supposed to sit. Her feelings were strange, really. She'd already worked through the idea that her father had a female friend, and during the fixing of Dayne and Katy's house, she'd even made peace with the idea. She was the one who'd called and invited Elaine to help in the final push to finish the work. But somehow having Elaine here — not for dessert but for the entire evening — felt strange and uncomfortable. Threatening.

Ashley told herself to stay calm, and by the time they sat down to dinner, she had let the subject go.

Once again they were at two long tables. The dining room was crowded, and laughter came from every direction. Ashley reminded

113

herself that the sound of everyone in one space, enjoying each other and life, was the reason for the dinner.

Still, Landon gave her a curious look after they sat down. "You okay?" He searched her eyes.

Ashley smiled at him and looked deep to the heart of the man who had never given up on her, never let her go no matter how hard she'd fought him. "Yes." She took hold of his hand. "I'm fine."

Landon held her eyes a little longer. He knew her too well to be tricked by her simple answer. But he also knew that this wasn't the time to make her open her soul. They could do that later. He gave her hand a squeeze.

"Devin's asleep?"

"In the portable crib." He laughed. "*One* of the portable cribs. When this many of us are together, we need a whole room for little beds."

Ashley watched her dad reach for the hands on either side of him. Which meant that somewhere beneath the dinner table, he was holding Elaine's hand. Ashley refused to let the thought take root. Everyone always held hands around the Baxter table. Instead she focused on the people around the two tables. Brooke was sitting beside

114

her husband, Peter, and their young daughters, Maddie and Hayley, who had recovered well enough from her drowning incident a few years back that she could sit at the table and eat with the rest of them. Near them were Erin and Sam and their little girls — Clarisse, Chloe, Amy, and Heidi Jo.

Ashley savored the sensation of Landon's hand in hers. She smiled at him and then gazed into the eyes of Cole, the son he'd taken as his own. Finally she looked at Katy and Dayne and at her younger brother, Luke; his wife, Reagan; and their preschool-aged son, Tommy, who was holding tight to the hand of his little adopted Chinese sister, Malin. And Kari and Ryan with their kids, Jessie and RJ, who was still in a high chair.

They were the kind of family others longed for, even with their quirks and funny moments of slipping on cucumber slices or crying over the mashed potatoes. The people surrounding Ashley were the ones she loved most in all the world. If her mother were here, she would've done the same thing — taken stock of the faces and young families around the room, grateful for each.

Her father prayed, and afterwards Cole looked around the table at his cousins. "I start basketball next week!"

"Me too!" Maddie raised both hands in

the air. "Hot Shots!"

Hot Shots was a program sponsored by the city that allowed kids through sixth grade the chance to play basketball before the competitive levels of club or high school sports. Ashley and Landon had stayed for a few of Cole's practices. She looked at Brooke. "How's her team? I mean, what's the coach like?"

"She wants to win, but she's been good with the girls." Brooke glanced at her husband, Peter. "Wouldn't you say?"

Peter hesitated. "The woman played at Indiana University ten years ago. That sort of drive for hoops never leaves your blood." He looked doubtful, as if the whole idea of getting kids involved in basketball in hoops-crazy Indiana wasn't the smartest thing. "I guess we'll know more when the games start."

Ashley shared a concerned look with Landon. She didn't want to say too much with Cole sitting next to her, but she was having her doubts too. She met Brooke's eyes over the top of Cole's head. "Our coach said he'll be disappointed if we don't take first place."

"Yeah." Cole looked at Ashley and then at everyone around the table. "Coach says at the end of practice everyone has to make their layups, and if we don't, then we all run lines."

That wasn't all, but Ashley would talk about it with Brooke later on. For now, she hoped they could talk about throwing a wedding shower for Katy, who was sitting at the other table with Dayne and their dad and Elaine.

Cole was going on about one boy on the team who couldn't make a layup if his life depended on it and how the whole team had to run lines because of him. "Sometimes after practice he cries." Compassion laced Cole's tone. "I feel sorry for him, 'cause he told me his dad likes basketball a whole lot, and his dad gets mad at him when he misses."

Ashley had seen this for herself. It was another reason she wanted to talk to Brooke. Organized sports were the norm for kids anymore, and Cole and Maddie were both athletic enough to play. Besides, like many kids in Indiana, they loved basketball. But she and Landon were new at this. They could use all the help they could get.

Ashley waited until Cole took a break to eat a few bites of turkey. "So, Erin, when do you leave?"

"Tomorrow." She made a sad face. "Things are crazy at Sam's work, and the

117

girls need their routine."

Ashley felt for her sister. This was the hardest part of their holiday gatherings — eventually everyone had to find their way back to work and home and their regular routines. "When do you come back?"

"Summer." Erin gave her husband a questioning look. "Maybe."

"The company's going through tough times. There could be pay cuts." Sam looked at the others and then down at his plate. He'd seemed troubled this trip, and now his attitude made sense. He had a lot to deal with, supporting Erin and their four girls.

"There's always the university." Ashley tried to sound hopeful. "You could teach engineering or finances. Either one, really."

"I've thought about it." Sam looked up. Weariness hung in every word. "I guess I keep thinking I'll make it through to the management level, and then the struggle will be worthwhile."

Brooke was sitting on the other side of Sam. She smiled at him. "At least we get to see you a couple times a year."

Ashley realized something. Erin and Sam would be going back but not Luke and Reagan or Dayne. Luke and Reagan were looking for a house south of Indianapolis, where in December Luke would start his new job

118

as a full-fledged attorney handling Dayne's affairs for the firm there. It was a dream position, and Dayne was paying extra so Luke's salary would be far more than the usual starting pay.

Ashley glanced at the other table. Luke and Dayne were caught up in some funny bit of conversation. The two looked so much alike, and now they had the beginning of something more, a bond that deep inside both of them had always wanted.

Again Ashley thought of their mother and how she would've loved this weekend, everything about it. She would've been standing at the front of the crowd of people in the backyard of the lake house waiting to welcome Dayne and Katy as they arrived from Los Angeles, and she would have added her own decorative touches to make the house a home. Here, now, she would've been practically bursting with joy. Dayne and Luke, her two sons, were at peace and at home, where they both belonged.

I hope You'll give her a way to see this, Lord . . . to know that everything's working out the way she always prayed it would.

Ashley sighed and finished her dinner. At the next table, her dad was saying, ". . . and then we walk through the cosmetic section of some department store, and this woman

119

practically ropes Elaine into a demonstration of *lip stain,* whatever that is."

"I could've gotten away, but I have to admit . . . I was curious about any kind of makeup with the word *stain* in it." Elaine allowed a quiet laugh. She wasn't nearly as talkative as their mother had been, but she laughed easily.

Ashley had noticed, and the fact that she liked to laugh reminded her that Elaine was good for their father. Even if her presence still felt strangely out of place. She gritted her teeth and swallowed the sorrow welling inside her heart.

When the dinner was over, the guys made good on their promise. They took care of the dishes while Ashley and the rest of the women joined their father in the family room. A few of the younger kids played on the floor while everyone else settled into the chairs and sofas.

"I'm stuffed." Kari held her hand against her stomach. "I can never get enough of Mom's mashed potatoes." As soon as she said the words, a look of alarm filled her face, as if maybe she shouldn't have mentioned their mother with Elaine sitting here.

Elaine crossed her legs. Her expression looked unfazed. "You're right." She aimed her comment at Kari but not in spite. Her

120

tone was kind and gentle. "I've always loved your mom's mashed potatoes. In fact, I use her recipe at home."

Across the room, Kari visibly relaxed. "Me too."

"Everyone loved how your mom cooked, Kari."

"Yes." Their dad's eyes were wistful. Not at all the way they would've been if he had feelings for Elaine.

Ashley studied him. Maybe she was making more of his relationship with Elaine than was actually there. Cole and the older kids were at the dining room table coloring, and Ashley was about to ask Brooke more about the Hot Shots basketball.

But Katy moved to the edge of her seat. "Dayne and I are meeting with a wedding coordinator tomorrow in Indianapolis."

In the blur of being in charge of Dayne and Katy's house renovation and trying to finish the surprise before Thanksgiving, Ashley hadn't had time alone with Katy since they'd been back. "So the wedding's in Indianapolis."

"No." Katy smiled. "That's just to throw off the paparazzi. We don't want the press to find out, so we're working with a woman Dayne knows from Hollywood. She's the best at keeping things a secret."

Ashley tried to imagine how Katy must feel. Just a few years ago she had been running the children's theater group in town with no romantic prospects on the horizon. And now she was engaged to America's heartthrob. Ashley smiled at her future sister-in-law. Talk about a fairy-tale ending.

"Where's the wedding, then?" Brooke had a cup of coffee in her hands. She looked at peace, something she'd been missing for years. But now that she and Peter shared a strong faith and had come so far with Hayley, there was a quiet wisdom to Brooke. And a lightheartedness that had never been there before.

The smell of warm pumpkin pie drifted into the family room. Katy grinned and lifted her hands. "We have no idea. We'll talk about that when we meet this lady."

"We'll help keep it a secret." Ashley glanced at her sisters and found approval all the way around the room. "We pulled off your home makeover without letting the press find out. Just tell us what to do for the wedding."

"Thanks, Ash." Katy couldn't have sounded more sincere. Their eyes met and held. "You have no idea how much that meant to Dayne and me. The house was on the verge of collapse, and now . . . well, now it looks brand-new." She looked around. "We'll never forget what you all did for us."

"That reminds me." Ashley felt her excitement building. "We need to plan a wedding shower."

Reagan had been quiet, but now she perked up. "We should have a special gathering like the one you threw for me in New York City."

"What was it like?" Elaine was caught up in the conversation. She didn't know any of them very well, and she probably saw this as a chance, a beginning.

"It was the most precious time." Reagan's eyes shone with the memory. "Everyone shared a Scripture that meant something to them, one that would be helpful for Luke and me once we were married."

"I like that." Katy's face took on a dreamy look. "I still can't believe we're getting married. Even after everything that's stood in our way."

"At my daughter's shower, we had every guest bring a single page with the secret to marital bliss." Elaine uncrossed her legs and tucked her feet neatly beneath her chair. "We took the letters and placed them into a scrapbook."

"Oooh, that's good too." Katy looked at the others. "Hearing what's worked over the years. That would be priceless."

Erin and Kari agreed that a book of thoughts and advice on marriage would be a perfect theme for the shower. Reagan added that maybe they could do both — a presentation of a special Bible verse and the single page of advice.

Ashley wanted to be excited. Elaine's idea was good and romantic, but somehow it made Ashley ache again from missing her mother. This moment — with Dayne finally home and about to begin his married years — should've been shared with their mother. She had been instrumental in pulling together Reagan's shower. She had even written Luke a poem the night before his wedding. It focused on how quickly a child grows up and how the little lasts in life can often go unnoticed.

A lump formed in Ashley's throat. Never mind that Reagan was laughing about how she had been scared to death before her wedding, not sure if the Baxter women would like her, and never mind that Erin was saying as long as she had a few weeks' notice she could take a few days to come back to Bloomington for the shower and help with the wedding plans.

The atmosphere around the room was vibrant, the way Ashley had felt just a few minutes ago. But now, in her own corner, a wave of tears fought for release. Was she the only one missing Mom? Her dad was saying that if they had a luncheon shower, maybe Elaine could help with the cooking, and Ashley wanted to shout no. That could never do — having Elaine help in a place where only Ashley's mother should be.

Suddenly Ashley couldn't take another minute. The planning and excitement, as if their mother never existed. She needed to be alone, to wrestle with her feelings and find a way to come out on top, in control before she broke down. She forced a smile and swallowed her sadness. "I'll be back." Then she passed the kitchen and headed upstairs to the bedroom at the far end of the house, her parents' bedroom.

The box of letters from her mother was still on the shelf in the closet, but she wouldn't look for it, wouldn't bring it down. Everything in the box belonged to her father. He had said he'd put together a scrapbook of letters when he had the time. Ashley had learned her lesson before — the box was off-limits.

But the bed wasn't. The bed where her mother had lain dying of cancer just a few years ago.

Ashley sat on her mother's side and put

her hand on the pillow. "Mom . . . I miss you. . . . Why aren't you here?"

Her whisper was the softest sound, caught in a cry that came from deep inside her. She ran her hand over the cotton pillowcase. This was where her mother had helped Ashley plan her wedding, where she had told her how grateful she was that Landon was finally going to be part of the family. It was where, on a day when her mother wasn't feeling so weak, she had done up the buttons of Ashley's wedding gown, one button at a time.

They had bonded here, connected at a deep level. And all the while Ashley had prayed for a miracle — that her mother might beat cancer and live to see not only the wedding but the lives of her children unfold around her.

The tears came then, streams of them. Hot and tender, they trickled down her cheeks as her eyes remained fixed on the pillow. Her mother should've seen the birth of Devin and the way her town had picked up the pieces after the tornado last spring. She should've been at Dayne's side after his accident, and she should've been at the front of the group of people when Dayne and Katy came home from Hollywood to their new house on the lake.

She should've held Hayley's hand as she walked outside with the other children — slower, yes, but so miraculously healed that she no longer needed a wheelchair or even a walker. Little Hayley, whom her mother had prayed for day and night. The miracle was happening, but Mom wasn't here to see it.

Ashley closed her eyes and imagined the scene downstairs. Here they were planning a wedding and a shower for Katy Hart, celebrating the astounding faithfulness of God to bring Dayne into their lives — and not just for a meeting but forever.

She hugged herself and wished that one more time her mother could hold her, rock her, and tell her everything was going to be okay. But instead, downstairs in the seat next to her father was a woman who didn't really belong. She was her father's friend, but the way they looked today during dinner was too much like . . . too much like the way he'd looked with her mother. Comfortable and happy and connected . . .

But not in love. Certainly not.

Her father would never really love anyone the way he'd loved her mother. Or would he? Was it even possible that somewhere not too far down road he would call his kids and make the announcement that he was starting over, trying love one more time with Elaine Denning? Friendship was one thing. She was glad her father had a friend, truly glad. But love?

A sick feeling welled up inside her. A feeling that had come over her several times in the past week.

If that happened, they could never look at their father and see Mom at his side — the way Ashley still saw her. If Elaine was there, then the picture would change entirely. It would be Dad and Elaine, not Dad and Mom. And even though Mom was gone, that would feel like betrayal. Ashley was sure it would feel that way to all the Baxter kids. Their parents had been so tightly knit that no one could ever take their place with each other.

But if her dad made that decision, there was nothing any of them could do about it. So maybe that was what frightened Ashley now, what made her sad. Maybe they'd shared their last holidays with Dad sitting alone at the head of the table, wandering outside after dinner to stand at the porch railing and stare across the Baxter property the way he did whenever he missed Mom.

With Elaine here, it was as if they'd all moved on. Another wave of tears filled her eyes and made its way down her cheeks.

That was the hardest part, really. She wasn't ready to move on, and the truth was, she didn't have a choice. If her dad was ready to start a new season — with someone who could quickly become more than a friend — then Ashley could only accept that fact.

She lowered her face to her mother's pillow and pressed her forehead against the cool case. Her mother had been right here in this very spot. She'd loved here, and she'd fought for another day here. "God . . . why?"

There was a sound at the door, but Ashley didn't want to move, didn't want anyone to see she was crying. She allowed herself to go limp, and she wrapped her arms around the pillow and beneath it. She felt tired and more emotional than she'd been in months. The door opened, and someone came into the room. "Who is it?" Her voice was muffled. She figured it was her father, wondering what she was doing.

"Ashley?" But instead, the voice was Landon's. He must've seen her climb the stairs. He sat beside her and put his hand on the small of her back. "What's wrong, baby?"

She sniffed and sat up, her shoulders slumped. She looked at him and saw again the unconditional love, the love that told her it didn't matter why she was crying. He was there for her regardless. She put her arms around his neck and leaned her head on his chest. "I miss her."

"Ah, honey . . . I had a feeling." He ran his hand along her back, soothing the pain inside her. "I watched you at dinner and in the other room with the women. Every time you were quiet, I thought you might be thinking of her."

"It's Elaine." Ashley squeezed her eyes shut, and the sorrow inside her built. "I want her to feel accepted, but . . . when she's here, I can't see Mom." She lifted her head and looked into Landon's eyes. "You know?"

"Mmm-hmm." He kissed her forehead.

That's what it was, why today had been so hard. Saying good-bye to their mother had been one thing, but her memory would live on in the rooms of the Baxter house, in the familiar places and chairs and moments. But with Elaine around, everything changed. Almost as if her mother had been replaced.

Ashley pressed her cheek against her husband's chest again and allowed a few quiet sobs. "I miss her . . . so much."

Landon could've told her that missing someone was normal or that it was time to move on. He could've said that God had at least blessed them with all the wonderful years they had with her mother, and he could've said that her dad deserved this time with Elaine, time to find friendship and companionship and even possibly something more. All of those things were true.

But all he did was hold her and let her cry.

Ashley savored the warmth of his body against hers, the way their hearts connected without a word. Because sometimes a heart needed to grieve so it wouldn't shrivel up and die from sadness. Tears were a way to bring new life to a soul barren from loss. And Landon — in his uncanny ability to love — understood this.

Which was one more reason why Ashley would love him until the day she died.

CHAPTER SEVEN

John was aware that Ashley hadn't returned and also that Landon had gone after her. As far as he could tell, none of his other daughters had registered her absence. Which was just as well. All night it had been clear that Ashley wasn't herself. Whatever was going on in her heart, Landon was the best one to help her through it.

John figured Ashley was struggling with Elaine's presence this evening, but he could only pray for her in that matter. Recently she had made great progress in accepting his friend, but the holidays were bound to be hard. Not just for her but for all of them. Tonight none of the others seemed troubled, and only Erin had pulled him aside and asked if something serious was going on.

"Are you and Elaine . . . seeing each other?" Erin's tone hadn't been accusatory but curious and maybe a little sad.

"Not in the way you mean." John leaned

in and kissed his youngest daughter's cheek. "We're friends. We enjoy spending time together."

Erin didn't hesitate. "Good." She took hold of his hand. "I'm glad for you."

And that's the way Ashley felt most of the time. At least that's what she'd told him ever since the big work day at Dayne and Katy's lake house. Ashley had called Elaine and invited her to help.

"You deserve her friendship," Ashley had told him later. "I understand."

John watched his daughters talking to Katy about the pending wedding shower. Ashley might understand, but her feelings ran deep in every area. Her emotions were bound to vary as Elaine spent more time with the Baxter family. He looked beyond the family room to the kitchen, where Elaine was making coffee. She got along with everyone — in part because she and Elizabeth had been friends for so many years. All those conversations when Elizabeth had shared about her children and their spouses, about her grandchildren, made it easy for Elaine to fit in.

He leaned back in his chair and gazed out the front window. A fiery red sunset splashed a brilliant glow on the field outside, and for a moment it resembled one of

Ashley's paintings. He sighed. *Dear God, my precious Ashley is hurting. I can feel it. Help her understand this next season for each of us. And help her know that we will never lose our connection to Elizabeth. No matter who comes and goes from our lives.*

There was more he wanted to say, more in his heart that he needed to share with his God and Savior. But John heard a high-pitched, singsong voice come up alongside him.

"Hi, Papa."

He looked down into the beaming face of Hayley — Brooke and Peter's younger daughter. There would never be a time when he wouldn't look into Hayley's eyes and remember how she had looked in the hospital bed, hours after nearly drowning. Back then her doctor had talked to Brooke and Peter about signing papers so that Hayley could be an organ donor once her body gave up the fight.

But God had other plans for little Hayley.

She was six now, and there were only small signs of the brain damage she suffered while underwater. A slurred word or a limited vocabulary. Her slightly slower way of going about things. But she was still making progress, getting better at feeding herself and using a crayon in her special-education

134

classes. They had their precious Hayley back. She was a miracle. Proof that God would always determine the number of a person's days — whether they lost a battle to cancer far earlier than anyone had hoped or made a recovery from a near drowning that no doctor or medical knowledge could explain.

John put his hand on her shoulder. "Hi, baby. How are you?"

"Good. I helped Cole catch a bird." She pointed toward the patio door. "Come see, Papa."

This was what he loved about having children around him — the way they took him back to the days when he and Elizabeth were raising a young family. Living out in the country meant there were always adventures, and often those adventures involved rabbits or frogs or birds. Ashley and Luke had been the animal finders twenty years ago. Now it was Cole and whichever cousin he could get to help him out.

John chuckled and eased himself out of his recliner. "Okay, Hayley, show Papa what you found." He took the little girl's hand, and they headed for the patio door. On the way, he caught Brooke's eye, and she smiled. He let Hayley lead him down the few steps to the back porch.

As soon as he was clear of the house, John spotted Cole in the dusky night air. He was chasing what looked like a wounded bird, grabbing at it and missing. "Papa . . . I found this bird in the bushes. I think . . ." Another swipe and Cole missed again. "I think Jingles the cat hurt him."

Hayley squealed and clapped. "Catch him, Coley. Catch him quick!"

The commotion must've been heard through the open patio door, because in seconds, the other grandchildren piled outside to see about the fuss. Maddie and Jessie joined in the chase, and Tommy tumbled out and tried to keep up. Seconds later Erin's oldest, Clarisse, joined them, waving her arms and trying to catch the bird.

John felt sorry for the wounded creature. No question it was hurt, but now it was also terrified.

"Here, birdie." Cole was using his sweetest voice to lure the creature, but even that wasn't working.

"Let's try something else." John held up his hand. "Let's make a circle around him. Everyone stop running, okay?"

The kids were breathless, but they did as he asked. All except little Tommy, who stopped, pointed his finger at the flapping bird, and pretended to shoot it.

Reagan was in the doorway, and she hurried outside and swept Tommy into her arms. "Let's not shoot the little bird, all right?"

Tommy started to fuss but then stopped, mesmerized by the drama still unfolding.

Luke came outside and joined the circle, and eventually the bird — probably sensing it was cornered — stopped in the middle and stared at them, its chest pounding from the struggle.

"Good little bird." Cole started toward it.

"Wait, Coley." John looked at Luke. "There's a box near the garage door. Get it and we'll see if we can make a cage for him."

Luke jogged off, and John looked at his grandkids. "Stay really still so you don't scare him." The air around them was chilly and smelled of burning leaves. John spotted Elaine in the doorway, stifling a smile. It felt good knowing she was here, that she was seeing him with his grandkids, seeing how they interacted with one another.

"Okay, Papa." Hayley nodded. "Really still."

Luke returned a few seconds later with the box. He handed it to John, and John crept up on the bird, the box in one hand, his fingers spread open on the other. "Come on. Don't be afraid." He sounded like Cole, but that was okay. As he reached the bird, the little thing didn't put up a fight. It hopped into the box, and in a rush the kids crowded around to peer in at it.

"He needs a hospital." Maddie used her arms to keep the other kids from crowding in too close. Her parents were both doctors, and lately she seemed to think that she had been born with some sort of genetically given medical understanding. "Right, Papa? He needs a hospital like the sick people who come and see Mommy and Daddy."

John knelt and took the trembling bird in his hands. It had definitely had an encounter with Jingles. Its right wing was damaged, and its feathers were missing on and beneath it. It also had a slight puncture wound on its chest. But otherwise the bird seemed pretty unscathed.

"No hospital for now." John studied the faces of his grandkids. In their earnest eyes he could see his kids, the way they'd looked decades earlier. He smiled at them. "Let's cover him with a warm towel and let him rest."

"What about some dinner?" Maddie raised her brows. "Want me to get him some turkey, Papa?"

"Birds don't eat birds, silly." Cole rolled his eyes at Maddie.

Of all the kids, Cole and Maddie were the most competitive. John put a stop to the conversation before it could get out of hand. "The bird isn't hungry. Thanks for thinking about him." John patted Maddie's hand, then stood and lifted the box. "He only needs a little rest. Then tomorrow or the next day, after his wing has a chance to heal, we can set him free."

Dayne and Katy were out on the patio now too. Dayne seemed particularly intent on the happenings, and John understood his interest. Rescuing an injured bird or catching a frog or a snake was part of life at the Baxter home. But not in Hollywood.

Eventually the kids settled down, and the group went back inside. Maddie's expression told anyone interested that she was still bothered by Cole's comment. She lifted her chin and gave her cousin a demeaning look. Then she held out her hands to the other cousins. "Let's pray for the bird. All birds need prayer."

Cole glanced sarcastically at the remainder of the turkey in the kitchen, but before he could say anything, John took his hand and gave him a stern look. "Yes, let's pray for the bird."

Even Peter and Ryan, the stragglers still washing dishes in the kitchen, joined them. John looked at Elaine, silently welcoming her into the circle too. She took her place beside him, and as the group came together and everyone closed their eyes and bowed their heads, Elaine took his hand.

Once in a while he and Elaine held hands. It was an act of friendship, a way of talking without words. But here, with the whole family except Ashley and Landon gathered around, the feel of her fingers against his seemed to usher in the start of something new and right and good. Something John wasn't sure he was ready to think about just yet.

Peter prayed, asking God to heal the bird's wing and let it fly free one day very soon.

When they were finished praying, the group doing dishes returned to the kitchen, and the girls, John, and Elaine went back to the family room. The commotion among the children died down too, though John had a feeling that Cole and Maddie were still exchanging barbs under their breath.

John tuned in to the conversation among his daughters and Katy.

Kari was saying that since they didn't know when and where Dayne and Katy's wedding was going to be, maybe they should

140

have the shower the day before.

"The shower in the day and the rehearsal at night?" Katy was sitting cross-legged on the floor, feeding a bottle to Malin, Luke and Reagan's daughter.

"Exactly. That way whether we're at your lake house or in the Bahamas, it'll work out." Kari laughed. "Not that you'd get married in the Bahamas."

"We might." Katy gave a slight shake of her head. "Dayne says anything's possible. So long as the paparazzi don't find out."

"It's beautiful there. Especially Nassau." Elaine clearly felt comfortable among his family. She sat in a chair across from John, her attention on his daughters. "My husband and I had our tenth anniversary there."

John could've hugged her. By talking about her husband, she reminded them that this wasn't her plan either. That being here as John's friend wasn't how she'd wanted to finish out her years. Both of them had been cheated out of the happily ever afters they'd dreamed of and counted on. Now they had each other. Hearing her mention her husband made it even more understandable.

Erin sat next to Katy on the floor. "How would you get everyone to the Bahamas?" She was holding her youngest on her lap. Amy was sleeping, her pale blonde hair half

141

covering her face.

"Dayne says we'd lease a jet." Katy made a look as if the entire experience was beyond her comprehension.

John chuckled under his breath. Whatever happened with the wedding, it would be remarkable, unlike any Baxter wedding they'd had before. But because so much was up in the air, it was important that they settle on a date. That way the family could at least set that week aside, no matter where they ended up having the celebration. "Will you have a date after you meet with the wedding coordinator?"

"Yes." Katy looked relieved. "My parents have been asking the same thing." She lowered her voice, as if someone with a camera and a tape recorder might be lurking just outside the door. "We'll probably have a couple dates, actually. One that we leak to the press, and another that we leak to only some of the press. The real wedding date will come before either of those. Apparently it's part of Wilma's plan."

John laughed, and his daughters began talking at once. As they did, John saw Ashley and Landon returning from upstairs. Landon gave her a quick kiss, then turned into the kitchen.

Ashley smiled and entered the family

room. She took the spot on the other side of Katy, sitting on the floor. John could tell she'd been crying, but she also made an effort not to look sad. She included Elaine as she made eye contact with the others. "What did I miss?"

"We're still talking about the shower." Kari leaned against the arm of her chair and angled her head. "Maybe we'll have it the day before the wedding, so that wherever and whenever they get married, we'll at least all be together."

"Dayne's talking about maybe leasing a jet and having the whole group fly to the Bahamas." Brooke had been quiet, but she sounded excited at the idea. "Talk about your movie scripts."

Ashley grinned. "This is going to be fun."

John's heart felt warm as the girls' conversation picked up pace. Ashley seemed okay about whatever had troubled her before. And she was right — the wedding would be a special time for everyone, no matter where they had it.

Everything about the night was filled with joy and laughter and anticipation, and even as the kids and their families said good night, and as Erin and Sam and the girls headed up to the guest rooms and Dayne found his place in the far room at the end of the house, John had the sense that this would be a beautiful season for the Baxter family.

Beautiful and memorable.

Kari pulled John aside as she left. "Ashley's fine. She talked to me." She reached up and hugged his neck. "She's just missing Mom."

John thanked her for the update. It was what he'd secretly hoped — that Ashley's sadness halfway through the night had less to do with Elaine's presence and more to do with her mother's absence.

Elaine was the last to leave, and when she had her coat on, she stood before him and smiled. Her eyes held a gratitude John hadn't expected. "Thank you."

"For what?" He reached out and took her hands, though the feeling was different from before, when they'd been in the prayer circle. This time it was two friends saying good-bye, nothing more.

"For including me tonight." Her voice was soft. "It meant a lot."

John stopped himself from saying that she was his friend and the kids needed to get used to that fact. *Friend* seemed to be a word Elaine bristled at. Instead he gave her a look that held more depth than before. "I liked having you here. We all did."

"Ashley?" Elaine wasn't angry or hurt. Just perceptive. A sad smile played on her lips. "She was struggling."

"She was missing Elizabeth."

Elaine's expression told him that she understood. "Ashley's a special young woman. It can't be easy talking about weddings and knowing that her mother won't be here to celebrate with all of you."

"Nothing about loss is easy." He tightened his hold on her hands. "You should know. You've dealt with it longer than any of us."

"Long enough to know that even after the darkest night, God's mercies are new every morning."

They were the words she left him with. She hugged him, not too long or too close, and then she bid him good night. After she was gone, when he heard her car heading down the driveway, he felt the hint of sorrow, of loneliness that had been coming more often lately whenever she left for the evening.

John went to the kitchen and finished putting the last coffee cups into the dishwasher. He liked Elaine, liked the way he felt when he was with her and the way she added bits of wisdom to the conversations between his kids. He liked her tender laugh and her strong faith. There was no denying it.

And as he turned in for the night, he realized that he'd gotten through an entire family get-together without aching for the loss of Elizabeth. Because Elaine had been lending her quiet strength and support all evening.

Before John fell asleep he read chapter 3 of Lamentations, where Jeremiah was crying out in agony for the ways he was hurting.

There was the verse Elaine had alluded to, the idea that God's mercies were new every morning. He was great in His faithfulness, because night — no matter how dark and dreadfully long — never lasted forever.

As John closed his Bible and set it on his nightstand next to the photograph of Elizabeth, as he lay down and closed his eyes, across the horizon of his heart he glimpsed something he hadn't experienced in years of sadness and nightfall.

A beautiful, breathtaking, hope-filled sunrise.

CHAPTER EIGHT

Dayne had been dreading this moment.

Since he'd arrived in Bloomington before Thanksgiving, he hadn't looked at a single tabloid, hadn't wanted to or needed to know what the rags were saying. His hours were full, sharing the joy of what his family and their friends and the CKT kids had done to renovate the lake house. After that, there'd been Thanksgiving and Laughter and Leftovers with the Baxters.

Real life — the one he lived in the public eye — felt a million miles away.

Now it was Monday, and he and Katy were on their way to the meeting with Wilma Waters in Indianapolis. Dayne wanted to know if the press had found out that he was engaged. He had to be prepared, especially since he hadn't told anyone outside his family that he wasn't planning to return to Hollywood until the filming of his next movie.

Since leaving Los Angeles, Dayne hadn't even talked with his agent. The guy knew he was with Katy and his family, and he was probably trying to keep things quiet for him. Especially since Dayne had only recently been out of physical therapy.

Now he was driving Katy's car, and for the first time in a week he felt conscious of his fame, his familiarity. He wasn't the oldest Baxter son enjoying time with his family. He was Hollywood's heartthrob, facing whatever was waiting for him outside the safe confines of Bloomington. The realization left him moody and quiet, the way he hadn't been since midway through his physical therapy.

"Are you stopping?" Katy seemed unnerved, anxious about his attitude. They had talked last night about making the stop, but it hadn't come up since he'd picked her up at the Flanigan house.

"We have to." Dayne adjusted his sunglasses. The day was bright and blue, but frost hung on the grass and plants as they headed north. He wore a baseball cap and the familiar hooded sweatshirt, the kind he always kept on hand in case he needed an escape, a way to hide. He pulled the car into the lot of a convenience store and parked in the middle, in a spot with no cars on either side. "I'll wait here."

"Be right back."

Dayne watched Katy walk across the lot and into the store, and he admired the way she wasn't conditioned to look over her shoulder for paparazzi. She was a normal person still, a regular person. Someone who could walk into a store and buy a few magazines without causing a ruckus. It was one of the conveniences people took for granted, one that Katy would be giving up when she married him.

After a few minutes she came out and smiled at him. It was a tentative smile, and he reminded himself that whatever news the tabloids held, Katy deserved his best attitude, his happiness and kindness. Especially on a day when they were driving to Indianapolis to meet with the wedding coordinator.

He clenched his jaw and then relaxed it. *God, help me handle the press. You know my feelings for them. Since the accident it's more of a . . . a hatred. I know it isn't good for me, but I don't know how else to feel.*

Forgive, My son. . . . Forgive as the Lord forgave you. . . .

The words filled Dayne's soul and mind, words he'd read in the Bible just this morning. A verse he had no idea how he was going to live out — not when it came to the paparazzi. The photogs had almost killed him. Forgiving them would take an act of God.

Katy opened the door and climbed in. "You're not on the cover of any of them!"

A slight breeze of relief blew across his conscience. "Good." He leaned over and kissed her. "Sorry."

"Why?" Her eyes had a dreaminess that hadn't been there before. She touched her lips to his again, then pulled back, waiting for his answer.

"I've been in a lousy mood." Dayne nodded to the bag on her lap. "Not looking forward to whatever's in there." A slow smile filled his face. "But that isn't fair to you, Katy. I can't wait to start planning our wedding." He kissed her one more time. "You know that, right?"

"I do."

"Exactly." He felt his eyes light up for the first time today. "Those are the words I can't wait to hear."

Katy giggled and clicked her seat belt into place. "Should I look?" Her hands settled on the bag of magazines.

"Yes." He pulled back onto the street. "No sense hiding from it."

" 'Dayne Matthews and His Brother

Make Up,' " Katy read the headline out loud. She gave Dayne a nervous smile. "So far, so good."

"Yeah." He raised an eyebrow. "Keep reading."

Katy found her place. " 'Sources say the feud between Dayne Matthews and his brother, Luke Baxter, may finally be over.' " She shook her head and mumbled under her breath, "Finally over? The two of you just met, for goodness' sake."

"That's not sensational enough." Dayne smiled, but inside he felt his anger rise again. What right did they have to print one word about him after driving an oncoming truck into his path? He kept his attention on the road. "Go on."

" 'According to a source, Luke Baxter is no longer employed at a Manhattan law firm but has been transferred to Indianapolis, closer to his family. A clerk at the firm in Indianapolis, a member of the Meritas network, said that Baxter will be working exclusively on Dayne Matthews' legal affairs when he starts his new position in December.' "

"Nice. We've got a leak, and Luke hasn't even had his first day." Dayne chuckled. "There's no getting around them."

The story explained that Dayne had

151

wrapped up his romance movie with Randi Wells and that the film was expected in theaters in early spring. " 'Dayne's next movie doesn't start shooting until May or later. Sources say the director for *But Then Again No* hasn't cast the female lead opposite Dayne as of yet. Some sources say he will marry former mystery woman Katy Hart before filming begins.' "

"There it is." He tightened his hold on the steering wheel.

Katy gave him a blank look. She let the magazine fall to her lap. "I'm not surprised really."

Dayne sighed. He needed to let go of his anger, of the tensions the tabloids had caused him since his accident. He'd taken them in stride before. He reached out and took Katy's hand. "You're right. The surprising thing is that we're not on the cover."

"At least not this week." She smiled at him, and her eyes were full of understanding.

He sighed, and the sound filled the car with tension.

"Hey . . . we'll get through this."

"I know. Bob gave me some verses about forgiveness." He felt himself relax. "I looked at a few of them this morning."

"And . . ."

"I can't stay angry. I know that." Dayne took off the baseball cap and tossed it on the console between them. "But I can feel the pain in my leg with every step, Katy." He kept his tone in check. "I don't want photographers chasing us the rest of our lives." He felt weary. "I'm not sure what to do."

Katy was quiet for a few minutes. Then she took a long breath. "I think I might have an idea."

"About the press?" Dayne was surprised. Katy was especially hesitant around the cameras. Whatever plan she had was probably not one they could actually pull off. Not as long as he was making movies.

Katy turned in the seat so she was facing him. "What if we take an entirely different approach?"

"You mean like every time we see a photographer, we stop and smile for him?" Dayne laughed. The idea was certainly not what Katy had in mind.

"Actually, yes. That's just what I mean." She didn't wait for him to object. "Like I said, I'm more afraid of running."

He had to clench his teeth to keep from interrupting her.

"Say we tell them what they want to know. We schedule an interview with one of the

153

more reputable magazines. *Celebrity Life* maybe. We can announce our engagement, and you can explain that you're moving to Bloomington to live a more private life." She seemed to be holding her breath, as if she'd been considering this possibility for some time. "If they don't have to guess about us, maybe it'll take away some of the thrill. The love of the chase."

Dayne wanted to blurt out that he could do nothing of the sort. He could never intentionally give the press details about his life. But even as he was about to say so, Katy's idea gradually began to make sense. Even just a little. If the press wanted to know about their lives, they would hunt them down until they had the information. Accurate or not. But if they scheduled an interview and photos with one magazine, the others would find a few stock photos of the two of them and reword and run the same story.

Yes, they'd still want new photos, but so what? It was possible Katy was right. By making the information public, they would do away with the throngs of photographers chasing them through the streets of Malibu and Hollywood. He gave a slow nod. "Interesting."

"Thank you." Katy sounded like she was

proud of herself. "I'm right there with you. I don't want to be chased forever. So if we give them what they want . . ."

"And if I tell them I'm moving to Bloomington for privacy . . ."

"I mean, they aren't going to send a photographer to Bloomington more than a few times a year. And when they do, we can stop and smile for the cameras." Katy ran her thumb along the side of his finger. "That's a small price to pay for sharing my life with you."

Hope filled Dayne's heart, and a love that knew no bounds filled him to the core. "How can I be marrying you, Katy Lynn Hart?"

She grinned. "I love when you use my whole name."

"I'm practicing for the altar." He felt the burdens from earlier lift. "All morning I've worried about the press. If they're speculating about a wedding, then keeping it secret will be harder than we thought."

"But if we give an interview announcing our engagement, and if we throw them off by telling them the wrong month . . ."

"It could work." They were at the exit for downtown Indianapolis. Dayne eased Katy's car off the freeway. He made a few turns until they were in the Hyatt parking lot. "I can't believe you love me."

Katy closed her eyes and kissed him. "I love you, Dayne."

"I'm the luckiest guy in the world." He returned her kiss. "We better go. Wilma's waiting for us."

She handed him the baseball cap. "Keep your head low."

"Thanks."

He put the cap on. They climbed out and held hands as they made their way quickly to the back door of the Hyatt. Wilma had arranged to meet them there, and as they walked, Dayne flipped open his cell phone and called her. "We're heading in."

"Okay. I'll be just inside."

Dayne closed his phone and dropped it back into his pocket. He looked around the parking lot, but he didn't see anyone looking for him, no paparazzi lurking anywhere. He put his arm around Katy. "No press; it's a good sign."

"Everything's going to be fine." Katy smiled up at him.

He wanted to shout that yes, it was. The wedding they were about to plan and the future they would build together were going to be better than any movie script. Because of Katy, he'd found new life with God and with his birth family. And one day after they got married, they would find another kind of new life.

The family he would share with his forever love, Katy Lynn Hart.

His Katy.

Chapter Nine

It was anything but normal to meet with a Hollywood wedding coordinator to talk about planning a secret wedding that might possibly include boarding the guests onto a private jet and whisking them off to a place like the Bahamas. But for Dayne, Katy tried to act nonchalant.

He had been struggling with his feelings about the paparazzi since the accident, but over Thanksgiving he found a new sense of peace. The break was just what they'd both needed. Now, though, it was time to face the future, which meant finding a way to deal with the press, both in person and in attitude.

Katy held tight to Dayne's hand as they headed through the back door of the Hyatt. A wiry woman met them. Katy knew from Dayne that Wilma Waters was in her midfifties, but she didn't look a day over forty. She wore tight black pants, black stiletto heels, and a black button-down cotton shirt, which was untucked. Her short hair was blonde, and she had red manicured finger-nails. Wilma's eyes were clear, blue, and kind. She was the picture of artistic profes-sionalism. Katy liked her immediately.

"Dayne, you look marvelous." Wilma took Dayne's hands and kissed first one cheek, then the other. She turned to Katy. "And you must be the mystery woman the tabs are in love with!"

"This is Katy Hart." Dayne smiled, and pride shone in his eyes. "Katy, this is Wilma Waters."

Katy shook the woman's hand. "Nice to meet you."

"The photographs don't do you justice." Wilma stepped back and surveyed Katy. "There isn't a wedding dress I can think of that wouldn't look stunning on you." She motioned for them to follow, and the only thing faster than her pace was her constant stream of conversation. "I've booked resorts in three beach communities without giving any names including mine, because at this point my name is synonymous with the weddings of top celebrities and . . ."

By the time they took their seats at a round table in a small meeting room, Katy was dizzy trying to keep up.

Wilma stopped suddenly and looked at her and then at Dayne. "I'm going too fast again, aren't I?" She winced, and a nervous laugh slipped from her throat. "Sorry. I get so excited about weddings."

Beneath the table, Dayne took Katy's hand. "Let's start at the beginning." He leaned back in his seat. He looked more relaxed than he had earlier in the car. "Neither of us has done this before."

Katy felt a chill run down her arms. It was really happening. They were here because she and Dayne were going to be married. So many times life had taken them on a crazy ride to where Katy had often doubted that they would ever see this day. But here they were. She focused on the energetic woman across from them.

". . . and not much parking, which wouldn't be an issue if we flew in the guests, but even so we need three locations, three options. A place that will help make this the wedding you both want." Wilma grabbed a breath. "Have you decided on that much?"

Katy felt a sense of peace warm her heart. With Wilma's reputation and her mandate from Dayne to keep the wedding a secret, Katy figured they might have little to say about where the wedding would be held. But clearly Wilma wanted this to be their celebration. Katy gave the coordinator a tentative smile. "I'm not sure we've got three places in mind." She turned to Dayne. "Do we?"

"We wanted to think through some of this with you —" Dayne sat a little straighter — "since you know what places make a secret wedding possible."

"True." Wilma nodded, her expression thoughtful. "Well, I can tell you right now we can't do a church wedding." She made an apologetic face. "Sorry."

"That's okay." Under the table Dayne squeezed Katy's hand. "God will be with us wherever we get married."

"And we sort of wanted something outdoors, anyway." Katy shared a look with Dayne.

"Outdoors and secluded." Dayne's expression showed the anxiety from earlier today. "If that's possible."

"Very possible." Wilma made some notes on a pad of paper in front of her. "So let's start with Bloomington. That's where you live, right, Katy?"

"Yes."

"Actually," Dayne cut in, "it's where I live too. The media doesn't know yet, but I'm staying with family, and before Christmas

161

I'll move into the lake house I'll share with Katy."

Wilma looked up from her pad of paper. "So what are the possibilities in Bloomington?"

Katy took the lead. "There's the lake house. It's newly renovated, and the yard is big enough for a large wedding."

"Good." Wilma made a few more notes.

"And there're the people I live with. They have seven acres, and we could easily hold an outdoor wedding there." Those were the two options she and Dayne had discussed. "Beyond that, the city has the lake and a few parks. Nothing very secluded."

"All right, I'd like to make a suggestion." Wilma folded one hand over the other. "You want around a hundred and fifty people. Is that right?"

"Yes." Dayne cleared his throat. "Katy's family and friends in Bloomington, several of the theater families she works with, and everyone in my birth family." He hesitated. "And my manager and agent and my close friends from Hollywood."

Wilma shook her head the way Katy had seen Jenny shake hers when one of the kids had an outlandish request, like whether a snake could be brought into the house. "If you want that many guests, Bloomington's

162

out of the question. The press will know about the lake house in a matter of weeks."

Katy bit her lip and tried to hide her disappointment. The lake house would've been a beautiful place for the wedding. But Wilma was right. It would take just one photographer following either of them back to the house, and the news would be on the front page of the tabloids: "Dayne Matthews Buys House in Bloomington." She stifled a sigh.

Wilma looked at her. "As for your friends' house, that's an option. But I'd say it's an option we use as a decoy."

Dayne blinked. "Decoy?"

"Yes." Wilma tucked a strand of her golden hair behind her ear. "I said earlier that we need three options. Here's why." She explained that they would have a first option — one that they would make a heartless attempt to cover up. A second option would feel secretive and seem secretive, one that even the guests would fall for. And then a third option. She smiled. "The place where the actual wedding will be held."

Three plans for three places? All the while certain that only one would actually pan out? Katy wasn't sure she could keep it all straight. "Who do we tell about the third one?"

"No one." Wilma held up one finger. She looked at Katy and Dayne, and her eyes made it clear that she was serious. "Absolutely no one. Not your close friends, not your family. No one at all."

"Isn't that kind of . . . awkward?" Dayne made a face. "I mean, we trust our families."

Wilma sat back and tossed her hands. "You want a secret wedding or not?" It was the first time she'd shown any edginess. But it was a confident edginess that told them she could give them what they wanted if they cooperated. "Tell your families you want to surprise them. It'll be an adventure for everyone."

It took a few seconds, but Katy could feel herself warming to the idea. "What about the dates?"

"Yes." Wilma flipped her book to a calendar section. "Let's take care of that right now."

The three of them talked for fifteen minutes about Dayne's filming schedule and the need for three dates to match the three locations. Delays had changed the start date on Dayne's next film to mid-May.

"When do you want to get married?" Wilma had her pen poised over the calendar.

Dayne looked at Katy and silently asked her to object if she'd changed her mind.

164

"We'd been thinking April or May. But now we're leaning toward March sometime. We want time in Bloomington before I shoot my next film."

"Perfect."

A few more minutes of conversation and Katy and Dayne agreed that March 18 would be the best time for the actual wedding, the one no one would know about.

Wilma circled the date. "Dayne, we need to talk about the press." Her tone filled with sympathy. "I haven't seen you since your accident, so before we go much further, I'm sorry. The paparazzi caused the wreck, and you were caught in the middle. I don't blame you for wanting a private wedding." She clenched her jaw and made a subtle shake of her head. "I want this celebration kept from the press as badly as you do."

"Thanks." Dayne tensed up, probably because of the mention of the accident. "We appreciate everything you're doing."

"That said —" Wilma tapped her pen on her notebook — "we need an interview with the press or they'll be rabid trying to find out information."

"Exactly what we talked about on the way here." Katy slid her chair a little closer to Dayne's. As she did, she felt his body relax again. "*Celebrity Life* magazine, maybe."

"Good." Wilma jotted something down. "I'll call the editor tomorrow morning. You'll need to fly into LA sometime in the next few weeks and use the interview to announce your engagement. Explain that you're considering a wedding in late April, before the start of your next film."

Dayne chuckled. "So basically lie?"

"Yes." Wilma made no apologies. "These people will eat you alive, Dayne." She turned to Katy. "The two of you should know that more than anyone. If you want a private wedding — and you're entitled to that much — then you'll need to tell them things that simply aren't true. Later on it'll only look like you changed your mind." She shrugged. "Besides, you *are* considering a wedding in late April. That's what we're doing right here."

It didn't matter how Wilma spun the plan; Dayne had called it. Wilma wanted them to lie. Katy felt a knot forming in her stomach. Lying went against her nature. Honesty was the cornerstone of everything she believed in, everything she tried to teach her young acting students. The best actor was the one who was the most honest with the character. But in this situation, they had no choice. Wilma was right. The press would be relentless until they thought they knew when and where Katy and Dayne would get married. They couldn't have a private wedding without saying something to throw the tabloids off the track.

"But we tell our guests the real date . . . right?" Dayne sounded resigned about the lying. He had probably processed the idea and come to the same conclusion: there was no way around it.

"Good question." Wilma took a deep breath. "Here's what we do. . . ."

The plan was fascinating, a coordinating of dates and events that would require hours of work on the part of Wilma and her two trusted staff members — her husband and her daughter. Katy tried her best to follow along. Four weeks before the actual wedding, Katy and Dayne would alert their guests to keep a certain date or dates open for a prewedding party. Then, forty-eight hours before the wedding, invitations would be hand delivered by Wilma or one of her staff to each guest.

"The invitation will tell them when and where to meet." Wilma smiled, confident. "That way there isn't time for the press to figure out what's going on."

"They'll think it's for a prewedding party?" Katy couldn't imagine how elaborate the plans needed to be.

"Most of them will have an idea that it's something more. But we'll never come out and say so." Wilma flipped a page in her book.

At the same time, there was a knock at the door.

Wilma cast them a knowing look. "Come in."

"Hello." A woman stepped into the room. Her dark hair was pulled back tightly into a bun, and she wore a skirt and a suit jacket. Her name tag declared her the banquet manager. "Your salads are ready, Ms. Waters." As she shot a few furtive glances toward Dayne, her cheeks turned a deep red. "Should I have them brought in?"

"Yes, very well." Wilma smiled at the woman. "Thank you."

When the woman turned and left the room, Wilma lowered her voice and leaned across the table. "Renting this room for today was a good idea. She'll tell everyone in the kitchen you're here. Mark my words, someone will leak this to the press, and they'll all have you getting married at the Indianapolis Hyatt."

"Then why are we here?" Frustration colored Dayne's words. "I thought we're aiming for something secret?"

"We're doing this on purpose." Wilma allowed a quick laugh as though she was proud of what she was pulling off. "Indianapolis is close enough to Bloomington, close enough to a major airport. The Hyatt has beautiful banquet rooms, and since it's out of Southern California, you'll never have the numbers of photographers that you'd have in LA." She patted the table between them. "This is option one."

"Here?" Katy was surprised. This wasn't the sort of place they'd ever considered for the wedding. "Will people believe us?"

"Coming from the viewpoint of a tabloid, a more remote place than Indiana doesn't exist. This hotel has a traditional feel and enough glamour to fit the bill." Wilma turned the pages of her book to the calendar section again. "We'll ask the banquet manager to keep things quiet, and we'll tell her we'd like to book a room for —" she moved her pen over the small squares — "April 22. We'll book the most beautiful room they have and pay the woman handsomely for letting us meet here. We'll have a hefty cancellation fee, but it's a small price to pay for the diversion."

"I love that you've got this all figured out." Dayne grinned. "What about option two?"

"Now that might be a tough one." She narrowed her eyes, as if the next tier of the plan was going to take her most brilliant work. She turned her attention to Katy. "Tell me about these friends of yours, the place where you're living."

Katy swallowed. The entire elaborate ordeal felt like it was taking on a life of its own. But Jenny had already offered her house, so letting the conversation take this direction seemed fine. She told Wilma that the Flanigans' house was seven thousand square feet and had huge areas for entertaining.

"Would you like to be married there?"

"Yes, but . . ." Katy looked at Dayne, then back at Wilma. "I thought you said Bloomington would be hard."

"It will be. If you want privacy, it's out of the question. But to make the plan believable, it needs to feel like the kind of place where you'd consider getting married. That way you can talk about it with family and friends as if maybe — just maybe — you might hold the event there."

Katy released Dayne's hand and leaned her forearms on the table. This was getting uncomfortable. "Lie to them, too?"

"No." Wilma seemed to sense that lying didn't come easily for her. "Only hint that this might be where the wedding will be staged. And then —" an intensity filled her face — "pick one or at the most two people who could help make it seem like a wedding might actually take place there. Remember, your close friends and family will think it's a secret, a surprise. Any hints you give about having a wedding at the house where you live will be good-natured red herrings."

So Katy could tell Jenny and Jim Flanigan that she and Dayne would be dropping hints that the wedding might be at their house. To help play along, Jenny and Jim could talk about ordering a truckload of folding chairs or getting the yard ready for a big event. People would see this and think that, hey, maybe the wedding was going to be at the Flanigans'.

That way if someone got wind of the happenings and leaked the information to the press, there would be no damage done. Because option three was something no one would know about until the day of the wedding.

"Now for option three . . ." Wilma's eyes sparkled. "Think outside the box. The West Virginia mountains, a lodge in the Canadian Rockies, the Caribbean. Somewhere meaningful." She paused. "Somewhere half a day's flight from Bloomington where your guests could fly in, stay for a few days, and witness your wedding."

Katy felt her eyes glaze over. She looked at the blank wall in front of her. Wilma was saying that the wedding could be anywhere they wanted. A beach or a mountain hideaway, someplace in the United States or a different country. How crazy was that? She looked at Dayne. "Any ideas?"

His expression was empty for a few seconds, but then his features changed and his eyes lit up. "Mexico. That would mean a lot." He gazed at Katy, beyond the surface to the deepest part of her soul. "I gave my life to Christ in Mexico." His voice grew soft, as if he'd forgotten about Wilma. "It was there that God told me to go back home and marry you." A soft glow fell over his face, and it was as if they were alone in the room. "What do you think? A beach somewhere in Mexico?"

Tears nipped at the corners of Katy's eyes. "Bob lives in Mexico too. He and his family would feel very comfortable there."

Dayne covered her hands with his before turning back to Wilma. "I love it. Now we need a beach."

"Let's take a look." Wilma pulled out a laptop from her bag and powered it up. As she did, there was another knock at the door.

Directed by the banquet manager, a staff member wheeled in a cart. From it he served a chicken Caesar salad to each of them. As the waiter served Dayne's plate, he grinned. "It's nice to have you here, Mr. Matthews."

"Thank you." Dayne returned the smile.

Before the staff left, Wilma stood and approached the banquet manager. "Please advise your staff again. In planning this event we need the utmost confidentiality."

"Yes, madam." The woman practically bowed. "We'll do everything we can to see that no one knows you're here or that you're planning a dinner with us."

A dinner. Katy smiled to herself. When the staff was gone, she looked at Wilma. "Is that what you told her? That you were planning a dinner?"

"Yes." Wilma sat back down and spread her napkin across her lap. She looked proud of herself. "I said I was planning a dinner to honor two special people, clients of mine."

"The manager didn't know it was me until she came in earlier." Dayne seemed like he was enjoying himself, caught up in the scheming. "Brilliant. I love it."

They finished eating their salads while Wilma found an online map of Mexico. "A straight shot would take you to Cancún."

She drew an imaginary line from Bloomington south. "I'd guess you could be there in less than four hours by jet."

"You're saying . . . have the guests meet at the airport? And then take them to Cancún?"

"Right." Wilma had her game face on now. She seemed more serious, and the details were coming faster than before. "The guests learn about the date in time to make plans, and then they get their forty-eight hour notice to meet at the Indianapolis airport to fly to Cancún. We tell them what to bring — black tie, evening attire, bathing suits, that kind of thing."

Katy sat back against her chair and exhaled. Hollywood people might be used to these sorts of surprise weddings, the kind where you board a mystery jet for a destination you didn't know about until that hour. But what about the families from CKT? She closed her eyes for a moment, and when she opened them, Dayne was watching her.

"It's a lot, huh?"

"Yes." She looked at Wilma. "Sorry. It sounds wonderful. I'm just not sure . . ."

Wilma tapped her fingers on the table between them. "Don't worry about a thing. That's my job. It's why you hired me."

Katy wanted to say that she hadn't hired

her. Rather, Dayne had taken care of that. In fact, in less time than it took to have lunch, the entire wedding had begun to feel complicated and dramatically out of hand. She faced Dayne. "What do you think?"

The calm in his eyes told her the answer before he opened his mouth. "Like Wilma said, she'll take care of everything." The ends of his mouth turned upward. "What about Cancún?"

Wilma was busy finding images from that stretch of beach. "The entire Mayan Riviera is amazing. I know a small five-star resort half an hour south of the airport in Cancún." She went on about how she could make a phone call and reserve the entire place for the weekend of the wedding. "We'd fly the guests in on Thursday night. You could have dinners or parties and a rehearsal on Friday and the wedding on Saturday. Guests would fly home midday Sunday."

Katy opened her eyes wide. It sounded like something from a fantasy. Of course, this was the life Dayne led, and it was something she needed to get used to.

Wilma was asking whether the idea was something they liked, something they could be excited about. "I won't make the call unless you want Mexico."

"Well —" Dayne breathed out, but it sounded more like a laugh — "can we get back to you? Maybe in a few days?"

Wilma looked like a party girl with a popped balloon. She found a smile and closed her laptop. "Of course." She handed her card to Dayne. "You know where to reach me."

They talked another few minutes about the *Celebrity Life* interview. Katy agreed that Wilma should go ahead and schedule the interview. The only thing they had on their schedules for the next few weeks was furniture shopping. A trip to Los Angeles would work out fine, especially for a few days.

Even so, as they left the meeting, Dayne seemed edgy again. Wilma was parked out front, so they parted ways in the hallway. Dayne took the lead toward rear exit and stopped in the doorway with the door partially opened. There were only a few cars in the back lot and not a sign of the press.

Dayne took Katy's hand, and they hurried to her car. "The hotel manager must really want our business."

"That . . ." Katy waited while he opened her door. She slid in, and when he was beside her she snapped her seat belt in place. "Or there aren't enough photographers in Indianapolis to get someone out here that quickly."

Dayne locked the doors, grabbed the wheel, and hung his head. "Why do I feel like I'm constantly having to apologize?"

"Hey . . ." She was still reeling from the meeting with Wilma, but Dayne had more at stake. Even though she'd spent every day after his accident praying and dreading the possibilities, she'd also had longer to forgive. Now she needed to be careful how she reacted to the wedding plans. Otherwise his anger toward the press would consume him.

Dayne turned just enough to see her. Then he gestured toward the back entrance of the hotel. "All that running around and plotting and having options . . . it's because of the paparazzi. Same as my accident." He flexed the muscles in his jaw and stared straight ahead. "It isn't fair."

"No." Katy silently prayed for the right words. "But we have options here."

"Like what?"

"A smaller wedding." She took hold of his arm. "I don't need a big wedding. We can have a party later with the CKT families. If it's just us, the Baxters, my parents, and the Flanigans, I'll be fine."

His expression told her how much the situation was affecting him. "You want a big wedding. I heard you tell Ashley the other night after dinner."

"But I could forget the idea —" her voice fell a notch — "if that's what you wanted."

"It wouldn't help." Dayne leaned back and let his hands fall to his lap. "Without Wilma's plotting, the paparazzi will find us. Like you said, if we keep running, they'll have more reason to chase us."

"Exactly." Katy was convincing herself as much as him. "So we let her walk us through it, and we pray for privacy." Her tone sounded more upbeat. "That's all we can do, Dayne."

"In there, I was actually starting to like the idea of a wedding with a hundred and fifty guests being flown secretly to Cancún." He laughed, but his tone held no humor. "Then I started thinking about flying to LA and having a formal magazine interview while trying to pull off a secret where if one person leaks the wrong information, the whole thing goes up in smoke." He met her eyes and held them. "All of a sudden I could think only one thing."

"What?"

"That you were crazy to ever say yes." Dayne framed her face with his hand, his fingers barely touching her skin. "You deserve a big wedding, Katy."

"All I want is you." She'd been feeling the

178

swirling rush of everything that lay ahead, but here — with her heart melting from Dayne's touch — she didn't care about the details. Let Wilma handle them. "These are the happiest days of my life. Wilma can make the plans, and we'll go along for the ride."

He clenched his jaw and studied her. "I need you, Katy." He brought his other hand up to her face, holding her like she was a great and priceless treasure. "If the planning gets me all . . . I don't know, all tied up, say something to remind me that we'll get through it."

Katy laughed and looped her arm around his neck. They would play nice with the press, granting the interview, and they would help each other through the tricky times — when the extent of their planning seemed downright ludicrous. She tenderly pressed her cheek to his. This close she could smell his cologne, his shampoo. His nearness was intoxicating. "Hey, I know what I'll say. And whenever I say it, you have to promise to let go of the anger." She drew back and touched the spot over his heart. "Otherwise it'll eat you up in here."

He smiled at her. The passion in his eyes was just below the surface. " 'Forgive as the Lord forgave you.' That verse is always coming up." He ran his thumb lightly along her brow. "So what's the code word?"

"That's easy." She rubbed her nose against his. "Wilma."

They both laughed, and Katy straightened back into her seat.

Dayne started the engine, and the rest of the way home they didn't talk once about paparazzi or pending trips to Los Angeles or the idea of having three options just to pull off a private wedding. They didn't mention a private jet or keeping secrets or how they would survive between now and March 18.

Instead they talked about the Baxter grandkids, about the bird with the hurt wing and Dayne's father catching it in the box as though he were a pro at the job, about his sisters' ideas for a wedding shower and Luke's excitement over his new job. And all the while they reminded each other how extraordinary life had become, how wonderful it was that they wouldn't just share Thanksgiving weekend together with the Baxter family . . . his family.

But an entire lifetime.

CHAPTER TEN

In her years of being a coach's wife, Jenny Flanigan had on occasion seen a football player cry. When Jim's star NFL running back blew out his knee in a career-ending injury and when a veteran tight end was traded after ten years of service. But she had never seen a player so completely broken as Cody Coleman.

He had been released from the hospital Sunday morning, and he'd slept most of that day. During that time, Jenny and Jim explained to their kids that Cody was out of danger for now. "But he has a drinking problem." Jim's tone was very serious. "We'll talk about it with him, try to figure out a way to help him."

"Will he still live here?" Justin looked worried.

Jenny's heart hurt for her kids — all of them. They'd been talking about whether Cody would have to leave because of his bad choices. Even Bailey had asked about it.

"He'll stay as long as he's willing to get help for his drinking." Jim seemed as devastated as the kids. "Drinking is a choice, and if Cody won't get help, he'll need to find somewhere else to live. Let's pray it works out, okay? Maybe we can learn something from this."

"Yeah, like never drink when you're in high school." Ricky nodded, his expression deeply serious. He looked at his brothers for approval, and they responded with a round of affirmations.

At dinnertime, Jenny had heard Jim talk to Cody from his bedroom door. "Time for dinner."

From inside the room came Cody's groggy voice. "I'm not that hungry."

"I don't care if you eat, but I'd like you to come to dinner." Jim sounded gruff. "And by Tuesday or Wednesday, you need to get back to school."

Cody's words were muted, but from her spot in the kitchen, Jenny could hear his response. "Yes, sir. I'll be there."

Relief filled Jenny. She wanted this to be a turning point for Cody, not a point of separation.

Everyone sat down to this year's final meal

of leftover turkey, potatoes, and peas. Cody was subdued and clearly embarrassed, and for the most part, he avoided eye contact. The kids, probably sensing that Cody didn't want to talk, made conversation among themselves.

Only Ricky mentioned the incident. During a lull, he looked at Cody. "We prayed for you." The look in his tender young eyes was part hurt, part gratitude. Jenny watched her youngest son. He felt betrayed, angry that Cody would drink again after telling Jenny and Jim he wouldn't. For a minute it looked like Ricky might ask why Cody did it, why he drank himself nearly to death. But instead he turned his attention back to his dinner, and the topic didn't come up the rest of the meal.

When they were done eating and the kids had cleared their plates and left the room, Jim focused on Cody. "We need to talk."

"Yes, sir." Cody was still dragging his fork through what was left of the little bit of food he'd taken.

"Look at me when I talk to you." Jim sounded like the coach he sometimes was on the field when the team was down two touchdowns with time running out.

Jenny kept her mouth shut. Jim knew better than she did how to handle this.

Cody lifted his gaze. "Sorry."

Jim rested his elbows on the table. "Why don't you tell me what happened that night."

"Sir . . ." Cody swallowed, clearly struggling. "I wonder if we could . . . if we could have this talk on Wednesday night."

Jim looked suspicious. "Why Wednesday?"

"What I did was stupid; I need time to think about it."

"You need to do more than think about it." Jim seemed to realize he was being harsh. He relaxed his expression. "You better pray God gives us both a plan. Otherwise we can't have you here, Cody. I won't have you drinking around my kids."

Tears filled the boy's eyes. "I understand."

Jim gritted his teeth, obviously struggling over Cody's request. Finally his shoulders fell a little. "Fine. We'll talk Wednesday. Until then you can catch up on your homework until you're ready to go back to school. I want you in bed by ten o'clock each night."

"Yes, sir." Cody's brows were raised, his eyes nervous. "I'll do the dishes."

"That's a good idea."

Jenny watched Cody collect the remaining plates and silverware from the table.

When Cody was gone, Jim gave her a

defeated look. "Was I too hard on him?"

"No." Jenny reached across the table and held Jim's hand. "Maybe we can pray with him before he goes to sleep."

"Okay."

"Hey." Jenny felt for her husband. "Don't be hard on yourself. I think he learned something over this."

"We'll see."

Jenny hoped Cody really had learned something, and she'd prayed about it that night when they put their hands on Cody's shoulders and lifted their voices to the Lord as well as over the next two days when Jenny and Jim wondered whether Cody truly understood the seriousness of what he'd done. In some ways, their hands were tied. Cody wasn't their son, so they couldn't deal with him the way they would if he were one of their own kids.

For instance, Cody had a clunker four-door sedan and a cell phone, things his mother had given him before she was arrested. Cody worked Saturdays at the local batting cage and made enough money to cover his expenses. But his car and cell phone gave him the freedom to get into trouble. If he were a Flanigan son, Jenny was sure they would've grounded him from both.

But in this situation they would have to rely on reason and divine intervention.

"Pray for me that I'll have the right words . . . the right attitude," Jim had told Jenny. "I can be too gruff with the guys. I know that. I'm just so mad about this — my whole team drinking."

Jenny understood. Cody was a leader on the team, and his bad example over the years had contributed at least somewhat to the decision by the other captains to drink at the Thanksgiving party. Jim had kept his feelings to himself since Sunday, but they were apparently brewing deep inside him. Waiting until today to have the talk was a good decision.

On Wednesday evening, Cody sought Jenny and Jim out before dinner. "After we eat, let's talk, okay?"

The meal was quiet, the way their dinners had been since Cody was home. When it was over, Bailey took the boys into the family room. She gave Jenny a look that said she'd be praying for the best. She had admitted she was worried about Cody, worried he would disconnect with their family and fall into a hole too dark and deep to ever climb out of.

They moved into the living room, and Cody sat at the far side of the sofa. Jenny took the chair by the fireplace, and Jim sat next to the piano in the chair closest to Cody.

Cody ran his tongue over his lower lip and anchored his elbows on his kneecaps. He looked scared to death. "First —" he swallowed hard — "I want to say I'm sorry. What I did was . . . totally wrong, and I . . . I want you to know that —" His voice cracked, and he hung his head low between his shoulders. After a few seconds, he pinched the bridge of his nose and shook his head. He didn't look up. "I'm . . . I'm sorry."

Jenny felt tears in her own eyes. She wanted to go to him, sit beside him, and put her arm around him. But she would follow Jim's lead. Cody was his player, and the two shared a special bond. When it was time for hugs, Jim wouldn't hesitate.

After an agonizing minute, Cody finally dragged the back of his hand across his cheeks and lifted his head. Futility defined his expression. "Drinking . . . it's all I've ever known."

Jim's eyes softened some. "But it has to stop. You must see that."

"Of course." Anger flashed in his eyes and left a trail of hurt. "My mother mixed drinks for me and my friends when I was twelve.

Twelve years old."

A pit formed in Jenny's stomach. If only they could've rescued Cody sooner, called social services and had Cody removed from his house. "Was your mom using drugs back then?"

"Definitely." Cody waved his hand. "She had a drawer full of needles, bags of powder. She tried to hide them, but I knew where they were." He folded his arms. "I knew she was stealing, too. Sometimes she did it right in front of me."

"That wasn't fair, and it wasn't right." Jenny wished the woman were here now to see what her selfishness and sickness had led to for her son. "You should've stayed when you came the first time."

"I know." Cody stared at his knees. He had been a freshman the first time he spent three weeks with them. He and his mother lived in an apartment a few blocks away, and it was nothing for Cody to walk over. Back then, same as now, Jim had been the father figure Cody never had.

"So let's talk about the party. . . . What happened?" Jim leaned back in his chair. He crossed his ankle over the other knee and waited.

"Karl's parents were out of town. He had basketball practice, so he stayed home alone." Cody shrugged, but the gesture held no defiance. He wrung his hands and tried to meet Jim's eyes. "Karl asked the team and a bunch of girls over, told us there'd be lots to drink."

Jenny glanced at her husband. This was what he'd feared, what his three captains had confirmed in the hospital waiting room. Jenny wasn't sure how the rest of the school year would unfold, but Jim had a plan. Something about the retired police officer who volunteered as security at the Clear Creek games. Either Jim's players would stop drinking or they wouldn't be on the team. She was sure about that much.

"Let's get a few things straight." Jim narrowed his eyes. "You're an alcoholic. You told me that months ago, remember?" He pointed to an empty chair. "You sat right there and told me you'd blacked out again, drunk so much you nearly died. You said you needed another chance to live here and that you would never, ever touch a drink again. Remember that?"

Cody seemed to shrink a size. "Yes, sir."

"Still think you're an alcoholic?"

The boy didn't hesitate. "Yes, sir."

"So one of the guys asks you over and says there'll be lots to drink, and what should you have done?"

"Gone to the Baxters' with you."

"Exactly." Jim looked restless, as though he was ready to get up and start pacing. "Not only that, but you should've told me about Karl." He jabbed his finger in Cody's direction. "You know how I feel about drinking. And if someone had been killed that night, one of your teammates or someone they might've run into, you would've lived the rest of your days knowing you could've done something to prevent it."

Jenny felt sorrow in her throat. Jim — more than many people — understood drinking and the cost it demanded from a person. His own story of loss was one that he wanted to share with Cody soon. It was painful for Jim to tell, but Jenny had a feeling that Cody would be changed by it.

She agreed with Jim, but it was tough for any teenager to come clean about the wrongdoings of a teammate. Let alone a teenager with Cody's upbringing. She slid to the edge of her seat. "Did you consider that? telling us the truth?"

Shame shrouded Cody's face. "Not really." He turned to Jim. "The guys have been drinking since the season ended."

"And you?"

"No, sir. Not until Thanksgiving."

"Okay." Jim ran his fingers through his

hair and sighed. "So we've got a couple problems. Big problems." He straightened. "I'll deal with the team, one way or another. I'm not coaching at Clear Creek just for the wins. But you, Cody. You're my biggest problem of all." Emotion crept into his tone. "Do you know how serious things were on Friday?"

Cody stared at the plush carpet between his feet. His regret and sorrow, his humiliation and fear were plain. Jenny had seen Cody sorry before. But nothing like this. When Cody lifted his eyes, he looked more frightened than ever before. "I almost died."

"If they'd pumped your stomach an hour later, you wouldn't be here." Jim stood and sat next to Cody on the sofa. "You need help. There's no other option."

Cody's chin quivered. He nodded, but he was clearly too emotional to speak.

"Jenny and I found an alcohol intervention program through church."

"I want that." He faced Jim. Then he pulled his cell phone from his jeans pocket. "I went and had my number changed." He handed it to Jim. "Check the names."

The surprise on Jim's face matched that in Jenny's heart. The idea of Cody making changes on his own was the best news so far, further proof that he was serious.

Jim flipped the phone open and clicked some buttons. After a few seconds, he glanced at Cody. "It's a short list."

"Just you and the youth pastor at church and the number to the prison where my mom is. The others are kids who don't drink ever."

Jim handed the phone back. "Brandon Reeves, the kicker?" He sounded doubtful. "He's pretty social."

"Never, Coach. The guy's as clean as they come." Cody took the phone. "Him and JJ Warrick. Everyone knows where they stand."

Jenny clasped her hands. "So have them over, Cody. We have a hot tub and a pool table. Guys like that are the ones you need as friends."

He raised his phone. "That's why I kept their numbers."

"Let me tell you what we know about the alcohol program." Jim folded his hands. Jenny knew that he'd done the research on Monday, and he'd been waiting since then to share it with Cody. The program took place in the evening. For the first two months, participants were required to come four days a week. The meetings lasted an hour, and afterwards there were thirty-minute private sessions with one of the volunteer counselors — all professionals from the community who gave up a night each week to work with the program.

"Everything they teach and everything they walk you through is all done in Christ's strength." Jim seemed to search Cody's eyes. "There's no other way to stand against this enemy."

Again Cody looked smaller than usual. Not the bigger-than-life football player everyone knew him as. Even so, his tone was steady. "I know that, Coach."

"After the two months, they recommend attending a meeting twice a week. And that's forever, Cody. Alcoholism never goes away. It lies in wait, looking for the moment when you think you've got it beat."

When Jim finished talking, Cody gripped his knees. He drew a sharp breath. "When can I start?"

"Tomorrow night." Jim pursed his lips. "If you're ready."

"I am." Cody's gaze shifted and he hesitated. After several seconds he looked at Jim again. "I have some bad news, Coach."

Jenny felt her heart skip a beat. Bad news with Cody could be just about anything. Had he gotten one of the girls at school pregnant or done something terrible between the party and coming home on Thanksgiving night? Jenny held her breath.

"You wanna talk about it?" Jim didn't look fazed. With all that he'd found out about his team in the past week, whatever else Cody wanted to say was probably not going to shock him.

Cody pressed his knuckles against his forehead. He released a shaky sigh, and when he looked up, he found Jenny's eyes this time. "I checked with the counselor at school. My grades are horrible. Worse than I thought."

Jenny exhaled. Having bad grades was a problem they could work through. "What's your grade point average?"

"Just under a 1.5." He squinted. "The lady was straight with me. I have a couple fails and Ds. She said I had no chance at a scholarship."

"What about summer school?" The disappointment shone in Jim's eyes.

Jenny felt it too. Jim had hoped Cody might get a scholarship to a Division II school. He'd talked to a few college coaches who were friends of his, and they'd promised to consider Cody. He was a strong enough football player that if he had even average grades, he could get a full ride somewhere.

But not with that GPA.

"Actually, Coach, I made a decision."

Cody straightened his back. This time he didn't waver a bit. "At the end of the school year, I'm enlisting in the army. I'll leave for boot camp in late August."

The army. Jenny wanted to beg God for Cody's protection before another minute passed. But she wanted to show her support too. The army would be good for Cody as long as he stayed away from drinking.

Memories rushed at her of the times when TV networks had run specials about the terrorist attacks on New York City.

Every time, Cody would get up and leave the room. "I can't watch it." He'd shake his head. "That's my country they're hitting. No one does that to the USA."

Some kids were born patriotic, and Cody Coleman was one of them.

"I'm proud of you." Jenny stood and went to him.

Cody rose and so did Jim. "I'm proud too. I think it's a good decision." Jim patted his back.

There wasn't a lot to say. Cody had already made up his mind. He had a semester of school and one summer left, and then he'd be a soldier. In the meantime, Jenny and Jim and their kids were the only family Cody would have. It wasn't time to debate

the decisions that had led to this moment.
It was time for a hug.

CHAPTER ELEVEN

Tears trickled down Bailey's face, and she stepped back from her hiding spot. She'd wondered what was taking so long, what her parents and Cody could possibly be talking about. And as she left the boys watching ESPN in the family room and tiptoed down the hall, she wondered about the hushed tones, the serious voices.

Her parents were going to give Cody a choice: either he could enroll in a program for people with a drinking problem and stay with their family, or he could move out and find a solution on his own. Bailey hadn't talked to Cody privately since he came out of the hospital, but she knew him well enough to know what he would do. He'd take the program, clear and simple.

So why all the talking?

She'd reached the end of the hallway and stood next to the open door of the guest bathroom. She felt a little wrong about listening in, but once she caught part of the conversation, she couldn't pull away, and now she knew.

Cody was joining the army.

She brushed her knuckle beneath her eyes and sniffed. Three boys from Clear Creek High — guys who had been seniors when Bailey was a freshman — had enlisted after graduation.

One of them lost his leg when he stepped on a land mine. He'd been home for nearly a year now, taking classes at Indiana University. When Bailey and her family saw him at the market once, Bailey had looked away. She didn't know if he'd recognize her, but if he did, she wasn't sure what she would say. He'd run track and done 4-H and mowed his dad's fields every summer. The idea that he didn't have his left leg was unthinkable.

And now the same could happen to Cody. Or worse.

Bailey shuddered and turned from her hiding place. As she did, her phone vibrated in her pocket. A text message. Bailey waited until she was in the kitchen; then she leaned against the counter and opened her phone. The message was from Bryan Smythe — the fourth day in a row that he'd texted her.

She'd prayed about Bryan a few times in the past week. When they talked, she told him she didn't want a boyfriend. Because it was true and because she wanted to test him. If he knew she wasn't interested, then maybe he wouldn't keep contacting her.

But her preference didn't seem to change Bryan's mind. In fact, every time she mentioned her intentions to stay single, he practically agreed. "We're too young for serious relationships," he'd told her yesterday when they talked. "If we put God first, He'll make everything else fall in place." She could hear the smile in his voice. "Besides, I'll be here waiting, whenever you're ready."

Talk like that was enough to make her lie awake thinking about Bryan, the way she had last night. Because maybe he was the real deal — the realest one of all. If he was willing to wait as long as it took until she would agree to be his girlfriend, then he wasn't like any of the other boys she knew. Except maybe Tim Reed. But Tim never acted interested in her for longer than a few days at a time. Before she fell asleep last night, she'd felt like God was telling her that she needed to spend more time with Bryan before she could make up her mind.

She clicked *OK* and read the message. *Hey, beautiful . . . I'm out driving around trying to think how I can get through the night without seeing you. Think you could help?*

Bailey sniffed and wiped at what remained of her tears. She felt a smile tug at her lips. Her fingers flew across the keypad, and her return message took shape. *You might just be beyond help.* She hit Send and took a glass out of the cupboard. She filled it with water, took a sip, and felt the familiar vibration of her phone.

She opened it again. *How 'bout we meet at the end of your driveway in five minutes? I won't stay long. Just long enough to see the stars in your eyes.*

Bailey felt a rush of adrenaline. Meet Bryan now? In the cold dark night, when lights-out was just around the corner? Her parents would never go for such a thing. But then . . . they were caught up in the conversation with Cody. And Bryan only wanted to see her for a minute.

She reread the message. *Just long enough to see the stars in your eyes.* Her heart pounded hard against her chest.

She had to say yes. It wouldn't take long. She'd be back inside before her parents knew she was gone. Besides, she wouldn't even leave the property. Their driveway was long enough that she could meet Bryan without anyone hearing his car, then get back inside without her parents knowing it.

She could tell her mom later, the way she always did with things that involved her friends.

The thrill of the secret meeting was too much to risk her parents saying no. Bailey opened her phone and tapped in her answer. *I'll be waiting.* Then she slipped on her coat and her shoes and went to the opposite side of the house.

As she passed by the family room, Ricky noticed her. "Where're you going?"

"Outside." She kept walking.

"Outside where?" Ricky was on his feet. "It's cold out."

The other boys were looking in her direction.

"I have to say hi to a friend real quick." Her tone told them that was the end of the conversation. She slipped through the doorway into the mudroom and left through the side door that served as a second front entrance.

It was freezing outside, and her breath hung in the air. Bailey stuffed her hands deep into her pockets and hurried toward the driveway. Her teeth chattered, and she thought she saw the shadow of a coyote just beyond the hedge that ran the length of the driveway.

A rustling in the grass on the other side of

her path made her jerk her head. She stopped and squinted, but the sliver of the moon cast no light on the yard. She quickened her pace. Her mother would be furious with her for meeting Bryan like this. What was she doing? And what was Bryan thinking?

His words from their last conversation ran through her head. *"All that matters is my relationship with God. . . . Girls can come later. . . . I read my Bible when I first wake up and before I go to bed. . . . Me and God, we're tight."*

"Okay, Bryan . . . so does God want you sneaking around to see me?" Bailey whispered and kept walking. She was nearing the road when she saw headlights crest the hill that led to their house. A few seconds later, a small, four-door Honda turned into her driveway.

Bailey felt herself relax. Bryan was here; no coyote would get her now. She ran the rest of the way to his car as he killed the engine and turned off his headlights.

He stepped out, shut his car door, and leaned against it. "Hi."

Even in the pitch dark she could make out his smile. She stopped a few yards from him, and suddenly she realized she was breathless. She couldn't tell if it was from the cold air or the run or Bryan's nearness. She hugged herself and decided it was all three. She felt shy and daring and guilty. "Hi back."

"I have a question." He stuck his hands in his jeans pockets. He wore his black North Face jacket, and he'd never looked better as he angled his head. "How do you expect me to see the stars in your eyes?"

Bailey giggled. The moment was like something from a movie. She felt dizzy with the way he looked at her, the way his words reached someplace deep in her heart she hadn't known existed before. She took a step closer. "What's that supposed to mean?"

"It means that if you stay so far away, I won't see what I came here to see."

Bailey forced herself to breathe out. How could one guy be so completely romantic? She was shivering more than before, but her cheeks felt like they were on fire. She took a few steps closer. "You can't see my eyes anyway. It's too dark."

"I can see you're cold." Bryan held out his hands. "Come here. I'll keep you warm."

Bailey sucked in a breath. In all the time she'd known Bryan, the most she'd done was give him a quick hug good night. They'd never lingered in the moonlight or stood on her porch. A picture filled her mind: her family riding the Blue Streak at Cedar Point last summer. The drops on that roller coaster seemed to last forever, and Bailey's stomach had flip-flopped like never before. She felt the same way now with Bryan so close.

Bailey took another step closer. "Aren't you cold?"

Bryan came to her, hooked his fingers through the belt loops on her jeans, and took a few steps back toward his car, gently pulling her with him. He leaned against the door again and drew her into his arms. "Mmmm. That's better."

His hands came up around her lower back, and she put hers around his neck, the way she usually did when she hugged someone. Only this lasted way longer than a usual hug. She could feel Bryan breathing, feel his chest rising and falling. His breath mixed with hers. Her teeth were still chattering but more because she was scared. "I'm . . . not cold now."

"See . . . I told you." His speaking voice was as golden as his singing voice. Bailey had noticed that every time she'd seen him on stage. But here, it was as if he were talking straight to her soul.

Something about it scared her. She wanted

to pull away and tell him thanks for coming. Time for her to go inside. But another part of her couldn't slip free from his arms even if she tried.

Bryan seemed to sense she was uncomfortable. He moved his hands to her shoulders and eased her away a few inches. Her eyes were adjusting to the dark now, and she could see that he was staring into them. "Just like I thought."

"What?" Bailey used her singsong voice, the one she pulled out in callback auditions. Otherwise he was bound to hear the fear in her tone.

"You're even more beautiful with stars in your eyes." Bryan dusted his thumb across her cheek. "I've been thinking about you, Bailey. Do you know that?"

She lowered her chin. Was he going to kiss her? If so, what was she supposed to do? Tell him she wasn't ready? Run like the wind to the house? She gulped, shy and nervous. Her parents would be furious if they saw her out here like this. She released her hold on him and took his hands from her shoulders. "I better go. My parents don't know I left."

In the distance a coyote started yipping, and another two or three joined in.

Bryan slid his fingers between hers.

"Okay." His smile made her melt. "I just wasn't sure I'd survive another night without seeing you."

It still felt as though he might kiss her. And that couldn't happen. Not in the dark when she hadn't even told her parents he was coming over. They weren't dating or going out. Besides, she didn't know *how* to kiss, which way to turn her head or anything. She wanted her first kiss to be special, something she remembered forever. Not something secret and spur-of-the-moment.

Bryan was pulling her closer again, and she felt a surge of panic. She needed a distraction. She could ask him how his Bible reading was going, what chapter he was in, and whether he had prayed about coming over before he did it. But somehow it didn't seem like the time.

Instead Bailey gave his fingers a squeeze, then released his hands. She hugged him again, much more quickly this time, hoping he would get the hint. She needed to get inside. "Thanks for coming by."

"You don't have to give it back." Bryan folded his arms.

A few feet separated them now. She stopped and studied him, shivering in the cold darkness. She had no idea what he was talking about. "Give what back?"

"My heart." His lips held a slight smile. "It's been yours for a long time." He nodded toward her house. "Go on. I don't want you to get in trouble." He made no move to get in his car. "I'll watch till you're safe inside."

It was the nicest thing any guy had ever said or done for her. "Bryan . . . that's so sweet."

"Not as sweet as you." He grinned. "Go on. I'll see you tomorrow — in my dreams or in person."

Bailey giggled and then turned and ran all the way up her driveway to the side door. That was the sort of thing Dayne Matthews would say in one of his movies. And she was the lucky girl Bryan was saying it to. She felt like dancing as she ran. Tonight was incredible, even if she did feel a little guilty.

With any luck, her parents would still be talking to Cody. When she reached the porch, she turned and waved. Then she climbed up the three stairs and slipped inside. Once she closed the door behind her, she leaned against the wall. Her heart was pounding so hard that she thought she might pass out.

She bent over and dug her elbows into her knees. After a few seconds, she finally grabbed a full breath. She straightened and waited until she wasn't breathing so hard. Then she took off her coat and headed through the mudroom and into the main part of the house. The boys were still watching SportsCenter.

Silently, Bailey took one of the high stools at the back of the room near the pool table. No sign of her parents. Which hopefully meant they were still talking to Cody. She leaned her head against the wall and closed her eyes.

Bryan Smythe was amazing.

Every time he opened his mouth, he practically spoke in rhyme. Her mind was still spinning with the sweet things he'd told her. And that last part . . . about taking his heart with her when she left. Wow. The other guys she knew could barely figure out a way to hold a conversation.

"You were gone a long time."

Her eyes flew open, and she jumped down from the stool. Ricky was standing in front of her, his hands on his hips. She tried to recover. "Not . . . not too long."

Suspicion colored his eyes. "What friend was it?"

"Bryan Smythe." There was no point lying. "He wanted to say hi."

"Did you ask Mom?"

Bailey felt her heart skip a beat. "Was

Mom looking for me?"

"No. Still . . . you have to ask to go out at night."

"I know, bud. I'll tell her about it later."

Ricky looked doubtful. He shrugged and went back with the other boys.

Bailey realized she'd been holding her breath, and she let it out slowly. *Calm,* she told herself. *Act calm.* She wasn't lying; she would tell her mom about Bryan's visit later. She went past the kitchen, through the dining room to the living room, where her parents were. They sat on either side of Cody, their hands on his shoulders, heads bowed.

They were praying, and Bailey knew better than to interrupt. She tiptoed back through the dining room and was about to join the boys in the family room. But instead she poked her head in and waved at them. "I'm going to bed."

Connor seemed to just notice her. He was that way around TV — completely absorbed. "Hey . . . come sit with us."

"Not tonight." She waved again. "I'm tired." Without waiting for whatever he was going to say next, she skipped up the stairs, turned left at the top, and darted into her room. For five minutes she sat on the edge of her bed and replayed in her mind everything Bryan had said.

She was just about to hit the bathroom so she could brush her teeth when her phone vibrated. She jumped and flipped it open at the same time.

Another text from Bryan. *Tonight was great. I thank God for you, Bailey Flanigan. Sweet dreams . . . I know mine will be.*

She flopped onto the bed and stared at the message. Was the guy for real? He was so nice! What guy said those things? Especially the part about thanking God for her. If it wasn't for lines like that, she might still wonder whether he was genuine or just great with his words.

But if he was thanking God, then of course he was real.

She made a dreamy sound and read his message once more. *Sweet dreams . . . I know mine will be.*

Suddenly she couldn't wait to see him again. She hit Reply and worked her fingers across the keypad. *Mine will definitely be sweet. Thanks for coming by . . . even though it was freezing . . . lol.*

A few seconds after she sent it, she received another. *I was only cold when you walked away. Next time we'll have to hug a little longer.*

She giggled and closed her phone. No need to answer that one. Besides, she always found it better if she didn't send the last text in a conversation. Let him wonder a little. That's what her mom always said. She hesitated, and a slight gasp filled her throat. Her mom! How was she going to tell her all that had happened in the last half hour? Even if her parents finished talking with Cody and her mom came up to her room, she couldn't explain everything Bryan had said or everything she felt.

And she wasn't 100 percent sure her mom would understand, anyway.

Bailey brushed her teeth, washed her face, and slipped into her nightshirt. Ten minutes later — a record time — she was beneath the covers with the lights off, thinking of every kind thing Bryan had said and how it felt having his heartbeat against hers. They hadn't done anything wrong. She was old enough to have a friend stop by to say hi, right? She dismissed the thought and went back to replaying Bryan's words about the stars and his heart and the sweet dreams he was going to have.

She could always tell her mother later.

CHAPTER TWELVE

John didn't spend much time at Elaine's house. Somehow going there felt strangely forbidden, much more like a dating relationship. The feelings came from his old-fashioned roots. Back in his dating days, a man didn't go to a woman's house if she lived alone. He might pick her up at the front porch, but he wouldn't go inside. Propriety ruled.

Going over there today was different. His motives were purely born of friendship. She needed his help, so he would go. Period.

Today was the second Sunday in December, and Elaine's new television still wasn't working right. John figured it was a wiring issue, something wrong with the connections. But in the meantime, Elaine couldn't watch football. And Elaine was crazy about football. She was the proud owner of an NFL Sunday Ticket package, which gave her access to every professional game played each week. She knew stats and players and had a definite opinion that the Colts would win the Super Bowl.

Or maybe *opinion* wasn't a strong enough word.

John had been going to church twice each week — once on Saturday night with Elaine and again on Sunday morning with his kids. Elaine would've done just about anything to keep her Sundays open. Twice in the last four weeks, John had joined her, watching Sunday football and sharing dinner at her house.

But then her television broke, and her kids bought her a new one during one of the day-after-Thanksgiving sales. It worked the first week, but a few days ago Elaine had tried to adjust something and lost the picture. When John returned from church this morning, he had a long phone message from Elaine. Could he please come over? Her TV needed work. She still had no picture, and she really needed one. Preferably before kickoff. Oh, and could he stay for dinner? She made homemade lasagna, and they could wrap the gifts they bought for their grandkids.

John smiled when the message ended. For a woman who didn't usually talk much, the message ran a full minute. It almost made

her sound nervous, like a schoolgirl searching for a reason to ask him over. He called
her, and there was a laugh in his voice as
she answered the phone. "So basically
you're inviting me over for the rest of the
day and evening."

"Basically." Elaine's light laugh filled the
phone line. "I guess that would've been
quicker."

They chatted for a few minutes about
practical things — that he would bring a
few rolls of wrapping paper and that she
had plenty of Scotch tape. Now he'd found
the bag of Christmas presents and paper
and put them by the garage door. He
grabbed a spare set of TV cables in case
hers were defective.

Before John left, he stopped in his bathroom and glanced in the mirror. A few old
bottles of cologne sat on the counter near
his sink. He picked up one he hadn't worn
in a while and spritzed it on his neck. Elaine
had casually commented a while ago that
she liked cologne and that many men their
age no longer cared about smelling nice.
But he wasn't wearing it for her. He was a
professional, a doctor who spent his day
around people. He would've worn it with or
without Elaine in his life.

Definitely.

As he set the bottle down and hurried to the garage, his cell phone rang. The caller ID told him it was Ashley. He popped it open. "Hello?"

"Hey, Dad. . . . I meant to catch you after church."

"Oh . . . sorry." John opened the trunk on his car and heaved the bag of gifts inside. "What's up?"

Ashley hesitated. "Are you okay? You sound out of breath."

"Just packing my Christmas surprises into the car." He chuckled. "It's a big load this year."

"Hmmm." Ashley sounded confused. "Where're you taking them?"

"Over to Elaine's. We're having a wrapping party."

She exhaled loud enough to be heard. "Anyway . . . I wondered if you wanted to join us for dinner at Kari's house. Brooke and Kari and me and our families. It won't be a late night. Kari and I are getting over some kind of flu bug."

"Sorry to hear that." John felt his heart stir. His kids were so kind to him since Elizabeth's death. Especially Ashley. "Thanks for the offer, honey. I'll have to take a rain check."

Ashley didn't seem upset. They talked a

few more minutes while he climbed into his car and backed out of the garage. He was halfway to Elaine's by the time they finished their conversation. He made the rest of the drive in silence, asking himself the questions Ashley had avoided.

What were his real feelings for Elaine, and why was he looking forward to spending the rest of the day with her? He pulled up in front of her single-story house and stared at it. This wasn't the house where she'd spent her married years. Elaine had sold that a decade ago after her husband died.

"Too many memories," she'd told him. "I keep the memories in my heart, but I need to live somewhere that matches where I'm at. And living life without my husband meant entering a new season. So I needed a new house."

The place was older and neatly kept with a large, nicely manicured front yard. Elaine's neighborhood was quiet and stately. John felt comfortable here. He tried not to notice that his pulse was faster than it had been back at home. He was looking forward to the day; that's all. Also it was gray and damp and freezing outside. Snow was in the forecast.

He took a deep breath of early winter air. He'd made the right decision about the day.

Kari, Ashley, and Brooke deserved a dinner by themselves. Especially since things were quieter than they'd been in a while.

Erin and her family were gone, and Dayne had moved into his lake house. He and Katy had purchased enough furniture for Dayne to have the basics, though they were still busy getting each room set up. Luke and his family were living in a rental south of Indianapolis, a place where they'd stay for six months while they continued looking for a house. Their furniture had arrived weeks ago, so they were settled and getting ready for Christmas.

Elaine's kids were in Indianapolis and Michigan, so she would've been alone today if he hadn't come. Spending the day with her would be good for both of them. He unloaded the bag of presents from the car and was about to set it down and reach back inside for the wrapping paper when he heard her voice.

"Need some help?" Elaine stood in the doorway grinning at him. "You look like Santa Claus."

"After Thanksgiving, I feel like it." John had put all the gifts in one oversize black yard bag, which now seemed about as big as him. His hands were too full to wave off her help, but he peeked around the bag.

217

"Stay there. I've got it."

She laughed and skipped down the steps. "I'll get the wrapping paper at least." When she passed him, she touched his shoulder. "Thanks for coming. Peyton Manning's going to make history this year, you know. I can't miss a minute of that."

"No problem." John kept walking toward the open front door. "We'll have everything up and running in no time." He stepped inside and looked around the room. The gifts Elaine had purchased lay spread out on one of her matching living room sofas. He set his things down on the other.

"It's freezing out there." Elaine returned with the wrapping paper and set it on the closest chair. "Feels like snow."

"That's what the news said." He caught his breath and smiled at her. "Okay, show me what you did to the TV."

John took apart the wires leading from the receiver unit to the television, VCR, DVD player, and two sets of speakers — one in the front of the room, one in the back. While he worked, Elaine made coffee, and they talked about their kids and grandkids. Elaine's were healthy. One of her kids was coming down for Christmas Eve, and the other would join her the week after.

"How's Hayley?" Elaine sat on the arm of

the old leather sofa she had in her TV room. "She looks better every time I see her."

John was lying on one hip, looking for the right place to plug in the cable. He sat up a little and looked at Elaine. "She's amazing. There's no medical explanation for how a little girl could be underwater as long as she was and be doing so well."

"It's a miracle."

"Yes. Brooke said she's starting to read, which means her brain is still healing." John found the right jack and made the connection with the cable. Then he sat up and turned to Elaine again. "To think I was ready to give up on her." He always choked up when he remembered those dark days immediately after Hayley's near drowning. "I thought there was no hope for her. She'd be blind and bedridden all her life. I begged God to take her home." He squinted against the pain of the memory and allowed a sad smile. "I guess God showed me."

Her eyes held fresh compassion. "He has a way of doing that. . . . How about Tommy? Is Luke having an easier time with him?"

John laughed. "He's all boy; that's for sure. Typical toddler, testing his boundaries." He stood and found another cable in the pile near the entertainment center. "He's still shooting people; only now when he does it he appears to be blowing a kiss. Then at the last possible second, he makes the shooting sound instead."

Elaine tried not to laugh. "I don't envy Luke and Reagan. Those years are a lot of work."

"They are. Luke found a Growing Kids God's Way class at their new church in Indianapolis. They might not agree with everything about the program, but I think it'll help." He chuckled. "Let's just say Luke and Reagan are both looking forward to it."

"And Ashley . . . is she okay?"

Elaine hadn't asked about his middle daughter since Laughter and Leftovers. If one of his kids struggled with the friendship between John and Elaine, she had told him she wouldn't worry about it or ask questions unless he brought it up. But clearly Ashley's emotional breakdown that night was still troubling Elaine.

"I should've told you." John sat back down on the floor. "She's fine." He looped one arm around his knee and leaned on his elbow so he could see the panel at the back of the TV. "She's been dealing with a flu bug or something. She looks like she's lost a little weight."

"Things are good for her at home?"

"Better than ever. She and Landon are

giddy in love. I mean . . . I can't believe that daughter of mine almost drove away the best thing that ever happened to her." He grinned and leaned toward the television. "I'll be thanking God forever that Landon was stubborn enough to stay."

"They have something special." Elaine sounded wistful. "Just like Kari and Ryan."

"Brooke and Peter too. They're just more businesslike. More left-brained, I guess. Now that they've worked out the trouble over Hayley's drowning, they're very close." John examined the cord, and in the shadows he tried to make out the labels beneath the jacks. "It's Sam and Erin I worry about. They have four beautiful daughters, but sometimes I wonder if Erin's really happy. She doesn't say much, especially since Elizabeth died."

"It's like that with my oldest. Gives me lots of reason to pray."

"Amen."

At the end of the hour, after talking about each of their children and grandchildren, John connected a cable from the receiver to the TV. Then he stood and put his hands on his hips. "That should do it." He pushed a few buttons, and the picture came to life.

Elaine clapped and looked at her watch. "Fifteen minutes to spare."

They watched the game while the smell of Elaine's lasagna filled the house.

When it was over, when the Colts had notched another victory and Peyton Manning was another step closer to making history, Elaine slipped a MercyMe CD into her stereo. Then she flipped a switch near her gas fireplace, and a flame sprang to life. "Have you heard the song 'Homesick'? It's on this CD." She moved some of her gifts to the coffee table and sat on the floor in front of it.

"Yes. It's beautiful. Talks about losing someone and feeling homesick for heaven."

"Mmm-hmm." She used her remote to start the CD. "Used to make me cry every time I heard it."

John wasn't sure what to say. The song still brought tears to his eyes; how could it not? He set some of his gifts on the floor at the other end of the coffee table and dropped to the carpet. That way they each had a work space. He paused long enough to catch her eye. "You can listen to it without crying now?"

"I can." Elaine shifted her gaze to the front window. "I hear it, and I have that love still, that . . . I don't know, that fondness for my husband and all we lived through together. The memories and laughter and lov-

222

ing. But I'm almost happy for him, I guess. He's where he's supposed to be." She lifted her hands and smiled at John. As she did, she looked especially attractive. "And I'm here. Because God's not done with me yet."

John held her eyes for a moment. "I like that." He felt lighthearted, with none of the maudlin heaviness that usually came with talk about Elizabeth or the loss he'd suffered. He smiled. "I like that a lot."

They wrapped Fisher-Price toys and LEGO box sets and Little House on the Prairie books. Nerf guns and miniature piano keyboards and building blocks and a couple of LeapFrog games. They talked about Christmas, their favorite traditions, and Katy and Dayne's pending wedding. All the while MercyMe played in the background twice through, and the fire crackled at the far side of the room.

An hour into their wrapping project, snow started falling. Winter was upon them now, no question.

By the time they finished dinner, John wasn't sure how to feel. He couldn't keep the smile off his face. Everything about the day was just what he needed, especially with Christmas so close. But what did that say about his feelings for Elaine? Or his feelings for everything Elizabeth had meant to him?

Before he left, he hugged Elaine a little longer than usual. "I had a great time. Your lasagna was perfect."

Her cheeks looked pinker than before. "The least I can do for someone who fixes my TV before kickoff."

He laughed. "It wasn't hard. Just a few loose connections."

"That'll be us one day." Her eyes sparkled. "A few loose connections."

They both laughed, and John realized how wonderful it felt. He bade her good-bye, and he was still chuckling when he reached the car.

On the way home, though, his uncertainty returned. He sighed and stared straight ahead at the road. *God, where's this going? I have no idea if I'll ever be ready for more than a friendship with Elaine. So am I wrong to spend a day with her?* He felt sad at the thought of cutting off the relationship again. *I don't know how to look at all this, God. . . . I need Your wisdom. Please . . .*

My son . . . My Word is truth.

The response echoed quietly in his soul, and John felt a surge of clarity. God was so faithful, so good. Of course that's where the answers would be — for this and for any dilemma he'd faced before or since Elizabeth's death. God's Word. The only truth that would never change.

John remembered then what he'd read that morning in his Bible. He'd been in chapter 3 of Ecclesiastes. The entire chapter spoke to him, underlining the truth about God's timing, His way of directing His people's days. It spoke of there being a time to mourn, a time to dance, and a time for every season in life. As John read it earlier, he had thought of his children.

But now he was remembering the Scripture with a fresh and startling understanding. Especially the first verse: "There is a time for everything, and a season for every activity under heaven."

Wasn't that what Elaine had said earlier when they were wrapping presents? Her husband was in heaven, where he was supposed to be. And she was here because God wasn't finished with her yet. The time for John and Elizabeth had come and gone — though every good thing about it would remain with him until he took his last breath. But this season . . . this time in life without her . . . was something new. Every season was meant for an activity, according to the Bible verse.

Maybe this season was meant for him and Elaine.

Even thinking the idea made a chill pass

over him. Not because he was thrilled with the idea, but because it terrified him. Not the friendship part but anything that might come after it.

John silently thanked the Lord for reminding him of the Scripture and making it clear that it could apply not just to his kids but to him. No matter how hard ushering in the activity of the next season might be.

He felt himself relax. The day had been wonderful, and as he finished the drive home, he replayed his time with Elaine. It wasn't until he walked through the front door that he realized something that shocked and saddened him. He must be making more progress than he thought toward the next season of life. Because in the course of the late afternoon, MercyMe's "Homesick" had played at least twice.

And John's eyes never even got damp.

CHAPTER THIRTEEN

Katy had been looking forward to the date all week.

Back when she was single, she used to dream of going with someone special to one of college sports' most unforgettable experiences — a basketball game at Indiana University's Assembly Hall. She and Rhonda, her CKT choreographer, used to talk about the fun they'd have and how they couldn't marry a guy who didn't enjoy a college basketball game every now and then.

She heard the knock at the Flanigans' door. She hadn't seen Dayne much yesterday and not at all today. He was working out details with his agent, figuring out premiere dates and film schedules.

Katy used the time to get her hair trimmed and catch up with the Flanigans. Tonight they were with their kids, and Cody was at a movie. Cody was doing great, attending his alcohol classes and never veering far from anyone in the Flanigan family.

Katy ran to the door, her purse over her shoulder. She felt pretty with her fresh haircut. She wore a red sweater, jeans, and a pair of knee boots.

When she opened the door, Dayne took a step back and gave a low whistle. "I was hoping we might get through the night without getting stopped by anyone. But not with you looking like that. It'll be 'Dayne, who? Let me get an autograph from your mystery woman.' "

Katy laughed and gave him a teasing look. "Stop." Her heart beat a little faster beneath his gaze, and she wondered if she would ever get used to the way he made her feel. She doubted it. "Mystery woman! By now everyone knows it's just plain old me."

"Hmmm." He gave her a polite appraisal with his eyes. "Nothing plain about you, Katy Hart. Country girl, yes." He raised a single eyebrow. "Plain, definitely not. And I like your hair."

"Thanks." Katy took his hand and shut the door behind her. "Know what?" The cold air contrasted with the warmth of his fingers against hers as they walked to Dayne's new 4Runner. She felt intoxicated by his presence, his love. By the fact that in a matter of months, he would finally be her husband.

"What?" He opened the door for her and kissed her cheek. "You live for these moments, same as me?"

"That." She grinned as he shut the door. When he climbed into the driver's side, she faced him. "But this whole date thing — I love it, Dayne." She snapped her seat belt in place. "I guess I never thought we could date . . . like regular people."

A quiet laugh came from Dayne, but it sounded a little doubtful. "We're hoping, you mean." He tugged on his baseball cap. "If I pull it low enough, I'll need you to lead me around."

"Which I'll do." She gave him a hopeful smile. "I think it'll be okay."

She looked out the windshield. They'd spent the last three weeks without a single paparazzi moment. A few times when they were furniture shopping in Indianapolis, someone had recognized Dayne and asked for his autograph. But no one called the press or no one cared enough to send a photographer. The time together without all the attention had been unbelievable, dreamy even. It gave them both a glimpse of how life might be someday when Dayne finished his movie contract.

Katy wanted to go to the game in the

worst way, but Dayne was right — being at an IU basketball game would be different. The game was televised, so there was a chance a cameraman could spot Dayne and their presence would be broadcast to the nation. Still, Katy had wanted to go so badly that Dayne had agreed. Their seats weren't on the floor. They were twenty rows up, and they were going with Luke and Reagan, who had found a babysitter for the night.

Dayne wore a long-sleeve polo shirt and the requisite baseball cap. Tonight was an experiment of sorts. Bloomington was going to be their home, so they'd have to get used to navigating the nightlife — and that meant restaurants and an occasional game at the university. One day soon, the whole world would know that Dayne Matthews lived here. If the situation played out the way it had with other celebrities who moved to Middle America, the novelty would wear off, and after a year or so they'd be able to live their lives almost like any other people.

They drove through town to the Encore Café on Sixth Street, a warm little restaurant with an eclectic mix of fresh food, private booths, and the best French bread in Bloomington. It always had live music and various students sipping coffee and eating dessert over an open textbook or two.

Katy figured no one would care about Dayne at a place like that, especially with the private booths.

"Hey." Dayne glanced at her. His expression told her he didn't care about whatever hassle they might face in the hours ahead. "I want this date as much as you do. We'll find a way to make it work."

They pulled into the parking lot, and Katy spotted Luke's car. "They're already here." That had been the plan. Luke and Reagan would get here first and grab a booth. Less time for Dayne to be noticed that way.

Inside the restaurant, it took just a few seconds for them to spot Luke and Reagan. Katy took the lead and motioned to the hostess that they were meeting people who were already seated.

Dayne kept the bill of his hat low, his gaze down. They took their seats without any incident.

"Victory!" Katy licked her finger and pretended to chalk up a point. "See . . . people have better things to do in the Midwest. No one's looking for celebrities."

Reagan shot a look at Katy. "Unless they recognize *you* first."

Katy hadn't thought much about that. Yes, her face had been in the tabloids for a few weeks. But lately there was only an occasional mention — mainly about whether Dayne was planning to marry her. And they'd made a plan to handle that issue the first week of January. Wilma had already set up the meeting with *Celebrity Life* magazine.

"How's my favorite attorney?" Dayne took the seat next to the wall of the booth. He adjusted his cap so he could see Luke better. "You all moved in at the office?"

"Definitely." The gratitude in Luke's voice was unmistakable. "What you've done for us, Dayne . . ."

"We think about it every day." Reagan reached across the table and patted Dayne's hand. "It's changed our lives."

"I heard that your mother was getting married." Katy had gotten the scoop from Ashley the other day.

"Yes." A hint of sadness crept into Reagan's tone. "I'm happy for her."

Years had passed since the terrorist attacks on New York City. Reagan's father had worked on the eighty-ninth floor of the north tower of the World Trade Center in New York City. He never made it out.

Katy snuggled close to Dayne. "Ashley says he's a friend from her high school days."

"A guy she dated for two years back then." Reagan tilted her head. "Life can be a strange thing."

Katy didn't share the rest of what Ashley had said — how her heart was breaking for Reagan and how difficult it would be if she ever heard news that her dad was remarrying.

Luke and Dayne launched into a talk about the law firm and how Luke was getting familiar with Dayne's investments and his contracts.

When the waitress came up, she did a double take at Dayne. But he became very involved in the menu, and by the time he ordered, the waitress looked like she no longer wondered if he might be Dayne Matthews. After all, what would Hollywood's top actor be doing at the Encore Café?

Katy smiled as she walked away. "Victory number two." She looped her arm through Dayne's. "See? It's like you're a real person!"

"Thanks." Dayne laughed, and the others at the table did too. He touched Katy's face and gave her a quick kiss. "Actually, thanks for making me try it." He gave Luke a wary look. "I could see this becoming a circus."

The conversation turned to Luke and Reagan's kids. Luke slipped his arm around Reagan. "The class we're taking at church is amazing."

"It's like we have another way to teach our kids." Reagan held up her hands as if to say, *Who knew?* "Everything's better because of it."

Beneath the table, Dayne put his hand on Katy's knee and gave it a gentle squeeze. His look said that he couldn't wait until the conversation about children involved them, too. They had so much ahead, so many years of learning and growing and falling deeper in love. Katy smiled at him. Maybe someday she'd believe she wasn't dreaming. That after everything they'd been through, this really was her life, the sunrise of all that was to come.

Their meals arrived, and they talked and laughed like old friends. Once in a while Katy would spot Dayne looking at Luke, drawn to him. Each time she breathed a silent prayer of thanks that God had allowed them to find this friendship, this relationship. It was more than she had dreamed. Especially after Luke found out he and Dayne were brothers and the aftermath that followed. His comments to the paparazzi had hurt Dayne to his core. But the pain was behind them now.

When they were finished eating, they hurried out to their cars and headed to the campus. Ten minutes later they were in line with the other fans, standing close together to keep warm.

Dayne whispered near Katy's ear, "This is my favorite part."

Katy was standing in front of him, the two of them facing the same direction. Dayne had his hands around her waist, and when the line inched forward, they moved as one. She leaned her head back against his chest. "Mine too."

The closer they came to the entrance, the more the atmosphere around them seemed to buzz with excitement. Indiana was ranked sixth in the nation, and as with other seasons, they had a shot at the title. Even Katy's CKT kids followed the Hoosiers. The town was crazy for their basketball team.

When they finally found their seats, Katy smiled. "We did it. Three victories and the game hasn't even started. How about that?"

Dayne grinned, but he slumped lower in his seat than usual and kept the hat in place. "Pretty sure the Hoosiers will notch another win."

"Definitely." Luke leaned forward and rested his elbows on his knees so he could see Dayne. The two brothers were sitting beside each other, with Katy and Reagan on the outside seats. "This could be the year." He looked out at the floor. "The team's clicking in every area."

"You played, didn't you?" Again Dayne had that look in his eyes, the look that said he loved having a brother. He'd told Katy as much. He wanted to know everything about Luke, all that he'd missed by not being part of the Baxter family.

"I played in high school and on Indiana's intramural team. Too busy with schoolwork for this sort of commitment." Luke grinned and glanced at the players in red and white stretching on the floor. "It would've been fun, though."

"They didn't have basketball at the boarding school." Dayne didn't sound upset by the fact. "Sometimes I wonder what would've happened if they did." He rubbed his chin. "I think I could've been pretty good."

"Well then . . . I'll take that as a challenge." Luke nudged him in the ribs with his elbow. "Dad has a hoop near the garage, you know."

"I noticed that." He winked at Luke. "Name the time. A little one-on-one ought to show me where I stand."

The game was a blowout from the first quarter, but Katy loved everything about it — the band, the cheerleaders, the dance team, the way the student body — decked out entirely in red — jumped to its feet every time the Hoosiers had a breakaway, and the thundering noise when Indiana pulled off a slam dunk or an alley-oop. Katy loved basketball, but since she'd been in Bloomington, she'd been so involved with theater that she'd made it to only a handful of games. Usually with Rhonda.

Katy settled back into her seat. Thoughts of Rhonda reminded her that she needed to call her friend, maybe have lunch with her. Last time they were together, Rhonda had seemed down. Short, almost. As if she assumed Katy was too busy for her, so she wasn't going to take up too much of her time. If Rhonda was feeling insecure or frustrated, Katy wanted to know. Rhonda's friendship meant too much to lose.

Dayne managed to go unnoticed even through halftime. While Luke and Reagan went for popcorn, Dayne kept his hat low and stayed in deep conversation with Katy about the strategy of the Indiana coach and the reasons he liked driving the ball downcourt over a methodical four-corners offense.

At one point when he was talking about a full-court press versus a zone defense, Katy laughed. "You think I'm actually following

237

any of this?"

He touched his nose to hers. His eyes danced, the way they had so much during the past few weeks. "Does it matter?" He breathed his answer near the side of her face. "You're helping us get through this game."

Katy giggled and kept listening. She understood the real reason for his attention. Halftime was when a roaming camera could catch a glimpse of him, the time when someone might recognize him and start a buzz of attention.

When the third quarter started, Dayne breathed out long and slow. "Another victory."

"Yep. And an education on basketball." She grinned across the guys at Reagan. "You missed a fascinating conversation about points and point guards. Guarding and forwards. Reverse dunks. That sort of thing."

"Hmmm. We should've stuck around."

The good mood carried through the game, and as Dayne and Luke had guessed, the Hoosiers beat Kentucky by twenty points. Even so the crowd stayed on its feet for the final minute, cheering and waving towels and pom-poms as though March Madness had somehow found its way to

December.

On the way out, as they were walking on the concourse toward the main doors, Katy noticed Dayne being less careful about keeping his face low. She was catching Reagan up on the wedding and the latest information from Wilma Waters.

Meanwhile, the guys were in front of them talking about how Indiana had a shot at the title. "I thought that assistant coach was going to come onto the court after that third quarter call."

"Traveling doesn't get any more obvious than that." Dayne laughed and tipped his head back.

Katy saw it coming before Dayne did. As he lifted his head, a group of college-age girls was walking toward them. Two of them stopped at the same time, and one of them pointed at him. "Dayne Matthews!" she shrieked. "Hey, that's Dayne Matthews."

Katy checked behind them and farther down the way. They were trapped, but at least there were no photographers anywhere. The camera crews were on the court.

Dayne turned to Luke and tried to ignore the girls, but they weren't about to be denied. The entire group was bouncing up and down now, clustering in toward Dayne.

He stopped and fiddled with the bill of his hat.

"Dayne . . . Dayne, can we get your picture?" One of the girls ran up and took hold of his arm. She handed her miniature camera to her friend. Her entire body was shaking. "Take it. Quick, take the picture."

Dayne looked over his shoulder and cast a helpless look at Katy.

She smiled as if to say it didn't matter. They could handle this distraction. Katy led Reagan a few feet away and waited.

The girl was still bouncing. She steadied herself long enough to put her arm around Dayne's waist and smile while her friend snapped the photo. This started a round of picture taking and finally a group photo. As they were finishing, one of the girls took a notebook from her bag. Another found a pen in her purse.

"Can we have your autograph, Dayne?" A brunette moved in as close as she could. "You're better-looking in person. But you hear that all the time, right?"

One of the girls ran her hands over his arms. "I didn't think you'd be so built."

Dayne kept taking steps back, creating space between him and the girls. Katy noticed, and she was silently grateful. She trusted Dayne, but it was nice to see he didn't enjoy this kind of attention. It came with the territory, but that was all. He would always do his part to keep his distance.

One of the girls took hold of Luke's arm. "Hey, you're his brother! The one in the magazines." She squealed. "Girls, this is his brother!"

Luke looked uncomfortable. He glanced at Reagan, but he seemed to realize that it wouldn't be smart to break away from Dayne and join the two of them. This way at least Katy could avoid getting attention. Her face would definitely be familiar to girls like these, girls who probably read the tabloids.

Reagan chuckled. "Easy, girls. They're both taken."

"Don't worry about it." Katy laughed quietly. It made her realize how much she was already used to the strange life of being in love with Dayne Matthews. "They'll be gone in a minute."

"I know." Reagan's tone dripped with disbelief. "I mean, I can't believe you have to deal with this all the time."

"I don't. Dayne's usually pretty careful." She watched him, the way he signed his autograph, keeping room between him and the closest girl. Katy looked at Reagan. "Guys can't stand girls like that. They like

241

the ones that are hard to get." She grinned. "Like us."

"True."

The trouble was, the girls had created a level of excitement, and now other groups of people were walking by, noticing that Hollywood's Dayne Matthews was in their midst. Couples and groups of guys stopped only for a moment, then went on their way.

But just as Dayne was finishing, another group of girls approached. They squealed and laughed and bounced and pulled out their camera phones. One girl fell to her knees and covered her mouth, too shocked to take another step. She kept shouting, "Dayne Matthews! . . . I can't believe it's Dayne Matthews."

"Oh, brother." Reagan laughed again and rolled her eyes in Katy's direction. "I'm not sure I could take it."

"It isn't his fault." Katy folded her arms. Her heart went out to Dayne. He had almost been killed by the paparazzi, by the public's fascination with celebrity. Even so, he wouldn't turn away a fan the way some actors would. He could very easily hold up his hand, look away, and keep walking. People would think he was a jerk, but he could do it if he wanted to. Lots of celebrities did.

But not Dayne. He understood the fascination, and though he didn't want to feed it, he respected and cared about his fans enough to give them this time.

"These are his fans. They're the ones who buy the tickets to the movies." Katy leaned against the cool brick wall. "He wouldn't have a job without them."

Reagan nodded. "I never thought about it that way."

Katy looked at Dayne just as he gave her another helpless look. She waved, wanting him to know she was fine. He could do what he needed to do and then they could leave.

Finally, after signing maybe thirty autographs and taking at least that many pictures, Dayne ducked close to Katy and took her hand. "Let's get out of here."

The thing with Dayne's celebrity was that he was ridiculously famous. So though the crowd of girls had passed, they were moving on to tell their friends about him, and if he wasn't careful, there could be a crowd looking for him.

Dayne pulled his baseball cap low and walked as fast as he could while allowing Katy and Reagan to keep up. He still had Katy's hand in his, but he turned his attention to Luke. "If a mob shows up, I'll make a dash for it. You stay with Katy and Reagan."

Luke didn't look surprised. After all, he'd been with Dayne during the trial in LA. He'd seen the tricks Dayne had to pull to make a getaway. He saluted Dayne. "Got it, Bro."

They managed to get to the parking lot without attracting any other fans, and when they reached their cars, everyone agreed it had been a great night.

Before they left, Dayne hugged Luke. "Let's do it again soon, okay?"

Their conversation was quiet, and Reagan was already in the car, so she heard none of it. But Katy was still standing near the passenger door.

"I'd like that." Luke held Dayne's gaze. "Hey . . . I'm glad we found each other. If I don't say it often enough, I'm thinking it."

Dayne smiled. "I know, Luke." He pressed his fist to his chest. "I can feel it." He waved and walked around to open Katy's door.

Never mind the inconvenience of an occasional outburst of fan adoration. Katy would've stood there all night if it meant being with Dayne Matthews. His fans only knew what he was capable of on the screen — the bigger-than-life persona. The tough guy and tender lover that he could become on film. They knew his look and his walk and his voice. They knew the heartthrob Dayne Matthews.

But they didn't know the sound of his laugh as he watched Cole chase a frog down the driveway or how he teared up when he talked about Elizabeth Baxter, the birth mother he'd known for only an hour before she died. They didn't know his dream of living in the lake house and having family barbecues and raising a houseful of children. And they certainly didn't know how much he loved his family. His new family. The fans didn't really know Dayne, and they didn't know his heart.

Only Katy knew that. And she would keep knowing him a little better — the way she had tonight, watching him with Luke — as long as she lived.

CHAPTER FOURTEEN

Dayne couldn't wait to be alone with Katy. Not in the car driving and not distracted by talk of the game and the good time they'd had with Luke and Reagan. All that was wonderful. But he had an idea, and all night he'd forced himself to wait until they were alone so he could tell her about it.

Not that the idea was new. But this time it was serious. Very serious. He'd spoken with his agent and the director of his next film. Now he needed to talk to Katy.

When they got to the Flanigans', Bailey was out front talking to some guy standing near a small car. She seemed to jump when they pulled into the driveway, and by the time they reached the circular drive at the front of the house, the guy had climbed into his car and was pulling away.

"Quick good-bye." Dayne peered through his window, trying to make out the driver. "Who's the guy?"

"Bryan Smythe." Katy's tone told him she was leery of the kid. "He's been coming on strong to Bailey, but Jenny and I don't think he's for real. He talks big about God and God's will and the Bible. But he wants to spend most of his time outside talking to Bailey by his car."

"Hmmm. Beware of guys who spend too much time outside." He nodded for emphasis. "Up to no good. Especially around a cutie like Bailey."

"It's hard, too, because usually Jenny and Bailey talk about everything." Katy frowned. "But Cody is taking up a lot of Jenny and Jim's spare time. It's almost like they're forgetting about Bailey."

"They probably think everything's fine with her. Cody's the one with the crisis."

"For now." Katy sighed. "I have a bad feeling about Bryan."

"He's one of the CKT kids, right?" It was coming back to Dayne.

"He's great onstage. I guess I just worry that he's a player. He says a lot of smooth things, but I'm not sure he's sincere. Bailey talked to me about him the other day, and some of what he told her sounds like nothing but a bunch of lines."

They went inside, and Dayne saw Bailey dart down the hallway, give a quick wave in their direction, and disappear up the stairs. Like Katy said, Jenny and Jim were talking with Cody in the family room. The boys must've been in bed already.

Dayne nudged her arm as they walked through the family room into the kitchen. "Wanna sit outside?"

She teased him with her eyes. "Didn't you just say beware of guys who spend too much time outside?"

"Except me." He gave her his best schoolboy smile. "You can trust me."

"Not without a cup of coffee." Katy took two mugs from the cupboard and tossed a bag of instant coffee into each. She used the hot tap to fill the cups. She added cream to hers and a spoonful of sugar to Dayne's.

They walked to the closet and grabbed an extra layer of coats and scarves and a stadium blanket. Then they went outside and sat on the porch glider. Dayne was practically bursting with his idea. He only hoped Katy would be as excited about it.

When they were side by side, Katy spread the blanket over their laps. "The snow's so pretty. I love how it shines in the moonlight."

"It's pretty cold for this LA boy." He shivered and slid closer to her. "I'm hoping I'll get used to it. Maybe in five years."

"Faster than that." She giggled and turned to face him. "Like I've already gotten used to all the girls."

"It isn't just girls. It's fans." The line was something he'd said before, but they both knew it wasn't true. He couldn't keep a straight face. "Okay. You're right."

She made her eyes big. "Dayne . . . Dayne . . ." She was teasing him, using the high-pitched voice of the girls at the basketball game earlier. "I can't believe it!" She put her hands over her mouth. "You're Dayne Matthews!"

"Okay, okay." He eased her hands down from her face and leaned in to kiss her.

"Mmmm." She met his eyes. "Imagine their reaction if you would've done that to one of them."

"Never." Dayne kissed her again. "And you're right. If you can get used to a scene like that one, I can get used to some snow."

A light laugh came from Katy. "You haven't seen anything. This puny snowfall's just the beginning."

Dayne pulled the blanket higher on his lap and put his arm around her. "As long as I've got you to keep me warm."

"That . . . or we could have our talks inside." She brushed her cheek against his. "Of course . . . it might not be this fun."

249

He was quiet, drawn by the nearness of her. But he couldn't let himself get distracted. He needed to talk to her. The director wanted an answer in the next day or so.

"Dayne?" She tilted her head up to him.

"What?"

"Why do I have the feeling you have something to tell me?" Katy looked deeply at him, past the teasing and lightheartedness of the moment to the place where only she was allowed. "Something on your mind?"

"Me?" He kissed her slower this time, then feigned an innocent look. "Nah. I've just been waiting the whole night for this moment; that's all."

A slightly worried look darkened her features. "Something wrong?"

"Not at all." Dayne put his hand alongside her face. "Everything's more perfect than I ever dreamed, Katy. I mean it."

"Good." She searched his eyes. "I have to agree with you on the perfect part."

He couldn't wait another minute. "I talked to the director the other day, the one doing my next film."

"You told me." Katy raised the corners of her mouth. "Remember?"

"I didn't tell you what we talked about." Dayne touched his knuckles to her cheek.

250

" 'Cause we talked about you."

"Really?" She wrinkled her nose. "About the wedding, you mean?"

"No. About how I've found a solution to the issues I'm having with on-screen love scenes."

Katy squinted at him. "You're not serious."

"I am." He started at the beginning. "The director's a great friend of the guy you read for, the director of *Dream On.*"

No question he had her attention now. She pulled the blanket up close to her chin and let him explain.

Since the leading lady who'd originally been cast opposite Dayne had checked into rehab and was asking for a year off, the role was still open.

"What about Katy Hart?" Dayne had asked the director. His name was Stephen Petrel, a former screenwriter whose Academy Award–winning scripts eventually earned him the chance to direct his own films. Now he was a legend. America lined up to see his films. Dayne was actually nervous bringing up Katy to him. He usually had very specific ideas about who could and couldn't play a certain role.

But as soon as Stephen heard Katy's

name, his tone changed. "You think she'd do it?"

Dayne wasn't sure, and he told Stephen as much. All he could do was ask, and if Katy said no . . . he could beg. Because after marrying her and sharing a honeymoon with her, he could think of a dozen reasons why he'd want to spend every waking moment on a set with her. That she was genuine and honest and breathtaking in front of the camera were only a few of them.

"So it's up to you." Dayne held his breath. "Star in it with me, Katy. It'd be the perfect way to start out — side by side on the screen."

Her eyes were wide, and she lowered her chin into the blanket. She was clearly considering the possibility. "What's the plot?"

Dayne reached for her hands. "It's a love story." He brought her fingers to his lips and kissed them. "But not as good as ours."

"Oh, brother." Katy laughed. "Now you sound like Bryan Smythe."

He made a face. "That bad?"

"Yes." She nodded. "Seriously, Dayne. Tell me."

"It really is a love story."

"Obviously." She gave him the sweetest slightly sarcastic smile. "You're starring in it. Of course it's a love story. It's girls like the ones we saw tonight who pay to see your films."

A laugh caught in his throat, and he couldn't hold it in. "Sorry." He took a deep breath and launched into the story. "It's called *But Then Again No.* It's about a guy and a girl who had been inseparable in high school. She gets pregnant, but they're young, so they put the baby up for adoption and wind up on opposite sides of the country."

"End of story?"

"Beginning." Dayne wanted to make her fall for the project the way he had. "It starts when their daughter takes an internship at a magazine only to find that her managing editor's her mother. She becomes driven to get her parents back together."

"And she does." The sparkle was back in Katy's eyes.

"She does but it's complicated."

Katy raised her eyebrows. "Complicated can be good."

"Yes, it can." His tone softened. "Two people falling in love even though they couldn't be any more different."

"So the movie tells us whether love's enough to bring them back together. . . ."

"Exactly."

She pursed her lips. "I like it."

"You'll love the script. It's brilliant. Stephen wrote it himself."

Katy tilted her head. Doubt crept into her eyes. "He really wants to consider me?"

Dayne didn't want to tell her exactly what the director had said, because it would scare her. He'd basically said that based on the rave reviews he'd heard about her and the fact that her chemistry with Dayne would be impeccable, if Katy impressed him on the first audition, the part was hers. Dayne held on to that information for another time. "We'll be in LA in January for the magazine interview anyway. We could stop by the studio, and you could read for him." Dayne lifted his hands. "Nothing more than that."

"He won't want me." Katy pulled one knee up and hugged it. "I have no real experience."

"For this part, that could be a good thing. Because there's a side to the female lead that's hard and jaded. But when she's with her love, she's as guileless as —" he let himself get lost in her eyes — "as guileless as you."

For a minute they said nothing. Katy rested her head on his shoulder, and he was drawn into the steady rhythm of her breathing.

After a while she looked up at him. "What about working together? I mean, if by a long shot I won the part?"

Dayne shifted so his face was closer to hers, and he kissed her. "I can't imagine anything better. The film's a must. I'll be in Los Angeles for six weeks and three more in Arizona for the location scenes." He ran his fingers down the length of her arm. "We have three choices. You stay here, and I leave for more than two months. Or you follow me around, staying with me in the Malibu house and hanging out on the set. Watching me do a thousand love scenes with someone else. Spending all those weeks on the sidelines."

"Not bad." Katy nuzzled her face against his. "Anytime I'm near you I'm happy."

His lips found hers, and it took a few seconds to remember what he'd been saying. "The third option is that we —" he kissed her once more — "get to do this —" another kiss — "and call it work."

"One problem." She worked her fingers into the roots of his hair and back along his neck.

"What?" His voice had fallen to a throaty whisper. Desire filled him.

Katy released her leg and slid closer to him. "I couldn't possibly take money for doing something I love so much."

Dayne moved so there were a few inches between them. He steadied himself. "I think you have the lovin' part down."

Her eyes held an innocence he doubted she was feeling. "Practice is always a good thing."

"Not always." Dayne wagged his finger at her. She was only teasing him, stretching out their pending good-bye. He kissed his fingers and pressed them to her lips. "It's late; I have to go." He stood. "Can I tell the director you'll read for the part when we're out there in January?"

Katy didn't look ready for Dayne to leave, but she moved slowly to her feet. "Yes. I'll do it for you." She smiled, clearly struggling the same as him. Saying good-bye was never easy, but in three months they'd never have to say good-bye again. Not like this.

Suddenly her words registered inside him. "You'll do it?" He'd expected her to say no, to tell him that she would be there and watch from the outside, but that after the stalker and the way the paparazzi had nearly killed him, she couldn't put herself square in the limelight.

What had come over her? Dayne hugged

her but not with the passion of a moment ago. Rather with a grateful heart, because the young woman in his arms was willing to climb out of her Bloomington box and take a step that could change her life. Forever. As long as she took the step next to him, it could only change things for the better.

As Katy held on to him, he found his answer. The reason she was willing to read for the director or take a part in a movie even though she was nervous around the press. He knew what had come over her, because it filled her voice and her touch and her eyes as deep as her soul.

Katy loved him, and he loved her. Period. And no movie, no audition, no stalker, and no amount of fame could ever do anything to change that.

CHAPTER FIFTEEN

Tip-off for Cole's first basketball game as a Peewee Cougar was at five o'clock sharp Friday evening nine days before Christmas. Many of the Baxter family and all the Flanigans were present for the event, and Ashley couldn't have been more proud. She stood and clapped, her hands raised in the air. "Let's go, Coley! Come on, Cougars!"

Next to her Landon was on his feet too. "You can do it, buddy." He cupped his hands around his mouth. "Remember what we talked about!"

The brief talk had taken place half an hour before they left for the game. Landon stooped down so he was face-to-face with Cole. "You love basketball, right?"

"Yes." Cole had his game face on, serious eyes, his brow lowered in conqueror mode. "I love it like crazy."

"Okay then." Landon stood and messed up Cole's hair with his fingers. "Go out and play like you love it. Don't be afraid, and remember that anytime God gives you a gift, you need to use it to the best of your ability. So when you get out there . . . play for Jesus."

"Okay. Thanks." Duly advised, Cole pumped his fist in the air, took a running leap, and banged his chest against Landon's. "Chest thumps! That's how they do it in the pros before a game, Daddy."

Ashley could've dropped to her knees and melted into a puddle. Every time Cole called Landon *Daddy,* the sound took her breath away. How many years had she and Cole lived alone, wondering if a daddy would ever be part of their lives? But now they lived like those days had never happened . . . in all ways but one.

Never for a single day would Ashley forget how blessed she was, how much God had gifted her with the reality of Landon Blake in her life.

Now, as Cole took the court, he looked back at Landon and pumped his fist again. His grin told them that he remembered his daddy's message to play like he loved the game and play for Jesus. Ashley turned to her dad and Dayne and Katy, who were sitting directly behind her. She lowered her voice so the other parents couldn't hear her.

"He's *starting*." She pointed at Cole taking his place at the middle of the floor. Then she tugged on Landon's sleeve. "I knew he had a gift."

Ashley waved at Kari, Ryan, and their two kids at the far end of the bleachers. Kari wasn't feeling well again. They wanted to be near the exit in case they had to leave. Kari noticed her and smiled, and Ashley mouthed, "Cole's starting!"

She looked out at the court and then at Landon. "Can't you just see Cole suiting up for the Hoosiers? I mean, look at him, Landon. Look at the way he's holding the ball. He's a natural out there. It's a gift, seriously."

"Ashley, the game just started." Landon gave her a comical look that said she was being ridiculous. "Any kid who can walk straight has a gift for basketball. This is Indiana, home of the Hoosiers." He put his arm around her shoulders. "We might want to give it a game or two before we alert the media."

Ashley laughed, but even as she did, Cole stole the ball, dribbled down the court, and made a layup. "See!" She jumped up and down on the bench and raised her hands in the air. She cheered and clapped. "Way to go, Coley! That's my boy!"

Ashley looked around. Everyone else was sitting on the bleachers. She gulped and quickly took her spot beside Landon.

"Remember, Coach Troy told us to cheer for the *team*." He gave her a friendly reminder–type smile and nodded at the bench. "All those little boys haven't even gotten on the floor yet."

"True." She slumped down a little and analyzed herself. She hadn't expected to feel this way about watching Cole play.

In the row beneath her were Jenny and Jim Flanigan with Cody Coleman and the rest of their kids.

The players moved up and down the court attempting something vaguely like an offense but rarely scoring. Ricky Flanigan was in the starting group with Cole, and this time as the other team took the ball down the court, Ricky sliced in, stole the ball, and passed it to Cole.

"Go, Coley!" Ashley was on her feet again.

Landon took hold of her sleeve and gave it a gentle tug.

She sat back down, and as she did, Cole took a wrong step and fell to the floor. The ball bounced off the heel of his new tennis shoes and rolled out of bounds.

"Sub out, Coach!" A loud voice from somewhere behind them boomed across the gym. "Give the boys on the bench a chance!"

Ashley stifled a gasp. Was the guy serious? She turned to Landon, astonished. "Did you hear him?"

"Yes." Landon's expression told her she might as well get used to it. "Welcome to third-grade sports."

Anger welled inside Ashley. "How dare he say that?" she hissed in a frustrated whisper. "It was a direct attack on Cole."

Landon whispered back at her, "Maybe his boy's bound for the pros too."

She slumped a little more and turned to face the court. Cole was fine, back up and trying to steal the ball from the Peewee Bulls. The boys passed the ball, celebrating a little with each actual catch. But when it came time for the closest Bulls player to throw the ball toward the basket, it fell about four feet shy.

A chorus of parents on the other side of the bleachers clapped. "Good try. . . . Way to work it around!"

Ashley watched them, learning. Yes, that was it. The encouragement should come in a general way. Nothing too personal. That way no one would feel left out.

Ricky had the ball, and Ashley spotted Jim Flanigan sliding to the edge of the bench, poised to stand. "Go Cougars! Take it all the way!" he shouted.

Landon leaned in. "Notice he didn't mention Ricky's name."

"Thanks." She gave him a quick, semisarcastic smile and kept her eyes on the Cougars.

Ricky passed to a little boy near the baseline, and for a moment it looked like he might shoot. A round of parents' voices encouraged him to do so, but the child passed it over the top of the key, and one of the Bulls snatched it from the air.

"Go Bulls," their parents yelled.

"The kids are tired, Coach. Make a switch already!" It was the grouchy guy from the top of the stands.

Ashley didn't want to turn around and look at him. That would be too obvious.

About that time, as if he'd heard the dad complaining, Coach Troy called a huddle with the five boys still on the bench. Ashley was sitting close enough that she could hear. "Ready, guys?"

"Yes, Coach!"

"Yes, sir!"

"Yeah!"

The boys' voices blended together, and Coach Troy sent them to the scorer's table to check in. At the next loose ball, the ref

blew his whistle, and the five Cougar players on the court took the bench, while the
waiting group ran onto the floor. The ref
helped the boys match up with the player
they were defending, and the game was in
action again.

The Bulls had the ball on the first posses-
sion after the substitution, and the five of
them had barely set up in front of their net
when the loud voice behind them kicked in
again. "Be aggressive, Billy! Get in position." The guy groaned. "Not like that.
Front your man, Son. Do I have to come
down there and show you?"

Ashley couldn't resist. She peeked over
her shoulder, and suddenly she figured it
out. This was the man who had made a
spectacle at one of the practices. The parents
who stayed to watch had been standing
along one side of the gym. Coach Troy was
going over the offense — how one player
would pass to another, while at the same
time a player near the baseline would cut
across, thus shifting the players and possibly creating an open shot.

But the man responsible for today's out-
bursts didn't like that offensive plan. He
stormed halfway across the gym floor and
waved his hand in disgust at Coach Troy.
"This is Indiana, friend. You can't teach a

set offense in Indiana. They'll run you out of town."

Coach Troy had picked up the basketball, held it beneath his arms, and stared at the man. Ashley remembered thinking he was probably too shocked to speak.

"You heard me." The man was tall and hefty. He looked mean, his face ruddy and angry. "It's a running game here." He brushed his hand toward the coach and slowly returned to his place. "If you can't teach the transition game, you shouldn't be here."

Ashley couldn't believe the man that day, and by the looks on the faces of the other parents, neither could they. But it wasn't until after that practice that Ashley realized who was paying the price for the man's intensity. As Ashley and Cole were on their way out, they passed the man. He had his son cornered in the first row of the bleachers.

"I don't care what you say, Billy. You weren't hustling." He thumped himself on the chest. "I played four years of D-I college ball, but you won't see a day at that level if you don't work harder." He must've been trying to stay unnoticed, because he kept glancing over his shoulder. The man apparently had no idea how loud he was;

every parent who walked past after practice that day shook his head.

Ashley had stopped and stared at the man's back. His tone was atrocious, and she considered going back and telling the coach. But it wasn't her business. Besides, the man wasn't *hitting* his son. Just hurting him with words. That much was clear as Billy nodded silently at the appropriate times, two trails of tears streaming down his little face.

Ashley wanted to grab the man and shake him. Before she left the building, she hesitated a few feet from the boy. "Good-bye, Billy."

"Yeah, bye, Billy!" Cole grinned. He didn't seem to understand what was going on, only that Billy didn't look happy. "Good practice."

Billy sniffed a few times. "You . . . you too."

The man hesitated, probably waiting for them to leave. Finally he shot Ashley a look. "We need a minute here, okay?"

Ashley glared at the man and cast the boy a sad smile. "I liked your hustle tonight, Billy."

"Th-th-thank you." He looked like he felt so bad about letting his father down that he could barely make eye contact. And what about his speech? Did he stutter all the time

266

or just when he was being yelled at?

The father had given Ashley a sardonic look. "Yeah, thanks. Why don't you mind your own business?"

Ashley hadn't been at another practice since, and until now she'd almost forgotten about Billy and his irate father. As it turned out, another boy — not Billy — won the rebound and dribbled the ball the length of the court for the layup.

But while the Cougars' fans were celebrating another score, Billy's dad shouted, "That should've been yours, Billy!" Then the man pounded down the bleachers and stormed to the far corner of the gym, near the Cougars' basket. From there he paced along a short line, five feet in one direction, five in the other.

"Look at him!" Ashley turned and shared the horror of the moment with her dad and Dayne and Katy. "If he goes to his car, I'll be scared. He'll probably come back and shoot someone."

"The ref should say something." Her father was clearly bothered also. "Poor little guy."

Billy looked terrified, and the players on the bench, including Cole and Ricky, were noticing the drama playing out between the boy and his father. Whereas Billy had been focused on the action, doing his best to keep up with his teammates, trying to appear aggressive, now he seemed entirely distracted by his father.

The Bulls missed, and the tallest boy on the Cougars caught the rebound. He immediately passed it to Billy, who started to dribble toward the Cougars' net. In that moment, Billy looked very smooth. It was possible to see that maybe the father's genes — if he had indeed played college basketball — had been passed on to his son.

"Yes, Billy. . . . That's it!" His dad clapped loud and dramatically. As angry as he'd been before, he was jubilant now. His hands shot straight in the air. "Finally!"

But the closer Billy came to his father, the slower and more nervous he looked. As he neared the three-point line, he panicked and threw the ball directly into the hands of a Bulls player.

"What?" His father pressed his hands against the sides of his head. "Ugh! You're killing me, Billy!"

Billy's eyes were wide, and it looked like he was crying. Billy slowed while his teammates passed him on their way down to the Bulls' side of the court. Then the poor child stopped and shrugged at his father. "Sorry, Dad," he shouted. "I'm sorry."

The man's face was beet red now. He pointed at the opposite side of the court. "Don't stand there! Get it back. Hurry!"

Everyone in the gym was watching, and at the next out of bounds, the ref blew his whistle. He tapped both his shoulders. "My time-out."

Coach Troy used the moment to swap players, apparently trying to distract his boys from the drama that might explode across the court.

The ref walked purposefully toward Billy's dad. When he was maybe a foot from the man, the ref said something none of them could hear.

"He's my kid," the father spat back. His response echoed through the quiet gym. "If he's not hustling, it's my job to get him into gear."

The ref said something else and pointed to the door.

"You can't kick me out!" Billy's dad snarled. "It's a public school." His words were tough, but whatever the ref said must've hit home in some way because Billy's dad made a brush-off gesture at the ref. Then he walked to the foyer and leaned against the brick wall near the drinking fountain. Far enough away so he couldn't comment on the action but still in sight.

Ashley had worried that the crowd might recognize Dayne, though he wore an old crewneck sweatshirt, jeans, and a baseball cap low over his brow the way he often did. As it turned out, Billy's dad created more than enough distraction. The fans were far too caught up watching him to notice they had a movie star in their midst.

Kari and Ryan left with Jessie and RJ not long after. They waved, but Ryan looked upset. He glared at Billy's dad on the way out, and Ashley held her breath. Ryan was a coach too. If anyone would challenge the guy, it would be Ryan. Ashley watched Kari link arms with him and lead him toward the farthest door, steering him clear of the chance to say anything.

Ashley's heart beat faster than usual, and she felt nervous, anxious. A little sick to her stomach too.

Billy's dad kept his distance and didn't say another word the rest of the game, but when Billy was in, he paced and held his hands in the air or waved off the entire action on the court and turned his back, his body language telling everyone in the gym that he was beyond disgusted.

Ashley took hold of Landon's knee. Her anger bubbled inside her, looking for a way out, an answer for Billy. "The ref should kick him all the way out." Her heart raced inside her. She was so indignant, so worried for Billy, that she forgot to watch Cole.

And at that moment, a ball swished through the net, and the Cougar fans jumped to their feet. "Way to go, Cougars!"

"Nice shot!" Landon yelled.

In front of them, Jim Flanigan chimed in. "Good passing, boys!"

"What happened?" Ashley blinked. She had no idea. She'd practically forgotten anyone else but Billy was even playing.

"Ricky made a three-point shot." Landon chuckled and patted Jim on the back. "The boy has an arm."

"Thanks." Jim turned around and grinned. "Can't wait to see him with a football when he's older."

Frustration surged through Ashley. "What about Billy's dad?" She looked at the man. His face was still red, his glare directed at his son. "Isn't there something we can do?"

Jim turned around again and gave her a sympathetic look. The action was still moving up and down the court, but he was calm and collected. Same as Landon. They were the antithesis of the man across the court. "There's a dad like that on every team. That's youth sports, I'm afraid. Once in a while someone goes overboard, and a coach or a ref has to step in. But this guy . . ." He motioned toward Billy's dad. "In my years of coaching, I've seen a handful of them every season."

"It's worse at the high school level." Landon put his feet on the bench in front of him. "I remember some of my buddies telling me stories."

"It's way worse." Jim glanced at Landon and then Ashley. "I had a dad once who took copious notes and stats on his son every practice, every game. Kid couldn't do anything right. At the end of every game the guy would pull his boy aside and tear him to pieces."

"He'd hit him?" Ashley gasped.

"Not with his fists." Jenny turned around. "With his words. I was there; I saw it every game."

Jim made a sheepish face. "One time the team and I were still in the locker room, and the kid's dad started saying things about the coaches."

"Basically bashing Jim and the other coaches in front of the entire group of parents waiting for their kids." Jenny looked indignant at the memory. "I went up to him and told him he might try being a little more positive."

Disbelief filled Jim's expression. "The guy

actually pushed her, shoved her in the shoulders and told her the team was none of her business."

"One of the parents called the police, and the guy was arrested." Jenny shook her head. "They released him later, and the athletic director forced him to stay home for the next two games."

"Let me guess." Landon had his eyes on the game. "He was right back at berating his son."

"Exactly." Jim sounded defeated at the memory. "Here's the sad part. Ran into the dad a month ago and asked about his son. The dad had him slated for IU or Duke or Kansas." He shrugged. "He was a decent athlete, and I hadn't heard where he wound up."

"The father just shook his head." Jenny's eyes glistened. "He said they hadn't talked to their son since he graduated. He skipped college and went to mechanics' school."

Ashley's heart sank. "It destroyed their relationship?"

"Yep. Same as it'll destroy the one between Billy and his dad and between so many kids and their parents." Jim took a long breath. "I've worked with pro athletes long enough to know one thing: the ability it takes to make it at that level has nothing to do with parents badgering their child. Kids either have it or they don't, and usually it's something that becomes pretty obvious long before high school."

"That was the last time the kid played football." Jenny looked heartsick. "His dad ruined everything fun about it. Now the guy probably hates the sport."

"That's the thing." Landon clasped his hands and rested his forearms on his knees. "Sports can be so good for kids. But if parents start looking for the scholarship or the ticket to the pros, it can destroy kids."

Ashley was horrified. She swallowed hard and found Cole, sitting on the bench next to Ricky. The two were giggling and flicking each other's legs, being little boys the way they were supposed to. She reminded herself to ask Cole later if he really wanted to be in a gym on a Friday night playing basketball.

Because here, at their entrance to the world of youth sports, the last thing she wanted was to force him into something that didn't interest him. If he'd rather be at her dad's house catching night crawlers and watching them wiggle through a jar of dirt, then fine.

She shivered, and for the rest of the game she didn't jump to her feet once. Instead she clapped and cheered and encouraged, not just Cole but Billy and Ricky and Lance and Johnny.

The whole team.

After the game, Ashley positioned herself so she could watch Billy — shoulders sunken — as he grabbed his gear bag and trudged toward his father. He hung his head, and twice as he crossed the floor he stopped and wiped his eyes.

That was all Ashley could take, and she wasn't the only one. Before she could make a move toward the boy, three other sets of parents hurried to him and patted him on the back. Ashley was standing close enough to hear.

"Nice game, Billy," one of the dads said.

"Good hustle." Another stopped right in front of Billy and waited until the child looked up. "Remember, you play for the fun of it."

In the distance, Billy's dad was distracted by the ref, who seemed to be giving the man an unwanted lecture. Good thing. Otherwise the man would've come unglued at the idea of some other dad telling his son the game was about having fun.

Of all things.

As Billy reached his father, the man held up his hands. In a voice that was only slightly quieter than it had been during the game, he said, "What happened out there?"

At the same time, Cole came running up and hugged Ashley around the waist. "We got homemade chocolate-chip cookies for a snack!" He held up a plastic bag with three cookies inside. "And a juice pack! Isn't that great?"

Ashley felt a sinking sensation. She was judging Billy's father, but she'd been on the same track in the first few minutes of the game. Bragging that Cole was a starter and writing his future to include a stint of playing college basketball. Landon had been right to pull her back to her seat.

Cole was more excited about the cookies.

She rubbed his shoulder. "Chocolate chip is my favorite."

"I know." He reached into the bag, pulled one out, and gave it to her. "This one's for you."

Landon and Jim were walking alongside Ashley's father. They had slight smirks on their faces.

"Okay —" she held up her hands — "you were right. It's too soon to tell about the whole gift thing." She clapped a few times in as lackluster a fashion as possible and looked at Landon for approval. "See? I can be calm." Especially after the sickening display by Billy's father. "Go team."

Cole ran to Landon next, and the two swapped high fives. "I did what you said; I played for Jesus!" Cole pumped his fist a few times. "And it was so fun, Daddy." His smile faded, and he whispered, "But Billy was crying. Did you see him?"

"I did." Landon's eyes filled with sorrow.

"I think his dad's being mean to him." Cole's mouth hung open for a few seconds. "I heard him yell a couple times."

A *couple* times? So Cole had missed the man's blatant display of temper and fanaticism? Ashley silently thanked God. Cole's first experience in sports, his first basketball game, wasn't marred by the ranting of a lunatic father. He was having too much fun playing the game to do more than barely notice the guy. He had his buddy Ricky with him and a coach he adored and his family in the stands. All that and homemade chocolate-chip cookies.

When they reached the parking lot, Ashley saw Billy and his dad walking in the other direction toward a lone car. His father wasn't yelling at the boy anymore, but a lesson seemed to be in full swing. The man stopped every few feet and appeared to re-create missed rebounds and lost opportunities on the court. Ashley watched, Cole's hand in hers, and for the first time she didn't glare at the man.

She pitied him.

What a price he was willing to pay for the chance that his son might have a little athletic talent. Because one day not too far down the road, Billy would probably design jet engines or tend to patients, argue legal matters or drive a delivery truck, and he would hate the game of basketball. But that wasn't all.

He would hate his father, too.

CHAPTER SIXTEEN

The meeting was set for Wednesday, the last day of school before Christmas break. Jim Flanigan had been working behind the scenes with Joe Agueda, his retired police officer friend. Jim had a video screen and a DVD player set up in the locker room. Joe had promised to bring something with impact.

But there was something Jim had to do before he could meet the guys. He found Jenny on the phone in the kitchen. All around her, the kids were having their annual gingerbread house contest. The teams this year were Bailey and Connor, Ricky and BJ, and Shawn and Justin. The kids were talking at once, discussing the sugary white mortar that would serve as glue for the large gingerbread pieces.

Jenny was saying something about the next CKT show being *Oliver!* and how the owners of the theater couldn't sell it out from underneath them.

Jim drew a deep breath. Even in this crazy moment, he and Jenny needed time together with God. There was no other way he could face his players with the ultimatum he was about to present. He caught Jenny's attention and made a signal for her to wrap it up.

She nodded. "Hey, Ashley, I have to go." There was another minute of conversation, and Jenny hung up. She gave a sweeping direction to the kids. "Don't eat the glue."

"I thought it was frosting." BJ had enough on his fingers to cover half the roof of his house.

"It's more glue than frosting." She looked from one team's project to the next. "No one eat the stuff. It's bad for you."

"Makes your insides stick together." Ricky made a face. Then he burst into giggles.

"It's true." Shawn looked at his siblings. "Some ants in Brazil die every year because people spread flour near their anthills."

Jenny hesitated, looking like she wasn't sure if she was supposed to stay for the story or not. She took a step closer to Jim, her eyes on their oldest adopted son.

Shawn set his gingerbread roof down so he could illustrate his story with his hands. "The ants march over to the flour, and then, of course, they guess that it's food, so they eat it, and down in their stomachs it mixes with their digestive juices and gets so sticky their insides stick together." He gave a definitive nod. "It kills them."

Jenny's mouth was slightly open. She blinked and glanced at the three bowls of white frosting the teams were using as glue. "Bottom line: don't eat the glue."

Bailey made a face. "As if we would. The stuff stinks."

"I think it probably tastes as good as it smells." Justin leaned close to the bowl and took a long whiff. Then he shook his head. "But not if it makes your insides stick together."

Jenny held up her pointer finger. "Be right back."

Jim smiled to himself as he led her into the family room. "It's like living in a sitcom."

"Every day of the year." She wiped her brow and searched his eyes. "What's up?"

"The meeting with the team's in an hour." He felt an urgency just saying the words. "This'll be an ultimatum for many of them."

"Joe's still coming?" They'd talked about this twice in the last week. Jenny had already told Jim that she thought Joe would bring a lot to the meeting.

281

"He'll be there. He told me to eat light. The movie's already been approved by the school district, but it's hard on the stomach apparently."

"Good." She put her hand on his shoulder. "The kids need a wake-up call." She leaned up and kissed him on the lips, lingering there for a few seconds. "You know what it was like."

"Yes." He sighed, and suddenly he felt tired and old. "I hope a story from an old man about a day a long time ago can make a difference right now. When these kids need it most."

"It will." Jenny wrapped her arms around his neck and leaned against him. "You're doing a good thing here, Jim. God will meet you in that locker room tonight."

"Pray with me?"

She brought her hands down to his, and for the next few minutes they took turns asking God that the meeting with Clear Creek's football players wouldn't be merely a reprimand or another time when the boys felt like they were being lectured. But that what they saw and heard and committed to this night would change them. Maybe even save them.

As they finished praying, Jim paused. He ran his finger over Jenny's right thumb, the one that was shorter than the other. She could still use it, still write and work and play as if she'd never lost the top half. But it was missing. And it would forever serve as a reminder of all God had taught them that spring night when they were in high school. He brought her hand to his lips and kissed her scarred thumb. Then he continued his prayer. "And one more thing, Lord. Thank You for a wife who has stood by me in the darkest of times and the brightest. Thank You that she supports me and believes in me. I can feel her prayers in everything I do. In Jesus' name, amen."

Jenny had tears in her eyes when he drew back and kissed her good-bye.

On the way to school, Jim realized again how true his prayer was. Jenny had always believed in him, always encouraged him. Sure, they had times when they disagreed about the kids. He thought she spent too much money on Bailey and she was a little too forgiving when the kids left a light on or didn't clean their rooms. Jenny called Jim reclusive when he slipped off to watch a football game during a CKT party now and then.

There was a time when his faith hadn't nearly been what it was today. But even through those stages, Jenny was patient, gently sharing a Bible verse or complimenting him about his coaching and telling him she was praying for him in the same breath.

After Bailey was born, Jim had taken a harder look at his life and also his eventual death. He had realized that if he didn't wake up one day, he wasn't sure whether he'd land in heaven or hell. He joined Jenny at church and started going to a triple-B class. Basic Beginner's Bible study. He learned about God and grew closer to Jenny along the way.

Jim wasn't perfect. Once in a while he still yelled a little too loud at a player or grumbled about the school district's handling of sports schedules.

But for sixteen years he hadn't been afraid to fall asleep.

He could only hope that after tonight, the same would be true for his players.

CHAPTER SEVENTEEN

Word must've gotten out, because every player on the Clear Creek football team gathered in the locker room for the seven o'clock meeting. Christmas break had officially started, and today they'd gotten out of school before lunch. Jim wasn't sure how many guys would care enough to come back.

But here they were. Captains Tanner Williams, Jack Spencer, and Todd Carson. Brandon Reeves, the clean-cut kicker, and the small group of guys who hadn't touched a drink all season. And sitting by himself, a pale Cody Coleman.

Jim looked around the room, taking count again, meeting the eyes of the players grouped together on benches, leaning on lockers, and sitting on the floor. He'd been right the first time. They were all here.

Never mind that football had ended weeks ago. The locker room smelled the way it always did — of teenage sweat and heavy rubber mats and the faint hint of pine cleaner. The guys settled down, and even the whispers and occasional clang of a shutting locker fell to an expectant silence.

Jim stood in a back corner and studied his team, the guys who had hung on his every word during the season. *Let them listen now more than ever, Lord. Please . . .*

Jim had talked to Ryan about the meeting and Joe's Aguedo's involvement. Ryan was unable to attend, but he'd given Jim the go-ahead.

Jim had asked Joe to go first. Normally on the sidelines Joe was a jovial guy. The players had come to expect a handshake or a joke from him. But here, he looked like the steely-eyed, street-smart police officer he must've been in his glory days. He stood at the front of the room with his feet apart, arms crossed. "Coach asked me to share a little something from my days as a police officer, working the streets of LA." His voice was deep.

Jim saw a few of his players sit a little straighter.

"Word around school is that this team has a drinking problem." Joe made eye contact with Cody, then Tanner Williams. "Captains, leaders . . . going to parties, getting drunk."

His tone fell short of defeat but just barely. "Guys your age think you're invincible. Big, strong football players. Taking third place in regionals." He paced along the front of the room and looked at Jack Spencer and Todd Carson. "You think it'll last forever."

Jim studied his players. Some of them were staring at their shoelaces, probably counting down the minutes until the meeting was over. But Cody was listening. Tanner, too, and maybe a third of the others. Jim kept praying.

Joe stopped and faced them again. "You think you'll always have the privilege of wearing the Clear Creek blue and gray, because you're an athlete and the games and practices and girls clamoring for your attention will be one long joyride that'll never end. And like football players all over the country as far back as the sport itself, you think it's cool to drink. Throw down a few beers at a party, get so drunk people have to tell you that you climbed a tree in your underwear before you threw up."

A few quiet chuckles sounded from the players.

"Exactly." Joe smiled and pointed at one of the guys. "See? It's all a big joke, right? 'Lay off, Joe. . . . Leave us alone, Coach.' " Joe's smile dimmed. "Only here's the part that isn't funny." His gaze became hard and intense. "It isn't funny when you take a call at one in the morning and find the twisted remains of two cars that hit each other head-on at fifty miles an hour." He cupped his hands together and held them out. "All the brains in your head could fit right here in the palms of my hands."

A couple of guys looked down. But no one was laughing.

"That's right; look away. At those crazy drinking parties, no one ever talks about what it's like to see a teenage boy's brains splattered on the road, lying there between sheared-off bumpers and shattered glass and empty beer cans." Joe bit his lip and let his intensity settle down for a moment. "I can talk to you all night about what I've seen, about the hysterical parents rushing into an emergency room too late to say good-bye. All because a couple of football players thought it was cool to drink."

The guys were gripped now; Jim could sense it. God was working here, even if the players didn't know it yet.

Joe shook his head. "I'm not going to do that. There isn't enough time." He walked to the DVD player. "Everything you need to know about drinking and driving is right here in this film." He nodded to Jim, and

Jim hit the lights. Then Joe pushed a few buttons on the player, adjusted the sound, and took a spot along the side wall.

On the screen — before any credits or title or buildup — was a car full of guys. The driver and two of the kids in the backseat were drinking beer as they barreled along a two-lane highway. Music blared, and the only thing louder was the laughter from the kids as they shared a brief memory from earlier that night about a couple of girls and how easy they'd looked passed out on the sofa at the party they were at.

It was a typical scene — guys being guys. Jim guessed every player in the room could relate.

Maybe fifteen seconds into the film, the driver looked back at one of his buddies, and as he did he veered into oncoming traffic and the headlights of a minivan. The explosion of glass and metal and screeching tires played out as the camera appeared to catch in slow motion the horror happening inside the car full of teenage boys.

This part of the film was a reenactment, slow with blurred images. But when the wrecked vehicles came to rest and the noise died down, the footage became real. The video put everyone in the locker room inside a speeding police car, heading to the scene of a two-car collision with possible fatalities. One of the officers in the car was Joe Agueda. A voice-over explained that in an attempt to discourage teenage drinking and driving, a program had been started in Los Angeles. Student videographers were invited to ride along to late-night weekend accident calls.

In a rush of urgent adrenaline and action, the officers pulled up first on the scene. The video captured the officers as they scrambled from their cars and for a split second stopped cold.

"Dear God," Joe whispered in the film. "Check for survivors."

His partner ran to what remained of the car. "Two kids in the back. We'll need the Jaws of Life."

The carnage and body parts that lay scattered amid the wreckage were graphic and unspeakable.

Around the room, a few of the boys covered up the instinct to gag by coughing hard or shading their eyes.

"Don't look away," Joe bellowed. "This is cool, remember? Drinking with your buddies on the weekend. Climbing trees in your underwear."

No one laughed.

In the background of the video, a siren

began to wail and then another. From inside the minivan a baby wailed. As the camera focused on one body, the voice-over kicked in again. "Johnny Harris was seventeen. He was a junior for Western High's football team, a captain, a running back. Beneath his yearbook picture, taken a week earlier, he had supplied this caption: 'Carpe diem — seize the day.' Johnny wanted to attend college and earn a business degree. He loved fishing with his dad, playing video games with his little brother, and watching movies with his girlfriend."

The angle of the camera changed, and another body came into view. "Andy Bennett was eighteen years old. Quarterback at Western High, Andy hadn't been a drinker through high school. He was a senior, and his friends later said he figured it was time to have a little fun. His dream was to be an astronaut. . . ."

One by one, the voice-over gave an obituary for the teenagers, all dead on impact. Inside the minivan, a young mother also lay dead. Her two children — a baby and a toddler — survived the crash.

The video ended with the emotional footage of the woman's husband speaking at her memorial service. "She didn't live to see our babies walk or run or learn to read.

She'll never watch them grow up or head off to school or get married." He hung his head, tears pouring down his face. "I'll spend the rest of my life trying to understand this . . . trying to forgive."

The song "Far Away" accompanied a slide show of each of the teens — their school pictures and shots of them hanging out with friends or practicing the game they loved. Each set of photos ended with the graphic picture of the boy's body the way it looked in the wake of the crash.

When the song ended and the last image faded to black, Joe turned off the player. Around the dark locker room there was nothing but complete and utter silence. From his place in the back corner, Jim closed his eyes. Joe was right. The video was hard to stomach. But it was also exactly what his players needed to see.

After a full minute of silence, Jim flipped on the lights.

Joe was still at the front of the room, his own eyes damp. "I keep thinking, what if those Western High players were *you* guys? What if one of them was Cody Coleman or Tanner Williams or Jack Spencer or Todd Carson?" He looked at the teary eyes before him. "Or any of you." He paused, and his chin quivered. This was the softhearted Joe they were more familiar with. He gritted his teeth, sounding angry and passionate and desperate as he finished. "Don't drink, guys. Don't do it."

Joe moved back to the spot at the side of the room, and Jim took the cue. He walked between a few of his players and took his familiar place near the dry erase board. He turned to face them, and he wondered if they could hear the way his heart pounded. He still felt queasy from the video, but the timing was right. There was no time like now to tell his story, the one he rarely ever told.

"When I was a junior, I played football for my high school, same as you. I was a linebacker, good enough to get interest from top colleges." Jim leaned against the board. "I met my wife, Jenny, that year."

He didn't want to drag the story out. It was important that they keep the impact of the video. He moved away from the board and came closer, meeting their eyes. They were curious, which was good. They needed to know this part of his past.

Jim took a quick breath. "One night during spring break, a bunch of us met at a park near the school. It was a place where people hung out and drank." He clenched his jaw. "That night — for the first time —

I decided to join them. Too many years of saying no, of being the only guy who didn't drink."

Understanding flashed on Brandon Reeves' face. The way it would've flashed on Jim's back before that awful night.

"I had two beers, maybe three, by the time the night was over and it was time to go home. Jenny was there — keeping an eye on me. She didn't drink then, and she doesn't drink now. As we headed for my pickup, we were fighting. She was telling me she couldn't date me if I drank and what a waste it was when I'd stayed away from the stuff for so long." He glanced at a few of his players in the back row. "You know how it is."

Jim let himself get lost in the story. That night as he was climbing into his truck he'd realized that maybe Jenny was right. Maybe he'd had too much to drink, so he shouldn't drive. About that time his best buddy, Trent Tinley, was wandering around looking for a ride home. Trent and Jim went way back to the days of Little League T-ball and capture the flag on the elementary playground. Trent wasn't much of an athlete, but he loved football. He was brilliant at algebra and Spanish and easily the funniest guy Jim knew. Some people called them brothers;

they spent that much time together.

Jim could feel himself being sucked back to that fateful night. He'd called Trent over. "I can't drive, man. You do it; you drive. You can stay the night at my house."

"Sure thing. Maybe the chicks'll think this baby's mine." Trent had jumped at the idea. Times like this Jim could still hear his friend's voice, still see his grin. Jim felt a lump in his throat. He had replayed the next half hour a thousand times, hoping for a different ending.

But there wasn't one.

What had happened next would stay with him forever. Jim looked around the room at his players as he told the next part of the story. Trent had taken the driver's seat, laughing about some kid in his chemistry class who turned the clock ahead the last day of school before spring break, winning the early release of everyone in the class. His laugh had been contagious, and as they pulled out of the parking lot, Trent, Jim, and Jenny were all laughing.

What Jim didn't know, what he was too drunk to realize, was that Trent had been drinking too. Twice as much as Jim. But that wasn't obvious even when Trent hit the main road driving way too fast.

"Hey, slow down," Jim had told him. He

was sitting next to the passenger door, with Jenny between them. He had her hand in his.

Trent had reached over Jenny and slapped Jim on the knee. "Live a little, Jimbo. Let's see what this baby can do." Trent laughed as if that were the funniest thing he'd ever said. Then he eased off the gas. "Just kidding. I'll be careful."

Jenny didn't have her license, but her parents were strict. She whispered into Jim's ear, "Trent's been drinking, Jim."

Jim blinked at his players. They were hanging on every word, some of their faces marked by surprise and others by a knowing of having been in similar situations themselves.

Jim shook his head. "I told her not to worry. We were dropping her off first, and we'd be there in a few minutes." He sighed. "Back then we didn't have cell phones, no way to call home and find a way out of the stupid things people around you might do." Jim took a breath as the memory came more fully to life.

They were halfway to Jenny's house, driving on a stretch of curvy, narrow road, when Trent lost control. "Jim . . . help!" he shouted.

Jim grabbed at the wheel, but it was too

late. Those were Trent's last words. He overcorrected and the truck flipped twice, screeching upside down off the roadway and rolling ten feet down an embankment. The truck landed on the roof, and when it stopped sliding down the hill, Trent was dead. The accident had broken his neck, killing him instantly.

Jim let the memory return to its permanent place in the back of his mind. He swallowed hard. He would live with the regret of that night forever. If only he hadn't asked Trent to drive. "If I would've been sober that night, I could've driven Trent home. Maybe he'd be here beside me, telling you how dumb it is to drink." He felt his lip quiver a little, and he gained control. "Trent was my best friend. I miss him still."

The eyes of Tanner and Cody glistened with sorrow, and a handful of other players stared at the floor.

Jim wasn't finished yet. He filled his lungs and prayed for the strength to go on. Especially with Trent's smile so fresh in his mind. "The crash cut Jenny's thumb nearly off. By the time the paramedics arrived, Trent was gone and there wasn't anything they could do to save the top part of Jenny's thumb."

Cody leaned forward, disbelief on his face.

He had probably noticed Jenny's thumb before — he was around too much to have missed it. But now he knew the story behind her loss, and it looked like enough to knock him off his seat.

"When they got us clear of the wreck, I tried to stand, but I fell to the ground. I couldn't feel my legs. They took us to the hospital, and for the next two days the doctors thought I was paralyzed."

Jim would never forget his father walking into the hospital room, eyes swollen from crying. His dad gave him no lecture or harsh words. He only leaned down, hugged Jim close, and sobbed over what they'd lost in one night. Because of one stupid mistake, one bad night of drinking.

Two days later, the swelling went down around the disk in Jim's neck that had been crushed in the accident. All feeling returned to his arms and legs, and the next year he suited up with his team for his senior year of football.

"But I was never the same." Jim blinked back tears. "And I haven't had a drink since."

The room was so quiet that Jim could hear the kids breathing. This was the part that mattered most. He'd brought a stack of contracts to the meeting, and he picked them up off the small table behind him. "I prayed about this decision, and I don't mind saying so. We've done a pretty good job of taking God out of public education, but when a coach finds out most of his team is drinking, maybe it's time to ask Him back in."

There were a few nods around the room.

"I'm giving you a contract." Jim handed the documents to a few of the players and motioned for them to take one and pass the rest on. "Each of you will read the contract and sign it." His voice was strong now, strengthened by the passion he felt for the matter at hand. "You'll sign it or you won't play football at Clear Creek High."

The contract was simple. It gave a place for the player to print his name. Then it stated that the player was making a promise to not drink again while in high school. Not ever. If the promise was broken, the player acknowledged that he understood he would be removed from the team and not allowed to play for Clear Creek again. At the bottom was a place for the player's signature.

Joe took a bag of pens and walked around the room, handing one to each of the guys. "Remember the video," he told a few of them.

"This team is going to be known for doing things right. If you can't live with the rules, then quit now." Jim studied his players. He figured four or five of them would quit on the spot, unable to consider high school football without the wild parties. But other than a few slight hesitations, the guys silently read the contracts and signed their names.

"When you're finished, you can come up and leave your contract on the table. Before we leave here, I want you to know that Brandon Reeves is starting a team Bible study." Jim looked at his kicker. He was grateful for the kid and for the times they'd talked this week. "It'll meet Wednesday nights at my house."

Jim narrowed his eyes. The next part wasn't going to be easy. "Finally, I've asked our captains to step down. It's the off-season, and anything can happen next year. For now, Tanner, Jack, and Todd agreed that Brandon should be the team captain."

Brandon looked uncomfortable with the announcement, even though he knew it was coming. He was a quiet leader. This would thrust him into the spotlight more than anything he'd ever accomplish on the football field.

Jim registered the surprise on the faces of most of the players. But it wasn't surprise mixed with shock. Rather there was an understanding that Coach Flanigan was serious. The changes were far-reaching, and they affected everyone on the team.

"Brandon's offered to stay and pray with anyone who wants to circle up." Jim looked at the kids who he figured would struggle with the idea of prayer in the locker room. "This is optional. Don't go tell your parents that Coach said you had to pray. Brandon offered, and from where I'm standing, a lot of you guys could use a little help making some changes in your life."

The meeting ended, and the guys brought their signed contracts to the front of the room in silence, heads hung, eyes averted. Six players left immediately afterwards, the guys who Jim had suspected of drinking even during the season. The others stayed and formed a circle with Brandon.

"God, our team's really messed up right now." Brandon's voice was clear and ripe with sincerity. "We know how serious Coach is and how serious drinking is. Help every man on this team to live up to the contract we just signed." He paused. "And for the guys that just left, I pray You change their hearts. 'Cause I think we all need You pretty bad. In Jesus' name, amen."

The guys straggled out of the locker room,

though Tanner and Jack and Todd came up to Jim before they left and apologized again.

Tanner was clearly caught in the emotion of the meeting. He massaged his throat. "Tonight was exactly what we needed." He went to shake Jim's hand but changed his mind and hugged him instead. "Thanks, Coach."

Cody rode with Jim, so he was the last player left in the locker room.

Jim thanked Joe as they locked up and walked to the parking lot. "Your video was just like you said." Jim rubbed the back of his head. He felt drained. "I couldn't watch it again."

"I remember that night like it was yesterday." Joe's eyes seemed to hold the pain from that night. "I just hope it changes things around here."

When they were alone in the car, Cody leaned against the door and silently let the tears come. They coursed down his cheeks. After a long while he looked at Jim. "I'll never look at drinking the same again."

Jim felt a surge of emotion. Even though he'd gotten the principal's permission to have his players sign contracts, and even though he'd made it clear that the idea of prayer and Bible study was optional, there was no question about one thing. He'd put

302

his coaching job on the line tonight. If he lost it, if the whole thing blew up in his face, so be it. God would take care of the details. At least his own teenagers weren't tempted to drink, and he thanked God that he'd stayed in Bloomington so they could continue on with Christian Kids Theater.

As for the meeting, all that mattered were the words Cody had just spoken. Now Jim could only pray that rest of his team felt the same way.

CHAPTER EIGHTEEN

Katy held the meeting at a coffeehouse.

Ever since Dayne's accident, she'd been neglecting her role as director of CKT, and now she needed help with the theater kids at least until after the honeymoon. It was too soon to mention the fact that she might be busy filming a movie after that.

She needed to take stock of her support team and how committed they felt about *Oliver!* the upcoming show. Katy would be around for the entire season, and Dayne had agreed to help. But between planning their wedding and taking a trip or two to Los Angeles, they would need help. And then there was the spring season, which Rhonda would have to direct.

They also needed to talk about the rumors that the owners of the theater wanted to sell to a high-rise developer. The area coordinator had that information to share. In all, the future of CKT felt shaky. Katy's heart ached with even the possibility of the organization closing down. But they had to talk about it.

The afternoon was brilliantly sunny and freezing. Three inches of snow lay on the ground, but the roads were clear. Katy arrived early and breathed in the warm smell of coffee and fresh-baked croissants. She found a table and laid out the agenda for the meeting. She'd made copies for Rhonda, Ashley, Al and Nancy Helmes — the music directors, and Bethany Allen — the area coordinator. Dayne was in telephone meetings with his agent and the producer, but he might join them later. She had an extra copy of the agenda just in case.

It would feel good to discuss everything and make a plan. Otherwise, the time until her wedding would pass in a blur of wonder and starry-eyed moments. She was more in love with Dayne than ever, more certain that their future would be everything they ever imagined.

But Katy had a commitment to the kids and families of CKT, and with Wilma Waters planning the wedding, she needed to focus on the work God had given her. And whether it could continue after the coming season.

The coffee shop wasn't crowded. Just a few people hovered over newspapers or were lost in quiet conversation at a couple of the booths.

Katy left her notes at the table and went to order. There was no one else in line. "Tall latte, extra foam."

The college-age girl behind the counter held her eyes a few seconds longer than necessary, and when she brought back the hot drink, she hesitated. "Are you Katy Hart?"

"Yes." Katy paid for her coffee and smiled. "You must know someone in CKT."

"No." The girl looked starstruck. "It's just . . . I've seen your picture in the magazines, and I knew you lived here." Her hands trembled as she counted Katy's change. "You're dating Dayne Matthews, right?"

Katy felt her cheeks grow hot. This had never happened in Bloomington — someone actually recognizing her from the tabloids. Sure, people who knew her had noticed her picture in the magazines. They understood that she was of interest to the paparazzi now. But never this.

The barista held up her hand. "It's okay. You don't have to answer. I just . . . I can't believe you're actually dating him. He's the most gorgeous guy in the world."

A part of Katy wanted to hold up her left

hand and show the girl that she wasn't *dating* Dayne Matthews. She was *engaged* to him. But instead she smiled politely. "We're dating, yes."

She leaned closer, putting her hands on the counter, and lowered her voice. "What's he like? I mean, is he as dreamy in person as he is on the screen?"

A giggle formed in Katy's throat, but she swallowed it. If paparazzi were around, she wouldn't go into detail without Dayne taking the lead. But here, it seemed okay. "Dayne loves God and he loves me. That's all I can ask for."

The girl's mouth hung open. "He really loves God? I mean, they haven't talked much about that in the magazines."

"Yes, Dayne gives God credit for everything about his life."

"Wow." The girl looked like she might faint. She reached out and brushed her fingers against Katy's hand. "I just touched the hand of the woman Dayne Matthews loves. I can't believe it." She blinked and stood a little straighter, as if she'd just come to her senses. "You know what? Maybe I'll start going to church." She grinned. "I mean, if God's good for Dayne, then maybe He'd be good for me, too."

Katy took a step back. "God's good for all

of us." There was a couple in line behind her now, and she didn't want to make a scene. She waved at the girl and took her coffee back to her booth. How crazy was that? The girl was going to go to church just because Dayne did? A chill worked its way down her spine. The responsibility of living in such public shoes was enormous. More than she'd realized until this moment.

She sat down just as Ashley and Rhonda walked through the front door. Ashley wore a black wool coat and a scarf. Katy hoped the barista wouldn't recognize her, too. Ashley hadn't been feeling well for a few weeks. She didn't need a scene at the coffee counter.

Katy watched, but her friends ordered and got their drinks without incident. They spotted her and joined her at the booth. "Wait'll you hear this."

Ashley looked exhausted as she slid in and leaned against the wall. "I hope it's good. I could use a laugh."

"Me too." Rhonda's eyes held shadows that had never been there before. She kept her eyes from Katy's, almost as if she were doing so on purpose. She didn't elaborate, but they would talk later. Katy would see to it.

She told them about the girl at the

counter.

Ashley was as dumbfounded as her. "People practically worship him."

"He's a pretty great guy even without the acting gig." Rhonda smiled, but it didn't quite reach her eyes.

Katy studied her friend. Rhonda was right about Dayne, but her words were laced with a subtle bitterness. She took a sip of her coffee. "How's it going with Aaron?"

Rhonda shrugged. "We're friends. Nothing more, really."

Ashley looked surprised. "He worked the teen camp, right?"

"Yes." She managed a slight smile. "We had fun that week. But nothing came of it."

"I think he might be interested." Katy grinned at Rhonda. She wanted to snap her out of the melancholy mood she was in. "He comes by your work still, right?"

Rhonda laughed. "He does that." It was the first break in what felt like tension between them. "Not that he ever gets around to asking me out."

"Maybe he's shy." Ashley was still resting her head against the wall.

"I don't know." Rhonda angled her head thoughtfully. She kept her attention on Ashley. "I guess I keep looking for the excitement, the romance. I mean, Aaron isn't exactly Dayne Matthews."

"Rhonda, be careful." Ashley sat up straight. Her expression and tone said her feelings on this matter were strong, whether she was tired or not. "A guy doesn't have to be Dayne Matthews to make a good friend or a good husband. It's all about how you are together, what you each bring to the relationship that makes life better than it is without each other." Ashley seemed to gather herself and she smiled. "So maybe you should take another look at Aaron Woods."

"Maybe." Rhonda's voice was more upbeat than before, but her words still seemed to have a bite. "I guess we can't all date Hollywood movie stars."

Ashley looked ready to launch into a second round on the topic.

Katy wanted to change the subject. "Here." She handed them each a copy of the agenda. Otherwise she would've tackled the topic right alongside Ashley. This was what she'd feared — that Rhonda was probably jealous of her relationship with Dayne and her pending wedding and the fact that Katy's life was too busy to include Rhonda as often as before. "We have a lot to talk about."

"I'm glad we're meeting." Ashley rested

her forearms on the table. "Between getting the lake house ready and taking care of Devin, I don't know. . . . I felt like CKT wasn't getting enough of my attention."

"And definitely not mine." Katy saw Nancy, Al, and Bethany walk in. They motioned that they were getting drinks first.

"Tell us about the wedding plans." Ashley's eyes lit up some. "Are you still getting help from that coordinator?"

"She's wonderful." Katy tried not to notice how Rhonda looked away. "We're looking over our options." She reached out and put her hand over Ashley's. "You don't look good, Ash. You wanna just go home? I can catch you up on this later."

"I'm fine. That flu bug wiped out a lot of people. Kari's feeling the same way, and she got it about the same time I did." She perked up a little. "Landon's watching the boys. I told him I wouldn't be gone long."

The others joined them, and the meeting got under way.

"First, let's talk about *Oliver!*" This was the part Katy was most looking forward to. She'd loved the story of Oliver Twist since she was a little girl. Directing it now — with Dayne's help and in the season of their engagement — was going to be a great time for everyone involved. No matter what the future of CKT held.

"We're in for *Oliver!*" Al and Nancy Helmes sat next to Rhonda. "We might as well tell you now." Al exchanged a look with his wife. Then he turned back to Katy. "We're moving to Phoenix in April. Our kids are there, and it's warmer. We're buying a condo so we can travel."

Nancy's eyes were filled with mixed emotions. "Our one regret is leaving our friends in CKT. Leaving all of you especially."

Sorrow rushed at Katy and welled up in her throat. Al and Nancy Helmes had been doing music for CKT for years. Losing them in this season, when everything about CKT was so uncertain, made Katy feel defeated. Still she smiled. She reached across the table and clasped Nancy's hand. "We've loved every minute of the time you've given to CKT. If God's calling you away, then we'll pray for you and wish you well."

Tears filled Nancy's eyes. "Let's talk about *Oliver!*"

"The good news is Katy's directing." Bethany looked elated and relieved. "Her wedding will take place sometime after closing weekend."

Rhonda committed to handling choreography and the role of assistant director.

Ashley thought she could be in charge of sets. "With a little help from my brother, that is." A weary smile tugged at her lips.

"He's always wanted a job painting sets." Katy made a notation in her planner. "I think he's about to get his wish."

They all laughed, even Rhonda.

The tension Katy felt from her eased as they talked about *Oliver!* and what sets might work. "I talked to Bill Shaffer." Katy made a check mark next to the word *props* on her outline. "He pictures a bridge as the primary set piece." She drew a diagram to illustrate. "Stairs would come down on either side, allowing us to have the cast on the floor or the bridge or both — especially for the full-company numbers."

"That's ambitious." Al put his arm around his wife. "Make sure there's a railing on the stairs so the kids are safe."

"Definitely. Bill makes the safest sets I've ever seen." Katy tapped her pencil on the diagram where she'd drawn the stairs. "This will be the tallest set piece we've ever worked with, but Bill's a genius. He'll pull it off."

They talked about the music and the choreography. "Fagin's gang will have to be the guys who can dance. Most of the up-tempo songs are with that group."

"When are auditions?" Ashley had her pocket calendar out. She'd already made a few notes in the margins.

"First Friday in January." Bethany had her planner out also. "If we're going to finish the show before Katy and Dayne's wedding, we need to start a week early."

The judges would be Katy, Rhonda, and the Helmeses. "Kids will sing a one-minute song, like always." Katy felt a thrill at the thought. She loved everything about auditions. "We'll go over the results, and that night we'll call back the kids we want to look at. The second audition will take place the next morning."

With the details of *Oliver!* in place, Katy moved to the next item on her agenda. They would get tougher as she went down the list. "That brings us to the spring show." Bethany already knew what she was about to say, so she looked at Ashley and then Rhonda. "I've talked to Dayne, and I can't commit to being any part of that show. There's the wedding, then the honeymoon, and Dayne wants me to stay in LA with him when he shoots his next movie." She didn't mention that she'd agreed to read for a starring role. Either way she wouldn't be in Bloomington.

Bethany picked up. "We won't be making

any permanent changes — not as long as Katy feels she'll be back after summer for the fall show. But we'd like to ask Rhonda to direct the spring performance. The show's *Seussical,* and the kids are through-the-roof excited about it."

Katy watched Rhonda's eyes come to life. "Seriously?"

"Could you handle it with your work schedule?"

Rhonda worked in an office during the day. She grinned. "I guess this is where being single has its advantages." She tossed her hands. "CKT is nights and weekends. It shouldn't be a problem."

"Good." Bethany looked at her planner. "Now about your help. The CKT office in Cleveland's been around a lot longer than us. They've got a theater grad student interested in directing. I've already talked to him, and he's willing to move here for the spring show and summer camp season. And wait till you hear this. I talked to the Flanigans. Katy'll be out by then, and Jim and Jenny said the guy can live in their garage apartment."

"Are you serious?" Katy hadn't heard any of these details. And now, in a matter of seconds, all the pieces had come together. Rhonda would direct, and she'd have help from a member of the strongest children's theater groups in the nation. Not only that, but since the position paid practically nothing, he'd have a place to live. The same way she'd had a place when she came to Bloomington. "This is perfect. Tell us about the guy."

"I don't know much about him. His name's Chad Jennings. He's twenty-eight with a strong faith and a love for theater. His résumé is impressive." Bethany focused on Rhonda. "He wants to run his own company one day."

"Okay." Ashley held up her hands as if she couldn't take another minute of the conversation without speaking her mind. "I'll ask if no one else will." She paused. "If he'll be working with Rhonda, is he single?"

Everyone chuckled.

They finished their coffees and speculated a little longer about the possibilities for who might help Rhonda with the spring show.

Katy silently thanked God that the details had come together so quickly. "Something else. Bailey Flanigan's been taking dance for years."

"She's easily the best dancer in CKT." Rhonda's tone told them how excited she was.

Katy'd been mulling this over for a few

weeks. "She might be ready to choreograph a show."

Rhonda gasped. "That's a great idea. I could help her, but she'd have the freedom to be creative."

A buzz of conversation broke out around the table, and at the same time Katy saw Dayne walk in. Seeing him made her smile. He wore a wool jacket dusted with snow. Immediately he spotted her, and their eyes held. Katy felt her heart flip-flop. She couldn't wait to marry him. Every day felt like a year.

Suddenly she remembered the girl at the counter. She slid past Bethany and excused herself from the group. If the barista recognized him, all sense of normalcy would disappear from the meeting. And Katy didn't want Dayne distracted when the news from the meeting was so good.

The barista was busy making a drink, so Katy hurried to Dayne, took hold of his arm, and practically ran him back to their booth. Along the way she leaned up. "You smell good."

"Nice to see you, too." He laughed. "Did I miss something?"

"The barista. She's crazy about you." Katy let Dayne slide in first, next to Bethany, so even if the girl looked their way, she might not notice Dayne. When they were seated, Katy told the story — how the girl wanted to touch Katy because Katy had touched Dayne.

"Great." He turned to the others. "Okay, where are we?"

"You've got a job." Ashley looked past Bethany. Her eyes danced the way they always did when she was around Dayne.

"Sets?" Dayne looked like a hopeful first grader waiting for word on whether he was captain of the kickball team.

"Yep, you and me." Ashley high-fived him. "Bill Shaffer builds, you do the grunt work, and I paint."

"Grunt work!" Dayne's tone was thick with teasing. "My dream job!"

Everyone laughed. Katy loved the relationship Dayne and Ashley were building. More than any of the Baxter siblings, Ashley had wanted to meet her older brother. Katy remembered just how badly. And now they'd be working on sets together. It was a scenario neither she nor Ashley had ever believed possible.

Katy introduced Dayne to Al and Nancy and caught him up on *Oliver!* and *Seussical.* "So we're set for the winter and spring shows." Katy checked her agenda. This was the part she was dreading. "Next we should talk about the theater." Bethany had brought a report with the details. Katy had a feeling the news wasn't good. "Go ahead, Bethany."

Bethany rifled through her papers and pulled out three pages stapled together.

A quiet fell over the group, as if everyone feared whatever might come from this part of the meeting.

"I won't take a lot of time on this. I have a report from the owners of the Bloomington Community Theater. It confirms what we've all been hearing."

Beneath the table, Dayne reached for Katy's fingers and squeezed them gently.

"They're planning to put the theater on the market at the end of this coming summer." Bethany suddenly seemed overcome, and she closed her eyes. When she opened them, they were sad and watery. "A developer's interested in tearing down the theater and putting up high-rise condos. Since the property borders the park, apparently the deal's pretty lucrative."

Katy felt too sick to speak. She was getting married, Nancy and Al were leaving, and now they were likely losing their theater.

Rhonda was the first to recover. "That doesn't mean it's for sure, right?"

"They're putting it on the market. From

what they're telling me, they're sure about that."

"What about other theaters, other locations?" Dayne's voice was compassionate. He hadn't been personally involved in the theater, but he was probably thinking about how much CKT meant to Katy and the people in Bloomington.

"The only other theater in town big enough to house our productions is at the university. And their schedule fills up a year in advance." Bethany scanned a page of notes. "The administrator in charge said that returning theater groups have first dibs on booking for the coming year."

Katy felt tears in her eyes. There were a million memories in that theater. Sarah Jo Stryker singing opposite Tim Reed in *Tom Sawyer.* Bailey Flanigan playing the White Witch in *Narnia.* The sword fight rehearsal in *Robin Hood.* Hundreds of hours of frustration and sweat and tears and twice as many hours of laughter and song and dance. The theater was the place where she'd first seen Dayne, the place where he'd proposed to her.

She couldn't picture someone tearing it down and building condos.

"I've looked at this proposal so long I've memorized it." Bethany passed it to Katy.

"Right now our best option is to pray the owners change their minds." She cleared her throat, and Katy knew her boss was struggling as much as she was. "If they sell the theater, we'll have to consider closing down CKT. Of course, this is highly confidential. I don't want anyone outside of this group to know that this is even a possibility."

"We can't close it down!" Ashley looked about to cry too. "The Baxter grandkids haven't auditioned for a single show!"

"A lot of kids haven't." Bethany closed her planner and folded her hands. "I'm very upset about it. I had to let you know so you could join me in praying and looking for some other way to keep CKT going."

A sense of shock and somber sadness settled around the table. They closed the meeting by praying, because prayer wasn't only their best option. It was their *only* option.

Al offered to lead. "Lord, we're at a strange crossroads with Christian Kids Theater. In some ways these seem like the best of times, but then this could very well be the beginning of the end. And that's something none of us want — even Nancy and me." He coughed, and it sounded as though he was fighting for composure. "We beg You, God, to change the minds of the building owners. Bloomington needs its community theater, and the kids need CKT. So please, Father, change the minds of the owners, and if not, then please give our dear friends here a way to keep things going."

No matter how positive the meeting had been, the ending left a cloud that hung over all of them as they left. Hugs were exchanged, and though Katy could still see something wasn't quite right with Rhonda, her friend seemed better than before. "Let's talk soon." Katy searched her eyes. "I mean it."

"Okay." Rhonda's smile was sincere. "I'm sorry, Katy. I haven't been myself lately."

"That's all right." Katy hugged her. "We'll talk soon."

They escaped the coffee shop just as the barista noticed Dayne. "Hey," she shouted. "Hey, that's Dayne Matthews!"

Dayne took Katy's hand and hurried her through the falling snow to her car. There he pulled her close, and she slipped her arms beneath his coat and around his back. "It breaks my heart, Dayne."

"I know." He kissed the top of her head. "But aren't you the one who told me God never closes a door without opening a window somewhere else?"

She snuggled closer to him. "I don't want a window. I want CKT to stay in Bloomington."

"But what if —" his voice was as tender as it had ever been — "you make a movie with me and you love it? Your music directors are leaving, the owners of the theater want to sell, and we're just starting out. . . . Maybe CKT's time is up. Maybe that's God's plan."

The possibility had crossed Katy's mind, but she hated to acknowledge it. "Rhonda can run it. She looked so excited when she was asked to direct *Seussical.*"

Dayne rubbed her back. "I guess God'll make it clear in time."

They were going back to the Flanigans' to bake cookies for the Baxter caroling night set for tomorrow. But right now Katy didn't feel like cooking. She batted at a fresh round of tears. "We have until summer. For now I can't think about it."

"Because we've got *Oliver!* straight ahead of us, we do." He used his best Cockney accent, and he widened his eyes in mock exasperation. "And I've got me a boatload of sets to grunt about."

She laughed despite her tears. "I love you, Dayne Matthews. So much. You could make me laugh anytime."

323

Dayne stepped back and did a formal bow. "My pleasure, m'lady. Just doing me job." He opened her door. "Your carriage, madam."

Katy was still giggling when he shut the door and jogged across the snowy street to his 4Runner.

The rest of the night, Katy stuck to her decision and didn't think about CKT. They couldn't talk about it in front of the Flanigans anyway. Instead they baked cookies and sang Christmas carols and listened to the brothers practice for their piano recital in January.

Despite the happy evening, when she was getting ready for bed that night, Katy replayed the CKT meeting in her head. So much good news. But in the end, none of it would matter or make a difference. Not if by summer's end the theater was sold to a developer and torn down to build condos. She thought about what Dayne said. How maybe God was ushering in a new season for all of them. How maybe CKT had run its course. And that whenever the Lord closed a door, He opened a window. Katy agreed, even if she didn't want to.

If the theater closed, the adults involved would find transition into something new and exciting. But a question had plagued her all night as she heard Bailey and Connor rehearsing their audition songs upstairs and as images of Tim Reed and the Shaffer kids and dozens of others flashed in her mind.

What about the kids?

CHAPTER NINETEEN

John had been looking forward to this day for a month. Caroling had been Elaine's idea, something her family did every year. Now they were half an hour from leaving, and the kids were in the kitchen putting plastic wrap over the last few plates of cookies.

The sounds of laughter, conversation, and singing filled the house and mingled with the smell of fresh-baked cookies. Kari, Ashley, and Brooke had been here all day making Elizabeth's sugar cookies in the shapes of reindeer and Christmas trees and stars.

The atmosphere was something John would remember forever, and as Hayley walked to him, he made a mental note that next year they would do this again.

"Papa?" Hayley held out her Santa hat. "Can you help me?"

"Sure, sweetie." He stooped down and eased the hat onto her head. All the kids were wearing them, with Cole and Jessie and Maddie grabbing at one another's and playing keep-away with them near the Christmas tree. John smiled at his little granddaughter. "There, honey. You look perfect."

"Know what?" She made the pronouncement slowly, deliberately. But every word sounded like a miracle. "I can sing 'Silent Night'!"

"Good, baby." He kissed her cheek. "I can't wait to hear it."

John stood and made another head count. Ashley, Kari, Brooke, and their husbands, and kids; the Flanigan family and Cody Coleman; and Katy and Dayne. Even Luke and Reagan and their kids had driven down for the event. And Elaine, of course. She was helping Jessie find her mittens, which she'd been wearing half an hour ago when she arrived.

"Hey, Dad . . . where are we going first?" Ashley looked wonderful, much better than she had recently. Devin was on her hip, and she wore a red scarf and hat.

"Knollwood Retirement Village — the big one downtown." He put his hand on her shoulder. "You look festive."

"Thanks." She rubbed her thumb across a dirt smudge on Devin's cheeks and made a silly face. "Someone has to balance out the boys."

It took fifteen minutes to get the kids and plates of cookies into the vehicles. Elaine rode with John, and he noticed something different about her. She looked happier than she'd been during Thanksgiving. He glanced at her as he led the caravan down the driveway. "Thanks for finding Jessie's mittens."

"Cole hid them under the couch. He said he thought it would be funny."

John chuckled. He remembered the fishing contest with Landon last summer. "He comes by that teasing stuff honestly."

"I can tell." She smiled. "This'll be fun. Everyone all together caroling. We never had a group this size when my family caroled."

"I think we're strictly a no-talent outfit, but if you say they want *any* sort of singers, we just might fit the bill."

"The people at Knollwood have short memories and poor hearing." Elaine's voice was light and cheery. "You could sing the same three songs four times through, and they'd love every note."

"With a gaggle of kids in Santa hats, it probably doesn't matter if we sing a thing." John leaned back and focused on the road. The storm from yesterday had let up, and the roads were as clear as the sky. A chilly wind swept through town, and with the snow on the ground, it was starting to feel a lot like Christmas.

They were quiet for a few minutes, the comfortable kind of quiet John had come to expect from Elaine. John flipped on the radio, and the haunting refrains of "O Holy Night" filled the car.

Elaine gazed out the windshield at the starry sky. "I love this song."

"Me too." John didn't mention that this had always been his favorite, whereas "Away in a Manger" had been Elizabeth's. He merely registered the fact and smiled to himself.

A mile from Knollwood, Elaine drew a long breath. "Ashley talked to me tonight." There was a peace in her voice. "It surprised me."

"I didn't notice. What did she say?"

"She pulled me aside before we left and told me she was sorry for being so emotional Thanksgiving weekend. She was missing her mom; that's all." Elaine folded her hands, content. "She didn't want me thinking she was angry that I was there."

"Good." John felt a warm sense of satisfaction. He'd been enjoying Elaine's company so much this Christmas season, but always in the back of his mind he worried that her presence would be hard on his kids. Elizabeth had been gone for two and a half years, but there wasn't one of his kids who didn't feel like she'd died last week. He felt that way too. Just not as often as before.

"Jingle Bells" was playing on the radio as they parked and headed across the lot in the cold wind. John and Elaine waited near the door for the others, and when they were all together, they went in and signed the guest book at the front desk. The place smelled of fresh pine branches and cinnamon, and Christmas wreaths and decorations adorned every table and countertop. An enormous Christmas tree with sparkling lights stood in the corner of the foyer near a warm fire and a pair of overstuffed armchairs.

"Name of your group?" The receptionist looked at them over a tiny pair of spectacles.

John glanced at the ragtag party, complete with sleeping babies and toddlers, rambunctious kids, and more than a dozen adults. He turned back to the woman. "Call us the Baxter Bunch."

"Very good. You can head into the dining room. The residents are expecting you."

John and Elaine led the way, and sure enough, as they opened the double doors

330

into the eating area, he saw dozens of residents in festive sweaters and Christmas clothes, hands folded neatly in their laps. A few of the women had newly done hairdos.

The moment the residents spotted the children trickling in, a buzz arose from around the room. Some of them sucked in an astonished breath, and others motioned to their friends to take notice. Children had come!

One frail old woman, probably in her nineties, sat near the front. Tears filled her eyes as she looked at Cole and Maddie, who were holding hands in a rare moment of unity. The woman lowered her head and waved her gnarled fingers at the kids.

Maddie returned the wave, but she went to Brooke and half hid behind her. Cole, though, must've remembered the residents of the Sunset Hills Adult Care Home, because he went right up to the old woman and hugged her. She softly stroked Cole's hair, ignoring the tears on her weathered cheeks.

John was touched by the scene. Cole would always have a special place in his heart. The first four years of Cole's life — while Ashley was still figuring out how to be a mother — he had spent most of his time at the Baxter house under Elizabeth's gentle care. The tenderness he showed now was familiar in a bittersweet way.

When their group was finally arranged around the piano, Connor Flanigan sat in front of the keyboard. He'd brought along his Christmas songbook, but the group's only rehearsal had been an hour ago around the Baxters' old upright.

Connor was a handsome kid with dark hair and blue eyes. In the past year he'd shot up six inches, and now he was nearly six feet tall. His voice was changing too, and sometimes even with the best intentions and training, it cracked. During their quick practice, Connor had expressed concern about it, and John had assured him they'd all be praying for him. Connor's father had said something along the lines of what Elaine had said in the car: the folks at Knollwood couldn't hear well enough to be critical.

Now Connor whispered to the group, " 'Silent Night,' okay?"

John was pretty sure the kids in the front row didn't hear the announcement, but they weren't expected to add much vocally.

Connor began playing, and the music filled the room. As it did, several of the residents found handkerchiefs from their purses or pockets and dabbed their eyes.

" 'Silent night, holy night . . .' " The Baxter Bunch sang in unison in a key that was close to right. And all around the room the residents sang along.

John subtly reached for Elaine's hand, and because of the closeness of their group, he was sure no one else noticed. It felt right, here with so much emotion filling one room, that he could connect this way with the woman who had become very special to him. John looked at the faces of the residents around him. He could only imagine the stories each one of them had to tell. Stories of lives lived and children grown and love lost.

And maybe — for some of them — stories of learning to love again.

Ashley shifted Devin to her other hip and kissed his cheek. She could barely sing.

The residents watched them with rapt attention, bobbing their heads to the slow, steady rhythm of "Silent Night," happy tears streaming down some of their faces. In their eyes was a shining sweetness that said somehow the song had transported them back to long-ago Christmases when they were young and vibrant, surrounded by people they loved — the way the Baxter family was surrounded now.

" 'Sleep in heavenly peace. . . .' " Connor's voice cracked as the note went high, but no one laughed. No one in the audience seemed to notice. This wasn't a performance; it was a privilege to spend time with these older people, men and women with wisdom and experience that here in this place almost always went untapped.

Ashley stroked Devin's downy hair with her free hand. The residents reminded her so much of her dear friends at the Sunset Hills Adult Care Home. She still kept in touch with Lu, the owner. Of the residents that Ashley had cared for at Sunset Hills, only Helen was still alive. She was less lucid now than ever, the short, brilliant moments of clarity with her daughter, Sue, forever gone.

When they started the second verse of "Silent Night," Ashley focused on the members of the audience. At a far table was a couple — one of only a few in attendance. They had to be in their late eighties or early nineties, and they wore matching red sweaters. They sat side by side, their arms linked. Halfway through the stanza, the woman rested her head on the man's shoulder.

Sad, Ashley thought. Her parents would never share a moment like this. No matter how old her father lived to be, he wouldn't spend these quiet, reflective years in the company of the wife he so dearly loved. Ashley glanced at her father and Elaine. They were standing close enough together to be holding hands. But Ashley doubted they were that far along in their feelings for each other.

And even if they were, she could do nothing about it. She didn't want to do anything. Her father had a right to his own life. Landon had been helping her figure that out. When she talked with Elaine earlier tonight, she'd felt good. The woman was kind and pleasant, and in that way she reminded Ashley of her mother. But she was also very different. She kept to herself more and said less.

Still she deserved Ashley's friendship and respect, because that's how the Baxter family treated other people. Every one of them missed Mom, especially at this time of the year. But a person couldn't lie in bed the rest of his life and will himself to die of grief. Life was for the living. Landon had told her that also.

Next to her, Landon's voice was rich and on key. Just being in his presence made her feel blessed and humbly grateful. Their relationship so easily could've wound up differently. It made her think about sweet

Irvel, the resident at Sunset Hills who had most affected her. The woman had lost her husband, Hank, but she lived every day as if he were just down the road fishing with the boys. He might've died, but Irvel's love for him, her belief in his presence, never did.

It was the way Ashley wanted to spend her life, loving Landon the way Irvel had loved Hank.

Landon seemed to notice she was thinking about him. He leaned in near her ear and whispered, "You have the most beautiful hair. Has anyone ever told you that?"

"Hmmm." She smiled through fresh tears. "I was thinking of her too." Ashley focused on a woman who could've been Irvel. Dear Irvel had suffered from Alzheimer's and could easily forget what she'd said from one minute to the next. She had a fascination with Ashley's hair and commented on it sometimes eight times in an hour. It was something Landon had teased Ashley about when she had worked at Sunset Hills.

Devin had a pacifier in his mouth, but he took it out now and waved it at the audience. His joyful cries blended with the closing verse of the song, and several of the people clapped in response, delighted at his happy sounds.

Only then did Ashley spot the white-haired man in the wheelchair. He sat near the back of the cozy dining area. He was dressed in a pale blue sweater, one that hung slightly askew on his shoulders. He was alone, and as they finished the song, he wasn't only crying quiet tears. He was sobbing.

Landon gently elbowed her and nodded toward the older man. She told Landon with her eyes that she'd seen the same thing. For the next thirty minutes as they sang, Ashley couldn't take her eyes off the old guy. What was his story? Why was he so affected by their songs, their presence? Maybe he had regrets or family who never visited. Ashley had no idea, but she was determined to find out.

When they finished singing, they went into the second phase of their visit. The residents of Knollwood couldn't accept cookies. But they could take a hug or a handshake.

As Connor played the final notes of "Frosty the Snowman," the group fanned out into the dining room and made sure each resident received some personal time. Cole, Maddie, Hayley, and Jessie were wonderful, making the rounds and talking to everyone in the room.

After visiting with a few ladies at the closest table, Ashley passed Devin to her father and took Landon's hand. Together they worked their way to the back of the room, where the frail-looking man in the pale blue sweater sat alone, still sobbing in a silent, gut-wrenching way.

Ashley reached him first. She pulled up a chair beside him and put her hand on his shoulder. "Hi. I'm Ashley." She looked at Landon. "This is my husband, Landon."

The man seemed suddenly self-conscious about his tears and the way his nose was running. He fumbled around the table in front of him until he had hold of a napkin. Then he wiped at his tears and blew his nose. "I'm Eddie. Eddie Buckley." He held out a shaky hand and greeted each of them. Then he pointed to his belt buckle.

Ashley wasn't sure if the man was confused or maybe delusional, but she and Landon both looked at the buckle. Engraved on it was an insignia Ashley didn't recognize.

Landon figured it out first. "You're a fireman!" He patted the man's shoulder. "Right? Is that it?"

Ashley loved how the man's face lit up. "Yes. A fireman." He put his hand over his chest. "I'm a fireman."

Landon pulled up a chair on the other side of Eddie. "Bloomington Fire Department?

On Fourth Street?"

"Yes, sir. Hired in 1932."

"I'll bet you've seen a lot of changes."

Eddie tried to speak. He opened his mouth, but his eyes welled up again.

Ashley changed the subject. "How long have you lived at Knollwood, Eddie?"

A concerned look filled his face. He looked around the room. "You know where I live? Where the roses are? On that street with the roses?"

Ashley and Landon exchanged a look. Ashley knew how to handle a situation like this. It was exactly the sort of thing she'd done at Sunset Hills. "Yes, Eddie." She patted his hand. "I know that place. Is that where you live?"

"Yes." His features relaxed. "On Fourth Street. Where the roses are."

Landon mouthed to Ashley, "The fire station."

And then she understood too. Eddie thought he lived at the fire station. Ashley noticed that the rest of the group was still visiting with the residents. She was glad. She wasn't ready to leave Eddie Buckley just yet.

"Yeah, I know that place, Eddie. Tell me about the fires." Landon leaned in close, and it was clear that he didn't want to miss a word.

"First big one was a blaze at the Indiana Theater. Spread to the jewelers and the sporting goods store." Eddie was more composed now. "Lots of damage, but we saved the building. Did a good job."

"I heard about that."

"And then February 6, 1935." His words were slow and not altogether clear. But the memory of these fires was clearly vivid. "Big fire at the Monroe County Jail." He narrowed his eyes. "You heard of that one?"

"The roof collapsed." Landon knew his history.

Ashley sat mesmerized. Except for the decades that separated them, Landon and Eddie could've been colleagues. Brothers from the same fraternity, anchored at the same fire department.

"Roof fell and five of us ran for our lives." Eddie shook at the memory. "Wicked fire. I was one of the five who got out. Saved our lives but lost the building that time."

Landon's tone grew softer. "So . . . you remember the Greyhound wreck . . . 1950, I think."

Eddie lowered his brow, and gradually his mouth hung open and he started crying again. Deep, silent sobs shook him, and he held up his hand toward Landon as if he desperately wanted to say something.

Ashley considered changing the subject, but the man seemed so determined to speak.

Finally Eddie swallowed a few times and found his voice. "August 10 . . . 1949. Bus crashed and caught fire. I was there and . . ." His nose began to run again, and he fumbled for his napkin. "I had one foot inside the bus . . . one foot." He squeezed his eyes shut and sobbed a few more times. When he opened his eyes, it was as if he were seeing the fire happening before his eyes once more. "I heard the girl . . . crying, screaming for help. I couldn't reach her . . . couldn't get through the flames."

Landon helped Eddie use the napkin on his wet face. "Sixteen people died."

"Sixteen." Eddie squeezed his eyes shut and shook his head, clearly devastated. "I can . . . I can still hear her screaming."

Again Ashley was amazed. The man didn't know where he lived, but he could recount with vivid detail the events and dates of fires that had happened half a century ago. In her experience, this was always true. Whatever had made up the days of a person's life stayed with them in their final season. She was grateful for Landon's interest in the man, touched by the way he took time to listen and validate the old guy's heroics, his worth. Because that was all Eddie lived for now.

The stories and the belt buckle.

And of course, when people were passionate about their work — the way firefighters were — they were bound to spend their days reliving each call. Fighting fires wasn't a job so much as it was a calling, and Ashley could picture Landon like this far, far down the road when he was ninety-five — recounting the apartment fire where he'd saved the life of a little boy but nearly died in the process or the clean-up efforts at Ground Zero, where he'd spent three months looking for the body of his buddy Jalen.

Ashley could only pray that when that day came, she'd be sitting beside Landon, holding his hand. That when Cole and Devin were grown with families of their own and time had stolen enough from her that she needed a place like Knollwood or Sunset Hills, Landon would be with her. And at Christmastime, when carolers came with little children, she and Landon would watch through teary eyes as they sang "Silent Night," and Landon might share his fire stories with a young gun the way Eddie had.

If so, Ashley was sure of one thing. She

would be hanging on every word. Because these were the years they would remember.

As the group left Knollwood for a series of caroling and cookie stops at the homes of their various friends, she thanked God that when it mattered most, she and Landon were passionate about things that would stay with them forever.

Their faith, their family . . . and for Landon, the fires.

CHAPTER
TWENTY

All his life Dayne had dreamed of a Christmas like this one. He had worked on films with a Christmas theme and pretended to be part of a family with a wife and children and a Christmas tree. But he'd never experienced it firsthand. Never had a Christmas tree except the artificial one he put up each year in the living room of his Malibu beach home, never gone caroling, and never attended a Christmas Eve service. He certainly never imagined sharing Christmas dinner with the family he'd seen walking across the hospital parking lot that long-ago summer day, back when even finding these people seemed impossible.

He and Katy walked into the Bloomington Community Church Christmas Eve service, part of a group of almost twenty members of his family, and Dayne was completely captured. First the caroling last night and now this. Pew after pew of families entered the church — all together to celebrate the birth of Christ.

The way it should be celebrated.

Dayne kept his head low as they walked in. He'd been to church with Katy every Sunday since the one after Thanksgiving, and they always found a quiet spot near the back. He'd gotten a few double takes from people, but no one had stopped him or talked to him about his celebrity. He'd had no requests for autographs.

"I could get used to this," he whispered to Katy. "I feel almost normal."

Katy grinned at him. "I wouldn't go that far."

Dayne had his arm around her, and as they filed into a pew near the middle of the building, he could feel his heart practically bursting inside him — to be surrounded by his sisters and brother and their families, by a father who had loved him all his life without his ever knowing it.

As they sat down, as the soft refrains of "O Little Town of Bethlehem" played and the candles across the front of the church flickered in reverent wonder, Dayne remembered one Christmas in particular. He had been fourteen years old, too old to take part in the annual Christmas pageant at the Indonesian missionary boarding school and too young to attend the teenage Christmas party on the first floor of the west dorm wing. Neither his parents nor Bob Asher's parents made it home that Christmas weekend.

He and Bob were the same age, and that year — feeling like they didn't fit in anywhere — they'd found a couple of old chairs outside the cafeteria and spent Christmas Eve looking at the starry sky and dreaming about what Christmas might be like.

"I picture lots of red and green," Bob had said. "With a candlelit Christmas Eve service, the kind in the movies."

"Yeah." Dayne had watched a shooting star. "I picture family. Mom, Dad, and a bunch of kids around a Christmas tree. There're presents and music and homemade cookies, but none of that matters as much as the people." He turned to Bob. "Know what I mean?"

"A whole family. Sisters and brothers and aunts and stuff."

Dayne had smiled. "It'll never happen. But it's the Christmas I like to imagine."

The memory faded, and Dayne wove his fingers between Katy's. "I dreamed about this once."

Katy slid a little closer to him. "Recently?"

"When I was fourteen." How could he

ever have known back then that one day the dream would come true? Back when he had no connection with any family other than the two parents who only sometimes made it back from the jungle at Christmastime?

Being here made Dayne wonder how he'd ever go back to Hollywood.

Beside him, Katy whispered, "Isn't it beautiful?"

He studied her, and he saw the blonde small-town children's theater director standing in the middle of a group of kids, the concern on her face as she walked with him around Lake Monroe and warned him about Kabbalah, and the tenderness in her eyes the first time they kissed. He could see her in the occasional flash of lightning, with the electricity out at the Flanigans' house, and lying beneath a dusty old Christmas tree prop on the stage at the Bloomington theater, minutes before he proposed. And here, in the glow of soft candles and Christmas wreaths surrounded by the Baxter family.

"Yes." He smiled at her. "It's the most beautiful thing I've ever seen."

At the crack of dawn, the Flanigan boys scampered up the stairs to Katy's apartment and knocked on the door. "Wake up, Katy!

Merry Christmas!"

She'd lived with them long enough to know the routine. Without so much as a look in the mirror, she found her bathrobe and slippers and met the boys in the stairwell. "Let's go! Where're Bailey and Connor?"

Ricky looked disgusted. "We woke 'em up, but they said, 'Five more minutes! Go get Katy first!' " He glanced at his brothers. "On Christmas morning? Who wants sleep?"

The five of them hurried downstairs, through the family room, and up another set of stairs to Bailey's room. "Merry Christmas! Time to get up!"

Katy smiled at the older kids' reaction. All six of them had slept in sleeping bags on the floor of Bailey's room on Christmas Eve. Last night, in keeping with the other part of the tradition, they'd stayed up talking and listening to music until the early morning hours.

Now it was barely seven o'clock; no wonder Bailey and Connor were having trouble waking up. Even so, they sat up and stretched.

"Merry Christmas!" Bailey grinned at them through bleary eyes.

"I keep waiting for you to turn off lights

at midnight on Christmas Eve." Katy sat on the edge of Bailey's bed. "Silly heads, staying up all night and getting a couple hours of sleep."

Connor was up now, and in a few minutes he was as hyper and animated as his brothers.

When Bailey was on her feet, she motioned for the others to follow. "Time for the story. Come on."

Katy loved this part most of all. The fact that these six children — knowing they had presents waiting for them downstairs — would enjoy the idea of heading to their parents' room first. Because that's where Jim would read them the Christmas story from the Bible. Jim and Jenny stayed up late every Christmas Eve assembling an air hockey table or bicycle or some other toy and wrapping presents. As per tradition, they slept in sweatpants and T-shirts so they'd be ready whenever the kids woke up in the morning.

The kids picked up speed as they traipsed down the hallway, and they barreled into the room with a chorus of "Merry Christmas!" and "Wake up!"

Katy watched as the kids sprang up and landed on every available spot on their parents' king-size bed. Ricky nestled in between Jim and Jenny, and the other kids sat on the edge of the mattress or in the middle on their knees.

Jim wasn't completely awake, but he waved his hand at the crowd of kids. "A herd of elephants! We're being attacked by a herd of elephants!"

"Save me!" Jenny opened one eye, then pulled the covers over her head.

Ricky snatched the sheets and touched his nose to his mother's. "Merry Christmas, Mom!"

"Yeah." Justin tickled her toes. "Time to get up!"

A sharp squeal came from Jenny, and she kicked her feet free of further attack. She sat up and squinted at her kids. "Isn't it still the middle of the night?"

"Nope!" BJ leaned his head back and raised both fists in the air. "It's Christmas morning! The best day of all."

Jim sat up next. "I thought for sure you were a herd of elephants." He reached for Shawn, sitting closest to him, and rubbed his knuckles against the top of his head, while the boy laughed, delighted. "I was ready to take you on!"

"I'd just take you on back." Shawn wrapped his arms around Jim's waist and tried to push him back to the bed.

"No wrestling." Bailey gave her dad and brother a warning look. "Christmas morning shouldn't have wrestling."

"Until after the presents are opened!" Ricky giggled. "Right, Dad?"

Jim winked at his youngest boy. "Postpresent wrestling is definitely allowed." He sat up again and pretended to dust himself off. "Okay, who has the Bible?"

Bailey found it on the nightstand and handed it to Jim.

"Katy, come join us." Jim nodded to the padded bench at the end of the bed. "We have to all be together for the story."

Suddenly Justin gasped. "Cody! We forgot about Cody!"

An avalanche of children tumbled from the bed and landed on their feet, racing down the stairs toward Cody's room. Katy stayed with Jenny and Jim, laughing as they heard the pounding feet headed for Cody's bedroom door, directly beneath Jim and Jenny's room.

"Merry Christmas!" the kids shouted. The sound was so loud that Katy wished she would've made the trip downstairs just to see Cody's reaction. In seconds, they heard the kids marching up the stairs, and as they entered the room again, BJ was dragging a half-awake Cody.

"Ugh . . . is it really morning?"

"Come on, Coleman!" Jim laughed. "We let you sleep in."

Cody sat in the chair near the fireplace, and when the chatter and excitement died down, Jim opened the Bible and turned until he found what he was looking for. "Every year we do this," he told the kids. His eyes shone. "And every year we always will." He looked at the open Bible page. "I'm reading from chapter 2 of the book of Luke." He took a breath. " 'In those days Caesar Augustus issued a decree that a census should be taken of the entire Roman world. . . .' "

Katy watched the faces of the Flanigan kids. Even Cody Coleman's. Despite a few yawns, their eyes were bright and alert, engaged in the story. And it was an amazing story, really. A young pregnant girl with visions of angels in her head and her frightened, confused betrothed heading by donkey on an arduous journey to register for the census.

Had the people at the inn known that the King of kings was about to be born? that though they turned away the young pregnant girl, the child she bore would turn away no one?

" 'Today in the town of David,' " Jim was

saying, " 'a Savior has been born to you; he is Christ the Lord. . . .' "

Katy couldn't help but silently thank God for the scene playing out before her. Would that every family across the nation might pause on Christmas morning and first remember the reason for the celebration. She wished Dayne could be here, but she would tell him about the Flanigans' tradition later. He was having breakfast with John this morning, and then he would join her.

Jim was finishing the story. " 'But Mary treasured up all these things and pondered them in her heart.' " He closed the Bible and met the eyes of each of his kids. "What are you pondering in your heart this Christmas morning?"

Katy smiled. She loved this part, too. Every year since she'd lived with the Flanigans, Jim ended the story with that verse and then turned the question to the kids. Sometimes their answers were sweet and poignant. Other times they said things that the family would laugh about for days to come.

"I'm pondering how come Mary wore a long dress if she was riding a donkey all that way." Justin made a face. "I mean, a long dress? Wouldn't pants and a sweater've been more practical?"

"That's what they wore back then. Men and women wore garments with sashes at the waist." Jenny had her arms around Ricky and BJ. "But that's a good ponder."

"I'm pondering if baby Jesus got splinters laying in a wooden box." BJ flashed an anxious look. "That would hurt a baby a lot."

Jim's eyes grew more tender than before. "Jesus was a man who understood the pain of wooden splinters in His back. Both as a baby and later on . . . at the cross."

They all thought about that for a few seconds. Then Shawn pondered whether the animals would've known that the baby was actually God, the Creator who made them, and Ricky wondered why people gave presents to each other when it was Jesus' birthday.

"Jesus set the example." Jenny rubbed her son's shoulder. "He gave us the greatest gift of all when He came to earth as a baby. Now we give gifts so we can remember what sort of God we serve."

Bailey seemed distracted when she gave her answer. "I'm pondering what that star must've looked like over Bethlehem." She gave them a dreamy look. "And whether it was anything like the stars over Blooming-ton."

"Um . . . something bigger, I'm guessing." Jim made a face at her, and everyone laughed.

Katy studied Bailey a minute longer, even after the attention was off her. The comment probably had something to do with her fascination over Bryan Smythe. The guy was always talking to her about how the stars didn't compare to her eyes. That kind of thing. If he turned out to be genuine, then fine. Bailey was certainly entitled to be starry-eyed this Christmas morning. But Katy had doubts. She would talk to Bailey later for a report.

When the kids had each taken a turn, when Jim had finished teasing Bailey about the size of the Bethlehem star, an expectant silence hung over the room.

Jim raised his brows, his eyes dancing. "Are we ready to go downstairs?"

A round of cheers and hoots came from the kids, and everyone jumped off the bed and headed for the door.

"Wait!" Jim's voice boomed the way it did on the football field. When the kids stopped and faced him, he smiled and pointed at Jenny. "Your mother needs to go first. She's the picture taker."

The kids bounced in place while Jenny took her camera bag from the dresser and hurried down the stairs. After a minute she yelled up, "Okay, I'm ready!"

And then the kids broke free and raced down the stairs. Gone were the wide-eyed angel faces and the earnest comments on pondering the birth of Jesus. Now they were a whole lot more like what Jim originally thought they were.

A thundering herd of elephants.

Ashley didn't really believe it was possible, but she had to find out. She was three weeks late, and if she didn't take the test, she'd spend every minute wondering. Last night after the Christmas Eve service they'd stopped at the only market open in town for milk and eggs. With Landon waiting in the car with the boys, Ashley also bought a test.

The directions were still familiar, since it wasn't so long ago that she'd taken the last one. First thing in the morning, the test would be more accurate. Now, with the boys and Landon still asleep, Ashley crept out of bed, found the test package beneath her bathroom sink where she'd hidden it, and followed the simple steps.

Five minutes later she was staring through

teary eyes at a small white stick with two pink lines. She was pregnant! Devin was eight months old now, and she and Landon had talked about having more kids. But they'd never come to any real decision, never taken steps to plan their next baby.

So God had planned it for them.

Her hand trembled, and there, on the cold bathroom floor, she lowered herself to her knees. She didn't deserve any of what God had given her. Nine years ago she had walked into an abortion clinic in France intent on destroying life. But God had grabbed her and changed her mind at the last possible moment. She was grateful every time she looked into Cole's blue eyes.

The tiles pressed against her knees, but she didn't mind. She sat back on her heels and covered her face with her fingers. The pregnancy test was still in her hand. *Lord, another child . . . I can't believe it. New life forming inside me even now, this Christmas morning. Thank You isn't enough.* She thought about Cole and Devin, about the bond they were forming. She blinked and hot tears hit her cheeks. *Let this baby bring another shade of sunshine to our home. Thank You, God. . . . Thank You.* She wanted to add, *And please let it be a girl.* But she didn't dare.

Any child would be a delight, a miracle. Especially when she considered the distance she'd come from standing at the doorway of the abortion clinic to kneeling here in the bathroom of a home she shared with Landon, Cole, and Devin. As she finished her prayer and eased herself to her feet, the pieces of the past few weeks fell into place. No wonder she'd been tired and sick to her stomach.

An idea hit her then. She tiptoed back through her bedroom, past Landon — still sleeping — and out to a closet in the hallway. She opened it and pulled out a few pieces of tissue and a roll of wrapping paper. In a hurry, she wrapped the stick and found a red and green bow for the top. On the tag she wrote the simplest message.

To Daddy . . .

Dayne arrived just as the Flanigan kids had finished opening their presents. When the doorbell rang, Katy was in the corner buried under a blanket and surrounded by wrapping paper.

Bailey sprang to her feet. "I'll get it." She ran into the entryway, and Katy could hear her sigh as she opened the front door. "Okay. So do you know how many girls would like to open the door on Christmas

358

morning and find Dayne Matthews standing on the front porch?"

Katy quietly laughed to herself. Bailey was right, of course. Being in Bloomington this past month had almost made Katy forget that the man she loved was admired by women all over the world. Even so, Katy could hear the teasing in Bailey's voice.

The fireplace separated the entryway from the living room, so it was only a few steps until they came into view. Dayne grinned at Katy, and then he seemed to take in the magic of the room — the twelve-foot Christmas tree in the corner and the wall of windows that went all the way to the vaulted ceiling. Snow lay on the ground outside, and the house smelled like monkey bread — a secret cinnamon roll recipe Jenny always made at Christmastime. The kids waved hello to Dayne and then continued giggling and marveling over the presents they'd opened.

Katy waited until Dayne looked at her again. She could feel her eyes dancing as she lifted her hands. "You haven't seen Christmas until you've seen it here."

Dayne laughed. "I guess not." He found a chair across the room near the fireplace, and for the rest of the morning they shared in the Flanigans' Christmas.

Katy wasn't sure which she enjoyed more. The time together with everyone as they moved into the kitchen for coffee and eggs and monkey bread, watching the way Dayne saved a seat beside him for Ricky, or how the other boys gathered around Dayne to show off their new remote-control race cars.

She'd seen him on the set in Hollywood and here in Bloomington when he was on location — the Dayne Matthews the world knew. But here with the Flanigans on a cozy Christmas morning, he looked and acted as if he'd found his way home, as if life without the craziness and rushed pace, without the paparazzi and people pulling at him, was all he'd ever really wanted. And no wonder. He could breathe, be himself here.

"I'm loving this," he whispered as she walked past him to her seat next to the boys.

Katy smiled at him, and their eyes held longer than usual. "Merry Christmas."

Dayne looked like he wanted to kiss her, but the look was enough. "I thought Christmases like this were only in the movies." He was flirting with her, enjoying the brief moment. "I lived in Hollywood all my adult life, and I never had anything like this."

"That's because —" she touched his arm — "the good stuff Hollywood writes about *really* happens in places like Bloomington."

After breakfast, when the excitement died down, everyone gathered in the family room to watch *It's a Wonderful Life.* When they reached the part of the movie where the entire town comes together to convince Jimmy Stewart that his life had mattered to countless people, Dayne leaned close to Katy. "That's you . . . with all the CKT kids."

His comment touched her and reminded her that the students in CKT did indeed count on her. Already Bailey had told her that a few of the older kids had talked. They were worried that Katy might not stay at the lake house after she married Dayne and that she'd move to Los Angeles and get involved in making movies and forget about CKT altogether.

Katy couldn't see that happening. Not when her passion lay here. But after the meeting at the coffeehouse the other day, she had to admit that they might be facing the end of CKT. And if Katy went to Hollywood every few months while Dayne filmed or if — by some remote possibility — she even did some acting, then someone else would have to replace her at CKT. If God allowed a developer to buy the theater, the group wouldn't have a place to perform.

She couldn't think about that now — not

when everything about the day was going so well. She snuggled closer to Dayne.

When the movie was over, Katy and Dayne went to the Baxters' for dinner. Everyone was seated at two tables except Erin and her family since Sam had just two days off. The atmosphere was warm and full of laughter and conversation — much as it had been Thanksgiving weekend. Dayne's dad made hot cider in a huge pot, and the smell of fresh cinnamon filled the house.

Katy noticed Ashley and Landon whispering to each other during dinner. She and Dayne were sitting across from them, and she wondered what Ashley was up to. Her friend was so spontaneous, so full of life. Maybe she was going to present a painting to her dad — something she'd talked about working on a few months ago.

Katy studied the faces around the table, the people who would very soon be part of her family. She couldn't imagine sharing holidays and birthdays and the seasons of life with anyone other than Dayne, the Baxters, and the Flanigans, who would always be like family.

Her gaze settled on Kari and Ryan. Ryan was helping little RJ with his potatoes, and Kari was talking to Elaine. Kari still didn't look right — a little too pale and not as lively as usual. She'd had the flu the same time as Ashley, so maybe that was it.

Katy leaned closer to Dayne. She could live a hundred years and never get used to the feeling of him by her side, the warmth of his muscled arm or the sound of his voice. She gave him a quick smile, and he did the same. He was talking to Luke and Reagan, who were at their table too.

Luke raised an eyebrow at Dayne. "I received an interesting e-mail from your agent the other day."

"Yes." Dayne laughed. "About Katy?"

Luke grinned. "I wasn't sure I was supposed to say anything. He sounded pretty sure about it."

Katy set her fork down. "What about me?"

Next to her, Dayne put his arm around the back of her chair. "My agent's figuring out the paperwork. If you get the part, he'd like to be your agent too." He winked at Luke. "Which means Luke'll have two clients instead of one."

Swirling emotions filled Katy's soul. Dayne was more serious than she'd thought. She was still thinking about the coming months — the play run of *Oliver!* with CKT, the wedding and honeymoon, and then the movie — when Ashley and Landon moved to the front of the room. Landon had been upbeat and animated all evening, but now he looked ready to burst. Whatever they were about to say, Katy had the feeling it was something big.

Landon put his arm around Ashley. "We have some news." He smiled at Ashley, and it was as if there were no one else in the room.

At the other table, Kari uttered a soft gasp, and she and Ryan shared a curious look.

Landon turned his attention back to the others. His eyes glistened, and his pride was undeniable. "Ashley and I are going to have another baby. . . . I found out this morning."

"The baby should be born in August." Ashley's eyes were damp. "We thought this was a good time to tell you."

The family laughed, and a round of congratulations came from both tables.

Dayne glanced at Katy, and in his eyes was a reflection of everything she was feeling. That it would be amazing to stand among this family one day and share news that they were going to have a child. The idea was enough to take her breath. But before she could say anything, before anyone had the chance to even move beyond the applause, Kari and Ryan rose slowly from their seats.

A second silence settled over the room.

"We were going to wait until after dessert." Ryan chuckled.

Next to him, Kari brought her hand to her mouth and stifled a burst of giggles. "I can't believe this."

"Wait a minute. . . ." Luke's voice held a level of astonishment that reflected how they were probably all feeling. He looked from Kari to Ashley, then back at Kari. "Don't tell me two of my sisters are pregnant at the same time!"

"I found out a few days ago." Kari shrugged and put her arm around Ryan's waist. "We're due in August also!"

The announcement brought squeals from Brooke, Reagan, and Ashley and cheers from everyone else as it moved people out of their chairs.

Ashley made her way between the tables to Kari, and the two hugged. "I can't believe it!"

The others circled around them, patting their backs and hugging Ryan and Landon.

"Next year we'll have two babies for Christmas." John's voice sounded above the others. "Thank You, God!"

"I'm having a sister!" Jessie announced. She ran around in circles in the adjacent family room. "A sister . . . a sister . . . a sister!"

Cole ran in after her. "I'm having another brother." He pumped his fists in the air. "And brothers are better!"

They went a few more rounds before Landon stepped in and asked them to cool it. "No one knows yet. You can celebrate in a few months."

"God knows." Maddie stepped up to Landon and smiled. "Right, Uncle Landon?"

Landon grinned. "Okay, yes. God knows."

Katy took her turn hugging Ashley and then Kari, congratulating them and repeating how happy she was for them. But as the reaction died down, as people made their way back to their seats for coffee and apple pie, she couldn't help but feel a little envious. How long would it be before the announcement would be theirs?

She was slightly pensive even as Dayne drove her back to the Flanigans' later that night. On the way they laughed about Jessie dropping an entire apple pie and offering to pick out the broken glass so people could still scoop some off the floor and eat it. But the double announcement was still in her thoughts.

"You're thinking about something." Dayne

glanced at her as he pulled his 4Runner into the driveway. He reached for her hand. "What's on your mind?"

"Mmmm." Katy turned so she could see him better. "I was thinking about the babies." She smiled and let herself get lost in Dayne's eyes. "How wonderful for Ashley and Kari, being pregnant at the same time, having babies together. Going through all the stages side by side."

"I thought you were feeling that." Dayne placed his hands gently on either side of her face. "Wondering how long before it's our turn."

"We have a lot to get through first." She whispered the words.

"But our day will come." He kissed her, slow and tender. "God's brought us this far. He'll make it clear when it's time to be parents."

His nearness was making her feel dreamier about the here and now and less concerned with the future. She kissed him, a kiss that didn't last long but one that made her heart beat faster. The talk about babies reminded her of the intimate moments, the passion that lay ahead for them. She breathed close to his ear, "I can't wait. . . . Know what I mean?"

A soft groan came from his throat. He

367

held her a little tighter than before and kissed her again. When he drew back, he searched her eyes, looked to the depths of her soul. "How can you ask? Every night I wish I could take you home with me." He moved so there'd be space between them and leaned against the SUV door. The sigh that crossed his lips said that the struggle to honor her purity was one he wrestled with daily. He smiled and seemed to find a level of composure. "Which . . . is why we should talk about the wedding."

Katy pinched her lips together and exhaled slowly. "Definitely." She was grateful for Dayne's commitment to honor her. Grateful beyond words. And at a time like this, he was right. Changing the subject was a better idea.

"What's the latest from Wilma?" Katy leaned back too. As she did, she noticed that it was snowing. Not the usual hard, fast snow that could cover a front lawn in half an hour. But a slow-motion sort of snow with enormous flakes, floating and swirling in the glow of the Flanigans' house light. "We've got the flowers figured out — white roses and baby's breath — and the colors."

"Cornflower and . . . coral." Dayne angled his head, teasing her. "I think I have it now." He said he liked the fresh and tropical colors, and he agreed they'd look great set against the white flowers. But until recently he kept calling them blue and orange. "Anyway, yes. Wilma called and told me that we're on schedule. The things we're asking for are available at the resort."

Katy watched the snow for a minute. It was getting cold in the SUV, and she needed to get inside. They talked a few more minutes about the shopping she was going to do that week for bridesmaid dresses. Katy hadn't found a wedding dress yet, but she was committed to finding one sometime soon.

Finally, Dayne walked her up to the door and wrapped his arms around her. "Thanks."

"For what?" She snuggled close to him, wishing she didn't have to go inside.

"The greatest Christmas ever." His expression showed the depth of his sincerity. "I'll never forget a minute of it."

She pressed the side of her face against his. "It's only going to get better."

And it was true. Long after Dayne had driven away, Katy thought about the years ahead. They had so much to do before they could consider having a baby. The wedding and the rest of his movie contract. If she started a stint of acting alongside Dayne, then pregnancy could still be a long time away. But it would come. And one day — with the people they loved gathered around them — the announcement wouldn't belong to Ashley or Kari or any of the others.

For now she would focus her thoughts on the joy she felt for Ashley and Kari and their incredible news about the babies who would be more than additions to the Baxter family.

They would be her nieces and nephews.

CHAPTER
TWENTY-ONE

Jenny was worried about her daughter.

Their annual New Year's Eve party was in full swing, and Bailey was somewhere in the house, visiting with the handful of friends who were willing to celebrate the new year without a keg of beer. Bryan Smythe was one of the teens who'd come over, his attention on Bailey.

But Jenny had heard things about the boy that troubled her. Brandon Reeves, one of the guys on the football team who didn't drink at the Thanksgiving party, had stopped by last week and commented that he'd known Bryan for years. They'd played tennis in the same circles and attended the same middle school.

"I was sort of shocked when I heard him and Bailey were hanging out," Brandon had told Jenny. "He's changed a lot lately. Everyone knows it."

Jenny had asked how Brandon could tell.

"Easy. He's hitting on half a dozen girls. Bailey's just one of them. Some of the girls aren't . . . well . . . they aren't the best girls. If you know what I mean."

The news didn't set well with Jenny. If Brandon was right, Bryan was capable of great manipulation. For a kid with a silver tongue, that could be a problem.

Brandon's words replayed in Jenny's mind tonight, and she made a point of walking around the house more than usual, working her way past the circles of neighbors and friends to the living room, where a dozen teens were gathered around the piano. Connor was playing music from *The Phantom of the Opera,* and two girls were standing near the piano singing.

Bryan was next to Bailey on the couch, his arm around her shoulders. That wouldn't have bothered Jenny except for the look on Bailey's face. She was smiling, but she looked tense — too tense for someone enjoying a party with a guy she liked.

"Hey, Mrs. Flanigan . . . those meatballs were the best." Bryan grinned at her. "I'm always telling my mom if she could only learn to cook like you!"

Jenny smiled but not on the inside. "Thanks. But I'll bet your mom's pretty good too."

"Well, either way." He talked louder than anyone in the room. As if he wanted people to hear what he had to say. "As long as you're cooking, I'll be here, Mrs. Flanigan. You're amazing."

She gave him a pleasant nod and noticed Tim Reed sitting on the opposite side of the room. He'd been quiet all night, and Jenny had the feeling he was upset about Bryan, about the way he stayed by Bailey's side and didn't seem to let her visit with her other guy friends.

"Tim, come here for a minute." Jenny motioned to him.

He hopped up and followed her into the dining room.

She found a bowl of noisemakers and handed them to him. "Can you pass these out when it's closer to midnight?"

"Sure thing." Tim was about to turn back to the living room, but then he stopped and lowered his voice. "Hey, what's with Bryan Smythe?"

Jenny peered into the room, but from where they were standing, Bailey and Bryan weren't visible. "I'm not sure. He's been coming around a lot. Calling, texting. I think he likes her."

"Looks mutual to me." A depth showed in his eyes, one that he rarely exposed. "I

373

thought Bailey was smarter than that."

Jenny's heart skipped a beat. "Why?"

"Haven't you seen his MySpace?" Tim laughed, but the sound wasn't the least bit funny. "Under occupation, he's got *player.* And he isn't talking about tennis. He also admits to smoking weed."

A sense of alarm filled Jenny's heart and throat. She was about to thank Tim, about to head back into the living room and ask Bailey to step outside for a talk. Never mind that it was twenty degrees outside. Bailey needed to know what Tim had seen on MySpace. But before she could make a move, Cody entered the dining room from the other side.

"Can I talk to you?" He noticed Tim and took half a step back. "I mean, if you have a minute."

"I do." Jenny turned to Tim. "Talk to her, okay? And pray for her."

"I will." Tim held her eyes a beat longer. "I pray for her all the time anyway."

Jenny hesitated, and a smile lifted the corners of her mouth. "I didn't know that. Thanks."

"Anytime."

Tim left and Jenny went to Cody. He'd been doing great since he'd been out of the hospital and started the alcohol classes. And

374

at least as impressive was the fact that the entire football team seemed changed by Jim's talk with them that night in the locker room. Most of them were supposed to stop by the party sometime tonight.

Cody leaned against the doorframe. Only then was the worry in his eyes obvious. "I found out something. I wanted to talk to you first, then Coach."

Jenny resisted the urge to sigh. She loved helping Cody, but she was beginning to sense that she was neglecting her own kids.

Bailey, for one. So much was happening in her life, and prior to Cody's struggles, Bailey had shared with Jenny every conversation and nuance within each of her friendships. Now they could go days without so much as a heart-to-heart.

When Jenny asked her about it, she would only brush off the possibility. "I'm fine," she'd said yesterday when Jenny brought up her concerns. "I know Cody needs you. Besides, auditions are at the end of this week. I'm working on my song and talking with friends."

Jenny wasn't so sure that was a good thing.

She studied Cody for a few more seconds. "Let's go to the office." She led, and once they were inside, she flipped on the lights

375

and shut the double doors. "What's going on?"

He looked down at his shoes and fidgeted with a paper clip sitting on the edge of the desk. "I can't believe I'm doing this."

She folded her arms. "Tell me, Cody."

"It's the team." He ran his hand over his forehead and into his hair. His angst was painful to watch. "Bunch of guys are drinking tonight. Coach said if anyone drank, he wanted to know."

Someone might as well have poured wet cement on her shoulders. *Please, God . . . not this again. Please . . .* "Are you sure?"

"Yep. If I tell him, he'll go there. I know he will."

This wasn't how the night was supposed to play out. Anxiety added to the feelings of frustration and futility. If Jim broke up a player party, he'd have to kick kids off the squad. And if he did that, he'd be in hot water with half the parents and a few members of the administration. Jenny swallowed hard. "If he asked you to tell him, then tell him. God will take care of the details."

Cody nodded. "The guys'll hate me for sure."

"At first." Jenny touched his arm and

376

found a sad smile. "Either way it's the right thing."

Together they found Jim, and Jenny watched the anger and disappointment fill his expression.

"I need directions to his house." Jim grabbed a piece of paper and a pen. Once Cody had supplied the information, Jim stood and hugged the kid. "We'll all get through this. I just don't want to be talking about it at a funeral home."

"I keep thinking how I felt before I passed out. You know, Thanksgiving night." Cody looked paler than before, still terrified at the memory. "When I thought I was gonna die." He shrugged. "I care about those guys; that's all."

When Cody was gone, Jim turned to Jenny. "I have to do this."

"I'll pray." Jenny bit her lip. She wanted to ask him to be careful, remind him that whatever he said or did, even if he only accused a player, the kid could tell his parents, and the parents could have him fired. It happened all the time to coaches trying to raise the bar for their athletes.

But Jim already knew the possibilities.

Now it was a matter of trusting God for the outcome.

■ ■ ■ ■

Jim's heart pounded against his chest as he made the short drive to the party. He had with him his cell phone and a file with the names and phone numbers of every guy on his team.

The whole way there he questioned himself. Wasn't the video enough? Had he missed something along the way? some signal or sign about how to reach these kids? Or maybe the only way they'd stop drinking was if they felt the pain themselves. He exhaled and forced himself to relax. *God, be with me. Give me wisdom here so the guys understand why I'm doing this.*

My son, in this world you will have trouble. But take heart! I have overcome the world.

The whispered voice permeated his heart and mind and soul. It was a verse from John chapter 16, a Scripture he'd read a thousand times before, starting with the high school days after Trent died. Jim had read it again after Cody's alcohol poisoning. Now he was grateful for the reminder, one that felt as if God had spoken it here and now to give him the strength to carry out what he was about to do.

Jim pulled onto the street and had no

378

trouble spotting the right house. Dozens of cars were parked in front and in the driveway, even on the front lawn. Already he could hear the pulsating bass of music being played inside. One couple was making out against a tree near the curb.

He had a choice to make now. He could call the police and wait until they arrived. Then as the kids piled out, he could write down the names of his players and kick them off the team when Christmas break was over. But then he wouldn't know which kids were actually drinking. And the administration would insist on that detail.

Jim sucked in a full breath, and before he stepped out, he grabbed his phone, the folder, and a pen and checked the time — 10:45. The players who had chosen to break his contract would probably be partying hard by now. Jim walked past the kissing couple — neither of whom seemed to notice him. The scene reminded him of that long-ago night at the park and of the way kids who drank lost all sense of reality or their surroundings.

He strode up the walkway to the front door and knocked, but after a few moments it was clear that no one inside the party could possibly have heard him. The music pulsed and shook the house, and he could hear people yelling and laughing inside. He tried again, but after a minute he figured he had nothing to lose. He opened the front door and stepped inside.

The room was full of kids swaying to the music and couples kissing, oblivious to everything around them.

Jim gritted his teeth and stayed by the door. Beer bottles littered the room, and in the kitchen kids were lining up to get beer from a keg. There were also bottles of what looked like gin and vodka open on the table.

He spotted Jack Spencer in a chair at the corner of the room. Jim's punt returner had one hand wrapped around a beer and the other arm around a blonde girl, giggling on his lap.

Jim hadn't been sure how he was going to handle this. Now it seemed obvious. He opened his folder, and on the blank sheet of paper he'd stuck inside he wrote: *Jack Spencer — drinking a bottle of beer.* Then he found Jack's parents' numbers. He called their home first, and on the second ring, kids started to notice him.

"Coach!" The shout came from a big kid dancing with a girl half his size. He'd played football his first year but dropped out. The dizzy look in his eyes told Jim he was probably working on his fourth or fifth beer. At least.

The call went to Jack's parents' answering service. Kids were stopping, turning his way, but Jim didn't care. Acting more calm than he felt, he hit the End button on the phone and dialed Jack's father's cell phone number.

By the time a man answered, Jack was on his feet. He tried to set the beer down on the fireplace mantel a few feet from him, but he missed. The bottle crashed to the floor and shattered, spraying beer and glass on the hearth below.

"Hello, this is Coach Flanigan, Jack's football coach."

"Yes." The man sounded irritated and confused. "I know who you are."

For a few seconds Jack looked helplessly at the mess he'd made; then he straightened and stared at Jim. His eyes were near circles, and around the room other kids were slowly figuring it out. Coach Flanigan was here at their party!

Jim searched the group, looking for other players. So far he saw none. At the same time he pressed his phone closer to his ear. "I'm afraid I have bad news." He explained where he was. "Jack's here and he's drinking, Mr. Spencer. You need to come pick

381

him up."

The man sounded as if he might argue, but he caught himself. "We'll be right there."

With each passing second, the significance of Coach Flanigan standing near the front door was impacting everyone in the front room and kitchen. Someone turned off the music, and everywhere Jim looked kids stood frozen, staring at him. Most of them with drinks in their hands. Suddenly it hit him. This was going to take longer than he thought. He couldn't let even one of these kids drive home drunk — player or not.

"No one's leaving without a parent." Jim's voice boomed through the front room and filled the house. He was no longer anxious or uncertain. This was exactly where he needed to be, and whatever the ramifications because of his presence, they would be well deserved. He put his hands on his hips and stood taller so everyone in the room could see him. "One kid leaves and I call the police."

The students stood stock-still. A few of them cussed under their breath, and he heard what sounded like a back door opening. If someone was trying to slip out, he wanted to know.

Jim hurried through the crowd, grateful

382

that no other players seemed to be at the party. But as he rounded the corner, he caught a glimpse of the one player he had hoped wouldn't be here. The kid who'd hung out at his house off and on since he was in grade school, the one Bailey had laughed with and grown up with and cared so much for. His tall frame was lunging toward the open door, and he had a beer in his hand.

"Tanner." Jim didn't grab the kid, didn't chase after him.

And Tanner Williams, his quarterback, didn't run. He stepped slowly back into the house and set the beer down on the nearest kitchen counter. He looked down for a moment, clearly embarrassed, devastated, though it was tough to tell whether his reaction was because he'd been caught or because he was truly sorry. Finally he looked up. "Coach . . ."

Jim held his gaze for several heartbeats. "I can't tell you how disappointed I am, Tanner."

Tanner said nothing, not that he was sorry or that it was a mistake. Nothing at all. There, in that instant, as Jim dialed Tanner's parents, he knew several things. First, the drinking trouble on his team wasn't going to disappear because of one team meeting, the way he'd hoped. If Jack Spencer and Tanner Williams had chosen to drink tonight — even after seeing the video and signing their names to a contract — then they would be kicked off the team. Jim and Ryan had already decided that was the only recourse. Jim would take care of the details the first day back to school.

Worse maybe was something he'd seen in both his players' eyes tonight — a subtle shading of an emotion he never would've expected from his star players. Not regret or sorrow or defeat.

But pure and utter indifference.

CHAPTER
TWENTY-TWO

Sometime after eleven that night, Bryan took Bailey's hand and casually walked her through the family room and kitchen toward the front door. He'd been trying all night to get her to take a walk, but she felt funny about leaving. Or maybe she felt funny about being alone with him. This was her family's New Year's Eve party, right? She should be inside with the group. Especially since most of the football team had shown up just after her dad left.

A dozen of her friends sat around their oversize coffee table in the family room playing Apples to Apples, and four more were gathered around one of the computers checking out everyone's MySpace pages. Connor and a group of his friends were in the living room circled around the piano, and the Baxter men were holding a pool tournament with complicated rules, intense competition, and lots of loud laughter.

Bailey's mother was in the kitchen with most of the other women, making coffee and preparing trays of chocolate-chip cookies.

They passed her four younger brothers playing with Cody Coleman on a computer. Cody had improved so much in the past month. He was laughing with Shawn, pointing at something on the screen. As Bryan and Bailey passed by, Cody turned. His expression changed in as much time as it took for her to breathe in. For some reason, he didn't approve of Bryan. He'd made that clear by his comments and tone of voice. Bailey made a note to ask him about it later.

"Maybe we should stay in." Bailey stopped a few feet from the door. "It's freezing out there."

"I'll keep you warm." Bryan seemed determined. He grinned at her, and his voice sounded velvety. "Please, Bailey . . ."

She was about to think of a better reason why it made more sense to stay inside when her cell phone vibrated in her back jeans pocket. With her free hand, she pulled it out and flipped it open. It was a text message from Cody. She glanced up, but his back was to her, his attention given to the computer screen and her little brothers.

"Who's it from?"

"Cody." She met Bryan's eyes. She didn't like that he cared, but she had nothing to hide. She read the message. *The guy's a player, Bailey. Don't go outside with him.*

Bailey felt anger slice through her. How dare Cody tell her what to do when he had nearly killed himself drinking? She uttered a quiet huff as her fingers flew over the keypad in response. *Like you'd care. . . .* She added, *lol,* just so he wouldn't think she was being mean. But she was mad all the same. Sure, her parents had warned her about Cody Coleman, and she knew he wasn't the kind of guy she'd marry. But still. She'd always had a crush on him. And until now he'd never even acted like she was alive.

Well, it was too late. She erased Cody's text and slipped her phone back into her pocket.

"What'd he say?" The teasing in Bryan's voice was gone. Now he seemed frustrated, as if he was trying not to be angry.

"Nothing." She would do whatever she wanted. Bailey and her mom hadn't talked in forever because she was too busy helping Cody and praying with Cody and listening to Cody. He could go to the moon for all Bailey cared. And besides, Bryan was a much better Christian than Cody could hope to be.

Bailey smiled at Bryan and used her eyes and the angle of her head to chase away his grouchiness. "It is kinda hot in here."

Bryan's brow relaxed. A smile lifted the corners of his lips, and his eyes began to dance the way they had earlier tonight. He released her hand just long enough to grab her coat and scarf from the rack near the front door. "It's not snowing. I already checked."

"Good." She allowed him to help slip her jacket over her shoulders. It was long and thick and made of wool, but even with it on — before they opened the door — Bailey felt a chill run down her arms. *We should stay inside,* she thought. *Just because I'm mad at Cody doesn't make it okay.* Almost as an afterthought, as Bryan took her hand and they went out onto the porch, she silently directed her next thoughts to the Lord. *Don't let me get pressured into anything, okay, God?*

Bailey sort of hoped He might give her an answer, but the only sound was the whipping wind through the trees along either side of the driveway. She pulled her coat tighter around her waist. "It's colder than I thought."

Bryan put his arm around her shoulders. He stayed close to her side as they walked down the steps and onto the circle drive. "I told you I'll keep you warm. Trust me."

Doubts flickered in her mind. Six inches of snow covered the ground, but the driveway was clear. They headed down the driveway, but tonight it seemed longer than usual. Much longer. Darker too. She stopped and gave him a nervous look. "We should go back. I didn't tell my mom."

He took her hands from her coat pockets and held them, running his gloved fingers over hers. "You're scared." His voice was kind and soft again. He sounded like the most trustworthy guy in the world. He looked deep into her eyes. "How come?"

"I don't know." Bailey felt her cheeks grow hot. "I feel guilty, I guess."

"You're still at home." Bryan pulled her a few inches closer. She could smell the leather in his jacket. "It was hot in your house. Besides, out here in the moonlight I can see your eyes better, all the way to your heart."

"Really?" His words warmed and calmed her. She felt her shoulders settle an inch or so. When he brought her a little closer, she didn't fight it. She had nothing to worry about. He was right; they were still in her very own driveway. "How come you're so nice?"

"I care about you. And I've missed you."

He released her hands and pulled her into a slow hug. "More than you know."

A gust of wind came across the driveway, and he stroked her back. His arms around her didn't feel suggestive or demanding — the way she'd seen some guys hug their girlfriends. "You're making me feel warm."

"I told you." Bryan leaned back and smiled at her. Then, as if he didn't have any other plans but to talk to her, he brought up CKT and how he wanted to study film in college. They talked about the rumors going around school that he liked half a dozen girls.

"All the girls are crazy about you." Bailey nuzzled closer to him.

"And the guys are crazy about you." He looked back at the house. "Including Cody Coleman."

"No." Bailey was having fun. She didn't want to talk about Cody. "He treats me like I'm his kid sister."

A smoky look came into Bryan's eyes. "You don't look like a kid sister to me."

The roller coaster feeling swirled her insides. What was he saying? And did he mean it the way it seemed? Was that a good thing? She swallowed. No words came to mind, so she kept her eyes on his, kept letting him look all the way into her heart. She was still lost in his eyes when he brought his face closer to hers.

"Bailey, can I tell you Happy New Year —" his face was so close now that she could feel his breath on her skin — "the way I want to tell you?"

Her heart was racing, and her throat was too dry to speak. Was he going to kiss her? Out here in the freezing cold on New Year's Eve?

Before any more questions had time to flash in her head, Bryan did it. He brought his lips to hers. Bailey wasn't sure what to do or even how to kiss. She wasn't sure she was ready, but it didn't matter. He was kissing her! He was kissing her and she was kissing him back, and even though she felt dizzy enough to fall over, the touch of his lips against hers was the most amazing feeling ever.

Fear and wonder and something like love mixed in her veins. So this was kissing! Her first kiss! This crazy, out-of-breath feeling . . . the heat in her face and the pounding in her heart. But was this what she wanted? Had she even told him it was okay to kiss her now?

Bailey eased away from him, and suddenly she felt angry at him and even angrier at herself. She wasn't going out with Bryan

Smythe, so how could she have kissed him?

A strange look colored Bryan's eyes. He took her wrists, then moved in and pushed his mouth over hers. When she tried to break free, he wouldn't let her, forcing the kiss to continue.

"Bryan!" Bailey took a big step back. She gulped in a mouthful of cold air, stunned, suddenly sick to her stomach. "What are you doing?" She took a few more steps. "Why would you do that?" She couldn't draw a full breath. "You know I'm not like that!"

"Hey . . . I didn't mean anything by it." The lost-in-love look in his eyes from a moment ago was gone. Now Bryan was all confusion and innocence. He held up his hands. "I thought you liked it." He laughed, but it sounded like he was making fun of her. "I wasn't gonna make you do anything you didn't want to do."

"But you were!" She was practically shrieking at him. "I took a step back, and you walked up and kissed me without . . . without knowing if I even wanted to kiss *you*. I tried to get away, and you wouldn't . . . wouldn't let me." She shook her head and moved farther away from him. "Everyone's right about you. Those words you say aren't close to the truth."

She glared at him and whirled around. No way could she get in the house fast enough. The wind hit her sharp in the face, but the sting in her eyes wasn't from the cold air. "I can't believe this," she muttered to herself.

He ran to catch up to her. "Bailey, you're overreacting. I didn't force anything on you." He laughed, but it sounded more like he was afraid. They were walking faster now. "I'm serious. It was just sort of . . . you know, natural."

Bailey stopped. "Go home!" Her arm shook as she pointed to his car. "I mean it — go home! I never should've come out here in the first place."

"It's ten minutes to New Year's." He tried another laugh. "You can't just kick me out. I mean, come on. That's acting like a kid sister big-time."

Her anger cracked just enough to give her tears a way out. "Are you kidding me? I don't care what time it is." She backed up a few more steps. "You talk about God and faith and how important it is to you, and then you do . . . you do that?"

There was a sound behind her, and she turned around.

Cody stood in the doorway. "Bailey?"

She looked at Bryan one last time. Then without saying another word, she ran up the steps and past Cody. She didn't want to talk to anyone, not when her heart was racing like this. She flew up the stairs, down the hallway, and into her room, shutting the door behind her and letting herself fall against the wall.

What had just happened?

In a single moment she'd gone from sharing her first kiss with Bryan Smythe to feeling like he would've forced more than a kiss if he could have. And now she felt cheap and used and lied to. He could see her eyes better in the moonlight? That wasn't why he'd taken her out in the cold, not at all. But she had been stupid enough to believe him, and now what?

Her tears came harder, faster. She needed her mom, needed to fall into her arms and tell her every embarrassing detail. And she wanted her kiss back too. Her first kiss. She faced the wall and buried her face in the crook of her arm. *God, why didn't You warn me?*

Then, with a rush of regret, the answer was as plain as the paint on her wall. The Lord *had* warned her. She'd felt funny about going outside from the moment Bryan suggested it. *I'm sorry, God. . . . I'm so sorry. Forgive me for being so blind. You warned me, and I didn't listen.*

The room was quiet — no out-loud answer from God. But she'd meant what she said. She was sorry. She would take back everything about her time outside with Bryan if she could. He had made a fool of her. The rumors at school that he'd gotten physical with one of the girls must've been true. Otherwise why would he even try to force her like that? Her head was spinning, and even though she was sorry, she still felt dirty. Bailey pushed herself away from the wall and into her bathroom. Her lips felt hot, and in her mind they looked different. *She* looked different.

Suddenly she felt a hand on her shoulder. "Mom . . ." She turned around, but it wasn't her mother.

It was Cody. He froze and stared at her tearstained cheeks, concern written across his face. "Uh." He looked like he wasn't sure what to do, how to help her. "I didn't mean to scare you. I just . . . no one but me saw you come up, and . . . what happened out there?"

Part of her wanted to order him out of her room. Okay, so he was right about Bryan. He didn't need to rub it in. Besides, she wanted her mom or maybe just time alone to replay what had happened and etch it into her brain so nothing like it would ever happen again. But the look in Cody's eyes caught her by surprise. There was no arrogance, no teasing whatsoever.

All the reasons Bailey had to be angry at Cody fell away. Even so, she couldn't talk, couldn't put into words what had just happened. More tears clouded her vision, and her nose was runny. She sniffed and lifted her shoulders a few times, trying to let him know that she was too upset to answer him.

"Come here." Cody held out his arms.

She hugged him, and the feeling was entirely different from earlier, when she was in Bryan's arms. Cody was only comforting her, the way Connor or her parents would have if they were here. But Bailey didn't want them to know she was up here crying. Not when the party was still going strong downstairs.

Cody held her for a long moment, then led her to the sofa at the far wall of her bedroom next to the window. He kept his hand on her shoulder until she was seated, and then he took the spot beside her. He didn't hold her hand or touch her arm, and he left some space between them. "Did he hurt you?"

"He . . ." Bailey couldn't tell him the truth. She'd never be able to look Cody in the eyes again. She never should've let

Bryan kiss her in the first place, but when he forced her . . . She remembered times when she and Cody had talked for a few minutes, and she'd teased him about the girls he'd kissed. "I couldn't be like you, Cody," she'd told him more than once. "Kissing any girl who comes along."

But now look at her. Bryan wasn't honest or trustworthy. She didn't know him well enough to share her first kiss with him, but she'd done it anyway and she knew why. Because he'd told her everything she wanted to hear — about seeing her eyes better in the moonlight.

Bailey hung her head. No, she couldn't tell Cody. "You were right." A teardrop fell on her jeans. She scratched at it with her fingernail. "He's not real." She waited for the barrage of told-you-so's, but it never came.

A sigh filled the room, and Cody crossed his arms. She could feel his anger rising. "If he tried something with you, I'll leave right now and level the guy." Fierce protectiveness filled Cody's voice. He started to get up.

"No." She lifted her head. "It was my fault. I never should've gone outside. You told me not to."

Cody frowned. "I've heard about him."

His eyes grew soft again. "None of it good, Bailey."

"I thought your text was just, like, you know, giving me a hard time."

"You aren't going to tell me what happened, are you?"

Before Bailey could answer, a loud burst of party horns and noisemakers came from downstairs. She could hear someone banging what sounded like pots and pans and other people hooting and howling. Above the noise she heard the deep voices of the football guys, shouting the way they did when they scored the winning touchdown.

Cody looked sad for her, but he smiled a little anyway. "Happy New Year, Bailey."

"Happy New Year." Her cheeks were dry now, and she slid her fingers beneath her eyes in case her mascara had run. When she checked her fingertips, they were smudged with black. "I must be a mess."

"It doesn't matter." He slid a little closer and put his arm around her. "As long as you're sure you're okay."

She sniffed again and nodded. "I can't believe I was stupid enough to believe him."

"Some guys are like that." Cody thought for a moment. "I guess maybe I used to be that way. Before . . ."

He didn't have to finish his sentence.

Bailey knew what he meant. Before the way he was living nearly killed him. "So . . . where's your following tonight?" Neither Cody's drinking nor his being sober did anything to change the number of interested girls.

But now he looked as innocent as Ricky. "No girls. Not while I'm figuring out how to stay clean, how to be closer to God. You know?" He lifted his hand off her shoulders and leaned into the sofa arm.

She nodded and fiddled with her fingers.

"Plus, I promised myself I wouldn't get involved with anyone until after I've put in a year of service."

Bailey was impressed. She sat a little straighter. "You still reading your Bible every day?" It was part of his alcohol program. But she wasn't sure if Scripture was still part of the solution.

"Actually —" he stood and snapped his fingers — "I'll be right back. I wanna show you something."

She leaned into the thick cushion and waited. Cody was more like her friend than he'd ever been before. Which could only mean that of course he was still reading his Bible. God was changing him, and maybe tonight — seeing her reaction to Bryan — was part of God's plan. A way for Cody to

399

see how some girls might've felt about him after a date.

Cody's footsteps sounded in the hall, and he jogged back in, holding his Bible — the one her parents had given him. He sat down and smiled at her. "I read this today. I think maybe it fits you, Bailey."

Cody opened his Bible. He was still catching his breath from the run down the stairs and back. The pages stuck together, and it took him a few seconds of flipping through them. "Listen to this." He found his place. "It's from Isaiah 43. 'Forget the former things; do not dwell on the past.' " He paused just long enough so their eyes could meet. " 'See, I am doing a new thing!' "

Bailey let the words soak in like water to her soul. After what happened tonight they were as powerful as if God Himself had walked up and given her a hug. "I haven't read that before." She tried to remember. "At least, I don't think so."

"It hit me pretty hard." Cody shut the Bible and set it on the floor next to the sofa. "I have a lot behind me I wanna forget."

Bailey realized something. Tonight she had lost a friend who had turned out to not be a friend at all. But she'd gained one in Cody. She leaned over and hugged him. "Thanks, Cody," she whispered near his

400

neck. "I'm glad you followed me."

She was just pulling back, just easing out of the hug, when her mother walked into view and stood in her doorway. She stared at them, her expression blank. "What's going on here?"

"Nothing." Cody was on his feet almost before she finished her question. He looked at Bailey and nodded. "See you downstairs."

"Wait. . . ." Bailey stood and reached for him, but he was already halfway to the door.

Cody turned around and gave her a quick shake of his head, and then he was gone.

Bailey looked at her mom. "Why'd you say that?"

Her mom looked on the edge of anger. "Watch your tone." She came a few steps closer to Bailey.

"I will, but, Mom, that was so embarrassing!" She put her hand on her hip. Her heart was skittering around inside her. Was it that obvious that she'd done something wrong? that she was no longer Bailey Flanigan waiting for her first kiss? that in one awful moment she'd let herself be played, and she'd fallen victim to the smooth-talking ways of a guy who was apparently really good at getting what he wanted?

Her mom exhaled hard. "What do you want me to say? We've been looking for you since eleven. Midnight comes and goes and no one can find you." She waved her hand toward the sofa. Her suspicions were loud and clear. "So I walk up, and here you are hugging Cody Coleman? What am I supposed to think?"

"We were just talking." Bailey couldn't stop her tears from springing up again. "I promise, Mom. I mean, how can you even think that? Cody and I are friends."

"Right." Her mom lowered her voice. "And it's my job to help you stay that way." The noise from downstairs was still loud enough to fill the house. "Come on." She put her hand on Bailey's shoulder. "I didn't think you were doing anything wrong. It's just . . . it's not smart to be alone in your room with a guy like Cody."

Bailey opened her mouth to tell her that Cody had changed, that he wasn't the guy who got around to all the girls the way he had before his alcohol poisoning. But before she could speak, her mother started again.

"And what happened to Bryan?" A bit of accusation was still in her voice. "He leaves, and you're up here with Cody."

Bailey wanted to scream at her mom, and she wasn't even sure why. Before, in this situation she would've sat her mother down and explained the entire story. She didn't know what had happened tonight, and how could she? But thinking about that only made Bailey angrier. Because if her mother hadn't been so busy with Cody and Christmas, maybe she would've known to ask if Bryan had done something to upset her.

Bailey lifted her chin and looked straight at her mother. "He went home. He felt sick." The lie felt good. Her mom had no time for the truth anyway.

"Hmmm. I'm sorry." Her mom leaned close and kissed Bailey's cheek. She was much calmer now. But as she left Bailey's room, she glanced back and raised her brow. "Cody, though . . ." She wagged her finger, as if she was trying to be more upbeat. "That's one you should stay away from. No matter how well he's doing."

Again Bailey's mouth hung open. Her mother was so out of touch that she had everything completely wrong. She brought her lips together and returned to her sofa. "I'll be down later."

"The party's almost over." Her mother sounded like she was pleading with her. "Your friends are asking about you."

"I said I'll be down." She was careful to keep her tone polite, but there was an edge to her voice all the same. "Five minutes, okay?"

Her mom hesitated. "I want to talk later. I feel like there's space between us."

"Me too." Bailey stared at her hands. Had she really given Bryan the impression that it was okay to force a kiss on her? She shuddered. "I'll come down, Mom. I promise."

When her mom was gone, she covered her face with her hands. It didn't matter if her mother was busy. Bailey didn't want to talk anyway. Not now. Not when she was sick about how the night had gone. She'd dreamed of her first kiss for years, and she'd always known she would share every detail with her mom. Because she and her mom were best friends — closer than any mothers and daughters she knew.

But she'd never pictured the details being what they were tonight.

She dried her tears and spent a half hour downstairs with her friends and family. Cody seemed to make a point of staying far from her. If she was sitting around the coffee table or watching a pool game, he was in the office with the boys. And when she went into the office to see what they were doing, Cody left for the kitchen.

Whatever. Now that her mom had made things uncomfortable, the friendship she and Cody had started would probably never have the chance to grow.

But that night when Bailey washed her face before bed, she was struck by a thought that shone a light of hope on her heart. Even if she and Cody never had another talk like the one they'd shared tonight, she would always remember sitting next to him on the sofa in her room, removed from the party and the memory of earlier tonight, and hearing him read a Bible verse she'd never heard before.

She let the verse run through her mind again. *"Forget the former things; do not dwell on the past."*

The words made her believe with all her heart that God had forgiven her and that with His help, she had permission to move on — away from the idea of a boyfriend or kissing or any of it.

And definitely away from sweet-talking Bryan Smythe.

CHAPTER
TWENTY-THREE

Auditions for *Oliver!* were set to begin at the Bloomington Community Church in half an hour, and Katy was organizing her notes on the judges table. Five minutes until the door opened, so for now chaos reigned in the lobby — the sort of chaos Katy loved. Kids warming up their voices, parents filling out audition forms, volunteers taking Polaroid snapshots of the kids, and half a dozen measuring tapes being passed around so that costume information could be collected.

Judging today would be by Katy and Rhonda and the music directors, Al and Nancy Helmes. Dayne and Ashley would help with the rehearsal process, and they'd make an appearance today, but they hadn't been involved long enough to help decide the cast.

One of the parent volunteers brought Katy the paperwork on the first ten kids ready to audition. She was looking it over, making sure the forms were filled out completely, when Al Helmes walked up and smiled. "Take a big breath."

"Are they ready?"

"For the last ten minutes. People are lined up outside the doors and all the way down the hall to the parking lot."

Katy grinned. "Good. I want this to be the best show we've done." She pushed back the thoughts that had blindsided her at random moments for the past few weeks — the possibility that this could be her last show with the CKT kids or that the theater could be sold out from underneath them by summer. Instead she nodded. "I'm ready."

Al saluted her and took long strides to the doors. When he opened them, a rush of people hurried down the aisle and into the pews.

Rhonda was among them, and her eyes met Katy's and held. When she reached the table, she touched Katy's elbow, never once blinking. "I owe you an apology." Her eyes were shiny. "I've felt . . ." She looked around, probably searching for the right words. "I don't know, left out I guess." She looked at Katy again. "But that's no reason to take my frustrations out on you."

Katy had prayed for this, asked God that

by the time they reached audition day her friendship with Rhonda might be what it was before. She leaned closer and hugged her. "Change is hard," she whispered near Rhonda's ear. "But I need my friend on my side."

"And I'm still here." She pulled back and searched Katy's face. "I guess I couldn't believe it. You marrying Dayne Matthews, and me . . . it's just hard."

This wasn't the time to tell Rhonda that God had a plan or that someday the pieces of her life would fall into place too. Katy gave Rhonda's hand a squeeze. "Thanks for being honest."

Nancy came up and asked about the music. Rhonda explained the setup for the day, and Katy listened too. The distraction gave Katy time to study her friend and silently pray for her. God did have a plan for Rhonda, no question. But things were definitely different between them. Not long ago they were both single, both wondering when God was going to bring the guys they'd been praying about since high school into their lives. CKT looked like it would go on forever, and change of any kind seemed years away. Now none of that was the same.

Katy sat down at the table, and Rhonda

took the seat next to her. "More than a hundred kids."

"Al told me." Rhonda reached for four yellow notepads on the table and passed one to Katy. Next to her, Al took one for himself and one for Nancy. The buzz around the room was at a fever pitch.

Katy grabbed the stack of the first group's audition forms and set it at the top of the table. "Well, here we go." She stood and clapped, the same clap she'd always used with the CKT kids, a clap that they repeated as a hush fell over the room. "Welcome to our auditions for *Oliver!*" She looked around the room, making eye contact with the people who had become like family to her — Jenny Flanigan sitting next to Bailey and Connor, Tim Reed's mother, the Shaffers, the Picks, and the Fitzpatricks. The room was full, with everyone watching her.

She instructed the first ten to take seats at the front of the room. Bailey and Connor were among those, along with a few kids she didn't recognize.

At the same time, she saw Dayne enter through a side door near the back of the room. He wore jeans and a thin, dark gray T-shirt, the kind that clung to him enough so she could see the muscles in his arms and sides, the way his upper body tapered down to his narrow waist. He'd worked hard to get past his injuries, and in the process he'd come out fitter than before, leaner and more toned. He slipped in and took a seat near the back. As he did, their eyes met and he smiled. This was his first audition to watch, and he'd told Katy that he'd been looking forward to it since Christmas, but he didn't want to be a distraction.

She gave him a look that said they'd talk later.

Bailey was the first to take the stage. She wanted the part of Nancy, the beaten girlfriend of Bill Sikes who delivered the most emotional impact next to Oliver. As Bailey took the stage, Katy was struck with how she was growing up. She was losing the young teenage girl look and becoming a beautiful young woman — willowy with the dancer's body she had earned with daily lessons or practices.

"Hi, I'm Bailey Flanigan." She took her time and made eye contact with the judges. "I'll be singing 'I'm Not That Girl' from the musical *Wicked.*"

Nancy Helmes peered at Katy, her brow lowered. "*Wicked*?" she mouthed.

Laughter stuck in Katy's throat. "It's a retelling of *The Wizard of Oz,*" she whispered. *Wicked* was the favorite musical of the day for theater kids, but the name often concerned people in CKT circles until they understood the premise. Jenny Flanigan had talked to Katy last week about putting together a CKT trip to New York City this June to see several Broadway favorites. *Wicked* would certainly be among them.

Bailey's song rose and grew, and she pulled off the one-minute performance flawlessly. Katy was mesmerized not so much by Bailey's voice — though she carried the song with a strong sound that was right on key — as by her acting. The song was about a girl who knew that the guy she loved was in love with someone else. It was deep and emotional and filled with a gripping resignation. Bailey conveyed the message in a way that was so convincing it left goose bumps on Katy's arms.

When she finished, the kids in the audience erupted into applause. They loved Bailey, and Katy was impressed. She always had to be careful when it came to Bailey and Connor — careful that she gave them the same consideration she gave the other kids. Early on she sometimes went a little too hard on the Flanigan kids so no one would accuse her of favoritism. But even if this had been the first time she'd ever seen

411

Bailey, Katy would have thought the same thing.

They just might've found their Nancy.

One after another the kids took the stage and presented their songs, and between groups, Katy would share a look or a smile with Dayne. A few of the kids had noticed him, but so far no one had approached him. The kids at CKT were getting used to Dayne Matthews. Besides, he'd be around often. They knew that. And today they were far too concerned with their auditions to worry about a movie star in the back row of the church.

Sometime around eight o'clock, the last student sang her audition, and Katy and the rest of the creative team moved to the coffee shop to talk about callbacks. At first Connor Flanigan seemed a possibility for Oliver, but a new boy had auditioned, a kid named Jacob with curly blond hair and the voice of an angel. He was fourteen, but he didn't look a day over eleven. With his soulful eyes and clear voice, Katy was pretty sure the boy would be given the lead part.

All that evening and into the next day the process continued, and by Saturday night the cast list was announced. Jacob was Oliver, Bailey was Nancy, and Connor — in his first big role since *Tom Sawyer* — was the Artful Dodger. Tim Reed convincingly won the part of Bill Sikes, showing more emotion than ever before. Katy could hardly wait to see the audience tremble when he learned his part.

Saturday night, Katy and Dayne went to dinner, and when they came home, the Flanigans were celebrating.

Ricky met them at the door. "Bailey and Connor both got good parts!" He did a victory spin and ran back toward the kitchen. "Yay for Bailey and Connor!"

Even before Katy could think it, she saw Jenny put her hand on Ricky's shoulder and still him. "They're all good parts." She looked down the hall at Katy and grinned. Like many CKT moms, Jenny had learned this lesson the hard way. The experience, the group camaraderie, the feeling of being part of something bigger than any of them could've done on their own — that was the beauty of being in a CKT production, not the number of lines a person had.

Katy smiled at Jenny, then turned back to Dayne. "Let's watch a movie in the rec room tonight." She looked over her shoulder at Jenny. "The Flanigans need their space."

"We better keep the door open." Dayne was teasing her, but he touched his lips lightly to hers. "I can't wait to marry you.

Have I said that lately?"

"Not in the last hour." She lowered her chin. She could feel her eyes dancing, the way they so often did when she was face-to-face with the man she loved.

Katy tried to keep some distance between herself and the Flanigans that night and later after Dayne went home. This weekend she was the director, after all. But silently she celebrated.

"It's fitting," she told Dayne when she walked him to his 4Runner that night. "All these years Bailey and Connor have worked so hard and played a lot of smaller parts. But now . . . when it might be my last show for a while, they get the leads. I'm happy for them."

He brushed his thumb along her cheek. "It's a strong cast."

"It is. I have a feeling the next ten weeks are going to go way too fast."

Dayne looked deep into her eyes. The cold night air was only tolerable because of his nearness. "Or not fast enough." He kissed her, and the sensation warmed her to the center of her being. "I'm counting down the hours till the wedding."

She rubbed her nose against his and closed her eyes, lost in the feel of his closeness. "Which means being busy with *Oliver!*

is a good thing."

"Very good." He kissed her again. "But for now the best thing you can do is go back inside."

Rehearsals were under way for *Oliver!* and Katy's days were as full as her nights. She'd found a wedding dress in Indianapolis, a beautiful, fitted, white satin gown with a simple, elegant train. Jenny Flanigan had been with her when she picked it out.

As Katy stood on a platform surrounded by mirrors, Jenny's breath caught in her throat. "Katy . . . Dayne'll faint dead away when he sees you in that."

"It's exactly what I pictured." Katy had looked on several other occasions, but no dress came close to this one. In it she felt like a princess, as if everything she'd ever prayed about or dreamed about regarding her wedding and her ensuing marriage was pictured in the way she looked in the mirror.

That night at the church building, Katy could barely stay focused on the rehearsal. She and Dayne were leaving for LA in the morning, set to meet with the writer from *Celebrity Life* magazine just after lunchtime. Then there would be a celebration dinner and the next day a meeting with the director of Dayne's next movie, *But Then Again No.* She wanted desperately to tell Dayne about the dress. But she held back. All he knew was that she'd found the right one.

Now Nancy and Al Helmes were with an ensemble group in the other room, and Katy, Dayne, and Rhonda were in the sanctuary blocking the scene in which Fagin and his young thieves teach Oliver how to pick pockets. Later, when the boys are all down for the night, Fagin sneaks over to his box of treasures, the ones he'd been skimming for himself.

It was the first time they were trying the false nose, a clay piece that was supposed to attach to the top of the very normal-size nose of Patrick, the boy playing Fagin. The goal was for Patrick to be as animated as the part called for without doing damage to or losing the false nose. Also, they had to be sure it didn't make him sound nasally when he sang.

Katy sat in the middle spot in the front row of the sanctuary with Dayne and Rhonda on either side. The kids were used to Dayne's presence now, and so far no paparazzi had made it to one of the rehearsals.

"Okay, let's run it from the top." Katy stood and motioned for the actors to take their places.

Fifteen young boys, including Connor, found their spots on the stage, the places where they were supposed to be sleeping. Patrick took the box of treasures and stared into it. He twiddled his fingers in a perfect Faginesque manner. But as he tiptoed downstage past the sleeping boys, he took a big breath, and without warning, his nose plopped into the box.

Dayne covered his mouth to hide a snort of laughter, and a chorus of giggles rose from boys onstage.

Katy took a deep breath and pulled her yellow notepad close. *Fix the nose,* she wrote.

Patrick didn't miss a beat. In the next few seconds, as he was sifting through the jewels and treasures in the box, he picked up the clay nose piece and deftly squished it back into place.

The move put Dayne over the edge. He dropped his head between his knees and fell into a round of laughter that was contagious throughout the room. Katy put her arm around Dayne's shaking shoulders and announced, "Take five everyone." She lowered her face near Dayne's. "Maybe Fagin doesn't need a big nose."

"Or maybe . . ." Dayne looked up, trying

to catch his breath. "Maybe he could find the nose in the treasure box and slap it on as part of the scene."

"Very funny." She raked her fingers through her hair. "Rhonda, ask Bethany if we can find another kind of modeling clay."

Rhonda was giggling too. She hurried off to find Bethany, and after a few minutes the laughter died down and they were ready to begin again. One of the numbers they worked on was "I'd Do Anything," in which the Artful Dodger — played by Connor — teasingly offered to give anything, do anything for the love of Nancy, played by Bailey Flanigan, who was performing brilliantly.

Katy figured she knew why. Bailey seemed better at home lately, less moody. She and Jenny were spending more time together, and Bailey appeared to have found a friend in Cody Coleman. For his part, Cody was continuing with his alcohol classes and staying close to home. All of it gave Bailey the chance to focus on her character. For that reason, even with weeks to go until opening night, the number was wonderful.

After the kids left the theater, after Rhonda and Bethany had packed their things and gone home, and after the parents had picked up their kids, Dayne gathered props and Katy sat at the director's table looking over the notes from the day.

The bridge would elevate part of the scene, because with seventy kids, people couldn't see the action upstage. Lighting would have to find a spot bright enough to highlight Dodger when he sang to Nancy; otherwise the audience would have to work too hard to figure out which one of Fagin's gang was doing the singing.

Katy stopped halfway down her page of notes as something caught her eye. She looked up, and Dayne was standing as far downstage as possible, his hand out-stretched toward her, a plastic long-stem rose in his mouth. With a dramatic flair, he removed the rose and held it to her. "M'lady . . . could I interest you in a dance?" His English accent was impeccable. "Please, m'lady."

Katy's heart melted, and she put her pen down. "Why, Dodger, you make a right fancy gentleman, you do!" She stood and curtsied, then walked to the edge of the stage, where she took hold of his hand.

In a single move, Dayne whisked her onto the stage. Then he dropped to one knee and stretched his arms out to either side. Main-taining the accent and with a voice that filled the room, he began to sing. " 'I'd do anything, for you, dear, anything . . .' "

Katy fanned herself, playing her part for all it was worth, caught in the moment, relishing it.

Dayne sang clear and strong, his eyes never leaving hers. " 'For you mean everything to me. I know that I'd go anywhere . . .' "

As Dayne sang the rest of the song, Katy grinned at him, impressed by the strength of his acting and enjoying the feel of being onstage with him. She thought about his next movie. Maybe auditioning for the part opposite him would be a wonderful idea after all. The time of their lives.

As the song wound down, Dayne fell to one knee again. " 'I'd do anything . . . anything for you!' "

She pulled him to his feet and flung her arms around his neck. "I love you! And you can play Dodger any day."

"Mmmm." He pressed his cheek to hers. "Only if you're Nancy."

Katy laughed, and it occurred to her that in the coming weeks, some of Dayne Matthews' finest moments wouldn't be on a silver screen for the whole world to see.

They'd be right here, on a simple wooden stage in Bloomington, Indiana.

CHAPTER
TWENTY-FOUR

On the private flight to Los Angeles, in the Town Car that picked them up, while they checked Katy in at the Hyatt, and all the way to his Malibu house, Dayne wrestled with what they were about to do. Giving in to the paparazzi, offering themselves on a platter to the very people who had nearly killed him. The idea still seemed crazy.

Only Katy's calm reassurance kept him from grabbing the keys to the convertible BMW in his Malibu garage — the one he rarely drove — and taking Katy for a three-hour drive up the coast instead. His Escalade had been totaled in the car accident, and now he had the 4Runner in Bloomington. He still wanted to buy another SUV for the weeks when he'd be working in Southern California, but that would have to wait. This trip was about making the announcement and getting Katy in front of the director.

It was warm and beautiful in Los Angeles. At nearly seventy degrees, it was a far cry from the snow and ice they'd left behind in Bloomington. They stopped at a Malibu deli, and Katy ran in for sandwiches, which they ate on Dayne's back deck. The paparazzi hadn't yet realized he was back in town, so they could sit outside and look at the ocean without worrying about someone taking their picture.

"How're you doing?" Katy put her hand on his knee and smiled at him. "The meeting's in an hour."

"Trying not to think about it." He set his sandwich down and stared at a pair of seagulls dipping low over the water. "I guess I just want to be back at the lake house or singing to you onstage at the theater." He turned to her. "You know?"

"I do." She took a sip of her iced tea. "I feel the same, but . . . what other choice do we have?" Her tone was gentle. "Much longer and they certainly would've found you helping run scenes for CKT. They'd hound us until they knew the truth."

Dayne gritted his teeth and looked at the blue Pacific again. She was right. He was who he was, and there was nothing either of them could do to change the fact. The hope was that once the information was public, the press would leave them alone, be less concerned about what happened next. Happy couples weren't of great interest to the paparazzi, right? Wasn't that the idea?

He sighed and reached for her hand. "I wish I could keep you to myself, keep this . . . this amazing thing we share just for us. So the whole world wouldn't need a front-row seat. Are you sure you really want this, Katy? this life I lead?"

"Look what we've had for the last nearly two months. There'll be times like that —" she gazed out at the beach — "and times like this. And, yes, I'll take all of it." She leaned close and framed his face with her hands. "I'm ready for what lies ahead. They can take all the pictures they want, as long as I have you."

Her words reassured him. He relaxed his jaw and smiled. "You're incredible; have I told you that?"

"Only twice today." Katy giggled. "Come on — we better get going."

They drove to the magazine office with the convertible top up. No point catching the attention of any photographers until they absolutely had to.

From the moment they met the reporter, Dayne felt uneasy. This was supposed to be the time when he felt most in control. No more running from the paparazzi; instead they were taking the story to the press. Giving them what they wanted in the sound bites and exact answers that he and Katy wanted to give.

But Dayne couldn't shake the bad feeling.

He sat next to Katy, the two of them holding hands. They had practiced their responses, and the interview went off like a well-rehearsed movie scene. Yes, Dayne met Katy at the Bloomington Community Theater, where she taught children's theater, and yes, it was love at first sight. Yes, he'd gone to Bloomington to meet his birth mother, who was dying of cancer, and no, he hadn't met any other members of his birth family on that trip. Yes, in the years since then he'd gotten to know all of the Baxters, and yes, he had a good relationship with all of them — even Luke.

When the reporter asked Dayne to discuss the conflicts between him and Luke early on, Dayne smiled and shook his head. "We never had any conflicts."

Willingly and purposefully, Dayne and Katy gave their answers, steering the interview away from any bit of controversy and focusing instead on the beauty of their love story, the thrill of their engagement.

Then the reporter directed a host of questions toward the timing and location of the wedding.

"We're really not sure," Dayne said with a straight face. "We've talked about a lot of options, but we're looking at a date sometime before I start my next movie."

The reporter had done her homework. She pushed harder, suggesting specific dates that lined up just before the new film dates for the movie.

Dayne laughed and shrugged. "We're really not sure."

The reporter gave him a look that said she didn't believe him. But the interview was such a coup that she didn't dare sour the moment. She smiled and moved on to Katy's dress. "Is it picked out?"

"Yes, but it's a surprise," Katy told her.

"What about flowers?"

Dayne grinned. He gestured in a wide-ranging motion. "White roses everywhere."

Dayne and Katy had decided that giving the reporter a handful of honest answers about the details of their wedding wouldn't hurt anything. The biggest secret was the date, and that was something they were entitled to keep to themselves. Even so, they weren't being dishonest by saying they didn't have an exact answer about it. If the press got wind of their tentative date, it would change. Wilma Waters was in charge of that part.

Again the reporter asked about the bigger details. "Do you have a location booked? Somewhere special we should know about?"

Dayne sank back into the sofa and smiled at Katy and then at the reporter. "We'll be married when the cameras roll in May. The rest will come together in time."

The reporter let it go. Next was the question they were certain she would ask eventually. "You're both Christians. Is that right?"

"Yes." The answer was obvious when it came to Katy. That had publicly been part of who she was since the trial, when her identity was revealed.

"You too?" The reporter looked at Dayne. "Didn't I read that somewhere?"

"Absolutely." Dayne gave a firm nod. This was what he had been looking forward to — the idea that if they cooperated with the press, then God could use their story, their relationship, to bring other people closer to Him. People like Dayne with colorful and imperfect pasts.

"So does that mean you're waiting until you're married?" The reporter's eyes twinkled as if she was most curious about this bit of information. It didn't take a detective to know that Dayne had violated this command of God's several times over. Once Katy and Dayne went public about their intentions, the paparazzi would love to find out that the two of them had somehow slipped up.

Dayne took the lead once more. "Katy's a virgin." It was something they had agreed would be a great example for young girls, a detail Katy was willing to share. Dayne pursed his lips, his tone serious. "I've had a lot of changes in my life, given myself back to God after many years away. Waiting until we're married is important to both of us."

The reporter seemed surprised and a little suspicious of this. She asked half a dozen more questions on the topic until she apparently gave up trying to find something fraudulent about their story. She turned her attention to Katy. "You were in a pilot movie several years back, and you read for a part in Dayne's movie *Dream On.* Is acting something you're considering in the future?"

They'd gone over this topic as well. Katy smiled and leaned a little closer to Dayne. "I'd consider it. We haven't made any decisions for sure one way or the other."

The interview lasted two hours and included a photo shoot. It was a cover story, no doubt, and the angle was clear from the questions that had been asked during their time with the reporter. Dayne Matthews was in love and marrying the small-town drama instructor, the one who had been his mystery woman.

When it was over, when they'd taken the last photograph and quickly found their way downstairs toward the back door of the building, twenty-some people were waiting for them. People they'd passed in the halls or who had gotten wind that an interview was taking place upstairs at the magazine's offices. Most of them had slips of paper and pens, which they handed Katy and Dayne with a chorus of requests for autographs.

A redheaded woman cried out, "Is Katy your girlfriend now, Dayne?"

Dayne felt his frustration grow. He hadn't had to deal with this since the accident. After his stint at the physical therapy center, he'd made an announcement with his agent that he had recovered and would continue to make movies. But then he'd gone off to Bloomington for Thanksgiving and Christmas, and other than the few minutes at the Indiana University basketball game, he'd been away from scenes like this one.

But next to him, Katy gave him a tentative smile. "Yes —" she directed her answer at the redhead — "we're dating." The look in her eyes clearly asked his permission to give in to these people, to meet their requests.

"Yep, she's pretty special." Dayne gave a slight nod as he reached for a piece of paper. After he'd signed it, he waved to the others. "Hi, folks." He used his movie voice, one that was clear and a little deeper than usual. "Another beautiful day in Los Angeles!"

After nearly fifteen minutes, Dayne finished signing autographs, though a group of women was speeding off the elevator in their direction. Dayne took Katy's arm and hurried her out the back door and to his car. When they were locked inside and Dayne had driven them halfway through the parking lot, he turned to her. "I'm not sure if I can do this, Katy."

She looked flushed from rushing. "Were there paparazzi somewhere? in the building?"

"No." He reached the street and turned right onto Wilshire. "There were more people coming from the elevator." He didn't want to take his feelings out on her. "Don't you see? It never ends. You try to be nice, but then the next wave of people wants the same thing. We could stand there all day, and someone would still miss out or think we were rude for leaving early."

Katy looked over her shoulder. "They're

running out into the parking lot."

"Of course they are." He exhaled hard. "Look, I want this to work, the idea of cooperating with the press, of being available when we're in Los Angeles." The uneasiness was back, worse than ever. "I'm just not sure."

Katy bit her lip, and for a moment she said nothing. Then she turned to him, and there was uncertainty in her expression as well. "I guess I don't see any other way. I mean —" she gestured toward the busy traffic all around them — "we can't run from photographers every time we come to LA."

"Which is why the magazine article seemed like a good idea to me, too. But being there . . . telling even a little of our private lives and knowing it'll be splashed across the front cover of *Celebrity Life* magazine gave me moments in that office when I wanted to scream."

She took his hand and eased her fingers between his. "I could feel that from you."

"What if we're wrong?" Dayne gripped the steering wheel with his other hand and stared straight ahead. "What if the paparazzi think we've given them open season on our lives?"

"For a time that'll be true. All the magazines will replay the story. But after that they'll leave us alone, Dayne. Because there's no more mystery, nothing to find out."

Dayne nodded, but doubts plagued him, thick and dense like June fog on Malibu Beach. "They'll want the date and location. They'll send people to Bloomington if it means getting the information."

"Which is why we have Wilma Waters." Katy sounded tired. "Please, Dayne. We have to try this. If it means smiling for the camera, I can do that. But I can't have them chase you again." Her voice cracked, and she pinched the bridge of her nose. "I can't live in fear about that. Paste my life in a magazine for the whole world to see. Fine." She glanced at him, and there were tears on her cheeks. "But I can't lose you."

Suddenly her motives for laying open their lives were as clear as the Indiana air. They were at a stoplight, and he stared at her, loving her. He brought her hand to his lips and kissed it. "That's it? That's why you want to be available?"

"Yes." She sniffed, and the terror she must've felt when he was in a coma shone clearly from her eyes. "This is your life — paparazzi and press and cameras and magazines. Either you work with them or they'll chase you. We know that."

Dayne didn't respond. He couldn't. The lump in his throat was too thick. It didn't matter how he felt, whether he was uneasy about being an open book for the press and having his love life laid out for the entire world to see. Katy needed this, because she needed him. When it came to meeting the paparazzi's demands, nothing else mattered to her.

Katy had sat by and watched while he nearly died; he couldn't put her through that again — not for the sake of making desperate attempts at privacy. Privacy that had never really been possible anyway.

The light turned green, and he drove until the next red. Then he turned to her and took hold of her other hand too. "I promise you, Katy, with every breath inside me, I'll work with the press from now on. If they chase me, I'll pull over and smile and wave. I won't let myself be in that kind of danger again."

"Really?" The fear was still in her eyes, but through it was a river of hope.

He came closer and kissed her, a tender kiss to soothe her fears and his. He drew back and searched her heart, her eyes. "While we're in LA, we'll sign the auto-graphs and do the interviews and smile for the cameras." He looked past a mountain of doubt bursting inside his own heart, doubts that somehow making themselves available would only incite the media, make the attention worse. He swallowed hard. "If this makes you more comfortable, we'll do it. I won't complain about it anymore."

They drove toward Dayne's house and stopped at a market on Pacific Coast Highway. Katy ran in and picked up ribs, carrots, salad, and little red potatoes. When she was back in the car, she said no one had recognized her. This was Malibu, after all. Everyone who lived here was in the movie industry one way or another. People didn't care to look twice at the other people in line. They were too busy with their own lives.

That night Dayne barbecued, and they talked about everything but the paparazzi. Because whether they gave in and allowed every photograph and interview or changed their minds and turned their backs and ran, they both could feel the wave of attention coming.

It would appear on the horizon of their recently quiet lives the moment the cover story hit. Dayne could only beg God that when it did, they could ride it out together. He'd seen what the glare of the media spotlight could do to people who made themselves available. Too often the remnants of a marriage were the only carnage left at the end of the day.

Dayne felt sick at the thought. As they finished eating, he studied Katy in the waning sunlight, and one thought stayed in his mind. He would rather die than let the media destroy what he and Katy had finally found together.

Stephen Petrel, the director of *But Then Again No,* was the most compassionate in the business. Dayne had no doubt that the movie would be replete with depth and emotion, a love story for the ages. That's how it was being talked about in the early buzz that surrounded the film, and he was sure that's how it would play out on-screen.

All the more reason why Dayne hoped Katy would give her best efforts in the reading she was about to do. The alternatives weren't something he even wanted to consider, and he'd told Katy as much last night before she headed back to her hotel. The movie was a love story, after all. How could he be dreaming night and day of Katy Hart while spending his days in the arms of the costar he wound up with?

Dayne and Katy stepped into the studio offices, and Dayne made the introductions.

Stephen shook Katy's hand and sized her up with a kind look. "You're very beautiful."

"Thank you." She blushed — something Dayne loved about her. The Hollywood women he knew, the ones he'd dated or spent time with on various movies, were very used to hearing people comment about their beauty. They took such compliments in stride, expected them even.

Not Katy. She angled her head, and for a moment Dayne saw her the way he'd seen her on the Bloomington stage that long-ago day when the CKT kids had just finished their run of *Charlie Brown.* Simple and irresistible with an uncomplicated beauty that had taken his breath.

Katy moved on from the compliment. "Dayne says you can tell us a little more about the film, the story line."

Stephen sat up straighter. "It's beautiful. This generation's *Love Story,* if I had to compare it with something."

The comparison sent chills down Dayne's arms. Stephen wasn't known for his flowery words and empty promises. If he saw *But Then Again No* as that big of a picture, then it would be a special movie indeed. Dayne wanted to hurry this part of the meeting along so they could get to the reading.

"Are you comfortable on a horse?" Stephen studied Katy. "Dayne says you rode when you were a schoolgirl."

"I did." Katy seemed confident. "Horses are easy for me."

"Good." The director went on to talk about how thrilled he was that they'd been able to get fourteen-year-old Jaclyn Jacobs for the role of the female lead during her younger years.

"Jaclyn is fantastic." Stephen rested his forearms on his desk. He told them that Jaclyn was one of the strongest child actors of their time. She was a pretty girl, tall with strawberry blonde hair and freckles. Her transparency in front of a camera made her perfect for the part. "She's a great kid too. Strong family, very grounded. She'd just as soon babysit for the neighbors as star in a big film. This is a small role for her, but she was passionate about it. We got the okay from her last week." Stephen smiled. "All that and she's a natural on a horse."

Dayne had heard of her. "Didn't she have an accident a while back?"

"Her horse rammed her into a wall, hurt her head." Stephen winced. "Tough blow. She had a helmet, thankfully, and she recovered after a week or so."

Katy frowned. "And she's still okay to get

436

on a horse?" She gave a nervous laugh. "I'm pretty sure I'd stay far away after something like that."

"Jaclyn's very sweet, but she's a tough girl too. She's very active. Even while she was recuperating, she played tennis in the mornings and walked her horse in the afternoons." Stephen pulled her head shot from a file and slid it toward Dayne. "She's the perfect younger girl in this story."

"Part of the story takes place when the couple's daughter is a young girl into horseback riding, right?" Katy sounded hesitant.

"Exactly." Stephen explained that the male protagonist was angry because of issues with his parents, and the female protagonist was mysterious because she was an editor who kept her emotions close to the vest. When he finished, Stephen stroked his chin. He studied Katy a moment longer, then turned his attention to Dayne. "I can feel it."

"Feel it?" It usually took a few weeks before Dayne was able to know exactly what a director meant in a moment like this.

"The chemistry." Stephen leaned back and folded his arms. "Intense chemistry between the two of you." He narrowed his eyes. "Physical love is good between you, I assume?"

Dayne wasn't prepared for the question. The mortification making its way through him was eased only when he caught Katy's quiet laugh beside him. He could tell she was embarrassed but not shocked. Hollywood would expect Katy and Dayne to be sleeping together.

"Uh . . ." Dayne cleared his throat and raised his pointer finger. "It's not like that with us."

The director looked confused. "I . . . I don't understand. I thought you were . . . I thought this was a relationship between you."

"It is." Dayne took hold of Katy's hand. He wasn't sure where to begin. "We're engaged, but we have a strong commitment to waiting, doing this God's way." He felt like he was rambling. "In other words, we're waiting until we're married."

Stephen's eyes opened wide. "I'm a believer also. I had no idea, Dayne. . . ." Slowly he gave a few distinct nods. "That explains the chemistry."

Dayne stopped himself from saying more, but silently he shared his shock with the Lord. Stephen was a Christian? That meant the film had a chance to not only be a beautiful love story but something life changing, a picture that would give people a true understanding of the sort of love found in 1 Corinthians chapter 13.

All the more reason why Katy had to have the part.

They talked a little longer, and then Stephen looked at his watch. "You ready to read for me, Katy Hart? I've seen your pilot movie, and I've talked to my friends in this town." He stood and led them into the hall. "I know what you can do."

Dayne felt his heart swell with pride. He would've fallen in love with Katy whether she could act or not. All he knew of her from the beginning was that she loved theater and kids and God. That was enough then, and it would be enough until they drew their last breath together. But the idea that she was also a talented actress in her own right was an added bonus. Dayne wanted her to have the role opposite him more than he'd wanted anything in a long time.

They walked into a soundstage, and Stephen positioned himself behind a camera located in the center of the room. He flipped a few switches, then grabbed a script from the nearest table and handed it to Katy. "Take a look at the first two pages. This is the scene where the female lead is explaining why she prefers work at the magazine to relationships." Stephen took a step back. "Spend a few minutes with it, and then we'll roll."

Stephen talked to Dayne about his last film and working with Randi Wells. "She's getting a divorce. I guess you know that."

Dayne had heard but only from the headlines in the tabloids. He needed to call her and see how she was doing. Or maybe Katy could call. The two of them had formed a friendship in the days after Dayne's accident. They were still talking about Randi and the struggles of living with an Academy Award–winning career while trying to maintain a marriage and young children when Katy signaled.

"Ready." She positioned herself in front of the camera. "Is Dayne part of this?"

"Yes, absolutely." Stephen pointed toward the spot near Katy. "You don't have to do anything, Matthews. Just give her someone to talk to. Let us feel the chemistry."

Stephen took his place behind the camera, peered through the viewfinder, and gave the okay sign. He pressed a button. "And . . . roll it."

Dayne looked intently at Katy, and before his eyes she began to transform. Passion and anger filled her expression, and she pursed her lips. When the words came, they didn't flow from her lips. They exploded. "I work because I have to work, okay? What do you know about my life?" Tears made her eyes damp, but she pressed on.

When the scene was finished, Dayne couldn't do anything but stare at her. Katy was so good he had goose bumps. He looked at Stephen and tried to find the words. "Okay, so maybe she can teach me a thing or two."

They all laughed, except Katy. She was still trying to come back out of the character. She looked at Stephen, clearly puzzled by their laughter. "Should I run it again?"

Stephen crossed the room. "Yes, my dear, I should say so. You'll run it again in May when we're shooting the scene on the set."

"You mean . . . ?" Now it was her turn to be amazed. She brought her hands to her lips, her eyes big. "You mean, you liked it?"

Again the men laughed, and Dayne put his arm around her. "Katy, you were so believable it was scary."

"Very believable." Stephen took his Black-Berry from his pocket and made a few taps on it. "I've got it penciled in now."

"What?" Katy was smiling, but she still looked like she was dizzy from the response to her reading.

"To send you a contract. I'd like you to consider the part, Katy. I can't imagine someone playing this role better than what I just saw here in a sixty-second cold read."

On the way back to the airport, Katy fell asleep on Dayne's shoulder, and Dayne replayed everything from the past few days. The meeting with the magazine and the conversation they'd had in the car on the way to his house. How terrified Katy was that the press would chase him into an accident again. And finally, the brilliance of her reading for Stephen.

But no matter how wonderful their time in Los Angeles had been or how hopeful their private and public future seemed, Dayne was still troubled by all that lay ahead with the press. The one thing he didn't want to think about was the starring role, the one the director had offered to Katy on the spot. Because doing a film like that together could be amazing or it could place them in too bright a light.

So bright that they might have trouble seeing the simplicity of a starry night in Bloomington or the wonder of God. Or even the love they felt for each other.

CHAPTER TWENTY-FIVE

The *Celebrity Life* magazine cover story caused shock waves that Katy hadn't anticipated. Now that she and Dayne had announced their intentions, it seemed that every publication in the world wanted to know exactly when and where they were getting married.

Paparazzi were stationed in Bloomington, camping out at the local Holiday Inn, determined to follow Katy and Dayne everywhere they went. Even so, Katy believed they were doing the right thing by being available. Early on they'd met with the photographers and explained that a true plan for the wedding really hadn't been set.

"You can take pictures of us coming and going, but the rehearsals for my kids theater are closed to the public," Katy had told them. "Also, we need to ask that you resist the urge to follow us home. There's a level of privacy that we're requesting here." She smiled at them, and she could feel the group of eight men being charmed. They didn't want to be enemies with Dayne and Katy; quite the opposite. If Hollywood's overnight glamour couple was willing to work with them, then they seemed willing to do their part.

A deal was struck. The photographers could get shots of Katy and Dayne coming and going to the theater and church as long as they stayed in the parking lot. Anytime Katy and Dayne had a few minutes, they would stop and pose for pictures, chatting with the photographers and giving them whatever tidbits might help them get their jobs done.

Dayne was going along with the plan, but he didn't like it. Katy could easily tell that much. "How long are we supposed to live like this?" He wasn't angry with her, but he obviously wasn't convinced that their approach was going to work.

"Just until the wedding." It was what the photographers had told Katy one day, and she believed them. "After that we'll be old news."

The constant presence of the paparazzi made it difficult to keep their talks with Wilma Waters secret, but they were finished meeting in person, anyway. As the days passed, a buzz bubbled just beneath the surface among the regulars at CKT. The Flanigans and other families could hardly wait for the wedding, even though they had no idea where the ceremony would take place.

They'd put out the first level of invitations, asking people to keep March 16 through 19 open, with instructions that another invitation would be hand delivered closer to the actual date. Katy expected that the press would get wind of the dates, though they wouldn't know the whereabouts of the wedding.

But for the first time since she'd come up with the idea, her kindness toward the paparazzi worked in their favor. The photographers seemed almost lulled into taking the easy pictures, gathering up the bits of information Katy and Dayne provided. And now it was opening night for *Oliver!* which meant that the wedding was two weeks away. Katy and Dayne dressed the way they might for a Hollywood premiere. She wore a glittery black dress, and he wore a tux he'd brought back from his Malibu house on their last visit.

The Baxters were all in attendance — including John and Elaine, who were spending more time together these days. Katy liked the way they were together, and she wondered — as did Ashley, Kari, Brooke, and the others — when John would see for himself that he had feelings for Elaine. Feelings that definitely seemed to go beyond friendship.

Katy made her way through the theater to check on Nancy and Al Helmes. "Everything all set?" She bent close so they could hear her above the excitement coming from the people filling the seats.

"Good to go!" Al gave her a pat on the shoulder. "If I haven't already told you, I'm impressed, Katy."

"By what?" She loved these friends of hers, loved the way they were almost like the parents in Chicago she saw so little of.

"By the way you're handling all the attention." He winked at her. "You'll make the perfect wife for Dayne Matthews. And things'll settle down eventually."

"Thanks, Al." She grinned at him, then at Nancy. "Let's bring down the house tonight."

On her way backstage, she saw Jenny Flanigan in the third row. All the kids were with her, and Cody Coleman had the seat on the end. Jenny cupped her hands around her mouth so Katy could hear her. "Jim's getting popcorn!"

"Pray that we're ready!" Katy felt her heart rate speed up. It was starting to hit her. In a few minutes the show would come to life onstage. The adrenaline rush from seeing that happen was always a factor just before the first show. "You never know on opening night."

Cody stood and moved close enough so Katy could hear him. "Do me a favor, could you?" He handed Katy a yellow rose. "Give this to Bailey for me."

Katy resisted the urge to raise her eyebrow. A yellow rose was very appropriate coming from Cody. He and Bailey had become good friends in the last few weeks, while Bryan hadn't called once. At least that was Jenny's take on the situation. Katy smiled at him. "I'll make sure she gets it."

She glanced at Jenny as she headed toward the stage wings. The look on her friend's face said Jenny was okay with Cody giving Bailey the flower. They'd all grown much closer to him since his alcohol poisoning. Cody seemed like a different person, and with the way Jenny said he was relying on God these days, he probably was.

The excitement continued to build as Katy zipped down the stairs and into the greenroom. The kids were putting the finishing touches on their makeup, smudging powdered cocoa on their faces so they'd look like dirty orphans, and adjusting their costumes and microphones.

Dayne was downstairs too, helping Larry Taie with the buttons on his Mr. Bumble costume. The kid was the funniest actor they had in CKT. He was perfect in the role, and he and Dayne had bonded in the course of bringing the show to life. Dayne saw great promise in Larry and had encouraged him to study acting in college.

"Okay, everyone." Katy clapped the rhythm the kids knew instinctively.

In only a few seconds, a hush fell over the greenroom, and the kids echoed the clap back to her.

"All right, let's circle up."

All seventy kids and fourteen crew members squeezed into a circle that took up most of the room. Dayne was at the opposite end, and just as Katy opened her mouth to make the final announcements, her eyes caught his. A sudden wealth of emotion built in her, and she brought her lips together and swallowed. Here they were, she and Dayne, doing the thing they loved without any cameras or paparazzi or national fame.

But was it the last time? the last time she'd ask her CKT kids to circle up before a show? the last time they'd share opening night in the Bloomington Community Theater? She blinked back tears, and one at a time she looked at each boy and girl in the circle — Bailey and Connor Flanigan, Tim Reed, Larry, Patrick, Sydney, the Shaffer kids, and the Picks. . . .

Dayne seemed to sense that she was struggling. He coughed, and the attention shifted to him. "Katy and I are very proud of all of you." His eyes shone, and sincerity rang in his tone. "You've worked hard to get where you are tonight. Now it's time to go out and show them what you can do, what God's given you the gift and talent to do. Tonight isn't about us. It's about giving glory to the One who brought us together." He glanced at Katy. "The only One who could've done that."

Katy was grateful to Dayne. If she could have frozen the moment, she would've crossed the room and hugged him. He knew her so well that they might have been friends for a decade or more. She found her voice. "Let's pray." She closed her eyes. "Lord, thank You for each one here. Help them remember their lines, and be with them that they might sing clearly for You. Above all, we pray that Your light will shine through us tonight. In Jesus' name, amen."

In her heart, she added another prayer that developers might not buy the theater and turn it into condos, and the kids might have the chance to continue with CKT, even if her position among them was replaced by Rhonda and Chad Jennings from Cleveland.

Before the circle broke apart, Tim Reed led the group in the song that had become as much a part of a CKT show as the lights and the stage. " 'I love You, Lord, and I lift my voice. . . .' "

Katy swallowed again. CKT couldn't be nearing its end. It was enough to think that this might be her last show without having to imagine one day driving by where the theater had been and seeing condos. She focused on the matter at hand, and when the song ended, she smiled at her entire cast. "Let's make it happen!"

A cheer rose from the kids.

As Katy made her way toward the stairs, Dayne fell in beside her. "Somehow I can't imagine you not doing this work, Katy."

"Me neither." She sniffed and kept her smile in place. This wasn't the time to mourn future losses. It was time to celebrate all they'd worked for. She looped her arm through his. "Here we go!"

The show began five minutes later and went along flawlessly through the curtain call. Patrick's nose stayed in place, and Bailey's angry interchange with Tim Reed's Bill Sikes character was something Katy felt in the pit of her stomach. There was no question that by the end of the show, everyone believed Bailey was an abused barmaid and not the innocent girl she was offstage. Connor was wonderful as Dodger, and Larry brought down the house with his funny leprechaun-like dance in pursuing the hand of the workhouse widow.

It wasn't until the play was over and they'd celebrated opening night with a party at the Flanigan house that it occurred to Katy: with this milestone behind them, the next one lay just ahead.

Their wedding.

Ashley stayed in touch with Katy throughout the run of *Oliver!* shows. She even left baby Devin with Kari and took Cole out of school so the two of them could act as ushers for one of the school-day shows.

"I don't get it," Cole told her that afternoon. "Why would they sell Oliver? You don't just sell people, Mom."

"No." Ashley thought about all that Cole would learn in the coming years, about the civilizations and generations who did indeed believe that people could be bought and sold. "No one should ever be sold like that."

"Because Jesus already paid the price for everyone. So that means people can't be sold again, because we're already sold to Jesus."

"Exactly." She loved the way Cole was growing, the way his thoughtfulness was starting to shape his worldview. "A lot of leaders would've done well to understand that through the ages, Cole."

She could tell by the look on his face that he wasn't sure what she meant, but he smiled anyway. "Exactly."

Later that night she shared his words with Landon, who pressed his fist over his heart. "That kid gets to me every time."

They were in the family room watching a basketball game on TV. Ashley kissed his cheek. "That's why I told you."

He cocked his head and studied her for a moment. "How're you feeling? You're not feeling sick like you were with Devin?"

"Nope." Ashley was glad. With Devin she'd had nausea morning, noon, and night. "This is my easiest pregnancy by far."

"Which'll make traveling a lot easier."

"I've thought about that. I think Dayne and Katy are going to whisk us off to some island somewhere."

It was fun trying to guess and allowing

the actual destination to be a mystery. Ashley and Landon talked about it with each other and with the other Baxters whenever they got together over the next week.

Then on Tuesday, March 14, a woman knocked on their door and delivered an envelope to them. "It's from Dayne Matthews. I believe you've been expecting it."

Ashley could hardly wait to rip it open. She thanked the woman and yelled for Landon. "It's here! The golden ticket is finally here!"

Landon had Devin on his hip. He hurried into the room with Cole in tow. "Is it the invitation?"

"Yes." Ashley held it up and did a little dance. She waved the envelope around and then tore off the top flap. " 'The honor of your presence is requested at the wedding of Dayne Matthews and Katy Hart, March 18, at the Riviera Resort in Cancún, Mexico.' " Ashley let out a squeal. "They're getting married in Cancún!"

The rest of the information explained that guests should pack swimsuits and casual clothes, as well as wedding attire, in one suitcase each and meet at five o'clock in the morning on Thursday, March 16, at the Indianapolis airport. From there they would fly by private jet to Cancún, where a bus would transport them to the resort, which had been rented exclusively for the occasion. There would be a bridal shower on Friday morning and various meals and gatherings throughout the day.

"Which means we have exactly one day to pack." Ashley paced a few steps toward the garage. "I better get the suitcases."

Landon looked at the front window. "Katy said the press are in town, right?"

"Yes." Ashley frowned. "They could be watching now." She peered out the window too. "If they are outside, we can't let them see us packing. We have to keep everything secret until the plane takes off."

By the next evening, Ashley had talked to her sisters and Katy. Everyone felt the same way — that three days on the Mayan Riviera would make for a dream wedding and a vacation at the same time.

It was time to celebrate. The brother they'd never known wasn't only found — he was getting married! And the sweet theater director who had become Ashley's friend was about to become something far more lasting.

Her sister.

CHAPTER
TWENTY-SIX

At the last minute, Jenny and Jim decided to take Cody Coleman to Dayne and Katy's wedding in Mexico. Originally he wasn't going, but he'd developed a strong attachment to the Flanigans since Thanksgiving. The time away would be good for him, a reward for his dedication to his classes and his growing faith.

By three o'clock Thursday morning, the Flanigans were awake and racing through the house.

"I'm bringing my stuffed dolphin." Shawn held it over his head as he ran down the stairs. "That's okay, right, Mom? Justin says I can't bring it 'cause there's no room in the suitcase, but I sleep with that dolphin every night, so it's okay, right?"

Jenny could barely keep the lists in her head straight. She waved her hand in Justin's direction. "Let him bring it. The dolphin's squishy. It doesn't take up much room." She raised her voice. "Bailey, get your suitcase down here. You're always last."

"I'll help her if she needs it." Cody was up, his duffel bag already sitting by the door.

For the first time Jenny heard it, sensed it in Cody's voice. Over the past couple of months, she'd seen Cody and Bailey getting closer, and she'd believed it to be nothing but a friendship. A brother-sister relationship. But here, in the midst of a crazy predawn morning, she had no doubts. Cody was developing feelings for Bailey, feelings she doubted he would act on any time before he left for the army.

Jenny hid her surprise with a smile. "Thanks, but she has to get her things together by herself. Otherwise she can't go."

"Hurry up, Bailey." Connor moved to the bottom of the stairs. "Mom says you can't go if you don't get down here."

"I'm coming. . . ." Her frantic voice came from her bedroom. "I can't find my curling iron."

Cody chuckled and turned his attention back to his bowl of cereal. "It's weird eating this early."

"Not for me." Ricky was the best eater in the family. He was finishing his second bowl of Cheerios. "Mom says we won't eat again till we get to Mexico."

Jenny smiled to herself. "Cody, why don't you check the boys' suitcase — all four little ones are sharing one big bag. Make sure they each have a bathing suit and flip-flops and their wedding clothes."

"Will do." Cody took a final bite of cereal and moved his bowl to the kitchen sink. He rinsed it and put it in the dishwasher. "Okay, boys . . . let's take a look at your suitcase."

Jenny's thoughts jumbled in her mind, and she pressed her fingers to her brow. "Vitamins . . . sunscreen . . . allergy medicine for BJ . . . nylons . . . hair spray." She muttered the list under her breath. "Bailey, do you have the hair spray?"

"Yes. Coming, Mom . . . really!"

Jim waltzed into the kitchen with a small suitcase. He lined it up next to Connor's and Cody's. "Everyone ready to roll?"

The chaos continued, but finally, they were loaded into the Flanigans' Suburban complete with six suitcases, three backpacks, vitamins, sunscreen, and plenty of hair spray. Even so, Jenny felt restless. "I keep thinking I forgot something."

"Not me, Mom." Ricky waved from the backseat. "You know, like *Home Alone.* You didn't forget any kids."

"*This* time." Jim gave her a wary look.

457

"There was the trip to Cedar Point."

"Ugh." Jenny let her face fall into her hands. "What a nightmare." They had been four miles from home when they realized BJ must've gone back inside to the bathroom. Because he was definitely missing. By the time they got back, he was sitting on the front porch with tears in his eyes.

"It's more fun in the movies," he'd told them. "I never wanna be home alone for real."

But that wasn't it this time. Suddenly she gasped. "My camera! I forgot my camera!"

"Nope." Bailey was sitting between Cody and Connor in the middle seat. "I remembered it for you." She patted her purse. "It's in here."

"Along with most of her bathroom." Connor laughed. "The thing's bursting at the seams."

Jenny allowed herself to relax. "I can't believe this."

"A wedding in Cancún?" Jim grinned. "I remember when the quarterback of one of my pro teams did something like this. Chartered a jet and took all the guests to Hawaii. I heard everyone had a blast."

"I can't imagine how excited Katy must be." She leaned back in the seat and set her purse on the floor. "I mean, did you really

458

think this would happen? that she and Dayne would find a way to work things out?"

"No." Jim didn't hesitate. "God's moved mountains for this one."

A smile tugged at Jenny's lips. She was tired and mentally drained from the effort of packing the family and getting out the door in time. But that didn't matter. They were on their way to Mexico with the Baxters and CKT families, on their way to witness Katy pledge her life and love to Dayne Matthews.

Nothing was greater proof of God's love than that.

Katy couldn't believe it was really happening.

Wilma Waters was in charge of checking in the guests at the counter for private air travel in the terminal adjacent to Indianapolis International Airport. Katy and Dayne personally greeted each family and offered them coffee and doughnuts.

Wilma asked the same questions to everyone. "Anyone follow you? Anyone ask you about today? Any photographers in the parking lot as you came inside?"

Wilma was pretty certain the paparazzi from Bloomington would figure something was up. They might even get as close as the airport. But they couldn't get into the private terminal without identification, so that would be that. They would know that Dayne and Katy's wedding guests were boarding a private jet, but they wouldn't have any idea where they were going.

Already Wilma had required a signed affidavit promising secrecy for the flight plans of the company's private jet. If anyone from the air travel company leaked information to the press — anyone at all — Wilma promised a lawsuit and said she wouldn't do business with the company again. It was a threat the company took seriously. Wilma didn't expect any trouble from the flight crew or people back at the corporate offices of the leasing company.

There wasn't a sign of trouble until John Baxter arrived. "We were followed," he told Wilma the moment he and Elaine joined the others inside the terminal. "Someone was waiting at the end of my driveway. They must've figured the wedding was coming soon."

"That's okay." Wilma checked her watch. "We'll be off the ground before anyone else figures it out."

Katy's nerves rattled. She found Dayne and clung to his arm. "A photographer followed your dad."

He touched her cheek. "We could be flying anywhere. If this is the first they know about it, they're too late." He slipped his arm around her waist and pulled her close. "You know what? God hasn't brought us this far just to see the wedding crashed by a bunch of photographers." He kissed her. "We'll be fine."

She nodded. He was right. They would be better than fine; they'd be perfect. Her private wedding was actually going to take place.

Katy and Dayne boarded the plane last, and as they did, the plane full of people erupted into applause ripe with excitement. She stopped, struck by the sight. Looking back at them were the faces of people she'd laughed and cried with — the Flanigans and all the CKT families she was close to. Her parents were on their way on a commercial flight from Chicago. She couldn't wait to see them.

Katy felt her eyes dance to life. Because she couldn't believe it. She sat next to Dayne in the second row, and within an hour most of their family and friends were sleeping. Everything about the flight and the fact that the wedding was about to happen felt surreal. When she was a little girl, she'd dreamed of being a fairy princess and marrying a prince. The way Cinderella did. And now here she was — being carried off in her jumbo-jet carriage with midnight a lifetime away.

"I keep thinking I should have glass slippers," she whispered against Dayne's neck. "Like someone's going to wake me up and tell me it's all a dream."

Dayne looked down at her, and the love in his eyes was enough to make her heart skip a beat. "It is a dream." He brought his lips to hers, and this time, sheltered from the watchful eyes of their guests, he kissed her slower.

By ten o'clock that morning they were on the ground with the entire party loaded into a series of buses. The planes coming from Hollywood and Chicago had landed half an hour before the one from Indianapolis, and now all the wedding guests were on their way to the Riviera.

Katy loved watching the people they'd invited, the looks of awe and excitement on their faces. Many of them had never been to Mexico, let alone the gorgeous eastern coastline of Cancún and its surrounding cities. Dayne's siblings sat with their families at the back of the bus. Their laughter rang all the way to the front. Wilma sat in the seat next to the bus driver, going over her notes like the lead contractor in a massive building project.

With every mile, Katy felt the thrill again and again. She and Dayne were really getting married, the way she'd only dreamed possible.

The weather in Cancún was warm and clear and beautiful, with temperatures expected to be in the eighties for the next several days and low humidity. It took four buses to get all the guests to the resort, and security was at a premium from the moment they arrived at the gates.

The Riviera was the most secluded resort along the Cancún coast. Palm trees and banana plants formed a forestlike fortress on either side of the entrance, and guards at the gates checked with Wilma that all four buses were part of the Matthews wedding party.

As with the jet leasing company, the Riviera had done business with Wilma Waters before. The management and staff intended to do more business with her in the future. Because of that, they were under orders to maintain heightened secrecy regarding the identity of the wedding party taking over the resort for the next three days.

The buses parked near the front lobby,

where stations were set up by last name. Guests got in the appropriate line and were given keys to their suites and a packet of instructions advising them of special dinners, showers, and meeting times.

Wilma had seen to all of it, and Katy pulled her aside once everyone had gone off to find their rooms. "I don't know how you pulled this off."

Where other people might look exhausted at this point, Wilma's eyes were bright and alert. She looked exhilarated by the challenge of planning the wedding. "I think we're really going to do it. All along my goal was to organize a big wedding without the media crashing it. We just might do it."

At this point everyone who knew the when and where of the wedding was already here at the resort.

Katy felt more relaxed than she'd felt since they first met with Wilma. "Even if they figure it out, they won't get past the front gate. I think we can all breathe a sigh of relief."

"Not yet." Wilma gave her an impulsive hug. "Not until you leave for your honeymoon."

The honeymoon.

Plans for the wedding had been so involved that Katy hadn't given much thought to the honeymoon. The destination was a surprise, something Dayne had planned. "Bring a bathing suit" was all he'd told her. Katy didn't care where they went. They could stay here at the Riviera, and the honeymoon would be perfect. As long as she and Dayne were together.

Dayne had gone off with his father and brother, because at Wilma's request, his room was near theirs. Katy's was across the hall from the Flanigans' and next door to her parents' — at the clear opposite side of the resort. That would give her more privacy to get ready for the wedding without any chance Dayne might see her.

Everyone had snacks waiting for them in their rooms, and after they unpacked, most people met by the pool. With only a couple hundred guests here, the resort felt wide-open — with space for people who wanted privacy and plenty of room for swimming or lying in the sun.

The Hollywood group included numerous A-list actresses and actors, all of whom found a smaller pool at the other end of the resort. Katy understood. They hardly ever had privacy, so why not take it while it was being offered?

Dinner that night was in one of the resort's ballrooms, and Dayne emceed the evening by having volunteers from among the guests play a version of Wheel of Fortune.

Afterwards, people fanned out toward the ocean, where some sat in beach chairs and watched the mild surf while others walked along the shore. Katy smiled when she saw Jenny walking on the damp sand, her arm around Bailey's shoulders. Whatever turmoil had suddenly reared up between them around the holidays was gone now.

Before they turned in that night, she and Dayne met with Wilma to go over the last-minute details. The shower would take place tomorrow at noon, and the rehearsal was set for six o'clock, followed by the rehearsal dinner. The guests who weren't in the wedding party would have the day to spend at the beach or at the pool. Everything was going according to schedule.

"So far, so good." Wilma grinned. "No paparazzi. Though word back home is that they're going crazy trying to figure out where the jet was headed." She gave a strong laugh and clapped. "I love it. Outwitting them with such a big wedding. But we're not in the clear yet."

As Katy fell asleep that night, she asked God to work miracles. *Keep the press away, Lord. It matters so much to Dayne, and because of that it matters to me, too. And please use our wedding to bring people closer to You and to each other.* She smiled, alone in the dark. The fairy-tale wedding she'd spent her life dreaming of was about to happen.

Her room was on the fourth floor, and she slept that night with her balcony door open, the sound of the ocean mixing with the warm breeze and filling her room. As she fell asleep, only one prayer was on her mind.

Thank You, Lord. . . . With all my heart, thank You.

CHAPTER
TWENTY-SEVEN

Darkness lay over the Riviera resort as John Baxter adjusted his bow tie. Elaine was ready, waiting in the next room for him. Katy and Dayne had chosen this hour for their wedding, the hour that symbolized everything about their relationship.

Sunrise.

Under the cover of night, the wedding pavilion and seating area had been set up on the beach. Flashlights had been left in the rooms so that the guests could find their way from their suite to the beachfront ceremony. Wilma had researched exactly when the sun would rise, when the light would first break the night sky.

John sprayed cologne on his neck and then went to find Elaine. She wore a dark gray, midlength dress, and in it she looked stunning. "Elaine . . ."

She stood and came to him. "You look handsome, John. The wedding's going to be perfect."

"I can't believe it's really happening, that my oldest son is part of our family, he's getting married, and . . . well —" his voice fell a notch — "you're here to share it with me."

She took hold of his hands. Her touch reminded him that though his heart had taken the greatest blow of all, though he'd nearly died from the pain of losing his Elizabeth, he was still breathing, still living. And Elaine was very much a part of what remained of his life.

He stared into her eyes, and he could picture the way it would feel in half an hour, having her beside him as morning dawned and the sun filled the sky. The setting for the wedding would be breathtaking: ocean waves and white sugary sand, blue-green water as far as they could see.

But Elaine was even more beautiful. Maybe after the wedding, they could take a walk and he would tell her. For now, he was too choked up to make his feelings known. It was wrong — and it always would be — that Elizabeth wasn't here, that she wasn't the woman standing before him, the one watching her oldest son marry the woman he loved.

Even so, this was his life — and his life involved Elaine Denning.

The way maybe — just maybe — it would involve her for the rest of his days.

Katy was filled with peace and joy she'd never known before. It was just after five in the morning, and she was in the bridal room with the friends who, all but Rhonda, were about to be her sisters. Kari, Brooke, Reagan, and Rhonda helped with her train, and Erin — who had flown in yesterday with her family — held the bouquet, waiting for the moment when Katy was ready.

And Ashley — the one who through her stubborn determination and unrelenting prayers had finally brought the Baxter family together — stood closest, adjusting her veil and humming Katy's favorite hymn, "Great Is Thy Faithfulness."

"It's true." Ashley's voice was low, filled with emotion. "I remember marrying Landon, the way God let my mother live to see that moment and how Landon never gave up on me." She smiled, but her eyes were watery as she looked at Katy. "All of that was God's faithfulness." She gave Katy a hug. "And this morning is too."

It was true; Katy knew it to the very depths of her soul. Dayne Matthews would love her until the day she died. He would fight for her and the special connection they'd found together. He would fight for it the way he'd fought back from the brink of death after his accident. If it took everything in him, he would honor and cherish her, working out the details of their marriage with every heartbeat.

The way she would too.

Sunrise that morning would take place at 5:53 a.m. At 5:40, Wilma Waters entered the room and stared at her. "Katy Hart, you are a vision. It's almost too bad the tabloids *won't* get a look at this wedding."

Katy felt a rush of joy. "Still no sign of them?"

"Not a photographer in sight except the one provided by the Riviera." Wilma wiped at her brow, as if the task had finally drained what was left of her boundless energy. Then she laughed, and her face came to life again. "Seriously, I can't take credit. This went way too smoothly for that." She pointed up. "I'm beginning to think there might be something to all that praying you've been doing."

"Yes." Ashley stepped up. "Before we're finished here in Cancún, give me a few minutes. If you didn't believe in prayer before, you will for sure after you've heard some of our stories."

A soft chorus of laughter came from the others.

But Wilma looked serious. "I'd like to hear about it. Katy and Dayne really have me thinking."

It was another victory, the perfect note to set out on. Katy wasn't sure if she could wait one more minute. "Are we ready?"

"We are." Wilma smiled, and her eyes shone with genuine emotion. "Even in the dusky darkness, the setting is beyond beautiful, Katy. Wait till you see it." She checked her watch. "Everyone's seated. The groomsmen are waiting with Dayne at the front. The eastern sky's already showing streaks of light."

"Okay then." Ashley touched Katy's arm. "As Katy would say, let's make it happen."

They filed quietly into a lobby, where Katy spotted her father. He had been ill much of the past ten years, and though they talked each week, their relationship wasn't what it might've been if they'd lived closer to each other. But here, before Katy, was the man who had made her believe in her dreams.

She walked up to him and whispered near his ear, "Remember, Daddy, all those times you told me I could be anything I wanted, have anything I wanted?"

"Yes, baby." Her dad had tears in his eyes.

472

"I meant every word."

"And you were right." She laughed, but only so she wouldn't cry. She touched her fingers to her lips. "Thanks for believing in me. That part stays with me no matter how far apart we are."

"You're beautiful, Katy. I couldn't be happier for you."

Only then did Katy notice the kids bouncing around the lobby near the door. Cole and Tommy were dressed in pint-size tuxedos, standing next to Maddie, Hayley, and Jessie, along with Clarisse and Chloe, Erin's two daughters who were old enough to be flower girls.

"I'm first, right?" Cole blocked Katy's path. "I told the girls I was first, but they don't believe me."

Wilma took over before Katy could say anything. "You'll all walk together. Cole, you and Tommy will walk at the center, with the girls on either side of you." She smiled at the five girls. "Do you have your baskets of rose petals?"

"Yes, ma'am." Hayley was the first to respond.

Her answer touched Katy and reminded her again of the hymn Ashley had been humming earlier. Hayley hadn't been expected to survive her drowning incident, but here she was — walking without assistance, able to function at nearly the same level as her sister and cousins. Yes, her sentences were still slower than those of the other kids. But she was whole and well and precious, all because of God's great and mighty faithfulness.

Katy massaged her throat, willing herself to control her emotions. She held on to her father's arm and realized she was trembling. And of course! She was about to marry Dayne Matthews — a man who was so much more than what the world knew of him. Only she had seen him struggle to recount the loss of his birth mother or the first meeting he'd shared with John Baxter. Katy alone knew the strength of the man, his will to live and find his place among the Baxters.

The importance of family.

"It's 5:48," Wilma announced. "Let's get started." She opened the door, and the sound of violins filled the lobby.

The music mixed with a gentle, warm wind and the sound of softly crashing waves. The combined effect made Katy's heart skip a beat.

Wilma directed the bridesmaids to head down the aisle, allowing ten seconds between each one. When they had all made their way through the doorway and down a winding path that would lead them toward the wedding set up on the beach, Wilma helped the children find a pretty formation, with two girls on one side of the boys and three on the other.

"Okay now —" Wilma touched Cole's shoulder — "don't walk too fast." She looked at Katy and her father. "I'll go in, and after a minute, the music will change. When it does, that'll be your cue." She smiled. "It's going to be perfect, Katy. Sunrise is in exactly two minutes."

When Wilma was gone, Katy's father smiled down at her, and she spotted a tear on his cheek.

"Daddy —" she reached up and wiped it with her fingertip — "I'm so glad you were well enough to come."

"I wouldn't have missed it."

At that instant the music changed, and Katy took a quick breath. "Here goes."

Theirs wasn't the traditional wedding march. Instead the violins and pianist set up on the sand played the theme from *Robin Hood: Prince of Thieves*: "(Everything I Do) I Do It For You." It was a song that had played often during Dayne's physical therapy. Something about it — the passion of the song and the love it sang about —

convinced Katy and Dayne that it would be the only truly fitting song for this moment.

The music played, and Katy and her father set out on the path. They rounded the corner, and the wedding scene spread out before them like something from a dream. Bunches of white roses cascaded from four-foot pillars along the outer edge of the seating area and at key points along the center aisle.

Only then did she realize that Dayne had a microphone. She hadn't known until *Oliver!* how talented a singer Dayne was, but here, now, she'd had no idea he was going to sing to her. She hesitated from the surprise and felt the sting of tears as he sang the first words of the song.

" 'Look into my eyes, you will see . . . what you mean to me.' "

She still had a long way to go up the aisle, but as she moved toward Dayne, she was lost in his eyes, so lost that she barely noticed the glistening lines on his cheeks. He was crying, her Dayne, the one who had loved her from the moment he saw her. Even so, his voice was strong and filled with passion. " 'Search your heart . . . search your soul . . . and when you find me there, you'll search no more.' "

As he reached the crescendo, as the music

filled the beach and Dayne sang about this being a love worth trying for, worth dying for, Katy was struck by something beautiful. Something she would remember as long as she lived.

From across the farthest reaches of the ocean, piercing for all time the darkness that had plagued their relationship, came proof that this was their moment, their time. Katy kept walking, her gaze locked on Dayne's. The love they shared was indeed worth whatever cost had brought them to this place. That much was as clear as the streaky yellows and pinks appearing before her eyes.

Nothing could represent her wedding day more than a sunrise — and not just her wedding day but every day that would follow with Dayne Matthews.

Because that was love, wasn't it? Waking up through the years and knowing with all your being that the depth of emotion and passion and connection that filled this moment wasn't something in the past but something new and fresh and alive.

Morning after morning after morning.

Dayne wasn't sure how he was able to stand. Katy was more beautiful than anything he might've imagined his bride to be. He couldn't take his eyes off her, couldn't do anything but sing every word, every line of the song as if he'd written it for her. Because he meant it that much.

The song was building, and he couldn't see anything but Katy. " 'Look into your heart . . . you will find . . . there's nothing there to hide. . . . Take me as I am . . . take my life. . . .' "

Katy reached her spot at the end of the aisle, and he realized that she was crying too. Not loud or with any trace of sadness but with tears of joy for all they'd been through to reach this place, all they'd survived together.

Let the paparazzi trail them. Let them write about every move they might make as husband and wife. Nothing — nothing in the world — would ever separate him from the love he felt for Katy Hart. If they needed to live on their own private island, he would go in a heartbeat before he'd let anything come between them.

His love was protection and passion and honesty and awe; it was a dusty-faced girl flat on her back on an old, dirty stage looking at him with wonder in her eyes and the flash of lightning between them on a dark, stormy night in Bloomington. He had never wanted anything in his life as much as he wanted Katy Hart, and along the way he'd found the One he did need more, even when he hadn't known it.

God and God alone had brought them here this morning.

It was a beginning, and it was only right that the sun was rising into the sky over his right shoulder as the song was ending. He finished it strong. " 'Everything I do . . . I do it for you.' "

As he lowered his microphone, the sky changed again, daybreak coming to life all around them.

Dayne's friend Bob Asher had flown in to take part in the wedding and to officiate the ceremony. He stepped forward now and looked at Katy's father. "Who gives this woman to be married?"

Katy's father kissed her cheek one last time before giving her away. Then he nodded in Bob's direction. "Her mother and I." With that, he tenderly took Katy's hand and gave it to Dayne.

The music was still playing softly in the background, repeating the chorus of the song. Before they began the vows, Katy and Dayne had something they wanted to do, something they had planned months ago. Together they walked to a small table set up near the piano. There on a white linen cloth were two vases full of dirt. Hers was soil taken from the flower bed near the front entrance of the Bloomington Community Theater. His was and from Malibu Beach.

They smiled at each other, and then Katy pulled a larger, empty crystal vase close. Gradually, they each poured the contents of their vases into the empty container. As they did, the two materials mixed and swirled together in the new vase.

When it was full, Dayne turned to their family and friends. He'd written something for this moment, but he didn't want to take a piece of paper out of his pocket and read. Instead he spoke from his heart. "Our worlds are very different, Katy's and mine. The sand and the soil show you that much. But here, with you and God as witnesses, we have found the miracle of oneness — one heart, one family, one faith. So that no matter what happens in either of our worlds ever again, we might be as difficult to separate as the soil and sand you see here."

Next to him, Katy squeezed his hand, and they moved back to the center of the pavilion area, where Bob said a few words about love and marriage and God's design in both. Dayne was focused, but every time he looked at Katy, he lost his ability to concentrate. It was the same way through their vows, Dayne caught up and mesmerized by

Katy's presence, the beauty that came from deep within her.

Finally Bob smiled. "I now present to you Dayne and Katy Matthews." He grinned at Dayne. "You may kiss the bride."

Dayne couldn't draw a breath, but that didn't matter. He lifted Katy's veil and held her face in his hands. The kiss didn't linger, but he would remember it all his days.

As he faced his family and friends, he wanted to shout to the heavens that they'd done it! They'd gotten married. And now she was his, and he was hers. It was more than he could take in.

At that moment he realized that the sky had changed again. The yellows and subtle pinks were brightening, and a hint of pale blue was filling in the gaps between the streaks. That was the beauty of a new day, wasn't it? A sunrise would change every few seconds, but with each change the picture only grew more beautiful.

The same way this was a beginning for the two of them, and changes would come. But as they did, Dayne was convinced to his core that the days would make themselves known the way the sky was coming to life here before their eyes.

With bright and breathtaking color and all the beauty of a changing sunrise.

A WORD FROM
KAREN KINGSBURY

Dear Reader Friends,

If you're like me, at this point you want to do a little dance or stand on the highest hill and raise a victory fist in the air. Dayne and Katy are married!

My eyes welled up as I pictured these two and all they'd been through, all that had led them to this place. And so you see that *Sunrise* is a new beginning not only for Dayne and Katy but for the Baxters and the Flanigans and all our dear friends in Bloomington, Indiana.

I know; I know. They're just fictional characters. But I think about them as if they're real. Just ask my husband. He's worried I might need counseling, but I tell him I'll be fine. Even if I spend time looking for Ashley and Landon when I visit Indiana.

What struck me most as I wrote *Sunrise* was the importance of new beginnings. Marriage is certainly a time of new beginnings, as anything can be when we allow God to work. An anniversary, a birthday, a first of the month. Since we are subject to a forgiving and gracious God, we ought to be intimately familiar with new beginnings.

God never planned for us to wallow in the mire of failed efforts or broken relationships, and He doesn't want us to flounder in the frog pond of unforgiveness and bitterness. He wants us to take hold of the promises He has to offer and make a new start. New beginnings are crucial if we're ever going to find victory in our life with Christ.

So though the characters are fictional, God is using them to teach me lessons that come straight from the Bible. Because the power of story belongs to God alone. Whether you're the reader or the writer.

Another lesson *Sunrise* taught me was the power of persistent prayer. Katy asked God for something some people might've thought too simple. She wanted her husband to enjoy their wedding without concern for photographers. And God delivered, as so often only God can do.

I wish I could tell you all that lies ahead for Katy and Dayne as they attempt to make peace with the paparazzi. I can only say that their love will be tested beyond the normal bounds, beyond anything they could've anticipated in this, the beautiful sunrise of their married days. Likewise, there's more to know about Ashley's story and Landon's, John's and Elaine's.

Maybe the saddest part is that there are just three books left with these precious people, the ones I've learned so much from. The ones tens of thousands of you have written to me about. Three more books. Look for *Summer,* then *Someday,* and finally *Sunset.* After that, we'll see if God allows more opportunity with the Baxters somewhere down the road.

If not, you'll simply have to check in on my Web site. I might start a Baxter update for those of us who want to know how these characters are doing when the books stop coming. In the meantime, I'll have other books, other Life-Changing Fiction titles you can journey through with me.

By the way, if any of you don't yet know the personal love and forgiveness of Jesus Christ, if for the first time you're hearing about Jesus and His powerful salvation and His plans for your life, please visit a Bible-believing church in your area and talk to the pastor about Jesus. You need to spend time in God's Word — the Bible — in order to know what the Lord wants from you and what He is offering free of charge.

If this book changed your life or led you into or back into a relationship with Jesus, please write to me and put *New Life* in the subject line. I'll be sure to read that letter and pray for you as you journey toward a deeper walk with our Lord.

Either way, I hope you'll take a minute and visit my Web site at www.Karen Kingsbury.com. There you can see what books are coming up or connect with other readers and book clubs. You can leave prayer requests or take on the responsibility of praying for people. People often tell me they haven't found a purpose or meaning to their faith. Maybe they're on the go a lot or their circumstances keep them homebound. Remember, prayer is a very important ministry. It was prayer that turned things around for Dayne and Luke, prayer that made the difference time and again in this series. Your prayers — either in the midst of a busy day or as the main focus of a home-bound one — could be crucial in the life of someone else, someone God wants you to pray for. Visit the prayer link on my Web site and make a commitment to pray for the hurting people who have left requests there.

In addition, I have two new pages on my Web site — one for active military heroes and another for fallen military heroes. If you know someone serving our country and you'd like to honor them, please click the appropriate links on the side of the home page and submit their photo, name, rank, and how people can pray for them. We can include more details if you have someone you'd like to honor on the Fallen Military Heroes page. The importance in our current war is not who is wrong or right, because war is complicated. However, the duty we all share is to honor and respect and admire our troops. They are heroes, and they deserve our utmost support and constant prayers.

On a personal note, my family is doing well, nearly through another year of homeschooling. It's a wonderful adventure full of laughter and precious memories. Kelsey is a high school junior, talking about colleges. Austin, nine, rarely wakes up in the middle of the night wanting to climb in the middle between Donald and me. Yes, I can feel the days moving too fast, and there's nothing I can do to slow the ride. But I am enjoying every minute all the same, trying to remember the lessons from *Sunrise* — look for the new beginnings in life and believe that this time God will help you see the light of day.

Thanks so much for sharing in this journey, the journey of the Baxter family. I pray that God is using the power of story to touch and change your life, the way He uses it in mine.

Until next time,
blessings in His amazing light and grace,
Karen Kingsbury

DISCUSSION QUESTIONS

Use these questions for individual reflection or for discussion with a book club or other small group.

1. What does a sunrise represent to you? Tell about a time when you got up early enough to watch a sunrise.
2. What area in your life could use a new beginning? What steps would you need to take to get that new beginning started?
3. Describe Katy's new approach to the press. What was at the root of her ideas?
4. What did Dayne think about opening their lives to the public? As their wedding neared, what were Dayne's fears about being publicly open with their lives?
5. Many Hollywood couples have fallen victim to the tabloids and wound up divorced. What advice would you give Katy and Dayne as they begin their married life in a very public way?
6. What do you think causes real Hollywood

marriages to receive so much scrutiny? What ultimately breaks up these marriages?

7. What concerns does Katy have about Christian Kids Theater? Have you ever been part of something good, something of God, and then watched it fall apart or close down? Describe that situation.

8. Can you understand Rhonda's feelings of discontent around Katy — especially in Katy's time of happiness? Explain how Rhonda is feeling.

9. Have you ever been jealous of a friend who seems to have everything all together? What typically comes of this jealousy?

10. What did you learn about Dayne through his playacting on the stage with Katy?

11. In what ways do you try to incorporate laughter and fun into your relationships — especially your relationship with your spouse?

12. Have you planned a wedding — yours or someone else's? What things are crucial to making the day come off the way you hoped?

13. Katy will need to make sacrifices in order to live alongside Dayne in his very public life. What are a few of those sacrifices?

14. What are sacrifices you've made on behalf of your spouse? How were those sacrifices received by the person you love?
15. After reading *Sunrise,* you know that Katy has been offered a leading role in Dayne's upcoming movie. In your opinion, what problems could come from this?

ABOUT THE AUTHOR

Karen Kingsbury is currently America's best-selling inspirational author. She has written more than 30 Life-Changing Fiction titles and has nearly 5 million books in print. Dubbed by *Time* magazine as the Queen of Christian Fiction, Karen receives hundreds of letters each week and considers her readers as friends. Her fiction has made her one of the country's favorite storytellers, and one of her novels — *Gideon's Gift* — is under production for an upcoming major motion picture release. Her emotionally gripping titles include the popular Redemption series, the Firstborn series, *Divine, One Tuesday Morning, Beyond Tuesday Morning, Oceans Apart,* and *A Thousand Tomorrows.* Karen and her husband, Don, live in the Pacific Northwest and are parents to one girl and five boys, including three adopted from Haiti. You can find out more about Karen, her books, and her appearance schedule at www.Karen Kingsbury.com.

The employees of Thorndike Press hope you have enjoyed this Large Print book. All our Thorndike and Wheeler Large Print titles are designed for easy reading, and all our books are made to last. Other Thorndike Press Large Print books are available at your library, through selected bookstores, or directly from us.

For information about titles, please call:
  (800) 223-1244

or visit our Web site at:
  www.gale.com/thorndike
  www.gale.com/wheeler

To share your comments, please write:
  Publisher
  Thorndike Press
  295 Kennedy Memorial Drive
  Waterville, ME 04901